W9-BXA-243

THE
SHELL
GAME

by *New York Times* Best-Selling Author

STEVE ALTEN

THE
SHELL
GAME

Jefferson-Madison
Regional Library
Charlottesville, Virginia

SWEETWATER BOOKS

Springville, Utah

30411 5668

© 2007 Steve Alten
All rights reserved.

No part of this book may be reproduced in any form whatsoever, whether by graphic, visual, electronic, film, microfilm, tape recording, or any other means, without prior written permission of the publisher, except in the case of brief passages embodied in critical reviews and articles.

The views expressed within this work are the sole responsibility of the author and do not necessarily reflect the position of Cedar Fort, Inc., or any other entity.

Cedar Fort books and its imprints carry no political agenda, nor are we aligned with any political party or candidate. Like the author, we believe the message within *The Shell Game* raises important issues that we, as a people and nation, need to address if we are to survive. Although the author has referred to real people and events, *The Shell Game* is a work of fiction.

ISBN 13: 978-1-59955-094-7

Published by Sweetwater Books, an imprint of Cedar Fort, Inc., 2373 W. 700 S., Springville, UT, 84663
Distributed by Cedar Fort, Inc., www.cedarfort.com

LIBRARY OF CONGRESS CATALOGING-IN-PUBLICATION DATA

Alten, Steve.
    The shell game / by Steve Alten.
      p. cm.
    ISBN 978-1-59955-094-7 (acid-free paper)
    1. War on terrorism, 2001—Fiction. 2. Terrorism—Prevention—Fiction.
    3. Intelligence officers—Fiction. 4. Conspiracy—Fiction.
    5. International relations—Fiction. 6. Nuclear warfare—Fiction. I. Title.

    PS3551.L764S54 2007
    813'.54—dc22

                              2007026515

Cover art by Erik Hollander
www.HollanderDesignLab.com

Cover design © 2007 by Lyle Mortimer
Edited and typeset by Erin L. Seaward

Printed in the United States of America

10   9   8   7   6   5   4   3   2   1

Printed on acid-free paper

OTHER BOOKS BY STEVE ALTEN

THE MEG SERIES

MEG: A Novel of Deep Terror
The Trench
MEG: Primal Waters
MEG: Hell's Aquarium (coming soon)

THE DOMAIN SERIES

Domain
Resurrection

THE GOLIATH SERIES

Goliath
Sorceress (coming soon)
The Loch

To personally contact the author or
to learn more about his novels, visit

WWW.STEVEALTEN.COM

The Shell Game is part of Adopt-an-Author, a free, nationwide reading
program for secondary school students and teachers.

For more information, visit
WWW.ADOPTANAUTHOR.COM

DEDICATION

This novel is dedicated to those who suffered on September 11, 2001 . . .

—to the courageous men and women of the Armed Forces, who risk their lives in the pursuit of liberty and freedom . . .

—and to those of us at home determined to safeguard those freedoms by demanding information and an open society, knowing that dissent and not acquiescence is the highest form of patriotism.

ACKNOWLEDGMENTS

IT IS WITH GREAT PRIDE AND appreciation that I acknowledge those who contributed to the completion of *The Shell Game*.

First and foremost, many thanks to my friend and literary manager, Danny Baror of Baror International; my agent, Matthew Snyder at CAA; my manager/producer, Belle Avery, and my terrific publicist, Lissy Peace of Blanco & Peace. Also, to my attorney, Joel McKuin of Colden, McKuin & Frankel, and to my advertising guru, Trish Stevens, at United Representatives.com.

Very special thanks to the great people at Cedar Fort who believed in this project and developed a new imprint to support it. My gratitude to Lyle Mortimer and Lee Nelson, to national sales director Tim Schulte, who fought for the book, and to editor Erin Seaward.

Although this is a novel, there is much truth in the details. My gratitude to those contributors who generously offered private accounts from their own lives that added to the authenticity and richness of the story. Many thanks to Richard Lawrence, Charles Jones, Nathalie Tarabadi (Enyotic Designs Ltd.), Dino Garner, Ian Primosch, Mike Worley (www.PolicePractices.com), Greg Croft seismic services (www.gregcroft.com), and Kevin Lasagna. While my research involved more than forty published books and two file cabinets worth of research papers, I wish to acknowledge two outstanding resources: Michael C. Ruppert's book, *Crossing the Rubicon: The Decline of the American Empire at the End of the Age of Oil,* and the feature documentary *Obsession: Radical Islam's War Against the West* (www.ObsessionTheMovie.com).

Very special thanks to those individuals who preferred their names not be made public, but whose information and guidance was invaluable—my heartfelt gratitude.

Thanks also go to my assistant, Leisa Coffman, for her talent and expertise in updating my personal web site as well as for all her work in the Adopt-An-Author program, and to Erik Hollander, for his tremendous cover design and graphic artistry.

Last, to my wife and partner, Kim, for all her love and support, to my parents, who have always been there to keep me going, and to my readers: Thank you for your ongoing support, correspondence, and contributions. Your comments are always a welcome treat, your input means so much, and you remain this author's greatest asset.

A PERSONAL NOTE
FROM THE AUTHOR

UPON READING THE MANUSCRIPT FOR *The Shell Game,* a trusted editor of mine, who has guided me through seven novels, most of which dealt with monstrous creatures, told me that none of the major publishing houses would ever publish this book. "It's not conventional fiction; the protagonist has to be more heroic and save the day . . . plus it's way too controversial. I just can't bring myself to believe the president of the United States would knowingly allow such a horrendous thing to happen."

My response was simple: "If I wrote a book back in August of 2001 about Saudi nationals training in American flight schools so that they could use box-cutters to hijack planes and fly them into buildings, would you have believed that?"

My editor friend thought about that for a moment and replied, "Okay, but you wouldn't have been able to sell that book either."

He's probably right.

But *The Shell Game* is neither standard fiction nor nonfiction. It was written as a cautionary tale, backed by disturbing facts and inconvenient truths that are used to project an all-too-real scenario down the path we have been lulled into taking.

Two long years of research went into the project; key bits of information were provided to me along the way by concerned fans of mine in the military, the oil industry, and the political arena, and by individuals who simply have suffered far too much. Some of the things they told me have given me nightmares, and, in fact, this entire project has taxed my nerves to the point of permanent damage. (Four months before the book was published, I was diagnosed with Parkinson's Disease.)

When we are the monsters in the story, then the horror becomes a little too real.

Right-wing political pundits will accuse me of being a conspiracy theorist—part of the "left-wing wackos." In truth, I am a registered Democrat, but I am far from liberal, and the Democrats feel my wrath in the story as well as the Republicans. To my delight, this book was published by a conservative group out of a traditional red state.

Red states, blue states. Utter nonsense. We are all proud Americans. So let me introduce to you two colors that better define the line of separation in the United States and the rest of the world: black and green.

Black is the color of oil and coal and the carbon dioxide it delivers into our atmosphere every day—70 million tons of it. Black is the ledger of the oil companies, created by billions of dollars in profits that support Middle Eastern governments, who care little about their own people and find their way into the hands of extremist groups. Those same billions of dollars allow the fossil fuel industry to lobby and coerce our politicians, who in turn allow them to continue to pollute. Black is the color of cancer and death, the color of minorities who perished in New Orleans because it was too costly to fix the problem, and the color of blood as it bleeds from a bullet wound and mortar fire. Black is the heart who loses a loved one in a war they know is unjust. Finally, black is the date that will appear on the calendars of all those who witness the blackest date in our history . . . when a nuclear device explodes in one of our cities, incinerating tens of thousands, radiating millions, and staining what remains of our civilization forever.

Green is the solution that can prevent the catastrophe. It is the color of clean energy and the new economy it brings. It is the color of our environment as we reverse the effects of climate change, reduce CO_2 emissions in the air, and soothe our planet's temperature.

Finally, green is the color of money, which is why green will never be allowed to positively impact our civilization as long as oil is black.

For those of you who will turn red (and blue) in the face arguing that climate change is not real, that oil is plentiful, and that our elected officials would never participate in anything nefarious nor cover up any details of wrong-doing, I have addressed the question of which information is real in *The Shell Game* in the last pages of the book. Read the story first so you can weigh the information in its proper context, then ask the politician who clamors for your vote in the next election to declare themselves as either a Green candidate or a Fossil Fuel candidate—

    —because look where red and blue have gotten us . . .

—Steve Alten, EdD

"The lie was dead. And damned, and truth stood up instead."

—ROBERT BROWNING

"The only thing necessary for the triumph of evil is for good men to do nothing."

—EDMUND BURKE

"Then the seven angels with the seven trumpets prepared to blow their mighty blasts . . ."

—REVELATION 8:6

THE STORY BEHIND
THE SHELL GAME

It dates back to the fifteenth century. Three shells, a flat surface, and a soft, little ball. The street vender performs his magic, maneuvering the shells in patterns of intersecting circles, then asks the viewing public where the ball is. Place a wager and lift one shell; expose the ball and you win. But the shell game is neither skill nor game of chance, but an act of deception, for the ball has been switched from the obvious shell through a sleight of hand, and any prior "winners" were all part of the con.

On a grander scale, the shell game is a democracy broken, cloaked by a veneer that alters society's perception of the world—lies based on spin, truth without fact. It is a hypocrisy that tears at the fabric of society—radicals who kill innocent people in the name of God, politicians who favor loyalty over competence, corporations that profit from bloodshed, and the media outlets who slant their broadcasts to meet the needs of their advertisers. It is legislation based on greed instead of need—health care systems that feed pharmaceutical companies instead of the sick, energy policies monopolized by the private sector and safeguarded by members of Congress who suckle off the teat of campaign donations. It is policies that protect the needs of the powerful and loopholes that encourage Wall Street raiders to seize worker pension funds—the system's reward for a hostile takeover. It is a federal budget that invests billions into weapons of mass destruction and pennies into its fighting soldiers, hiding the grim reality that one in three adult homeless males is a combat vet, that one in four veterans of Iraq and Afghanistan suffers mental health problems, that our nation's warriors have been left behind by an administration that wraps itself in the stars and stripes but refuses to provide adequate funding for our soldiers' needs.

Most of all, the shell game is about a society addicted to oil, the profits of which empower politicians and finance corrupt regimes, fund weapons that kill, build schools that teach hatred, and support terrorist organizations that target democracies.

But as in all great deceptions, eventually it is truth that exposes the con: that the end of oil is upon us, that there are no alternative resources in place, that an extremist ideology has grown stronger as a result of the failures of our appointed leaders . . . and then the reality of our course shall hit home.

The following work of fiction becomes nonfiction in or about the year 2012.

Be forewarned . . . our clock is ticking.

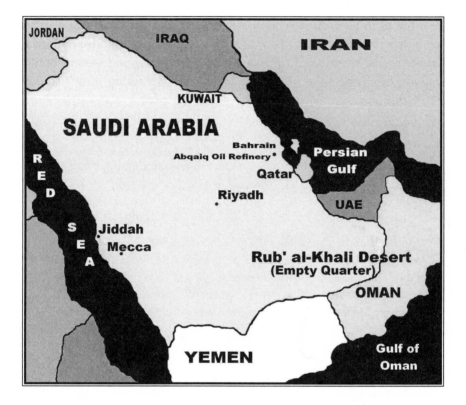

THE MIDDLE EAST

"Men, in order to do evil, must first believe that what they are doing is good."

—ALEXANDER SOLZHENITSYN,
Novelist and Nobel Prize winner

"The most honorable death is by killing. And the most honorable killing and the most glorious martyrdom is when a man is killed for the sake of Allah."

—HASSAN NASRALLAH,
Hezbollah Security General

"In the months that followed [September 11, 2001], I also made clear the principles that will guide us in this new war: America will not wait to be attacked again. We will confront threats before they fully materialize. We will stay on the offense against the terrorists, fighting them abroad so we do not have to face them here at home."

—PRESIDENT GEORGE W. BUSH
May 27, 2006

"After all this I saw another angel come down from heaven with great authority, and the earth grew bright with his splendor. He gave a mighty shout, 'Babylon is fallen—that great city is fallen! She has become the hideout of demons and evil spirits, a nest for filthy buzzards, and a den for dreadful beasts. For all nations have drunk the wine of her passionate immorality. The rulers of the world have committed adultery with her, and merchants throughout the world have grown rich as a result of her luxurious living.' "

—REVELATION 18:1–3

PROLOGUE

The hotel suite is richly decorated in cream-colored fabrics and matching carpet, the turquoise drapes drawn, blocking out the view of downtown Washington. A series of aluminum steam table pans situated on warming trays cover a small side table, the aroma of scrambled eggs, bacon, and hash browns filling the room.

Ignoring the hunger pangs growling in his stomach, Colonel Graeme "the Bull" Turnbull, U.S. Army, directs his harsh, blue-eyed gaze at the two civilians seated directly across the small conference table. Ryan Gessaman, a rugged man in his forties, wearing a dark suit and matching bow tie, is a senior assistant to Richard Perle, chairman of the Defense Policy Board. Perle, known around Washington power circles as the "Prince of Darkness," is himself a close personal advisor to former secretary of defense Donald Rumsfeld and a major investor in a number of defense companies. Perle is also co-founder of the Project for the New American Century (PNAC), a political think tank, established in 1997, that promotes American dominance in world affairs.

Turnbull does not recognize Gessaman's companion, an as-yet unidentified woman with thick, shoulder-length, blonde, curly hair and penetrating hazel eyes, her navy business suit partially concealing what appears to be an athletic physique.

"Colonel, are you sure we can't interest you in some breakfast?"

"No, thank you, sir."

"Well, if you change your mind . . ." Gessaman opens a sealed file. "I understand you're currently stationed at Camp Anaconda. How long have you been in Iraq?"

"Since the beginning. I started in Afghanistan with the 187th Airborne Regimental Combat Team, the 'Rakkasans.' We were the first boots on the ground. Same for Iraq. *Ne desit virtus*—"

"—let valor not fail," the woman translates. "When did Military Intelligence recruit you?"

"The day Psy Ops found out I spoke fluent Arabic."

"So you were with MI two years, then Counterintelligence. Looks like you were quite busy . . . over one hundred interrogations." The woman's eyes narrow. "Tell me, Colonel, what's the most interesting thing you ever learned from these 'sessions'?"

Turnbull frowns. "You don't want to know."

"Try me."

"Back in 2005, I reported that Bin Laden had escaped to the Hadhramaut of Yemen, that he was being protected by Sayyid tribesmen. The info went up the food chain, but nothing ever happened. Seems the Sayyids of the Hadhramaut are allied with members of the Saudi Royal Family . . . to go after him would have insulted our Saudi friends. Better to just pretend the number-one bad guy's hiding in a cave in Afghanistan than confront the real enemy, huh?"

The woman nods. "I share your frustration, Colonel. Off the record, CIA ran an assessment of the blowback of a Bin Laden capture. Sometimes bad guys are better left alive than dead."

"Is that why we're funding Sunni insurgents with ties to Al-Qaeda?" Turnbull watches their expressions drop. "Yeah, I know about that, most of the other grunts in MI do too. Fact is, 45 percent of these foreign fighters are Saudis, and half of them are involved in suicide bombings. You don't have to be a brain surgeon to figure out where these guys are getting their money and weapons."

"It's a complicated situation, Colonel," Ryan Gessaman replies.

"Not when you're getting shot at."

"Shiite radicals must be contained."

"Look, friend, let's get something straight: I ain't in politics and the old 'the enemy of my enemy is my friend' policy doesn't fly with me, unless your definition of history is any period of time less than five years old. We supported Bin Laden to keep the Soviets in check, we supported Saddam to keep the Iranians in check . . . now we're supporting Al-Qaeda to keep Iraq from turning into a Shi'ite nation? Ever wonder why we're not exactly being embraced these days?"

The woman stares straight ahead, saying nothing, her silence saying everything.

"Let's refocus on Iraq," Gessaman says. "The president has decided to go with a troop surge. Your thoughts?"

An icy glare crosses Turnbull's eyes. "You don't want to know my thoughts."

"Off the record."

"Off the record . . ." Turnbull smirks. "The commander-in-chief started a forest fire, now he thinks he can put it out with gasoline. Baghdad's a zoo, you have so many different factions fighting against one another that we need a score card just to know who to shoot. Troop surge? Where exactly is the president getting these troops from? The Boy Scouts? I'm working with soldiers that have been recycled so many times they're starting to demand air miles. My enlisted men are so fried that a third of them no longer have any business carrying a weapon, let alone participating in combat operations where their presence jeopardizes the welfare of an entire platoon. And the Reserves and National Guardsmen? Nice surprise, not telling them deployment doesn't officially begin until their boots hit sand, meaning the six months their unit spent at the MOB stations didn't count."

Gessaman interrupts, "Morale aside, Colonel, we're asking for your assessment of—"

"Morale aside? Disillusion and morale don't mix real well on the battlefield. Our guys want to complete the mission, they're no longer sure what the mission is. Last month my soldiers killed a guy setting a roadside bomb. Turns out he was a sergeant in the Iraqi army, the guys we're supposed to be training as our replacements! Who the hell are we fighting for? In the last ninety days, three of my PFCs committed suicide. These were brave, outstanding soldiers . . . when they arrived three tours of duty ago. Two were on antidepressants, the third had already attempted suicide ten weeks earlier. His mental health officer and I had personally signed a recommendation that the soldier not be returned to active duty. My CO's response was that we had troop shortages, request denied."

"Duly noted, Colonel," said the blonde. "We appreciate the severity of the situation, which is why you are here. Now, if you could refocus your comments on the activities of the enemy."

"I'm sorry, ma'am, I didn't get your name."

"No, you didn't. The insurgents, Colonel."

"Insurgents are a small piece of a larger puzzle. A year ago we were in the middle of a Sunni–Shi'ite civil war, now we're seeing growing signs of a Shi'ite movement designed to unleash a nationwide bloodbath aimed at American troops. The militias' objective is to lure us out of the green zone, then pin us down in hostile neighborhoods using Iranian-made rocket-propelled grenade launchers. As a result, we've now ceased all military sweeps. Meanwhile, the local Sunni population is slowly being killed off or sent packing. By invading Iraq, we essentially radicalized the entire Muslim community and turned a secular society into a Shi'ite nation."

"In your estimation, Colonel, what group is doing most of the damage?"

Turnbull looks hard at Gessaman. *They're playing head games, leading me somewhere . . .* "Which group is the worst? The Shi'ite Death Squads? The Mahdi Army? The Badr Organization? Take your pick. Essentially, the groups trained by the Iranians. Of course, if you happen to be a Shi'ite living in the South, it's the Sunni extremists, backed by our Saudi and Jordanian allies. These groups come and go as they please, controlling neighborhoods, sometimes entire cities, and the Iraqi militia and police give them free reign. The civilians are too scared to venture out of their homes, and areas that used to be mixed have now segregated into either Sunni or Shi'ite simply out of necessity. Add to that the perpetual shortages of water and electricity, plus an exodus of ten thousand Iraqis a day, and you've got an almost intolerable situation. But you already know that, don't you, Mr. Gessaman?"

Gessaman says nothing.

"Let's talk about you, Colonel." The blonde leafs through her own folder. "Both parents trace their roots to the Scottish Highlands, your family came to America just after World War II. Grandfather was a war hero—"

"Yes, ma'am. He fought Rommel in North Africa."

"According to your bio, you come from a long line of fighting men."

"The Turnbull clan has fought in every war since Longshanks invaded Scotland." The colonel smiles. "We were a wild sort, the only bunch of rowdies ever to have a bounty placed on the entire clan's head."

"Tell me about John Turnbull." The blonde flashes an encouraging smile.

"John Turnbull . . . now there was a crazy-ass ancestor. According to Scot lore, John was reputed to have killed more English during William

Wallace's raids than any other kinsman who wore the kilt. Used to bring a two-hundred-pound mastiff into battle. One time, John beheaded four English knights while his dog chewed on their arms. True story. Some time after that this little English dweeb by the name of Kerr beheaded the dog and John simply lost it. Forgot all his training and got his arm chopped off, then he lost his head. Literally. War is hell, huh?"

The blonde again makes it a point to reference her notes. "According to Scot history, for the next two hundred years the Turnbulls waged war on the Kerr's land."

"That we did. See, us Highlanders . . . we never forget a debt."

"Killed a lot of people in the process, I imagine."

"Nothing I'm proud of, mind you. But you do what you have to."

"Women and children too?"

The colonel's guard goes up. *She's a spook. CIA most likely. Careful, Bull, this one's a wolf in sheep's clothing . . .*

Ryan Gessaman jumps in before he can reply. "Colonel, you're right about Iraq, it's become a real quagmire. Was it a mistake to go in? We'll let history decide. But the problem that refuses to allow democracy to take root in Iraq is the same one that threatens America—Islamic radicals. And everything's coming from Iran."

"Ever hear the term 'Islamic Waqf'?" asks the blonde. "It refers to an old Islamic precept that states Muslims have the right to claim any territory their people have conquered by force. Any conquest, including the ones that date back over a thousand years."

"That's a radical interpretation," the colonel counters. "Waqf is the act of giving an estate to the leaders of Islam to manage to help the poor."

"Radicals are who we're dealing with, Colonel. America stumbled in Iraq, and radical Islam used the momentum to spread its tentacles throughout the Muslim world. Yesterday, Hezbollah assassinated Pierre Gemayel, a Christian Cabinet minister in Lebanon, one of the few leaders left who stood against Syrian influence. We're dealing with a dangerous ideology, fueled by religious hatred, that thinks nothing of slaughtering Muslim and non-Muslim civilians alike to achieve their objectives. These radicals have infiltrated at least fifty-five different countries, and they won't be satisfied until they've retaken or recaptured every speck of land, from Madrid to the Middle East and then some. Their influence is spreading quickly throughout the Arab world; the more radical the violence, the more power they wield."

Gessaman nods. "This is Nazi Germany all over again, only they're killing for Allah, which is far more powerful cause than the Fuhrer. Radical Islam is winning the war of minds through an extensive propaganda program. Children in Palestine, Jordan, Iran, and Saudi Arabia are being taught at an early age to despise the West. Textbooks and music videos depict Jews and Christians as blood-sucking animals, the westerners as Satan worshipers. We have videotaped footage of first graders chanting for Jihad and the opportunity to blow themselves up in Allah's name. And as bad as things may seem now, it's going to get a whole lot worse. Within the next five years we could be looking at Armageddon-like attacks that could lead to the end of open societies as we know them."

"Five years, Colonel," the blonde repeats. "Within five years, Iran will be producing enriched uranium. Think about how a nuclear Iran would change the Middle East. The Saudis would demand nukes, then Egypt, Jordan, Syria . . . nuclear detente. But that's not even the worst of it. How do we stop Iran from supplying nuclear weapons to terrorist groups? Is there any doubt these Islamic radicals would use them? Remember how helpless you felt on September Eleventh? Imagine waking up one day and learning a suitcase nuke just wiped out New York or Chicago or Philadelphia or Miami—"

"—or all of them at once!" Gessaman says. "Hijacking planes requires long-range planning and specific talents, and we still failed to stop it from happening, smuggling in a dozen fifteen-kiloton suitcase nukes would be a cakewalk. A dozen Hiroshimas, Colonel. Think Homeland Security could stop it? What about immigration? We can't even keep a thousand Mexicans a day from sneaking over the border, and six years after 9/11 our ports still remain virtually unprotected. And you know how Washington is when it comes to terrorist threats; the politicians always wait until something bad happens before they react. You think the Dems are going to be any better? Non-binding actions change nothing."

"Weapons of mass destruction . . . our population in imminent danger." Colonel Turnbull exhales an exasperated breath. "With all due respect, this smells like the same neocon fear tactic Cheney and Rumsfeld used back in 2002."

"Are you saying the Iranians pose no threat?"

"Lady, let me tell you something I'm guessing you already know. The most effective ally we had in fighting the Taliban *were* the Iranians. They had always considered bin Laden a terrorist and were already battling

Sunni Pashtun tribes in Afghanistan. The Iranians had been secretly providing us with military support and intelligence against the Taliban—up
until the moment George Bush did an abrupt about-face and declared
their nation part of the axis of evil, even though they had nothing to do
with 9/11."

"And what about Ahmadinejad's threats?"

"Ahmadinejad's nothing more than a blowhard . . . the Iranian equivalent of Ann Coulter. It was our reaction to him, coupled with the invasion of Iraq, that increased his popularity among Shi'ites. We gave him
exactly what he was after—a presence. We did the same thing forty years
ago with Castro, and look where that got us."

"And when Castro acquired nuclear missiles from the Soviets, we
didn't hesitate to act," Gessaman shoots back. "Ahmadinejad's missiles
are radicals carrying suitcase nukes. Imagine the worst-case scenario.
American cities destroyed without warning, tens of millions of people
vaporized, millions more dead and dying. Our economy destroyed, panic
in the streets."

"It's an absolute nightmare," the woman says, "and Iran is the linchpin. Rumsfeld screwed up Iraq, no argument, but the Neocons were right
about one thing: threats must be addressed before they arrive, sponsors
of terror, held accountable. We simply cannot afford to allow the nuclear
genie out of the bottle in the Persian Gulf."

Colonel Turnbull's heart races. "Why am I here?"

"You're here because you know the enemy, because you've seen what
they can do. You're here because you have access to resources we may
need." Ryan Gessaman closes his folder. "For a moment, Colonel, I want
you to imagine you're the new secretary of defense. Better yet, the next
president. Your top advisors have just told you in no uncertain terms that,
within the next five years, Iran will have enriched uranium to build and
supply nuclear suitcase bombs to radical extremists. How do you prevent
the terrorists from using those weapons to decimate our nation and western society?"

"A preemptive invasion, I suppose."

"Yes," Gessaman replies, "but with what fighting force? You said
yourself, Iraq's a disaster, our troops are burned out, the military is dangerously short on manpower, and the American people want out of the
Persian Gulf. Even if you went ahead, you'd need upwards of half a million troops to invade Iran, maybe more to maintain control, which none

of us truly believes can happen. Where do you get the troops?"

"You could institute a draft," the blonde suggests, playing devil's advocate.

Gessaman shakes his head. "The American public would never go for it."

"Okay," the colonel says, "so we don't invade, we simply take out their nuclear facilities, just like the Israelis did with that Iraqi reactor back in '81."

"A good suggestion," Gessaman states, "only there's potentially dozens of facilities, most of them unknown, many underground. Plus, there's the terrorist training camps, the military bases . . . no, if we do this it's got to be all or nothing. And remember what you said earlier: by invading Iraq we essentially radicalized the entire Muslim community. The days of preemptively attacking another country are over . . . unless there's just cause."

"You mean if they hit us first?"

"Exactly." The blonde's eyes bear down on Turnbull. "The world had no problem with us invading Afghanistan after 9/11. Last May, I sat in a top-secret meeting between President Bush and his most senior national security advisors about how to rewrite the rules of the Cold War. The old rules of deterrence don't apply when it comes to suitcase nukes. At some point before his presidency ends, Bush will announce that, should a nuclear suitcase bomb ever be detonated on American or Allied soil, the United States will hold the country who supplied the material 'fully responsible' for the aftermath."

Colonel Turnbull wipes a bead of sweat from his brow. "What does 'fully responsible' mean exactly?"

"The term was purposely left vague, allowing for a nuclear or other type of retaliatory attack. Should such an attack be directly linked to the Iranians through nuclear forensics, the outcome would change the geo-political landscape forever."

"Wait . . . you actually want them to hit us?"

"Of course not," Gessaman backpeddles. "But hypothetically, if they did . . . then the world would understand, then our response would be justified."

"Think about it," adds the blonde. "Eliminate Iran's crazy president and the radical mullahs and democracy suddenly has a fighting chance to take root. No more nuclear threat, no more Iranian insurgents into Iraq, and we deal the radical elements of Islam a death blow. We're talking about saving western society while allowing the Arab world to climb out of the Stone Age, once and for all."

Colonel Turnbull sits back in his chair, suddenly feeling queasy. "Let me get this straight: you want to allow an American city to be nuked in order to give us an excuse to turn Iran into a parking lot?"

"No. Only the desired Iranian targets. Nuclear facilities, military bases, terrorist training sites. A preemptive strike to prevent a dozen nuclear attacks on American cities."

"But to wipe out a million Americans?" The colonel mops sweat from his brow.

"Your grandfather fought in World War II," the blonde reminds him. "Imagine what would have happened if Roosevelt had waited another six months before entering the war. All of Britain would have been lost, the Manhattan Project would have been delayed, Hitler's heavy water experiments were nearly complete . . . Germany would have won the war."

"But allowing a nuclear attack . . . on American soil?"

"News flash, Colonel: Roosevelt *knew* the Japanese were readying an attack on Pearl Harbor, and guess what—he allowed it to happen!"

"I heard that; I just never wanted to believe it."

"Believe it," Gessaman states. "U.S. intelligence had broken the enemy's codes months earlier, we'd been monitoring their communications long before December 7. World War II was Roosevelt's Iraq. He knew Congress and the American people would never agree to engage in another battle in Europe, not unless something drastic were to happen . . . an event so terrible, so heinous that it would incite an emotional public response and illicit a massive call to arms. When he learned the Japanese were coming, FDR ordered the carriers out to sea and allowed the devastation in Pearl Harbor to take place. The president sacrificed thousands of innocent American men and women so that our country would be forced to go to war, a war the White House secretly provoked in order to give us a fighting chance to defeat an evil that was threatening the entire world."

The colonel's eyes grow harsh. "And Bush? Are you saying he allowed the events of September Eleventh to happen in the same way?"

Ryan Gessaman smirks. "Honestly, Colonel, I didn't think someone of your stature would be a conspiracy theorist."

The blonde leans forward, her Cheshire cat smile intended to dismiss his question. "Colonel, this is merely think-tank conversation; the Pentagon engages in this kind of rhetoric eight days a week. But let's face the facts: Islamic radicals want to get their hands on a nuke, and with Iran entering the game, the odds are suddenly even that the threat is very real. I think you'd agree we've been relatively lucky since 9/11, but our ports remain unprotected, and our border patrols fail almost every test we throw at them. Sure, we could sit back and pray our intelligence network will stop the next wave of attacks, only it doesn't take a team of terrorists to blow up a city; it only takes one suicide bomber with one atomic suitcase bomb. But if we control the variables, we can destroy the threat."

"What variables do you control?" Turnbull asks. "The Republicans lost both Houses, the Neocons lost Rumsfeld. Come 2008, another Clinton may be occupying the White House."

The blonde is grinning, but her hazel eyes are as cold as ice. "You're misreading the landscape, Colonel. Corruption scandals swung the pendulum away from the GOP in the midterms. That slide will be corrected in the next two years. The Democrats will talk a tough game, threatening to cut funding to the troops, but in the end they'll be so worried about the '08 elections that they'll back down and Bush will still do whatever he pleases."

She waves the conversation off. "Anyway, this is just talk. Before any action can even be considered, there must be a plan, and no one knows this area of the world better than you."

Colonel Turnbull clears his throat. "Nothing personal, ma'am, but I have a family that's barely seen me these past few years. I've done my time in hell, so if it's all the same to you, I think you'd better find another man for the job."

The blonde sits back, her face turning flush. "You think you've been in hell? You have no idea what hell is, Colonel. I have a great uncle who passed away a few years ago. When he was ten the Nazis rounded him up with his parents and sisters, his aunts and uncles and cousins, and the rest of the Jews in his village and shoved them into cattle cars. The lucky ones suffocated to death on the ride to Auschwitz. When they arrived at the death camp, the women were separated from the men and taken directly to the gas chambers. That was before the Nazis figured out they could run the ovens day and night by using the fat from burning human flesh as a fuel.

"I may seem cold-hearted to you, Colonel, and maybe I am. But when I go home at night I hug a husband who loves me and kiss my two young children whom I adore, and if I have to sell my soul to make sure they don't get incinerated by some lunatic in a turban who's been brainwashed into believing he's going to paradise for killing infidels . . . then so be it."

She pauses, looking out the window at downtown Washington. "Last week I was watching CNN . . . Glenn Beck was interviewing Benjamin Netanyahu. The former Israeli prime minister was asked what the Jews learned from the Holocaust. You know what he said? He said, 'When someone tells you they intend to annihilate you, you should believe them.' "

She forces a smile, regaining her composure. "I know you're a family man, Colonel; that's why you're here. For a moment I want you to imagine you and your family living in the Highlands centuries ago, at a time when Longshanks was readying his invasion of Scotland. If you knew you could save your country and countrymen by sacrificing a few clans while forever removing the English threat, would you have done it?"

Colonel Turnbull grinds his teeth, the nerves in his right quadriceps causing the leg to shake. "Okay, lady, you've got your man."

"If you want to get people to fight, you have to get them to believe there is a threat, that they're in danger. This is an integral part of Islamic propaganda."

—ITMAR MARCUS,
Palestinian Media Watch

"Bush and Cheney are ramping up the case for an attack on Iran, just as they did before invading Iraq."

—ROBERT FOX,
The First Post,
July 1, 2007

"Whoever fights monsters should see to it that in the process he does not become a monster."

—NIETZSCHE

"The American way of life is not negotiable."

—VICE PRESIDENT DICK CHENEY

"Iran's chief nuclear negotiator, viewed by the West as a moderator in Tehran, resigned before crucial talks with Europe this week over Iran's nuclear program, signaling that Iranian officials may have closed the door to any possible negotiated settlement in its standoff with the West."

—NAZILA FATHI AND MICHAEL SLACKMAN,
New York Times,
October 21, 2007

WINTER
2011

"The first angel blew his trumpet, and hail and fire mixed with blood were thrown down upon the earth, and one-third of the earth was set on fire. One-third of the trees were burned, and all the grass was burned."

—REVELATION 8:7

"Yeah, I was in the old Executive Office Building for those meetings, at one time or another all of us were. BP, Chevron, Conoco-Phillips, Shell, Exxon-Mobil, U.S. Oil and Gas . . . but only the top managers, the CEs were purposely kept away. That was the red flag, the 'plausible deniable' factor. All of us knew what was at stake, we'd seen the reports coming out of the Caspian Basin, all of which added a sense of urgency to Cheney's plan. Rumsfeld showed us SAT images of the oil fields while Wolfowitz did most of the selling, some nonsense about how our workers would be safe, how they'd be embraced, all the while pushing us for timetables on how long it would take us to get the oil flowing again, as if we had a crystal ball. The Brown and Root guys had detailed maps of Iraq's energy infrastructure, you could tell they'd been in it with the CIA lady from the beginning. It was one big circle jerk, and I just kept nodding, wondering what the hell we were doing here, I mean the Bushies had just taken office, and the scenario they outlined, no one actually believed it would happen. Five months later the planes struck the Twin Towers and everyone knew. The Senate Hearings that followed . . . what a joke. I mean, no one was even placed under oath."

—ANONYMOUS OIL EXECUTIVE,
on Vice President Dick Cheney's secret
Energy Task Force meetings

"On August 13, 2002, the CIA completed a classified, six-page intelligence analysis (dubbed "Perfect Storm") that described the worst scenarios that could arise after a U.S.-led removal of Saddam Hussein. According to then-CIA director George Tenet, it was relegated to the back of a thick briefing book handed out to President Bush's national security team for a meeting on September 7, 2002, where the Iraq war was Topic A."

—WALTER PINCUS,
The Washington Post,
June 2007

CHAPTER 1

Iran Claims Capability to Build a Dozen Nuclear Missiles

Associated Press: December 11, 2011

TEHRAN—Iranian President Mahmoud Ahmadinejad announced today that his country has succeeded in enriching enough weapons-grade uranium to build a dozen atomic bombs. "For more than a decade we have been pressured by the West and the Zionist regime to curtail our efforts to remain a liberated power. Thanks to our great successes in bringing nuclear power to our people, we have taken the next step down the path of independence. Iran's enrichment program now yields enough uranium to arm a dozen nuclear missiles—sufficient to annihilate the enemies that threaten our borders. The great nation of Islam will no longer be bullied by the West. The Zionist movement will be eliminated in one storm, the western powers that hold Iraq, in another."

The McKuin administration responded to the Iranian announcement by stating that Ahmadinejad's rule has succeeded only in taking his people down a "dangerous path of self-destruction."

Ahmadinejad's recent rise in popularity among his own people, fueled by the continued violence in Iraq, allowed him to change the Iranian constitution, extending his presidency.

DIRKSEN SENATE OFFICE BUILDING
ROOM SD-366
DECEMBER 12, 2011
9:06 AM EST

HEARING BEFORE THE COMMITTEE ON
ENERGY AND NATURAL RESOURCES
United States Senate
110th Congress

"The hearing will please come to order." Committee chairman David Keller grandstands a sweeping glance around the packed chamber, the senator from California reminding himself not to look directly into the C-Span cameras. "I'd like to thank everyone in attendance, particularly the senators who have chosen to join us here today for the first in a series of meetings that I hope will lead to real change in the role energy plays in our global economy, the environment, and the security of our nation. In light of the recent events in Iran, I can think of nothing as important.

"The questions we're going to be focusing on today concern the present and future energy needs of both the United States and the world as a whole, specifically dealing with oil and natural gas. If our witnesses would share their perspectives on these specific challenges, the committee and I would be most grateful. Senator Poschner, I believe you had some opening remarks?"

"Thank you, Mr. Chairman, and a special thank you to our esteemed panelists who have made themselves available for this morning's session." The republican senator from Virginia pauses for the applause, nodding to the lone woman and four men seated at the witness table below the main dais. Adjusting his wire-rimmed glasses, he reads from a prepared statement.

"Ladies and gentlemen, we live in unprecedented times. The world's population is growing by a quarter of a million people every day. Whether we're able to feed and clothe, educate, sustain, and maintain our population will depend upon our ability to meet global energy demands. Little has changed over the last twenty years. Fossil fuels still supply 85 percent of our energy needs, with oil leading the way. Each day the United States uses approximately 22 million barrels of crude, representing nearly a fourth of the world's 94 million barrel-per-day consumption. These staggering quantities are expected to increase at an annual rate of upwards of 2 percent, reaching 107 million barrels of oil per day by 2020 as the economies of China, India, and other Asian countries continue their unprecedented acceleration as industrialized nations . . ."

Ashley Brown Futrell III, affectionately known to family and friends simply as "Ace," stretches his left leg beneath the witness table. At six-four and 225 pounds, the forty-four-year-old petroleum geologist and one-time football star at the University of Georgia finds it hard to remain seated for very long in one position. His left knee crackles like gravel beneath a twice surgically repaired patellar tendon, and his joints ache from chronic arthritis. On good days he can recall every pass completion thrown during a meteoric college career, on bad days, only the pain.

Ace tilts his head hard to the right then back to the left until the vertebrae in his neck "snap" into place. Then, methodically, he pops each knuckle a finger at a time while stealing another quick glance at his watch.

Ten after nine. Six more hours 'til I leave for Dulles Airport. Figure an hour flight, then another hour to get my luggage and catch a cab into the city. Eight hours . . . eight long hours until Kelli's back in my arms. No more long trips, Futrell, no matter what she says. This is it. Ace palms his Blackberry, flipping through the stored images in his photo gallery. Kelli and their two children smile back at him, tugging at his heartstrings. He has thought about his wife every day during his travels abroad, the hardest times coming at the end of each eighteen-hour day when he lay in bed alone in some foreign hotel room, staring at the ceiling fan, wondering if she was all right . . . wracked with guilt over leaving her. Twenty-three days . . . at least a dozen times he had contemplated taking the next flight home, but his wife had insisted he stick it out. Tonight he and Kelli will finally share the same bed—a suite in Central Park—before driving home to Long Island tomorrow to see their kids.

He checks his watch again.

Ace had met Kelli Doyle during their junior year at Georgia—he the walk-on third-string quarterback suddenly thrust into the limelight, she the knockout blonde with the country-girl smile and the disposition of a back-room brawler. She had been an All-American on the women's lacrosse and field hockey teams, a tough-as-nails competitor who enjoyed physically humiliating her opponents. Ace and Kelli's relationship had lasted nearly until graduation, when Ace had gone through his "gray period." Kelli, always focused on the brass ring, had moved on without him. Six years later the flame was rekindled when they ran into one another at a fund-raiser in Orlando. Within two months they had married.

Fourteen years of marriage, most of it good. A house, cars, two wonderful kids, two well-paying careers—the American dream . . . all threatened by that damn lump in her left breast. Surgery, chemo, followed by a two-year reprieve before it had spread. The second round of chemo had knocked the fight out of her . . . but was it enough? He had wanted to cancel his trip, but she had insisted, promising him good news when he returned.

Three long weeks . . . never again. PetroConsultants can fire me if they want. Plenty of other jobs in the field. He turns to face the other four members of the panel. To his immediate right is Ellen Wulf, an associate director with the Energy Information Administration, to her right, Michael Bach-Marklund, a senior fellow for the Center for Strategic and International Studies. Next to him is Rodney Lemeni, an economist representing Chevron, Texaco, and Caltex, then Christopher Santoro, a consultant from the Cambridge Energy Research Association (CERA). CERA is a sister organization to Ace's employer, PetroConsultants, both falling under the ever-expanding IHS Energy Group umbrella. *Wonder if any of them have to travel twenty-two weeks out of the year?*

Senator Poschner drones on, "Listen to these stats. China is adding the equivalent energy demand of an entire mid-sized country every two years. Last year they added another forty-four thousand megawatts—more than our largest power company, and they still experienced blackouts throughout 60 percent of their country. In addition, India has—"

Ace shifts again in his chair, waiting for the senator to chew up his allotted time. He has worked as a petroleum engineer for PetroConsultants for fifteen years and has heard it all before—the statistics, the warnings, the recommendations, the endless debates. He has never doubted the sincerity of the senators present, not now, not six years earlier when he last testified before the newly installed, Democrat-led Congress. But convincing a committee to act is far different from passing sweeping legislation, especially when the White House was doing the Texas two-step with the fossil fuel industry.

Maybe I should just quit. Not like I haven't given it some thought. I'm sure I could find a position with any of the major oil companies . . . unless of course I burn the bridge right now, pull back the curtain, tell Congress what I really know . . . yeah, like that'll make a difference. Most of these bozos receive campaign donations from the six sisters of sludge, the ones that don't won't survive next year's election. Your call, Ace. Feed your family, or go down in one last blaze of glory . . .

"Thank you, Senator. That brings us to our first witness of the day. Ace Futrell is a senior administrator at PetroConsultants of Geneva, now part of the IHS Energy Group. Mr. Futrell's team has been collecting data as part of his organization's upcoming report on world oil reserves—"

What about a major university? I could probably get a teaching job. Of course, we'd have to downsize. Lose the cars, forget about that Disney cruise. Maybe I could pick up a few night shifts as a fry cook at McDonald's. Could be fun. They just bumped the minimum wage to $8.25, that should be enough to cover our cable bill. So what if we can't afford health insurance or college tuition or summer camp . . .

"Mr. Futrell, I know you've been traveling abroad these last few weeks. The committee greatly appreciates you diverting your trip home to be with us this morning. Mr. Futrell?"

. . . or gasoline or food—

"Hey, Ace, you're on." Ellen Wulf nudges his shoulder, snapping him back into reality.

"Mr. Futrell, I asked if you're ready to testify."

"Testify? Yes, sorry. Oh, and it's pronounced Fu-troll. As in petrol." Ace adjusts his microphone, then reads from his notes. "Mr. Chairman, Senators, it's an honor for me to be back with you this morning. I've been asked to address the topic of global oil production, specifically how much oil is left in world reserves. Having just returned from an extensive field trip to the Middle East, I have with me preliminary results from our latest data; however, before I share that information with the committee, I feel it's important we understand a few basic rules of the game. The first is a fundamental law of energy, the Law of Diminishing Returns. When the first wildcat rig is drilled, we know very little about what an oil field will yield, but by the time the last well is up, we pretty much know everything. The pattern is consistent and clear—every oil reserve peaks and drops in what M. King Hubbert, the father of petroleum geology, discovered to be a bell-shaped curve. The first oil pumped from a well is the cream, the easiest to access. Eventually the basin will peak, thereafter production will slow, the less the flow, the more difficult and costly it is to pump. And yes, while technology continues to increase the long-term potential of each reserve, even technology has its limitations."

You're boring them, Futrell. They're not here to resolve the oil crisis, only to spin it.

"Peak oil is a term that refers to the top of Hubbert's Curve, the point at which the fruit is still easily picked among the tree's lower branches. EUR Oil refers to the Estimated Ultimately Recoverable quantity of oil remaining underground, the key word here being 'recoverable.' Bottom line, Senators: It takes energy to get energy and, in this case, oil to recover oil. If it takes two barrels of oil to recover three barrels, you pump. But if the field is in decline and you're only able to recover two barrels or less for those two barrels expended, you can't continue pumping, not with a negative energy return on energy invested. Remember that, Senators. It means we'll run out of oil long before the last drop is ever drawn out of the ground.

"Hubbert correctly predicted crude oil production in the United States would peak between 1966 and 1972. The actual peak occurred in 1970, though it would take another full year before that fact became apparent. Since then we've gone from being the world's largest oil producer to its biggest importer, a role now being challenged by China. While we still have active reserves in the Gulf of Mexico, for the most part America's domestic supply is all but finished.

"What about the rest of the world? Hubbert predicted world peak oil would occur between the years 2000 and 2005. Have we peaked? No question about it. From 2003 to today, not a single new catchment has been discovered that exceeds 500 million barrels. Okay, so how much is left? That's a bit more difficult to predict, given that these national companies exporting oil tend to operate in secrecy and deceit. Kuwait, for example, recently lied about its reported reserves in order to protect their OPEC production quotas, a practice all too common among producing nations. Oil companies are just as bad. Because they have to pay taxes on reserves, they tend to report new findings in old fields, a practice that maintains stock prices but does little for world energy needs. Six years ago executives at Shell had to resign after they misrepresented oil reserves to stockholders by 4 billion barrels of oil . . . an 'accounting error' worth an estimated $136 billion."

Ace reshuffles his notes. "Here's a few hard facts that play into the equation. Our species uses a billion barrels of oil every ten days, and the United States is responsible for 25 percent of that. Instead of enacting policies that conserve energy, we continue to use more. America's demand for oil, as well as natural gas and coal, is expected to increase by another 40 percent over the next twenty years, and we're not the only nation using more energy. As Senator Poschner already mentioned, the energy demands coming out of Asia, specifically China and India, are enormous. Prior to 1990, China's energy needs grew only half as quickly as its gross domestic product, but over the last five years there's been a groundbreaking surge in China's economy that has caused their energy consumption to quadruple. We've contributed to that variable, our auto imports playing a key role in the mobilization of China's workforce. Of particular concern is China's recent shift from coal to oil and natural gas, a change necessitated by the effects of carbon dioxide emissions that have decimated air quality in their major cities. As a result, China's oil demand has risen from 14 million barrels per day in 2004 to its present levels of 19 million barrels, nearly equaling that of the United States. When one considers that China's population of 1.4 billion people is four times as large as ours, it staggers the imagination to think how high their demand could eventually go. And, like the United States, China receives most of its oil imports from Saudi Arabia, followed by Iran, Venezuela, and the Sudan."

Chairman Keller interrupts, "It's no secret we're in direct competition with the Chinese, Mr. Futrell. What this committee would like to know is how much oil is left, specifically in Saudi Arabia, which appears to be the only oil-producing nation that can sustain global increases in demand."

Ace nods. "Saudi Arabia is the key; there's no doubt. They possess five fields classified as super-giants, several of which have been pumping for close to sixty years. Ghawar is the mega-giant, composed of several super-giants. The field is 174 miles long and sixteen to twenty miles wide, and it's been online since 1951. To the Saudis' credit, they set the standard on maintaining their wells, with recovery rates at 75 percent—far and away the highest in the industry."

The Chairman interrupts again. "Yesterday, the committee heard a presentation by Mr. Nansen Saleri, the reservoir manager at Saudi Aramco. According to Mr. Saleri, the Saudis have tapped and untapped fields that could meet world demand beyond 2054. By the look on your face, you don't seemed convinced."

"No, sir, I'm not, and I'm not alone. Despite their public gestures, the Royal Family has clamped down on foreign inspections of both oil wells and tankers. As a result, our data reflects basin quantities that are antiquated at best. As to these untapped fields . . . we've been listening to that song and dance for years. These days, if the House of Saud told me the desert was dry, I'd probably bring a raincoat."

The remark sends smiles across the faces of a few of the Democrats in attendance.

Nicely done. The fast food industry can use a man like you . . .

Republican senator Bob Prichard, a staunch oil industry supporter from Texas, is not amused. "For the record, Mr. Futrell, the House of Saud has been a friend and ally to this nation for more than sixty years. Besides being our main supplier of cheap oil, they've also proven themselves to be a stabilizing influence among the other OPEC nations, as well as one of the few countries in the Middle East that supports our ongoing war against terrorism.

They also fund the teaching of radical Islam and hatred of the West, and fifteen of their nationals hijacked our planes. Ah, but what's a few thousand dead civilians among friends . . .

"I ask you now, sir, and for the record, are you in possession of any hard evidence that refutes the information presently being supplied by Saudi Aramco?"

"Hard evidence? No, Senator; however—"

"Thank you, Mr. Futrell."

Ace grinds his teeth, refusing to back down. "Senator, you invited me here to testify, not to debate politics. PetroConsultants accepts the fact that third-world nations routinely exaggerate oil reserves. In the last year alone Venezuela, Dubai, Iran, and Iraq have all been caught in lies. I'm not sure we're any different. After all, how many tens of billions of dollars worth of aid to New Orleans was secretly diverted to rebuild oil rigs damaged by Hurricane Katrina?"

Oops, did that just slip out? Ace returns the senator's glare.

Conversations break out as Senator Prichard's face turns a deeper shade of red. "Mr. Chairman, I demand you strike those comments from the public record, they have no bearing on—"

"Senator, my only point was—"

Chairman Keller interjects, "I think we've got the point, Mr. Futrell. If you'd conclude your testimony with your latest figures?"

Ace takes a deep breath, his blood pressure refusing to settle. "One final comment, if I may, Mr. Chairman, for the record. While the committee might eventually enact measures to replace some of the 40 percent of oil expended on power generation with natural gas, coal, nuclear, or some other form of alternative energy, there presently exists no short- or long-term solution to remedy our transportation and farming needs. Let me be crystal clear here: without the oil used in fertilizers and pesticides, corn yields would drop from 130 bushels per acre to thirty, the same would apply for our other crops, including the grain needed to feed livestock. It's gasoline that powers industrial tractors, allowing a mere 2 percent of our population to feed 300 million people, and it's gasoline that brings those perishable goods to market. When the oil stops flowing, the masses will go hungry—and that, Senator, is fact. The only way you remedy that nightmare is to invest now in renewable energy resources and enact major policy changes that radically replace our nation's infrastructure, something that will take upwards of ten years, mandating long-range planning and investment. In the opinion of many experts, it's long overdue."

Chairman Keller waits for the spectators' applause to die down. "Your recommendations are duly noted. Now, the estimates?"

Ace removes a sealed manila enveloped from his briefcase. "Mr. Chairman, Senators, based on all available supply indicators, it is PetroConsultants' belief that world oil levels peaked in the summer of 2003, fueled, in part, by unexpected losses incurred at Iraqi wellheads and insurgent attacks on pipelines in the wake of the second Gulf War. Based on current and projected demand, the ongoing war in the Middle East, the continued pattern of hurricanes affecting the Gulf of Mexico with increased ferocity, and the potential for more terrorist attacks that threaten key pipelines, we anticipate the world suffering serious depletions by the year 2017."

A hush falls over the chamber, followed by dozens of side conversations.

"Six years, Mr. Futrell?"

Ace nods. "Or perhaps, Mr. Chairman, even sooner."

"Secretary Rumsfeld also stated that he was giving a lecture to members of Congress, in the Pentagon, on the morning of 9/11 and warned them to expect the unexpected with future terrorist attacks. Shortly after that he was handed a note stating that the North Tower was struck. Shortly after that he was told the second tower was hit. He then claims he continues with this lecture until the Pentagon was struck at 9:38. This makes absolutely no sense. If the Secretary of Defense was lecturing to Congressmen about surprise terrorist attacks when he is told two planes have hit both World Trade Towers, it is beyond belief that he continues this presentation without reacting to this 'unexpected' terrorist attack. The fact that not one member of the (9/11) Commission chose to scrutinize this statement speaks volumes."

—MICHAEL KANE,
"Elephants in the Barracks: The Complete Failure
of the 9/11 Commission,"
Centre for Research on Globalization

"The most important thing for us is to find Osama bin Laden. It's our number-one priority, and we will not rest until we find him."

—PRESIDENT GEORGE W. BUSH,
September 13, 2001

"I don't know where he is. I have no idea, and I really don't care. It's not that important. It's not our priority."

—PRESIDENT GEORGE W. BUSH,
March 13, 2002

CHAPTER 2

"Mary Chris, I'm late! Where's the Sweet'N Low?" Aurora Police Area Commander Doug Dvorak searches through kitchen cabinets and drawers, leaving chaos in his wake.

"I forgot to buy some," his wife calls out from the bedroom. "Use the sugar."

"Can't! Just started that new diet."

"Then use honey."

"It's still sugar!"

"Then drink it black!" She enters the kitchen, a curling iron dangling from her chestnut hair. "Since when do you diet anyway; you're like a genetic freak as it is."

"I'm in training for the spring marathon."

"Good. You can run over to Wal-Mart after work and pick us up a new alarm clock."

"I told you, I can fix it." He fills his Chicago Bears coffee mug, making a face as he chokes down the bitter elixir.

"Then fix it tonight, I can't afford to be late again." She wipes coffee from his goatee. Gives him a kiss. "Be careful out there."

"Always."

♦ ♦ ♦

Situated forty-two miles west of Chicago, the city of Aurora is a community of 165,000 suburbanites, spread out over four counties, six school districts, and seven townships. The Fox River splits the historic downtown area into east and west districts. Aurora is home to a renovated movie theater as well as several churches and bridges that date back to the late 1800s.

Commander Dvorak oversees Area One, which encompasses the west side of Aurora and its downtown area. He also commands the city's bicycle patrol program and its special response team.

He is ten minutes from the police station when he receives the call from dispatch.

♦ ♦ ♦

Ray Henry has been the owner and general manager of Aurora Truck Rental since returning from two tours of duty in Iraq. Dvorak finds the former staff sergeant in his office on the phone, pacing behind his desk.

Henry waves him in. Signals, "one minute," as he jots down numbers on a note pad already filled with hieroglyphics. "Fine, fine. But you tell Jerry I want that truck back here in an hour with new front break pads or I'm taking my business over to Kendall." Henry hangs up. "Sorry, Doug. Appreciate you coming by. How's Mary Chris?"

"Good. So what's up?"

"Probably nothing, then again, my 'soldier-sense' is tingling. Had two customers come in late last night to purchase one of our trucks. Middle Eastern types, supposedly college students, living at the same address. First red flag was their driver's licenses, both from South Carolina. These days, Bin Laden could probably get a license from that security sieve. Anyway, they got real antsy when I told them I had to make copies for my records. Second red flag was paying me in cash—$17,500 to be exact."

"What kind of truck?"

"Seventeen footer, one of the temperature-controlled units used for hauling perishables."

"They say what they needed it for?"

"Produce, but I could tell they were lying. Here's a copy of their licenses." Henry hands him the photocopies.

Dvorak reads the names. "Jamal al-Yussuf, age twenty-seven. Omar Kamel Radi, twenty-nine. Okay, I'll check it out." He stands to leave. "Tell your girls I'll see them Saturday at soccer practice."

"Sure thing. But I didn't tell you the last red flag. Schmucks were wearing Cubs jerseys. Who wears a Cubs jersey in December, especially the way the Bears are playing? Am I right, or am I right?"

◆   ◆   ◆

The apartment complex is a two-story brick face, located six miles from Waubonsee College. Commander Dvorak verifies the refrigerated truck is nowhere in sight then locates the landlord, Dawn Darconte, a local woman in her mid-thirties.

"They rented the apartment back in October. Told me they were students."

"Ever give you any trouble?"

"No. They pretty much kept to themselves. And they paid for the year in advance."

"Isn't that a bit unusual for students?"

"Bit unusual for anyone."

"Ever see them carrying textbooks?"

"I work full time in a video store. They could be moving a library in and out of here and I'd probably miss it."

She leads him upstairs to apartment 2-D. He knocks several times. Waits.

No answer.

"When do you recall last seeing these guys?"

"Maybe a week ago. The tall one, Omar, he jogs in the mornings. I have a key. Want me to let you in?"

"Without a search warrant, I'd need consent of the occupant or evidence of abandonment. What about their car? Is it still out front?"

She peers over the rail. "Nope, it's gone."

Dvorak fishes inside his pocket for a business card. "Call me if they show up."

◆   ◆   ◆

Commander Dvorak was back in his office by eleven-fifteen. By noon he'd established that neither Jamal al-Yussuf or Omar Kamel Radi were officially enrolled at Waubonsee College. By two-fifteen that afternoon he learned that both suspects had closed their checking accounts at a local Citicorp branch, having purged each of more than $65,000. A check on the deposit histories of both men traced back four months, all monies originating from a bank in the Cayman Islands.

By six-thirty that evening, Commander Doug Dvorak had his signed search warrant.

"Tired of frequent blackouts, China has set up the world's largest electrical grid, more than doubling its electrical generation capacity from its 1995 level. It also built a magnetic levitation train outside Shanghai in 2003 that can travel at more than 300 miles per hour, while our own rail system is literally falling apart."

—*U.S. NEWS & WORLD REPORT,*
February 19, 2007

"This program gives consumers an opportunity to experience the highly fuel-efficient vehicles GM has to offer in the mid-size segment."

—DAVE BORCHELT,
Southeast General Manager of General Motors,
on GM's new fuel price protection program, capping gas
prices at $1.99 per gallon for one year. Eligible vehicles include
the Chevrolet Tahoe and Suburban (half-ton models only)
and the Hummer H2, which averages nine miles per gallon.
May 2006

"The U.S. House of Representatives has passed a wide-ranging energy bill that will require most utilities to produce 15 percent of their electricity from renewable sources like wind and solar power. President George W. Bush has vowed to veto the bill because it does nothing to encourage increased domestic production of oil and gas."

—JOHN M. BRODER,
International Herald Tribune,
August 5, 2007

CHAPTER 3

DIRKSEN SENATE OFFICE BUILDING
ROOM SD-366
DECEMBER 12, 2011
10:27 AM EST

HEARING BEFORE THE COMMITTEE
ON ENERGY AND NATURAL RESOURCES
United States Senate
110th Congress

"THE HEARING WILL COME TO ORDER!" Chairman Keller strikes his gavel until the room quiets. "Six years, Mr. Futrell? This committee's been assured by multiple sources on more than one occasion that world reserves should continue to meet demand until at least 2029. The Energy Information Agency's own Annual Energy Outlook Report stated that—"

"With all due respect, Mr. Chairman, EIA estimates are based on non-technical considerations. While the DOE's data on current and past supplies tends to be fairly accurate, future projections were concocted so they'd equate to anticipated domestic supply growth. They were political projections, Senator, nothing more. It's like asking an economist; all you'll get are unsubstantiated, sunny expectations."

More cross-conversations fill the chamber. Keller pounds the gavel until the sound echoes above the din. "We're moving on. The Chair recognizes Senator Ashton."

The representative from Alabama appears quite animated for a man stricken to a wheelchair. "Mr. Chairman, it is an undeniable fact that the world will eventually run out of oil, but to suggest, without evidence, that we'll actually run out of oil within six years is simply irresponsible. Last year I personally attended an energy conference hosted by the Center for Strategic and International Studies right here in Washington. I listened to testimony from numerous experts, including directors at Saudi Aramco, who presented us with in-depth maps of their oil fields. The Saudi's projections, backed by the U.S. Geological Survey, go far to refute Mr. Futrell's 'personal opinions.' Conservative estimates indicate reserves of six hundred billion barrels, not counting a significant part of the Rub' al-Khali Basin, which has yet to be drilled. As such, I formally request that Mr. Futrell's estimates be stricken from the public record."

"Seconded."

Ace sits back, a numbness creeping over his being as Republicans and Democrats argue whether to remove his statement from the event's recorded history.

Chairman Keller retakes control of the proceedings. "We shall table a vote on any motions until after the Committee hears testimony from the other panelists. Mr. Santoro, I'd like to hear your opinion on Saudi reserves."

"Thank you, Mr. Chairman." Christopher Santoro repositions his microphone, allowing him to stare down the table at Ace. "CERA has conducted our own study of the Saudi oil fields in question. We agree with Senator Ashton that these reserves hold more than 600 billion barrels, plus an additional 200 billion barrels in undiscovered resources, and perhaps another 100 billion in fields that have peaked but still hold reserves that can be pumped using new technologies. That's 900 billion barrels of oil, enough to meet global needs well beyond 2035. We also believe that, as technology evolves, oil companies will continue to drill deeper and more accurately, and I think even Mr. Futrell has agreed, no one does it better than the Saudis. By producing slowly and steadily, Saudi Aramco has expanded the life cycle of each of its big reservoirs, with depletion rates averaging a mere 1 to 2 percent a year. Sure, we'd love for the Sauds to open the valves and double production, but sending a glut of cheap oil into the market can also destabilize the industry. The Saudis realize this and use their vast reserves to stabilize prices. Still, as history has shown, whenever there's a crisis, be it a hurricane in the Gulf or a harsh winter in Japan, the flow of oil is always increased to compensate for demand. Based on CERA's studies, and taking into consideration new extraction technologies and alternative energy sources coming on line, we feel confident global reserves will last us beyond 2043, perhaps as long as 2050."

Several Committee members applaud the statement.

Rodney Lemeni, an economist from Chevron/Texaco, half raises his hand, adding, "I would agree with Mr. Santoro, provided the oil companies continue to receive the strong backing and support of the United States government."

Yeah, because the oil companies need a few billion dollars more of our tax money each quarter in order to keep the lights on . . . Ace raises his hand. "Mr. Chairman, so there is no confusion, our analysis of the data took into account all factors, including improved extraction technologies. Granted, we did not add the untapped fields located in the Saudi's Empty Quarter, the reason being—we've yet to see any geological or seismic evidence that shows us what's really down there."

"Yes, but given the vast fields and their proximity to the Ghawar, wouldn't you assume more of the same?"

"Sir, if I've learned one thing in my fifteen years in this business, it's this: if it doesn't smell right, something stinks."

"Senator Thornton, you wish to reply?"

Robert Thornton, the republican senator from Alaska, leans into his microphone as he addresses the Committee. "I want to thank all of our distinguished guests for attending this morning's session. After listening to Mr. Futrell's comments, I hope our friends on the Democrat side of the aisle are now convinced that drilling in the Arctic National Wildlife Refuge is no longer an option, but a critical necessity in meeting our nation's present and future energy needs."

"Response? Yes . . . Mr. Futrell."

Ace grabs the microphone, his psyche now fully engaged in battle. "With all due respect to Senator Thornton, while some 'experts' have tossed around quantities of 16 billion barrels of oil being found in ANWR, the U.S. Geological Survey's numbers are far more accurate, dealing with EUR Oil, not volume. There's less than a year's supply of recoverable oil in the Arctic, and it would take at least ten years to bring that supply to market. The Arctic supply is nothing more than a band-aid, and a small, expensive, and, in my estimation, a politically motivated one at that." *Now who's your daddy, Senator? Me or BP?*

"How dare you, sir!" Senator Thornton barks. "This is a bipartisan hearing, we're committed to seeking solutions, not votes, and I will not be chastised by a . . ."

A what? Future fry cook? Droplets of sweat drip from Ace's armpits, though he refuses to break eye contact with Thornton, whose entire re-election campaign is based on opening ANWR to drilling.

Chairman Keller allows him to ramble another minute. "Senator Henk?"

Mrs. Danelle Henk, the democratic Senator from Louisiana, offers a motherly smile to the panel. "Thank you, Mr. Chairman. I'd like our panelists to comment about non-conventional energy resources, specifically heavy oil and tar sands. It's my understanding these resources can yield significant supplies of oil."

Ellen Wulf is first to reply. "Senator, EIA projects the equivalent of 200 billion recoverable barrels of oil in Canada's Alberta tar sands. While processing tar sands isn't cheap, we believe the potential yield warrants the expense. There has also been talk about expanding a new field in Venezuela."

"Okay, Mr. Futrell, but keep it short."

Ace feels his face flush. "It's not my intent to be a naysayer, Mr. Chairman, but I feel it's important the Committee have all the details. Despite U.S. pressure, Canada has been hesitant to increase tar sand operations because of the nature of the job. Tar doesn't flow out of the ground the way oil does. The technology involves hot-water flotation to remove thin layers of oil from the sand, while adding a petroleum distillate to upgrade the tar to a synthetic crude. It's essentially an open mining pit operation, but it produces lake-size amounts of polluted refuse water. It's also costly in terms of energy, requiring upwards of twenty percent of Canada's entire natural gas production, which they've been understandably hesitant to sacrifice. In regard to Venezuela, while the Orinoco oil belt contains one of the largest known accumulations of bitumen in the world, the synthetic crude project has a low yield of only 5 to 10 percent based on current technologies. Once again, it comes down to economics."

"What about synthetic fuel, Mr. Futrell?" This from Senator Bill Rawlins, a veteran of the first Gulf War. "The Senate has been debating the virtue of subsidizing syn-fuel as long as I can remember."

It's a set-up question, and a good one. "Senator, syn-fuel is nothing more than a giant tax dodge created by a handful of greedy companies who found a way to take advantage of a tax incentive enacted by Congress back in the 1980s. Synthetic fuel is made using bromide and coal, but the companies running the fifty or so syn-fuel plants across the

United States, and I use the term 'plant' loosely, are simply spraying coal with diesel fuel or pine tar resin so they can collect enormous tax credits from a loophole the Senate refuses to close. The subsidy's buried in Section 559 of the Tax Relief Bill, and the syn-fuel lobby, which uses the Orwellian name Council for Energy Independence, spends about $2 million every year to keep it in place."

Senator Rawlins smiles in satisfaction. "Thank you, Mr. Futrell. Perhaps our friends on the other side of the aisle will take note of your comments."

Senator Keller registers the weight of the chamber. "This is an issue we need to address at a later date. However, since we are discussing fossil fuel alternatives, I'd like to hear from the panel on solar, wind, and other potential resources. Mr. Bach-Marklund."

"Thank you, Mr. Chairman, and thank you, Senator Ashton, for joining us at last year's conference. The Center for Strategic and International Studies has submitted its report on current forecasts in regards to alternative energy solutions to fossil fuels. Natural gas is the leading alternative fuel, currently supplying about a quarter of our energy needs and slightly less around the world. Natural gas can be burned cleanly in internal combustion engines, the challenge is in developing a storage capacity that renders it feasible to use in automobiles. Compressed natural gas lacks the range of a tank of gasoline, while liquefied natural gas requires extremely low temperatures for storage. At the same time, natural gas, like oil, is a finite resource. While EIA estimates supplies lasting until 2050, industry analysts agree we'll most likely run dry before 2025. That's because newer fields tend to be harder to find and are far smaller, depleting faster. Unlike oil, gas doesn't taper off. It just shuts down when depleted. Natural gas can be imported by cooling it into a liquid form at minus 260 degrees Fahrenheit, however LNG requires special tankers and ports, of which there are currently only three in the United States.

"Wind may be our most promising renewable source to fuel electricity, and the technology continues to advance, with the latest turbines capable of producing up to three megawatts. At present, wind supplies less than 2 percent of America's energy needs, though countries like Denmark have reached levels as high as 10 percent. To contribute significantly, the industry requires additional funding to resolve certain technological challenges, and much of our transmission lines will have to be revamped in order to bring wind power to the masses. As Mr. Futrell indicated, the commitment entails significantly altering our nation's infrastructure.

"Solar power currently supplies less than one percent of domestic needs. Like wind, solar is clean, renewable, and the technology continues to improve, with new thin-film panels and PV dye coatings showing real promise in reducing costs. The Swiss are close to completing their new Titania Dye Sensitized Cell, which could yield the most inexpensive photovoltaic panels yet.

"Hydroelectric power currently accounts for 3 percent of global energy needs—9 percent here in the States—but expansion is quite limited as the rivers that can handle dams have already been exploited. Micro-hydro projects utilizing smaller rivers and streams show promise to assist less-populated communities.

"Geothermal power remains stagnant. Nuclear power has also stagnated, due to costs, radioactive wastes, and the potential for these facilities to be targeted by terrorists. Nuclear currently supplies 20 percent of our electricity but less than 4 percent of our total energy needs.

"Of all the alternative energy sources available today, there are only two that can replace or supplement oil as a transportation fuel. The first is hydrogen fuel cells. While hybrids continue to sell well, shifting to a total hydrogen community requires a trillion-dollar upheaval in our infrastructure. Hydrogen is also very combustible, and big business is not apt to outlay substantial investments in technology unless they see a full commitment by the federal government.

"More promising is ethanol, or E85, a mixture composed of 85 percentethanol and 15 percent gasoline. In Brazil, E85 has already replaced pure gasoline at service stations. Most Americans don't know it, but all new American cars possess flex-fuel engines, meaning the consumer can switch back and forth between E85 and gas without service required. Whether ethanol is generated by cornstarch or sugar, it's a clean fuel, good for farmers, and good for the environment. But switching to an ethanol nation again requires a serious commitment by the federal government to make changes within our infrastructure, in this case, the farming sector."

"Thank you, Mr. Bach-Marklund. And I agree, this Committee must look into ethanol and some of the other alternatives you mentioned."

Look into? Ace smirks. *He just told you Brazil's been energy independent for years. Just be honest . . . as politicians, you have no interest in getting us off the Middle East needle, at least not while your campaigns are financed by the pusher's profits.*

"The Chair recognizes Senator Clinton."

The former first lady and presidential candidate nods to the Chairman. Her speech will be one of the few featured on the nightly news.

"Thank you, Mr. Chairman, and thank you to our panel for joining us here this morning. As we begin yet another debate on developing a long-term national energy policy, the short-term prognosis continues to look bleak for the majority of Americans. Never has the gap been greater separating our nation's haves from the have-nots. How can we continue to offer oil companies billions of dollars in tax incentives when the working man must pay upwards of five dollars a gallon for gas? How can we continue to subsidize electric companies when their constituents can barely afford to heat their homes in winter and cool them in summer? How can we continue to channel $8 billion a month into Iraq when 40 million Americans cannot earn a decent wage, provide food for their families, afford medical insurance, or receive a proper education? How can we continue the tax cuts that benefit our wealthiest few while refusing to legislate against the loopholes that encourage pension funds to be looted in corporate takeovers? As policy makers, we have a responsibility not only to set the nation's course in regards to energy, but to make sure that whatever legislation is enacted, it cuts a wide path that does the greatest good for the American worker."

Ace doodles over his notes, his thoughts slipping back to his travel plans. Following the usual script, the energy hearings have degenerated from fact-finding exercises to posturing and speeches. Congress will again banter back and forth politically for months but delay the "major impact" decisions until after the 2012 presidential election. The public will continue to complain about high energy and fuel costs, and the issue will certainly be debated in the fall, while behind the scenes the corporations with major contracts at stake will use their eight-figure donations to seed those candidates who share their "mutual interests." In the end, Congress will most likely pass an energy bill loaded with pet projects and "tax incentives" designed to encourage Big Oil to explore. Perhaps there will be a new port or infrastructure development or two "awarded" to the usual suspects. But in the end, there will be no impact-generating, long-term solutions, no major infrastructure commitments . . . nothing to stave off the 'big rollover.'

"Before we break for lunch, we have time for one last speaker. The Chair recognizes the Senator from Delaware."

Ace checks his watch again. *Nearly noon. Maybe I can excuse myself from the afternoon session . . . catch the 1:50 flight into La Guardia. With any luck—*

Senator Joseph B. Mulligan, another candidate vying for the Democrat Party's nomination, waits until the chamber quiets. "Mr. Chairman. I'm not going to read any prepared speeches today, but I do have a few comments. You know, my father was always a straight shooter, and if he was in this room, I think he'd say all this digging and drilling and data collecting is a yesterday-forever policy that's finally run its course. The American people are fed up . . . hell, I'm fed up with energy policies that rely on third world countries, half of which would rather see us dead than alive. In my opinion, it doesn't matter if oil will last us another day or another century, as long as we keep importing it, it jeopardizes the security of this nation. It's high time we stop debating and start making decisions that free us from this damn fossil fuel business, no matter which lobbyists we insult. Far as I'm concerned, if we'd invested half of what the war in Iraq has already cost us just in terms of tax dollars, we'd already have ample port facilities for liquid natural gas, something we've been kicking around in this chamber since back when I was a junior senator with a full head of hair!"

Ace stops doodling, his attention now fully focused on the speaker.

"And yes, while LNG won't keep our planes, trains, and automobiles running, as Mr. Futrell has so eloquently pointed out, it seems like it would help us conserve what little oil's left until solutions are at hand. Conserve. There's a word I haven't heard all morning. President Carter used that word to make a real impact back in '73 when OPEC decided to grab us by the short and curlies and shut off the spigot, thinking they could dictate foreign policy. President Carter also had a pretty darn good idea about investing in processing coal into a high-grade synthetic fuel and gasoline. My republican friends might rightly state that we could go back to the Ford administration when Vice President Rockefeller pushed a plan to develop alternative energy sources. Of course, Dick Cheney helped derail those plans thirty-five years ago and he and his cronies have profited quite well from those policies ever since. Personally, I agree with Mr. Futrell. It's high time we commit serious financial resources and properly seed alternative energy solutions—even with our runaway deficits, Senator Clinton. Because if we do it right—selecting the right policies to support the best technologies in a true bipartisan manner—then we ought to be able to stimulate the American economy by creating whole new industries. But we'd better do it now, because if we don't, the technology sure won't be there when the lights go off and there's no food at the grocery store."

Ace Futrell can't help but grin in admiration. Finally a senator . . . a presidential candidate no less, with the cajones to take on the big boys.

Poor bastard doesn't stand a chance.

"Life is what happens while you are busy making other plans."

—JOHN LENNON

"Washington Air Traffic Control Center knew about the first plane before it hit the World Trade Center. Yet the third plane was able to fly 'loop-de-loops' over Washington, DC one hour and forty-five minutes after Washington center first knew about the hijackings. After circling in this restricted airspace, controlled and protected by the Secret Service who had an open phone line to the FAA, how was it possible that this plane was then able to crash into the Pentagon? Why was the Pentagon not evacuated? Why was our Air Force so late in response? What, if anything, did our nation do in a defensive military posture that morning?"

—9/11 WIDOW KRISTEN BREITWEISTER,
from a testimony given before the Joint Senate
House Intelligence Comittee.
September 18, 2001

"Then the second angel blew his trumpet, and a great mountain of fire was thrown into the sea. And one-third of the water in the sea became blood. And one-third of all living things in the sea died. And one-third of all the ships in the sea were destroyed."

—REVELATION 8:8

CHAPTER 4

"UNIT ONE IN POSITION."

"Unit Two in position."

"Acknowledged. We're entering now." Commander Dvorak nods to his patrolmen. The lead officer keys open apartment 2-D, the second and third men in line coming in low, guns and flashlights drawn.

A quick search of the two bedroom apartment confirms the occupants have moved out. Dvorak enters, followed by another officer carrying a forensics kit. He looks around.

The L-shaped living and dining room area is small. A thirty-three-inch plasma screen television is mounted on an otherwise bare wall facing a second-hand sofa. The dining room light fixture hangs above empty floor. Brown curtains conceal a balcony overlooking the parking lot. The kitchen is overflowing with trash from fast-food joints.

"Commander, we found something."

Dvorak heads back toward the bedrooms and enters the master suite. One of his officers is holding up the queen-size mattress, exposing the box spring . . . and a laptop computer.

TAVERN ON THE GREEN RESTAURANT
NEW YORK CITY
8:03 PM EST

THE DINING ROOM IS ALIVE, ITS heated air recirculating an aroma of lobster bisque and filet mignon, its clothed tables spilling over with patrons bundled in sweaters, feeding among a sea of overcoats and parcels, fine paintings and chandeliers. Frosted windows glitter with holiday lights, everything multiplied in a frenzy of etched glass and mirrors.

Ace weaves past patrons and waiters as he makes his way through a twisting hall of mirrors into the Chestnut Room, the paneled dining area, one of three looking out onto a central garden.

Kelli Doyle is seated alone at a table for two, staring at her reflection in a large hourglass clock. The remains of her blonde hair, once thick, shoulder-length curls, have been reduced to dried strands tucked beneath a matching wig, set in a tight ponytail. Her weakened body slumps against the padded chair, seeking equilibrium against the pain, the scorching residue of her last treatment of chemo still swimming in her tissues, burning out the cancer and everything else the clear elixir has come in contact with.

She glances at the faint brown discoloration along the inside of her forearms—burn marks from her fourth and final cycle. Chemotherapy is an all-or-nothing endurance race against death as your body is eaten away from the inside out while your mind shuffles in and out of a dementia interrupted only by spasmodic episodes of vomiting. Only her self-imposed mission has kept her going, the morality of her choices giving her a newfound strength.

What doesn't kill you . . .

"Hey, stranger." Ace beams at his wife but gets no response. "Kel?"

The frail blonde looks up, her thin face creasing into a smile. "Hey, you." She stands, half-falling into her husband's arms. "You were gone so long—"

"But now I'm home for good. So? What did Dr. Eastburn say?"

Her eyes glisten. "Blood count's normal. I'm in remission."

Ace hugs her again, easing back as he feels her ribs caving beneath his grip. Kelli's two-year battle has taken an emotional toll on his psyche, each day lived with uncertainty, every joy hollow. Remission—a death sentence commuted.

"Ace, honey, you okay?"

He pulls away, Kelli's thick wool sweater leaving fuzz against his five-o'clock shadow.

"Am I okay? You just gave me the best damn Christmas gift a guy could ask for."

"Sit down, there's more." She reaches into her purse, pulls out an envelope, and places it on the table. "Merry Christmas."

Wiping a stray tear, he removes his overcoat and pulls his chair close to hers. "What's this?"

"Open it."

Ace peels back the flap and stares at the tickets. "A cruise?"

"To the Bahamas. Just the two of us. My mother said she'd watch the kids."

"Are you strong enough to travel?"

"I'll deal. I really need to get away."

"We both do."

She studies his expression. "What happened in DC?"

"Nothing. Same old same old." He scans the menu.

She pulls it away. "You're not getting away that easy. What did you say?"

"Nothing."

"Liar. You told them everything, didn't you? I knew you would. Good for you!"

"It means nothing. Half my comments were stricken from the public record, the other half refuted by the senators on the oil lobbyists' payrolls."

"Maybe I can help deliver your message." She squeezes her husband's hand. "Ace, I wrote a book."

"A book? What kind of book?"

"A tell-all memoir."

His heart beat jumps. "CIA stuff or White House days?"

"Both. Focusing mainly on a period I spent working with the Strategic Support Branch."

"You never told me much about that."

"The SSB's a clandestine espionage arm of the Pentagon created by Rumsfeld after 9/11. It was a neoconservative initiative, pushed by Dick Cheney, who believed Iran-Contra failed only because the CIA and Pentagon were involved and secrecy couldn't be maintained."

"These guys don't give a damn about the Constitution or the law, do they?"

"They have a 'vision' about how the Middle East should be realigned, and Iraq was only the beginning. The SSB allows the Neocons to operate in secrecy, outside the jurisdiction of the CIA. Just before Rummy decided to step down, I was brought in to help initiate . . . well, let's just call it a Middle Eastern contingency plan."

"Oil?"

"And Islamic extremists. I can't give you any details, at least not yet, just suffice it to say it was bad stuff."

"How bad?"

She looks him straight in the eyes. "As bad as it gets."

Ace feels his skin crawl. "And you want to go public with the information?"

"I didn't at first. It began as a Kabbalah exercise, sort of a written confession of my sins. Then, after . . . well, after I got sick, I started seeing it as something else . . . a way to warn people, a way to expose the plot before it happens so that it never happens."

"What plot?"

"I can't say."

"You can't say, but you're going to publish this information."

"Yes . . . I mean no, not publish, release, over the Internet. But I can't do it yet, I'm still gathering details, I've been out of the loop a bit over these last few years."

"Then how do you even know it's still happening?"

"The same reason you know we're running out of oil. You're in the trenches, you hear things. In order to do what I want to do, I'm going to need your help."

"My help? Against the SSB, the Neocons? The entire fossil fuel industry?" Ace massages the growing ache in his sinuses. "Kelli, I'm not Superman, I'm just mild-mannered Clark Kent, a regular guy trying to provide for his family."

"Every Clark Kent has a Superman in him."

"More Kabbalah?"

"It keeps me sane, and don't change the subject. I know you, Ace. You're as sick of these lying hypocrites as I am. How many times have you testified before Congress? How many times have you seen them do nothing? The system's broke, and it'll take all of us down with it . . . unless we act."

"And exactly how do you propose we do that? The Feds are in bed with Big Oil, the Neocons are in bed with the defense contractors, and the White House—and the rest of the world—is lining up to sleep with King Sultan. Remove Sultan and there's five hundred other royal a-holes waiting in line, daggers poised, to take his place, backed by about a trillion dollars in Saudi assets, a quarter of the remaining oil left on this planet, and, oh yeah, did I mention the White House? Or will you be rewriting sixty years of U.S. policy in your memoir as well?"

"I admit it's a challenge."

"No, going to the moon was a challenge. This is more like a massacre."

"Sort of like your first game, huh? Georgia versus Tennessee?"

"Save the speech."

"Your first game playing between the hallowed hedges. First Gary Archer breaks his leg, then his back-up goes down, forcing the coach to turn to third-string quarterback, Clark Kent."

"Okay, enough—"

"Down 17-3 late in the game, the Vol's defense blitzing you on every play. Ace, I swear, you had so many guys chasing you it looked like a jail break. The game was over, and everyone in Sanford Stadium knew it . . . except Coach Dooley and my man. Every time they sacked you, you just kept getting up, clapping and yelling, rallying the troops."

"Seriously, if you're looking to get laid tonight, I'm a sure thing."

"Then it turned. Another third and long, the pocket collapsing on you, when out of nowhere, 'boom,' you took off running . . . fifty-two yards, first down! They never saw it coming, the scrawny little white boy from West Virginia."

"I wasn't scrawny."

"Another run, another first down, and now you've got Tennessee's defense thinking. The coverage on your receivers loosens up, Mark gets loose in the end zone and you nail him with a thirty-yard laser—touch-down! Everyone's going nuts, but you're the calm in the storm, like you saw it all before it happened. Crowd's back in the game, our defense holds and you've got the ball again. With twenty seconds left you tied the game, you brought us back from the dead."

"We lost in overtime."

"My point is one man's effort against impossible odds not only changed the game, but changed our season. The team suddenly believed again, and you guys made it all the way to the Orange Bowl. Not too shabby for a walk-on. You had no fear. I really loved that about you."

"Loved?"

"Love. I meant love."

"We both know what you meant." He glances down at his sleeves and the set of three thin white scars that run along the inside of either wrist. Two inches long. Twenty-three years old—his scarlet letter.

"Guess every Superman has his kryptonite, huh, Lois?"

"Ace . . . I didn't mean—"

"Yeah you did. You say everything that crosses that conniving little brain of yours and you mean everything you say."

They pull away from one another as the waiter interrupts, "Good evening, sir. Something to drink?"

"Arsenic. Leave the bottle."

Kelli shoots him a look.

"Coke."

"Madam?"

"Another water, please."

The waiter leaves.

"Ace—"

"It was a long time ago, Kelli, a lifetime ago. Things change. I'm not the same person, this isn't a football game, and there's no *S* on my chest. Start mouthing off to the wrong people and there'll be bullets flying . . . and those will just be coming from the American side of the equation."

"I have something in mind."

"And I told you I'm not interested." He kneads his eyelids. "Look, I'm tired, we both are. Right now, all I want is for us to be together."

"It doesn't work like that. I have access to information that could change a lot of people's lives. We have a responsibility—"

"My first responsibility is to my family."

"All the more reason to—"

"Damn it, Kelli, I said no!"

Heads turn. Ace looks away.

Kelli stares at her husband. *Maybe I was wrong. Some scars run so deep they never fade.* She reaches out for his hand. "Hey, I'm sorry."

"You don't know when to stop."

"I said I was sorry. You gonna be grumpy all night?"

"This is dangerous stuff. After today, I'll be flying way above the radar, and technically you're still part of the machine."

"Exactly. I know where the mines are laid and the bodies buried."

"We're not discussing it anymore, end of story."

Her eyes grow harsh. "No, Ashley Futrell, let me tell you how the story really ends. Things are going to happen. Bad things. Nine-eleven kind of things, only on a different scale. Cheney's goal was always to make the Presidency omnipotent, and he used 9/11 to trample the Constitution.

Bush went right along with his agenda from the start. U.S. aggression fueled the popularity of Ahmadinejad, and Ahmadinejad's threats kept the Neocons in power. The world's become a tinderbox, and there are people on either side of the equation tossing matches."

"And some of those people you and your cousin helped get into office."

"Guilty as charged, and now I want to do something about it. Something radical. The clock's ticking, Ace, the question is—are you ready to get back in the game?"

◆　◆　◆

An hour later they're outside, breathing in the cold winter air. The appetizer of conversation had turned their meal into a chore, and barely a word had been spoken during the main course.

Ace raises his arm to hail a taxi.

"No, let's walk. Please?"

They head north, Central Park on their right, the night alive with Manhattan traffic and festival lights.

"Ace, I'm sorry I ruined our evening. It's just . . . I've been thinking about things."

"I can see that. Too bad you never gave these things a thought while you were working for the Bushies."

"Stop." She blocks his way. "No more cheap shots, okay? Let's just be together tonight, we'll sort the rest out in the morning."

Ace sees the urgency in her eyes. "Okay. No more fighting."

She points across the street to the northwest corner of 72nd and the Dakota Building. "That's where John Lennon was shot. Let's walk in the park, I want to see the Strawberry Fields Memorial."

Before he can object she's leading him east through Central Park. They follow a narrow path that opens to a clearing and a garden, made barren by the cold. A mosaic composed of inlaid stones from all over the world lies before them, a tribute to the late musician and peace activist. The word *Imagine* is visible in the moonlight.

Two women are leaving flowers, setting them among others that have accumulated since the last anniversary of Lennon's death, only a week earlier. The women nod to Ace and Kelli and head back up the path.

Ace stares at the memorial. "I can still remember the day he died."

Kelli nods. "He had the right idea. What do you think Lennon would do if he were alive today? Do you think he'd sit tight? Move to Montana?"

"Probably throw a concert, make people aware. Organize a political rally or something."

"You think it'd make a difference?"

"I don't know. Maybe against Nixon, but not with these guys. Their roots run too deep."

"Agreed. The only way we change course now is with a complete House cleaning. Both Houses. Eventually the Judiciary. We need to find politicians on both sides of the aisle who have the balls to make the radical changes necessary."

She moves closer, leans in, and kisses him passionately, surprising him.

After a long moment she pulls away and hugs him, tears in her eyes. "I love you, Ace. I know you've been suffering inside, and I know what happened years ago changed you, but the strength that made you special . . . it's still inside you, waiting to come out. I know that sounds corny, but isn't it time you found your way home?"

He starts to reply when shadows move, catching his eye.

The man is tall, at least six-foot-four. Long and lean. Tan complexion. Dressed in a dark raincoat, hands buried deep in his pockets. Dark eyes and heavy brows are just visible beneath the wool NY Giants ski cap. Clean shaven. European.

Ace's scalp tingles as he approaches. A heavy whiff of aftershave arrives first, followed by words that glide over a trace of Russian accent. "Never was a Beatles fan, you know. The Rolling Stones, they were more my liking."

A false smile.

A spark of light—

—a double whooft in the crisp December air, and sound is silenced.

Kelli's frail hand slips from Ace's grip. He catches her as she goes down, his mind racing to catch up with the fleeting moment, everything moving surreally, his pulse a timbering drumbeat in his ears, Kelli's pained expression frozen in time. His eyes instinctively search for the stranger—gone—even as a steady stream of blood slides between his fingers, warming the hand now pinned against his dying wife's back. He presses his face against her cheekbone as blood rises up her larynx, choking her last words.

A final heartbeat . . . and she's gone.

Ace gags on his emotions, unable to comprehend what has just happened, what is still happening. Reality explodes. He shatters the night with a guttural yell, unable to tear himself from his wife's broken body. He screams rebuttals at the fleeing killer, cursing, raging, his soul lost, his existence plunging into a maelstrom of insanity, an abyss so deep he will never find his way home.

For Ashley "Ace" Futrell, the tsunami has struck. The world as he knew it is gone—

—never to be the same again.

"Our society is run by insane people for insane objectives. I think we're being run by maniacs for maniacal ends and I think I'm liable to be put away as insane for expressing that. That's what's insane about it."

—JOHN LENNON

"The Iranian nation possesses the full nuclear fuel cycle, and time is completely running in our favor in terms of diplomacy."

—MAHMOUD AHMADINEJAD,
Iranian President,
on his country's uranium enrichment program,
expected to be ready by March 2007

"A blueprint (Rebuilding America's Defenses) written in September 2000 by the neoconservative think tank: Project for the New American Century, was drawn up by Dick Cheney, Donald Rumsfeld, Paul Wolfowitz, Jeb Bush, and Lewis Libby. The plan shows Bush's cabinet intended to take military control of the Gulf region whether or not Saddam Hussein was in power.

—MICHAEL MEACHER, MP,
U.K. Environmental Minister (1997–2003),
from "The War on Terrorism is Bogus,"
The Guardian,
September 6, 2003

CHAPTER 5

FBI–CHICAGO HEADQUARTERS
610 S. CANAL STREET
DECEMBER 15, 2011
1:37 PM CST

LOCATED IN DOWNTOWN CHICAGO IN THE U.S. Customs Building, the Chicago Division of the FBI consists of thirty-six squads assigned to investigate counterintelligence and terrorism, as well as organized crime, drug violations, violent crime, and white collar crime. Included in their state-of-the-art facility is the Regional Computer Forensic Laboratory (RCFL), used to examine and analyze computers and related systems in terrorism, child pornography, and other forms of Internet crime.

Computer Forensic Science is the discipline of acquiring, preserving, retrieving, and presenting criminal data that has been processed electronically. With personal computers averaging thirty to sixty gigabytes of storage capacity (thirty gigabytes of printed data would create a stack of paper sixty stories high), new methods of training must be combined with technology to aid an examiner in determining which files are critical, especially in accordance with time limitations and judicial constraints.

Of the seven forensic examiners currently assigned to the Chicago RCFL, Steven Klemz is the newest recruit. Klemz has suffered through six weeks of classroom training and more than two months of dealing with nothing but chat logs and cyber-porn. Then, three days ago, his director, Adrian Neary, handed him the laptop confiscated from the Iraqi suspects' apartment. Suddenly, the young recruit's life had meaning; he was being given a chance, he was in the game: counter-terrorism.

Agent Klemz' first action was to copy the laptop's files into a SAN, short for Storage Area Network, a single repository used by examiners to load large amounts of data. Time was of the essence. Director Neary wanted to return the laptop to the suspects' apartment, which was being watched by the local police department.

With the data now copied, Klemz began sorting through files and segregating e-mails, using a Netcase program to translate Arabic into English. He refused to leave the facility, eating his meals at his station, taking hour catnaps when waves of exhaustion would hit. Still he continued on, building a profile of the subjects through the web sites they visited and through their e-mail correspondence.

Both suspects were born in Iraq. Jamal al-Yussuf was a Shi'ite. His home, Baghdad. He was an artist and had been taking courses in graphic design. He was also a photographer; his web site portfolio was dark and horrifying—amputees lying in dust-caked streets, cloaked policemen armed with machine guns, explosions raining upon civilian neighborhoods, the strafing ripping out chunks of stucco. Through blogs and intercepted e-mails, Agent Klemz learned that Jamal had lost his father and grandmother in the opening air raids of the war. An eleven-year-old brother, Kudair, had been wounded with shrapnel from a car bomb, and Jamal had carried the boy two miles to the hospital, describing in horrifying detail how the boy's liver kept slipping out of his open abdominal wound between his fingers. The boy had died in the waiting room.

Omar Kamel Radi was a Sunni, tall, just over six feet, five inches. He had been a soccer goalie in Haditha, a farming town on the Euphrates River, and hoped to play for the national team. After the U.S. invasion, Omar's neighborhood became a battleground between American troops and Iranian insurgents. A roadside blast reportedly destroyed his family's home, with two children listed among the dead. The military offered no details of the account.

Two civilians.

Two men with motive . . . unleashed by the American invasion.

Suddenly, Agent Klemz lost his enthusiasm for the project. He stopped reading the e-mails, allowing the program to sort the correspondence using key words. Tonight he'd go home, eat a hot meal, sleep in his own bed. *I should give mom a call . . .*

The blinking red alert catches his attention—an encoded video file has been detected. Agent Klemz pages his director as the lab's computer resolves the encrypted codes and opens the file.

Clean-shaven and scarred from head to knees, Chicago FBI director Adrian Paul Neary had spent his first seventeen years with the FBI as a field agent working in conjunction with the DEA. Forced to accept a desk job after three suspects wielding barbed wire jumped him, Neary's body bears the evidence from the attack, including a jagged, two-and-a-half-inch tear in his chin that runs clear past his lip.

Neary joins Agent Klemz at his station, the two men staring at the videotaped footage.

The opening scene, taken by a handheld camera, is of a classroom of Arab grade-schoolers, ages five to seven . . . singing a song. Neary listens carefully. He translates: "Arabs are beloved and Jews are dogs."

"Is this what they teach their kids?"

"They indoctrinate them into hatred early."

The scene changes to a graduation ceremony. Suicide bombers, their faces cloaked in black masks, their vests holding plastic explosives. Chanting in Arabic: "Death to America, Death to Israel."

Neary shakes his head. "The psychosis of hate."

The next scene is far more disturbing. A small Palestinian girl is holding a Glock 9mm pistol, emotionally spent as she chants to a small public gathering, "I want to die Shaleed! I want to die Shaleed! I want to die Shaleed!"

Agent Klemz shakes his head. "She's no older than my seven-year-old niece. What are they teaching these kids?"

"How to die for Allah."

One of the suspects, Jamal al-Yussuf, appears next. He is dressed in combat fatigues, alone in a room, the walls bare, a cot positioned visibly in one corner. Facing away from the camera, he kneels in prayer. Bows. Turns to face the camera, an object held in his hand.

It is a child's skull.

Agent Klemz shudders.

Al-Yussuf rattles something off in Arabic at the camera.

Neary translates: "We knock on heaven's gate with the skulls of Jews . . . with the skulls of Americans."

"Lovely."

Neary pats his rookie on the shoulder. "Put out an APB. I want these nut jobs found."

"Change is avalanching upon our heads, and most people are grotesquely unprepared to cope with it."

—ALVIN TOFFLER,
Future Shock

"The military don't start wars. Politicians start wars."

—GENERAL WILLIAM WESTMORELAND

"We succeed, with Allah's grace, to raise an ideological generation that loves death like our enemies love life."

—RAED SAID HUSSEIN SAAD,
Al-Qassam Brigades Commander,
North Gaza

Book Excerpt:

To the Brink of Hell: An Apology to the Survivors
by Kelli Doyle,
White House National Security Staff Advisor
(2006–2010)

Frankly, I hope this scares the hell out of you.

I remember the moment it first hit me, the realization that something was terribly wrong. One moment you're fine, your mind consumed by the trivial, the next . . . Those first moments are the toughest, when mortality hits you like a ton of bricks. "Cancer? Can you operate? What about chemo? Well then, doc, what can you do?"

At some point, through tears and the tightness in your chest, you expel the words you never imagined having to ask: "How long?"

The doctor's answer is hard to hear, maybe harder than the death sentence itself, because even if he's wrong, even if he's off by a week or a month or even a year, it doesn't really matter—you know your clock is ticking. Of course, it's always been ticking; it's been ticking backwards ever since birth. We're born in an instant and die in an instant, our life, those precious moments in between, and like it or not, no one gets out alive.

When it comes to mortality, being human is both a blessing and curse. Aware of life's limits, we're forced to process something we can never fully comprehend. The first stage of coping with death is denial, a stage you'll be entering into momentarily. This will progress to blame, then anger. You'll punch the walls, kick the dog, and curse God, asking, "Why me?" Eventually, you'll negotiate and try to make peace with your maker because you'll need him now more than ever. And if you're a fighter, you'll fight for every last glorious moment.

That's what I want you to do, I want you to fight. I want you to act! Because the clock is ticking backwards, and the bells are tolling. Only they're tolling for you! They're tolling for your children and your parents and friends, and every loved one and acquaintance . . . every human being you know or knew or might never know. There are 6 billion of us who share this planet, and soon—very soon—every one of us save an elite few are going to perish.

That's right, a massive die-off. To most of you it will appear gradually, as gradual as climbing into a giant pot of cold water and turning on the burner. At first you won't know anything is happening, then slowly . . . slowly and painfully, like an IV drip of chemo burning into your veins, the realization will kick in that there's no escaping this death sentence, that the chaos that surrounds you won't be going away, that the food left in your refrigerator and on your shelves won't last very long, that you and your family are going to starve to death.

Or freeze.

Or be incinerated by a weapon whose impact you'll never hear. Or succumb to a virus you'll never feel. You will be as helpless as the victims of the tsunami that struck Indonesia the day after Christmas in 2004 or the lost souls of Hurricane Katrina, abandoned without food or water in flooded New Orleans . . . only this time there will be no rescuers, and CNN won't be covering the event, because there won't be any electricity to power their cameras. Shooting the messenger won't help. Call me a liar, repute my warnings, curse my existence—it won't change a thing. The brakes are shot and civilization is being diverted, instructed to gaze in the rearview mirror as we drive ourselves off a cliff, only you're too busy micro-managing your life to see what's happening.

Open your eyes! Read the signposts! It's already begun, the opening moves played out as if upon a great political chessboard:

The 1973 oil crisis—the first taste of things to come.

The Reagan-Bush years—moves within moves, corruption behind smiles.

Iran and Iraq—a fostered war designed to temporarily control the center of the board.

Saddam's invasion of Kuwait—the manipulation of a pawn.

The rise of Islamic fascism—a cancer spreading throughout the Muslim world.

Secret energy meetings—our path of self-destruction, mortared in greed.

The lies behind 9/11, the sacrifice of a noble knight.

The invasion of Afghanistan, a feint in the conquest of Iraq . . . a fateful plunge into the abyss.

The election of Hamas. The deceit of Hezbollah, the tentacles of Iran.

The smiling enemies in Saudi Arabia.

Attempted coups. Rigged elections. Laws "to protect the public," penned straight out of a George Orwell novel.

The board's still in play, but the outcome was decided long ago, and soon the final piece shall fall, but not the way the self-appointed autocrats would ever have predicted. When the house of cards collapses, everybody loses, from the rainmakers to the reign-enders, and the meek shall indeed inherit the Earth, at least what's left of it. As for me, I'll be long dead by then, and yet the cancer that riddles my body's been a blessing in disguise, for it has given me a newfound strength . . . an insight to set in motion my own little series of events that might stave off some of the impending doom and perhaps buy back my own auctioned-off soul in the process.

For me, it's too late. For my children, my loved ones . . . for you, I toll these final warning bells: the end of civilization as we know it is on the horizon, a tsunami of death on its way . . .

And you're asleep on the beach!

"As all those who write about civic matters show and as all history proves by a multitude of examples, whoever organizes a state and establishes its laws must assume that all men are wicked and will act wickedly whenever they have the chance to do so. He must also assume that whenever their wickedness remains hidden for a time there is a hidden reason for it which remains unknown for want of occasion to make it manifest. But time, which is called the father of all truth, uncovers it."

—NICCOLO MACHIAVELLI,
Discources

"Therefore, I have asked Vice President Cheney to oversee the development of a coordinated national effort so that we may do the very best possible job of protecting our people from catastrophic harm."

—PRESIDENT GEORGE W. BUSH,
altering a long-standing protocol by placing the vice president in charge of all federal programs and agencies dealing with terrorism.
May 8, 2001
(4 months prior to the events of September Eleventh)

"Then the third angel blew his trumpet, and a great flaming star fell out of the sky, burning like a torch. It fell upon one-third of the rivers and on the springs of water. The name of the star was Bitterness. It made one-third of the water bitter, and many people died because the water was so bitter."

—REVELATION 8:10-11

CHAPTER 6

GRAMERCY PARK MEMORIAL CHAPEL
NEW YORK
DECEMBER 16, 2011
10:22 AM EST

THE POLISHED WALNUT CASKET RESTS STARKLY upon its steel-wheeled chariot, its presence an emotional black hole that tugs at Ace's being. His insides tremble against the finality of its weight—he cannot bear to be in its presence much longer, nor contemplate standing by the gravesite in the coming hour as his wife is lowered into her final resting place. Too weak to move, he remains seated in his designated place of honor, his left arm draped protectively around his eight-year-old son, Sam, his right hand wedged in between the hands of his thirteen-year-old daughter, Leigh. Kelli's parents, Sharon and Bruce, are seated behind him, along with Kelli's grandfather, Fitch. Ace registers the strength of their presence, yet inside he remains an island of combusting rage.

From his seat he watches Kelli's first cousin, Jennifer Wienner, take charge of the precession. For years the two had been known around Washington's inner circles as Butch and Sundance, pet names anointed by the GOP's top political strategist, Karl Rove, who himself had been nicknamed Turd Blossom by the second Bush he had maneuvered into office. Kelli, of course, was Butch, a former CIA analyst promoted in 2006 as an advisor to the National Security Council, overseeing the Gulf Region. Jennifer was Sundance, a campaign strategist who trained under Rove to oversee election "hotspots," seats vital to maintain control of the Houses by the GOP. Following the midterm elections of 2006, Jennifer had left politics, accepting a highly paid lobbyist's position for a major pharmaceutical company specializing in flu virus vaccines. Like her cousin, Jennifer knew where the mines were laid and the bodies buried . . . along with the treasure.

Ace watches Jennifer as she shepherds each guest, accepting their condolences. Divorced and in her early forties, Jennifer is roughly the same age as her deceased cousin and cut from the same cloth. She greets each guest as if closing a deal.

"Jen, I'm working with the DeLay foundation. He sends his condolences and specifically wanted me to ask you if the police have caught the bastard yet. If there's anything we can do—"

"Jennifer, are you holding up? Katherine sends her love. She couldn't make it with the trial and all, but said she'll call you next week about financing another Senate run in Florida."

"Ms. Wienner, I am so sorry for your loss. Do you remember me? Laura Whisenant. We worked together on Saxby Chambliss's campaign back in '02. Ol' Max Cleland never knew what hit him."

Black suits, nameless faces. Crocodile tears and Cheshire cat smiles . . . everyone networking.

Ace registers everything. Tucks it all away, adding it to the rage that fuels his fire.

"You're the husband, right?"

He looks up, gauging the White House intern that has somehow managed to slip past Jennifer to invade his private island of grief—an Ivy Leaguer with aspirations of power.

"Richard Perle asked me to send his personal condolences. He would have liked to be here, but he's been so busy, with the war and all—"

"Maggot."

The man breaks into a nervous half-smile. "I'm sorry, what did you say?"

"Your ears not working? I called you a maggot. That is what you are, isn't it?" Ace's eyes bore through the false smile, causing beads of sweat to break across the man's forehead.

Sensing a disturbance in her universe, Jennifer moves to the approaching storm.

"Sir, if there's something I said—"

"Deaf and stupid too. You'll make a fine political aide."

"Ace, let me handle this—"

"No, Jen, let me." Ace stands, waving to the funeral director. "Mr. Goldstein, this viewing is officially off limits to anyone associated with Capitol Hill."

"Ace, don't—"

"Back off!" He turns to face the gathering crowd buzzing at the rear of the chapel. "If I can have the attention of the dirtbags exchanging business cards in the back. Yes, that would be all of you."

The room quiets.

"Thank you for your condolences, now if you leaches would please crawl back inside your limousines or beneath your rocks, Kelli's family and friends would like to say our good-byes in peace."

Stunned expressions. No one moves.

Jennifer shoots Ace a venomous look, then quickly herds the group outside.

Ace returns to his seat, receiving a nod of thanks from Bruce Doyle as he draws his children in close.

♦ ♦ ♦

A cold rain falls from a sky more brown than gray. Mourners huddle beneath a flock of black umbrellas, half-listening as a rabbi leads them in prayer and Kelli's casket is lowered into the ground.

Grief is an emptiness that only time can fill; in its waxing moments it can swallow you whole, in its waning respite it will rise to ambush you with a long forgotten memory when you least expect it. The death of a parent causes reflection, the death of child can shatter faith—

—the death of a spouse forces change.

Ace trembles as the casket bearing his wife's remains disappears from view.

What do you do when your existence is shattered in an instant, when the pain is so intense that you can't stand to be inside your own skin, when your every waking moment is consumed by endless emptiness? How do you go on when you are so sickened by life that you wish you'd simply disappear . . . the urge to drink your thoughts into numbness stayed only by your newfound responsibilities as a single parent, your children's pain far more important than your own, their innocence an emotional anchor that forces you to live out each hellish moment.

For days Ace Futrell had wept only in private; around detectives and doctors and among family and friends he had remained a rock. But as he whispers his last good-byes to his soul mate and sweeps his children up in his arms, he knows he will weep no more; as he climbs back into the limousine, another emotion will slowly seep into his being—one so cold it will suffocate his heart, one so deep it will replace his heart.

How do you quench a fire that burns inside you like a furnace, fueling an anger so hot that it consumes all thoughts, all logic, all tears?

There is only one way . . .

Revenge.

Today Ace Futrell's fury will cement his life's new mission—to find his wife's killer, to assassinate the assassin—

—to punish those responsible for destroying his family.

"What we want is not a united Arabia, but a disunited Arabia split into principalities under our suzerainty."

—LORD CREWE,
British statesman

"Oil is too important to be left to the Arabs."

—HENRY KISSINGER

"The truth is that the United States wants to eradicate our religious and Islamic identity."

—NAGI AL-SHIHABI,
Egyptian newspaper editor,
2004

CHAPTER 7

THE BOEING 747 JUMBO JET LANDS with a double thud, the spoilers—small hinged plates situated along the top portion of the wings—flipping up into the air stream to kill the plane's lift and keep the massive plane on the ground. Bypassing the airport's main terminal, the pilot taxies his aircraft to a private hangar—a temporary embassy for the visiting VIP and his traveling entourage.

King Sultan bin Abdul Aziz—ruler of Saudi Arabia, head of the Al-Saud family, absolute monarch of the world's largest oil-producing nation, and guardian of Islam's two holiest shrines—relaxes inside the jumbo jet's private sauna with two of the dozen "stewardesses" who have made the trip from Riyadh. As the 747 slows to a halt, the king exits the heated chamber and showers, his naked followers washing him down, then patting him dry.

Feeling refreshed, the king slips on a silk robe and enters his master suite, a chamber complete with oversized bed, fifty-two-inch flat-screen satellite television, and a crystal chandelier. Touching a keypad on his internal communications system, Sultan speaks Arabic to his son, Prince Bandar bin Sultan, ambassador to the United States. "Is he here?"

"Yes. He is in the hangar, waiting for an audience."

"Tell him I'm concluding an important meeting. Awaken me in two hours."

◆ ◆ ◆

Scott Swan finishes checking his e-mail on his Blackberry, glancing at the time: 4:47. The CEO of Tech-Well Industries, a defense contractor recently purchased by the Carlyle Group, has been waiting in the airport hangar office for nearly three hours, and his patience has worn thin.

Lousy Saudi bastards . . . no appreciation for the working man.

◆ ◆ ◆

The Carlyle Group is a private equity investment firm whose financial assets, estimated between $30 billion and $50 billion, are topped only by its members' abilities to directly and indirectly affect world policy. Founded in 1987 by David Rubenstein, a domestic policy advisor to President Carter, along with his partners William E. Conway, Daniel A. D'Aniello, and Stephen L. Norris, the Carlyle Group's list of partners, advisors, and associates reads like a global Who's Who of the rich and well-connected. Their power players include former Presidents George H. W. Bush and his son, George; former secretaries of state James Baker III and Colin Powell; former prime minister of Britain John Major; as well as former prime minister of South Korea Park Tae Joon; former secretaries of defense Donald Rumsfeld and Frank Carlucci (also a former deputy director of the CIA); as well as a growing list of ambassadors, heads of state, and regulatory agencies from around the world.

While political access helped launch the company, it was money from the House of Saud that helped propel the Carlyle Group to its present heights.

Carlyle's first transaction with the Royal Family took place in 1991 when Prince Al-Waleed bin Talal, the largest individual shareholder of Citicorp, purchased nearly $600 million of Carlyle stock. That investment opened the flood gates to the Saudis, who were shepherded by former President Bush, James Baker, and John Major, three world leaders who had supported Saudi Arabia during their terms in office. From that point on, Carlyle Group soon found itself selling everything from AWACS to weapon systems, the profits from which enabled them to purchase defense contractors LTV, Harsco, and BDM International, which they later turned around and sold to TRW, Boeing, and Lockheed Martin. In the wake of the first Gulf War, Carlyle's defense contractors won major contracts to support the Royal Saudi Air Force while the Vinnell Corporation, on the verge of bankruptcy, landed a big contract to modernize the Saudi National Guard (following a Carlucci trip to Saudi Arabia).

In recruiting key players from former White House administrations as well as from former subordinates from the Pentagon and CIA, the Carlyle Group has become more than just a successful investment firm. It has become a political arbitrage—a trading entity that relies on insider information and "the persuasion of access" to forecast political stability among foreign activities.

For "normal" trading to be legal, it must be based on publically available information. However when it comes to former presidents and secretaries of state, this black-and-white area often turns gray. The Carlyle Group uses this gray area as a hedge against the unknown, such as investing in foreign government bonds or accepting contracts in war-sensitive sectors like oil and arms. With direct access into the White House, Carlyle's advisors not only gain insider information, but they also have the ability to sway foreign and domestic policy. By "riding the board," Carlyle has minimized the risks in purchasing struggling companies, turning them around, and selling them for huge profits.

◆　◆　◆

Scott Swan tucks away his Blackberry and picks up a two-month-old issue of *TIME* magazine, the front cover depicting the world's continuing struggle to control the Avian Bird Flu, which again threatens to become a global pandemic. He skims through the article, a grin creasing his face as he reads about the pharmaceutical companies now working on a vaccine.

Stock's up another dollar, should split by next April . . .

He tosses the magazine aside as Prince Bandar bin Sultan enters the office. "Mr. Swan, my father will see you now. I am truly sorry for the delay."

The executive forces a smile. "Business is business." Swan kisses the prince on his silk-robed shoulder, then grabs his briefcase and follows him out of the office and up the portable steps leading onto the 747 jet.

King Sultan bin Abdul Aziz, now dressed in his own traditional white *thobe* and matching *ghotra* headpiece, greets his guest in the study. "Mr. Swan, *Masaa al-Khair*."

"*Masaa an-noor*."

"And how is your chairman?"

"He sends his best."

"But the chairman has chosen not to greet his biggest investor in person?"

"Due to the nature of this meeting, he felt it best I come alone. Officially, this is simply a social call between the two of us. It has nothing to do with Tech-Well or Carlyle."

"Understood." The king signals to his son and visitor to take a seat. "Still, I am very uncomfortable with certain elements of this transaction. I need reassurances if we are to proceed."

"Remember, it was you who came to us."

"The timing concerns me."

"Would you prefer to wait until your country is invaded by Iran or seized by an Islamic revolution?"

"I would feel more comfortable if President McKuin was not in the Oval Office."

"There is an election coming up."

"You wish to make jokes?"

Swan looks the king in his piggish eyes. "McKuin will not be a factor."

The king raises an eyebrow. "The vice president?"

"Your Highness, I am merely a conduit to those pulling the strings. I don't need to know nor do I want to. What I do know is that the world is at a crossroads and your kingdom needs stability. These are tenuous times, and it will get worse unless we act now. Difficult decisions have been forced upon us, terrible decisions; still, we do what we must. Historians not yet born will celebrate our courage."

"The House of Saud cannot be implicated—"

"There will be no loose ends."

"And if something does go wrong?"

"It won't."

"Now you speak for Allah?"

Scott flushes. "As I believe I made clear, I am a liaison, nothing more. However, I've heard there are contingencies . . . backups in case of unforeseen events. That is all I am at liberty to say." He stands to leave. "The Secret Service limo will be here to escort you to the White House at nine a.m. Your meeting with the president is at ten."

"Mr. Swan, I too have contingencies . . . the United States economy is my contingency. If anything does go wrong—a blogger selling conspiracy theories, a former CIA agent writing a tell-all book," the king's eyes blaze, "then the House of Saud shall pull the plug on our investments in your country in the time it takes to make a single computer transaction."

King Sultan's cherub face creases in a frigid smile.

Swan clears his throat, finding his voice. "Try not to keep President McKuin waiting."

BALTIMORE, MARYLAND

JAMAL AL-YUSSAF LIES IN THE STRANGE bed in the strange room, staring at the ceiling, the uneasiness he feels reminding him of his childhood back in Iraq. For as long as he could remember, his father had instructed him to sleep under his bed, that it was the best place to be in case the house came crumbling down or the American jets broke the sound barrier. Under the bed, Jamal would be protected from flying glass. Under the bed, he would be safe.

The year was 1991, and Jamal was seven years old. As he lay underneath his bed, night after night, he tried to think of what he had done wrong to deserve this. When the American planes came low and the sirens would go off, he would stick his fingers in his ears and sing his favorite songs as loud as he could, just as his mother had instructed. He had asked her once when he should stop singing. She had replied, "When I come and get you, Jamal."

Winters were the worst because it got dark out faster and turned very cold. Saddam had cut off electricity to give the enemy less to shoot at, and Jamal was not even allowed to turn on a flashlight to read. Night after night the family would huddle together, listening to the BBC on the radio, waiting to hear updates about the war. At some point water became rationed, and when the pipes burst from the bombings, Jamal's mother had to boil it to make it potable—without any electricity.

Then there were the shopping trips. The entire family would pile into one car and lie down in the backseat while Jamal's father drove through decimated streets to find supplies. On one occasion Jamal peaked out the window at the carnage, bodies wrapped in bloodied white sheets along the roadside, people crying and screaming over them. As the boy laid back in the seat he started to sing, wishing he was back in his safe place.

Twenty years later, Jamal registers that same familiar fear gnawing in his gut. Grabbing his pillow and blanket, he rolls onto the floor and curls up beneath the iron-framed bed, humming his favorite song until he falls asleep.

"The people can always be brought to the bidding of the leaders. That is easy. All you have to do is tell them they are being attacked, and denounce the peacemakers for lack of patriotism and exposing the country to danger. It works the same in any country."

—HERMAN GORING,
at the Nuremberg Trials

"It could happen tomorrow, it could happen next week, it could happen next year, but they will keep trying. And we have to be prepared."

—VICE PRESIDENT DICK CHENEY

"Iran is part of a movement that has already displayed more aggressive tendencies by coming here and killing us . . ."

—RUDY GIULIANI,
GOP presidential candidate

"A coalition of Shia and Sunni and Hezbollah and Hamas and the Muslim Brotherhood and al Qaeda wants to bring down the West."

—MITT ROMNEY,
GOP presidential candidate

"Osama will follow us home [from Iraq]."

—JOHN MCCAIN,
GOP presidential candidate

CHAPTER 8

MONTAUK, NEW YORK
DECEMBER 16, 2011
5:25 PM EST

THE BEACH HAMLET OF MONTAUK REPRESENTS a seventeen-square-mile track of land bordered to the south by the Atlantic Ocean, to the north by Long Island Sound. The Doyle-Futrell home is a contemporary two-story with cedar shake shingles located in the Hither Hills section, within walking distance of the beach. Inside, maple walls and bamboo floors maintain the beach-look, while the two stone fireplaces create a ski-resort effect—a practical aesthetic put to good use during Montauk's harsh winter months.

The mourners have gathered in the great room, warming themselves by the main fireplace, eating and comforting one another with memories of the deceased. Every so often Ace's name is referenced in hushed tones:

"He travels so much, who's going to stay with the kids? The housekeeper?"

"What about that live-in nurse of Kelli's?"

"No, she was part of a service. He'll have to get one of those full-time sitters."

"They should move. A beach town is no place to raise kids."

♦ ♦ ♦

Ace remains upstairs, alone in his study, listening to the wind howl at the storm windows. Bookshelves line the walls of his office. It is just after five, but it is already dark outside.

Leaning back in his leather chair, his eyes linger upon a family Christmas photo, taken years earlier, that sits on one corner of his desk. *Everyone smiling. Everyone healthy. Did I appreciate those times like I should have? If I could only turn back the clock—*

A double knock, and Jennifer opens the door. "Can I come in?"

He motions to the sofa. She closes the door behind her and takes a seat. "You hiding out?"

"The kids' friends are over. I needed a reprieve."

"Understandable. Can I bring you some food?"

"Maybe later."

"I'm here for you, Ace, if you need me. You know, with the kids."

"Thanks."

"What are you going to do? I mean, I know you and Kelli talked about it. I'm sure you made plans."

"We talked about it."

"And?"

"Things have changed." His eyes lock on hers, delivering the message.

"Ace, you're angry, and you have a right to be, but just let the police handle this."

"The police aren't handling anything, the FBI's in charge. Case closed."

"What's that supposed to mean?"

"Do I need to spell it out for you?" Ace gets up from his desk chair amd locks the door. "She was sanctioned, Jennifer. A few of her old pals in Washington, no doubt. Maybe some of the buzzards circling at the funeral."

"Is that why you went off? Ace, that's ridiculous. Why would they target Kelli?"

"You tell me?"

"This is crazy talk."

"Then I guess I'm crazy."

"No, but you're under a lot of stress. How about if I move in for a few weeks. I could help with the kids, let you get back to work—"

"I was fired."

"What?"

"They called this morning. Left the message on my machine. Apparently I ruffled the wrong feathers in DC. Nice of them to wait until the day of the funeral, knowing I wouldn't be home."

"What will you do? Do you need money?"

"We're okay. Your cousin earned a good living. Paid for it in the end."

"That's enough! There is no conspiracy—"

A knock. The locked door handle jiggles. "Ace, you in there?"

Ace unlocks the door for Bruce Doyle. His father-in-law looks pale. "Son, I think you'd better come downstairs."

◆ ◆ ◆

The four vans are parked on his front lawn. The occupants, all wearing black jackets with the letters *FBI* in yellow glow-lettering, are already unloading equipment. The team leader waits impatiently at the front door.

"Mr. Futrell, my name is Special Agent Geordie McGillivray with the FBI. I have orders to search your premises."

"Orders from who?"

"The Department of Homeland Security."

"Homeland Security? Why? What's this all about?"

"I'm not at liberty to say."

"Then tell me what you're searching for."

"I'm not at liberty to say."

"Then you'd better show me a damn search warrant!"

"Homeland Security is no longer required to have a search warrant when dealing with acts intended to intimidate or coerce a civilian population."

Jen shakes her head. "Damn Patriot Act."

"You think my family is out to coerce a civilian population?"

"I'm sorry, sir, I'm not at liberty to say."

Ace feels his blood pressure boiling over. "You keep using the term 'liberty.' I wonder if you really know the true meaning of the word."

Jennifer pushes her way into the conversation. "Is this in any way related to my cousin's death?"

"I'm sorry, ma'am, I can't answer any of your questions at this time. Now if you'd step back and allow us to search the premises." He nods to two armed FBI agents who barge their way in, each man carrying a heavy suitcase.

"Wait! I have a house full of guests. Today was my wife's funeral."

"My condolences. However, please be aware that all guests currently on the premises will be subjected to a search. Cooperate and we'll try to make this as least invasive as possible."

"Cooperate? You invade my home, refuse to tell me why you're here or what you're searching for, and you want me to cooperate? Ever hear of the Constitution, pal? It wasn't written to be used as a doormat!"

Agent McGillivray touches the walkie-talkie mounted over his right shoulder. "Security, we have a situation. North entrance."

Before Ace can react, another agent barnstorms the door, taser in hand. He points the black stun gun at Ace and fires.

Zap! The blue bolt of electricity instantaneously penetrates Ace's clothing and skin, jolting his central nervous system like a bucket of ice water. Purple lights flash across his vision, his body turning to electrified jelly as it hits the floor.

Special Agent McGillivray looks over the gathering circle of guests. "Anyone else have an objection? Good. Then in an orderly fashion I'd like you to line up against that far wall, arm's length apart. There's nothing to fear; this is a security matter that most likely doesn't concern you."

Sensation returns. Ace pulls himself up into sitting position on the floor, his fingertips still singed with hot electrical impulses. Through watering eyes he sees his daughter racing down the staircase.

"Dad! Why are they doing this? Dad, are you okay?"

Ace nods, his voice box unable to form words.

"Miss, I need you up against the wall with the others."

"Dad, they're taking everything! My laptop . . . all my CDs and DVDs! Why are they doing this?"

"Everything will be inspected and returned. Now line up with the others." The FBI agent grabs the thirteen-year-old girl by her arm.

Leigh twists free. "Get your paws off me!"

The security man wheels, aiming his stun gun at the teenager—

No! A wave of adrenaline drives Ace off the floor. Wobbly hands grab for the weapon, twisting the barrel at its moment of discharge—

—the blue bolt striking Agent McGillivray, who drops to the floor in spasms.

An elbow clubs Ace in his face. The former quarterback shakes it off, slamming the FBI agent against the hallway mirror, their images shattering on contact.

And then everything goes black as Ace Futrell sinks into a midnight sea of velvet.

"Normal FAA procedures for responding to even minor deviations from air traffic control protocols were followed routinely and without complication sixty-seven times between September 2000 and June 2001 before a new convoluted order was released by the Pentagon on June 1, 2001. That order inserted the secretary of defense into a decision-making and action protocol, normally the domain of senior military commanders. Why? It took only minutes for (scrambled) fighters to get there after (golfer Payne) Stewart's plane had missed only one turn and failed to respond to radio transmissions for just a few minutes (October 25, 1999). Why the enormous difference in responses between 1999 and 2001 when an obviously greater emergency existed and was widely recognized? . . . part of the (explanation) lies in a deliberately superimposed overlay of war game exercises being conducted by several governmental agencies on September Eleventh that inserted false blips into radar screens in the North East Air Defense Sector (NEADS), involved live-fly exercises with aircraft posing as hijacked airliners, and effectively confused and paralyzed all response by loyal interceptor pilots who would have seized the initiative that day, regardless of protocol had they known where to go."

—MICHAEL C. RUPPERT,
from *Crossing the Rubicon: The Decline of the American Empire at the End of the Age of Oil*

Book Excerpt:
To the Brink of Hell: An Apology to the Survivors
by Kelli Doyle,
White House National Security Staff Advisor
(2006-2010)

Before I worked for the White House and long before my years with the CIA, I had to decide between majoring in history or international relations. I can still remember my first college professor trotting out the worn cliche 'history is written by the victors.' Young and still impressionable, I believed it then.

I no longer believe it. In the war that is coming, there will be no victors, only survivors.

It may be you to whom I write these memoirs. If you knew how it all began, then maybe you wouldn't be so quick to repeat our mistakes. That I was there for many of these decisions allows me a unique perspective to shed light on what really happened.

It does not in any way exonerate me from the deeds.

Politics never interested me, but power . . . that was something different. To be counted among the elite, that was a goal I aspired to. Competition was in my blood; I was a two-sport athlete in college, our field hockey and lacrosse teams always ranked in the top twenty. For four glorious years, my world consisted of practice, games, travel, more practice, class, parties, and maintaining my GPA so I'd be eligible to continue the ride.

Go Dawgs.

As my final year at the University of Georgia wound down, I developed a bad case of senioritis—a dreaded fear of graduating and having to enter the real world. What was I going to do?

Marriage was an option. My fiancé was a shooting star on the football team, but while I loved him dearly, he was going through his own trials and tribulations that only served to push our relationship onto the back burner. Law school was a possibility, but my ego, still fueled by competition, was demanding something out of the ordinary. When Career Day came, I moved from booth to booth, yet only one choice stood out among the rest, one I had never even considered: the CIA.

The Company was, and still is, the most powerful and secret organization in the world. Its budget remains hidden even from Congress, and few really understand the extent of its powers. It has its own mercenary army, and it has its own corporations that influence wars and Wall Street. Enticed by my forthcoming degree in international relations (and three semesters of Arabic) the recruitment officer promised a training regiment that would challenge me physically, offering travel to exotic lands and an opportunity to serve my country.

That last part sealed the deal. I had competed in the Junior Olympics and World Games and my soul was wrapped in the stars and stripes. Two weeks after graduating from the University of Georgia, I found myself in Washington, DC, completing the exams necessary to receive my security clearance as a field officer. By fall I had begun officers training school. By the following spring, I was on 'the Farm.'

The Farm is Camp Peary, a military reservation located in York County, Virginia. The CIA and Special Ops use this heavily forested game preserve as a training facility. To free up the site's 9,275 acres, the Feds had to relocate two entire towns—Bigler's Mill and Magruder. The Farm has its own airport and is heavily secured, and with the exception of our after-hour get-togethers at Buck's Strip Bar and Steak House, Camp Peary's activities are kept away from the public eye.

And for good reason. Among other things, the Farm is where the CIA trains its assassins. The program combines guns and wits with clandestine field training exercises, and for its female recruits, a special treat—a jail cell interrogation that separates the GI-Janes from the Martha Stewarts. Being the former, I was able to "endure" and soon found myself fast-tracked for a battle looming in the Middle East.

The year was 1990.

The CIA does not make policy. Our job was to provide intelligence to the president of the United States and his policy makers, and once that policy is determined, our job was to execute it.

Yes, to the victors go history, but history and truth are two separate entities. I joined the CIA because I believed in what America stood for, I believed in the morality of truth. I could justify the coups on foreign governments and the tactics we used because, hey, we were the good guys, right? The end always justified the means . . . democracy's on the march. Let freedom reign.

It's hard to accept the truth. Lies don't shatter realities and dreams, only truth does that. And the truth was—the president lied.

All presidents lie. Roosevelt lied about Pearl Harbor. Lyndon Johnson lied about Vietnamese torpedo boats shooting at American ships in the Tonkin Gulf. Reagan lied about Iran-Contra. Clinton lied about his personal affairs in the Oval Office. I suppose even George Washington lied (he probably never even owned a cherry tree).

But it was the lies coming from the Bush-Cheney White House after the events of September 11, 2001 that led us to the invasion of Iraq and to a crossroads in western civilization that will affect you and your loved ones and a billion more innocent people.

Did the U.S. intelligence community know Al-Qaeda's attack was coming?

Yes.

Did they try to stop them?

Yes, but they were prevented from doing so. FBI field agents in both Minneapolis and Phoenix who were close to exposing the plot were repeatedly and purposefully bottlenecked from taking action by a single supervisor—Dave Frasca—who would later receive a promotion for his actions. Then, on the day of the attacks, the joint chiefs, under Vice President Cheney's personal direction, scheduled and conducted five separate war game drills that purposely pulled interceptor jets away from the northeastern airspace corridor while deliberately inserting false blips on air traffic screens to simulate, of all things, hijacked airliners. Military jets that routinely intercept aircraft within minutes were delayed an unfathomable eighty minutes. Most never even entered the fray. While dedicated pilots and air traffic controllers desperately tried to determine what was real from what was staged, an FAA administrator "accidently" destroyed the recordings of the day's tragic events . . . and he too was later promoted.

Those are facts . . . but only the tip of a dirty iceberg.

Of course, none of that information was ever brought up in the 9/11 hearings.

Intelligence agencies around the world knew when and how the attacks would occur, but their warnings were ignored. Wall Street investors certainly knew—a day before the attacks domestic and foreign investors placed an unprecedented number of "put calls" (a leveraged bet that a stock will drop) on the airlines and companies that would suffer devastating losses, in some cases more than ninety times higher than normal trading. These financial transactions netted upwards of $15 billion in insider trading that was halfheartedly investigated before they too were dismissed by investigators and the media, the latter manipulated by the Bush administration, who were dictating which stories to run and which to kill. Meanwhile, key members of Congress who opposed the administration's plans received packages of anthrax in the mail, the lethal spores later determined to have originated not overseas, but from labs used by the CIA.

One voice of opposition who refused to be intimidated— Senator Paul Wellstone—would conveniently die in a plane crash.

These "convenient coincidences" happened repeatedly throughout the events leading up to and following the activities of September Eleventh. Almost none were sufficiently investigated; almost all were cloaked in secrecy, stymied with retribution. Revealing passages in the 9/11 report were blacked out, and despite the biggest failure in intelligence history, no one has ever been reprimanded or punished.

Whether you prefer to believe in "coincidence theories" or "conspiracy theories," thousands of innocent American lives were sacrificed on September 11, 2001. But the real enemy was not just Osama bin Laden and his Islamic radicals.

It was our addiction to oil.

Oil has gone from a cheap energy resource that spawned an industrial age, a technological boom, and a population explosion, into a commodity that now determines foreign policy—and with it, the lives and deaths of millions of people. And yet it is a resource that is running out, the issue being one that has affected every president since Jimmy Carter.

So why don't we just replace oil? Alternative energy resources have received lip-service and scant investment, while trillions of our tax dollars have been, and continue to be, invested in fossil fuels and military options that ensure our drills are in position to secure every last drop.

When it comes to oil and its suppliers, our foreign policy gets twisted like an Orwellian pretzel. In his first major speech after the events of September Eleventh, George Bush declared, "You are either with us or with the terrorists." That black-and-white stance turned multiple shades of gray after the Shi'ites gained power in Iraq and Hezbollah rose in Lebanon, threatening our chief oil suppliers—the Saudis (lest we forget, the hijackers' country of origin). In an effort to stymie the Shi'ites in both Iraq and Lebanon, the Bush administration covertly began channeling billions of "rebuilding" dollars into Sunni resistance groups—otherwise known as Al-Qaeda.

That's right. Five years after they attacked the United States, the very terrorist organization we sought to eradicate was "hired" to quell a Shi'ite uprising unleashed by our own invasion of Iraq.

This memoir was not written to make a political statement or attack a political party. It was meant to expose the truth that surrounds our nation's addiction to oil, an addiction that funds our enemies, destroys our cities, and will lead to the annihilation of innocent millions.

"If it is desirable to alter the life of an entire people, is there any means more efficient than war?"

—CARNEGIE ENDOWMENT FOR
INTERNATIONAL PEACE,
1909

"This religion [Islam] will destroy all other religions through the Islamic Jihad Fighters."

—An excerpt taken from a Jordanian/Palestinian schoolbook

CHAPTER 9

Revolutionists Attack Saudi Air Base

Associated Press: December 16, 2011

RIYADH, Saudi Arabia—Rebels armed with explosives destroyed a squadron of F-15 fighter jets and two squadrons of Agusta Bell (AB) 205-S and 212-S attack helicopters housed at the Riyadh Airbase. Claiming responsibility for the attacks was Asraf, a new revolutionary group that claims to represent the collective oppressed will of the Saudi people.

In a statement published by the underground newspaper, Rai al-Nas, one of the group's leaders, said, "Ashraf opposes the hypocrisy of the Saudi monarchy whose Royals rob our citizens of our nation's God-given resources. Ashraf opposes the United States and other western nations who keep the Royals in power because they seek to control Saudi resources. Ashraf also opposes radical Wahhabi clerics whose brutality has enforced the reign of terror unleashed by the Saudi monarchy. Ashraf is willing to negotiate the sale of the people's resources to western nations once the seeds of democracy are sown in Arabia, but this can only be achieved by removing the Royals from their absolute power."

A Royal Saudi Air Force (RSAF) commander said that security would be beefed up at other military bases and believed arrests were imminent.

WASHINGTON DULLES INTERNATIONAL AIRPORT
DULLES, VIRGINIA
DECEMBER 16, 2011
8:25 PM EST

THE REFRIGERATED TRUCK HAS BEEN PAINTED navy-blue with canary-yellow trim. Two-foot-high white stenciled lettering identifies the purveyor as Middle Eastern Delicacies. There is an 800-number and a listing of assorted food samples. The stolen license plate is from Maryland.

Omar Kamel Radi is the driver, Jamal al-Yussuf next to him in the passenger seat. Both men wear uniforms identifying them as employees. Each wears photo ID tags. Jamal grips a clipboard holding a work sheet detailing an extensive food order, called in by King Sultan's head chef. Despite the frigid air coming from the slightly opened windows, both men are sweating.

Omar stops at the airport security gate. He wipes a bead of perspiration from his heavy brow as he lowers the window for the guard. "Delivery. Hangar 12-D."

The guard shines his light inside the cab. "Shut off the engine and climb out. I'll need to inspect your load."

♦ ♦ ♦

An olive-skinned man dressed in an airport security guard's uniform watches the scene play out from his motorized cart parked sixty yards east of the gate. Shane Torrence, a veteran field operative of the Strategic Support Branch lights a cigarette, then speaks into his walkie-talkie. "Food's here."

♦ ♦ ♦

Jamal al-Yussuf walks around to the back of the refrigerated truck, handing the guard the clipboard while Omar unlocks the back and yanks open the rolling doors, then extends and lowers the rear lift gate. A heavy scent of curry wafts out from the truck. The tall Sunni climbs inside, followed by the guard.

There are two aluminum refrigerated storage lockers secured to the floor, each eight feet long, six feet wide and four feet deep, the huge cases on wheels. Omar pops the four sealed fasteners and raises the lid of the first, revealing enough food to feed thirty people. There are beef kebabs and chicken dishes, pastries filled with potatoes and meats, and an assortment of appetizers, sauces, and desserts, all wrapped in plastic sheeting.

The guard's mouth waters. "Looks good. Open the other one."

The Iraqi complies. Inside are two whole lambs, their bodies skinned and seasoned, wrapped in plastic sheeting.

"Gross. Close it up."

Omar re-seals the storage containers while the guard takes out his radio and calls for a security car. "It's Becker at twelve. I need you to escort a delivery truck to Hangar D."

The two delivery men climb back inside the truck. The steel gate is retracted, allowing them entry onto the airport grounds. A white police car marked "airport security" leads them across the tarmac past rows of hangars until they reach building 12-D.

◆　◆　◆

SSB Agent Marco Fatiga watches the two vehicles approach the hangar that temporarily houses the Saudi 747. Like his associate, Shane Torrence, the Bronx native has been assigned to the two Iraqis as a "ghost."

A member of the Secret Service joins Marco outside the hangar. "Another delivery?"

Marco nods. "With these Arabs it's either food or women."

The truck is directed through the open hangar bay doors. Minutes later, a six-man Arab detail exits the 747. They off-load and wheel away the two storage lockers while the head of security signs the work order and pays the tall driver. "Wait here. The kitchen staff will empty the containers and bring them back out to you."

Twenty minutes later, the six Saudis wheel the "emptied" lockers out of the jumbo jet's cargo ramp. The two delivery men join them as they load and secure the containers in the hold of the refrigerated truck.

No one bothers to search the "empty" lockers.

Marco Fatiga hovers close to Omar as he attempts to bolt the vehicle's rear doors. The former soccer goalie's hands are shaking, making it difficult.

The SSB officer steps in and secures it for him. "Better ease up on the caffeine, young man. You don't want to get into an accident."

The two men's eyes lock for a brief moment. The driver nods nervously, then climbs inside the truck. Airport security leads the purveyor off Dulles's grounds.

Forty minutes later, the truck pulls onto Interstate 66, heading west.

TIVERTON, ONTARIO
8:12 PM EST

THE STEELBACK CANADIAN BEER TRUCK CONTINUES north along King Street through Tiverton, heading for Kincardine. The driver glances to his left at the Huron Wind Farm. Five massive 1.8-megawatt wind turbines dot the western landscape like giant white pinwheels. The former Air Force officer and CIA operative, now assigned to the Strategic Support Branch, shakes his head. "Clean, free, and simple. Never had a Chinaman's chance."

◆ ◆ ◆

Michael "the Turk" Tursi was born in Hinton, West Virginia, an old railroad town nestled at the foot of the Appalachian Mountains where the Bluestone and Greenbriar Rivers meet the New River. His mother, Mary, worked as an assistant principal and English teacher at the local middle school; his father, Patrick, was a police officer when he wasn't fulfilling his duties in the National Guard. For Michael, an only child, life was well regimented: homework and study were the priorities, followed by church and Little League sports. It was middle-class, apple-pie America, a lifestyle that suited Mike's parents but left their son wanting more.

Everything would change after the twelfth of June, 1977.

It was the last day of the school year, and Mary Tursi was patrolling the halls, trying to bestow a fleeting sense of organization to the final moments of chaos when she came upon thirteen-year-old George Nathanial, a boy she had suspended a month earlier for bringing a hunting knife to school in a failed attempt to impress a would-be girlfriend. This time George had smuggled in something more lethal—a .25-caliber handgun he had taken from his grandfather's footlocker. George would later claim it was never his intention to shoot Mary Tursi, that he just wanted to show the weapon to his peers, but as they struggled for possession of the gun, it discharged, fatally wounding the thirty-nine-year-old assistant principal.

When a teacher is killed, the effects ripple across the entire school district, creating a heightened sense of vulnerability that often takes years to subside. The effects on the victim's family, of course, are far more profound. To fifteen-year-old Michael, a young man raised to respect the law, the world suddenly made no sense. Bad things were not supposed to happen to good people. These were not the rules he had been taught to live by. For the next two years, Michael would spiral into a deepening state of depression, the one-time honor roll student failing his courses and quitting the baseball team, his father eventually resorting to having him home schooled just so he could attain his diploma. Psychiatrists were hired, drug therapies prescribed, but nothing seemed to help.

Desperate to return a sense of direction to his boy, Patrick convinced his son to enlist in the United States Air Force. Three weeks later, eighteen-year-old Michael Tursi found himself on a bus bound for Lackland Air Force Base in San Antonio, Texas.

Michael's first day began with his arrival on the base at one in the morning and ended twenty-three hours later the following night. Basic training is designed to separate the weak from the strong as recruits are torn down and built back up. Physical activity is punishing, made worse by the mental duress. Enlisted men not cutting it can be sent home. Every so often a few opt to kill themselves rather than be shamed into quitting. During Tursi's eight weeks, his squadron experienced one attempted suicide and one that succeeded when a recruit took a nose-dive out a third-story window during morning formation.

Basic training teaches recruits the proper method to fight and kill. Mind games are mixed in with the physically demanding regiment, adding new types of stress. For Michael Tursi, training succeeded in restoring his competitive will to excel, and he quickly realized the Air Force could open doors, doors leading him away from the life of mediocrity he had always dreaded.

One day, Tursi was ordered to an administration building, where he was placed in a room with only a chair, a desk, and a reel-to-reel tape player. A major informed him he was to listen to tapes, which included every language, and write down what he thought the speaker was communicating. It was a language aptitude test, and Tursi's scores were outstanding, warranting an assignment in Washington, DC, as an interpreter.

He would opt instead for electronics.

After graduating from basic training (bestowed with the nickname, the Turk), Michael was assigned to Sheppard Air Force Base in Witchita Falls, Texas, where he would spend the next fourteen months in training as an analyst technician for ballistic nuclear missiles.

◆　◆　◆

Tursi turns off the highway onto an access road leading into the Bruce Power Nuclear Plant. He stops the truck at the security checkpoint and waves to the approaching guard. "Paulie, how was the party?"

"I wouldn't know. Those events are strictly for the suits."

"Ah, who needs it, eh? Here, for you and the boys." Tursi reaches for the box of cigars on his passenger seat and hands it to the grateful guard. "Cubans, the real deal. Buddy of mine has a contact at the embassy. I was forced to quit years ago."

"Bless your heart."

"Any time. Listen, I'm running late. Gotta pick up those empty kegs."

"Sure, sure. Go on through."

Tursi waves, then enters the facility, heading for the loading dock.

◆ ◆ ◆

The Bruce Power Station, Canada's first privately-owned nuclear plant, is composed of two generating plants, each holding four CANDU nuclear reactors. Short for CANada Deuterium Uranium, CANDU reactors use natural, unenriched uranium in their design, requiring deuterium oxide, or "heavy water," as both a coolant and moderator.

Uranium is a high-density metal believed to have formed during a super novae more than 6 billion years ago when a star, ending its life cycle, collapsed in on itself and exploded, releasing radioactive decay and debris that eventually reached Earth. Uranium can be found in rocks and seawater and is the heat that occurs within the earth's crust.

Different forms (isotopes) of uranium are designated by the number of particles (neutrons) in the nucleus. When a uranium atom's nucleus splits apart, it releases a tremendous amount of energy. It also emits neutrons, which go on to split other nearby uranium nuclei, releasing more energy in what is called a fission chain reaction. Isotope U-235 (92 protons + 143 neutrons = 235) is used in nuclear fission because it yields an abundance of energy as heat when it splits. It is this heat that is used to make steam that drives a turbine in a nuclear reactor.

Of the two kinds of uranium found in nature, it is the rare U-235 isotope that is used in nuclear bombs. Natural uranium contains less than 1 percent U-235. In order to be usable in nuclear explosives, it must be enriched to 90 percent U-235 and only 10 percent U-238. The other fissile material used in nuclear weapons is plutonium-239, a substance made by bombarding uranium-238 with neutrons in a nuclear reactor. Virtually nonexistent in nature, plutonium is one of the most toxic substances known. Inhaling merely a thousandth of a gram will cause massive fibrosis of the lungs. Ten pounds of U-235 or slightly less plutonium is all that is necessary to reach critical mass in a nuclear bomb.

For a CANDU reactor to operate with unenriched uranium requires the use of heavy water as a medium. Heavy water is water in which both hydrogen atoms have been replaced with deuterium. The production of a single pound of heavy water requires 340,000 pounds of feed water. Because heavy water can also be used to enrich U-235 into nuclear-grade uranium, production and distribution of heavy water is closely monitored.

The world's largest producer of heavy water? The Bruce Heavy Water Plant in Tiverton, Ontario.

◆　◆　◆

Tursi drives past the commissary and rolls the big diesel until its left flank is lined up with the loading dock. Richard Weldon Small, the loading dock foreman, is waiting impatiently for him as he raises the vehicle's side gate. "There were . . . problems. My guy could only fill seventeen kegs."

"That wasn't our arrangement."

Small is sweating, despite the frigid temperatures. "We did the best we could. There was only a twenty-minute window."

Tursi looks over the twenty beer kegs, hastily arranged on five pallets. He walks to the fourth pallet and randomly selects a barrel. "Open it."

"We don't have time. My supervisor—"

Tursi unhooks a ratchet-like device from his belt loop and uses it to twist open the keg. From his ski jacket pocket he takes out a ten-inch chemical analyzer and dips the metal end into the barrel's clear liquid content. Checks the meter: deuterium.

"We've known each other six years. You don't trust me?"

"I don't trust anyone who's in a position to screw me." Tursi removes a thick envelope from his pants pocket. "Twenty thousand. Make sure your guy on the inside gets his, or you'll be looking over your shoulder the rest of your days."

Small leafs through the wad of bills. He nods nervously, then the two men roll the barrels onto the truck, securing them among the other ten kegs of beer.

Six hours and two rest stops later, Michael Tursi guides the beer truck across the Ambassador Bridge into Detroit.

"Those who would give up essential liberty to purchase a little temporary safety deserve neither liberty nor safety."

—BENJAMIN FRANKLIN

"FBI Director Mueller personally awards Marion (Spike) Bowman with a presidential citation and cash bonus of approximately 25 percent of his salary. Bowman, head of the FBI's National Security Law Unit, is the person who refused to seek a special warrant for a search of Zacarias Moussaoui's belongings before the 9/11 attacks. The award comes shortly after a 9/11 Congressional Inquiry Report saying Bowman's unit gave Minneapolis FBI agents 'inexcusably confused and inaccurate information' that was 'patently false.'"

—DOUG GROW,
from "FBI Performs a Nasty
Little Sequel to Whistle-Blower Saga,"
The Minneapolis Star Tribune,
December 22, 2002

CHAPTER 10

Ace sits up slowly, immediately aware of the dull ache in his head. His stomach is empty and still a bit jumpy from having thrown up in the police car. The heat from the repeated jolts of electricity is a waning memory, but it has left a bad metallic taste in his mouth.

There are two other men in the holding cell. A heavyset man in his fifties is lying on a bench, using his wrinkled sports coat as a pillow. A college student is on the floor, passed out cold.

Ace perks up at the sound of approaching footsteps. Using the iron bars, he drags himself off the floor just as the guard opens his cell door. With him is a lanky fellow in his mid-forties, his tight, curly gray-brown hair matching his business suit.

Jeffrey Gordon, senior partner at Cubit, Gordon & Furman, Attorneys at Law, greets his boyhood friend with a worried look and a quick embrace. "Bail's been arranged. Let's get you home."

"What about—"

Jeff shakes his head. "Not here."

◆ ◆ ◆

Ten minutes later, they are in Jeffrey's car, inching their way through rush-hour traffic.

"But how can they just enter my home without a search warrant?"

"Patriot Act, section 213: any federal law enforcement agency can enter your home or business, whether you are there or not or whether they tell you about it or not, then use any confiscated evidence to convict you of a crime. It's all legal."

"It's fascism, that's what it is! What the hell happened to the Fourth Amendment?"

"It got bulldozed back in '01. Section 202 states the Feds can read your e-mail, and section 216 allows them to intercept your cell phone calls."

"Damn. How the hell could Congress pass—"

"Cheney and Ashcroft rammed it through before Congress even read it. The bill hadn't even been printed when the vote was called. The bottom line is the Feds can basically do anything they want, as long as they claim the suspect is part of an ongoing terrorism investigation."

"Terrorism? Jeff—"

"I know, I know. What about Kelli? Was she working on anything that would give the powers-that-be a scare?"

Ace thinks back to the night his wife was killed. "I don't know," he lies. "When it came to her job, Kelli never told me much. Jeff, how much trouble am I in here?"

"The FBI dropped the assault charge after I threatened to go to the papers with the whole funeral thing. But you have to be very careful. I've represented other clients targeted by the Feds, and 'paranoid' is probably not a bad thing to be right now. Assume you're being watched 24/7, your phone lines tapped, your e-mail intercepted. In fact, just stay off the Internet until this thing blows over. And no financial transactions that look even remotely out of the ordinary. They'll have access to your credit cards, your bank accounts, everything. Hopefully this is just some White House official being paranoid about crossing Kelli years ago. You certainly ruffled a few feathers at the funeral."

Jeffrey turns onto the expressway and looks at his friend. "I heard you lost your job."

"Yeah. Ruffled a few feathers there too."

"Do you need a loan?"

"Thanks, no, we're . . . I'm okay. It's just piling up a bit right now. To be honest, I'm more worried about the kids."

"Gay and I are coming by later. We'll bring Jesse and Rayna. Meanwhile, let me do some poking around, see what I can find out."

THE WHITE HOUSE
WASHINGTON, DC
DECEMBER 17, 2011
2:20 PM EST

DAVID MCKUIN, THE FORTY-FOURTH PRESIDENT OF the United States, sits impassively behind the 1,300-pound wooden desk constructed from timbers salvaged long ago from the British vessel, *HMS Resolute*. McKuin is alone in the Oval Office, gazing absentmindedly out the glass doors that lead to the Rose Garden patio. The fourth heavy snowstorm this winter is set to hit the Northeast later this afternoon, and already two inches have fallen. The garden is blanketed in white beneath heavy gray skies, the forecast calling for ten more inches with temperatures dropping into the low teens.

People will die . . . Happens every storm. Traffic accidents steal a few, and a dozen elderly who can't afford to pay their electric bills will freeze to death.

McKuin is two hours removed from his meeting with King Sultan bin Abdul Aziz, and he can still smell the man's overpowering aftershave on his lapels. But there is something else lingering in the Oval Office air. *What happens when the lights go out permanently? When the heat is gone? When the stoves don't work and there's no food to be had in all of DC? How long will it take before the people march on Washington?*

McKuin is a Republican but far from a Neoconservative. He believes in God but refuses to pay lip service to the religious fanatics who wish to control the party. He has served in war and has been duly honored, but the politics of conflict and the abuses of resources sicken him. His election win in 2008 was based on his reputation as a centrist conservative. McKuin has earned a trust that extends over both parties, a trust that he has never been a puppet to big business, coupled with the public's belief that he could end the conflict in Iraq and return America's good name to global affairs.

Despite his efforts, problems across the globe are mounting, led by the hot spot in the Middle East. In Iraq, McKuin inherited a hornet's nest of sectarian violence between Sunni and Shi'ite, spurred by Iranian mullahs and Islamic radicals. The cancer has continued its spread throughout the region, America's military presence propping up a puppet regime—a finger in the dike of a massive Islamic wave that threatens Iraq, Saudi Arabia, Syria, and Israel.

The situation eats at the president's ulcer every day. The ongoing war in Iraq has dictated changes in United States–Middle East policy, which now backs "moderate" dictatorial regimes in Egypt, Jordan, and Saudi Arabia, who are using their fundamentalist Salafis to spread the Sunni-Shiite conflict into Lebanon in an attempt to destabilize Syria. Meanwhile, Islamic fundamentalism continues to spread throughout the region, while the popularity of Iranian President Mahmoud Ahmadinejad grows in leaps and bounds. Despite protests from the West, the Iranian leader has expanded his country's nuclear capabilities while supplying conventional weapons to Hamas and Hezbollah, all the while strengthening his relationships with China and India through increased oil exports.

The wild card in this equation remains Saudi Arabia and its royal dictators, who continue to play both sides against the middle in an effort to quell unrest both outside and inside their borders. While Iran's nuclear presence openly threatens the kingdom's borders, the House of Saud is rotting from within, its decay traced to decades of greed and abominable human rights abuses. Promises of open elections have dwindled into heavy-handed exploits generated more for public show than for democratic change. The Saudi people, once determined to participate in running their own country, have festered in servitude, all hope of breaking the Saud family's monopoly on power dashed—at least as long as the Royals are backed by industrialized nations importing oil. The gap between the Saudi masters and the impoverished masses widens with each passing day, and within this vacuum of discontent Islamic Fundamentalism grows, fueled by the Iranian-led slaughter of Iraq's Sunni populace.

Having refused to "squander" its nation's profits on basic services necessary to build a modern economy, the House of Saud has chosen instead to subdue the will of its people. To deal with the Islamic threat the Royals have resorted to bribing Muslim leaders, who have in turn been utilizing these newfound financial resources to attack the West.

The president knows full well there is a growing movement among members of his own party to quash the Islamic extremists, McKuin's vice president, Ellis Prescott, one of the main supporters. Invasion scenarios for Iran have been secretly drawn up and discussed, but the president refuses to be pushed into another costly engagement—one he knows is fueled in part by the neoconservative movement's desire to control the Middle East and its diminishing oil supply.

Unlike most of the hawkish radicals within his own party, the president understands firsthand what it means to engage in a poorly planned battle contrived by politicians. His experiences in the military have given him a far different perception of guerilla warfare, and he will exhaust all other means before flexing his military might in Iran, especially with American forces being stretched in Iraq. The roots of Islamic radicalism stem from economic inequality, military occupation, and authoritarianism, and McKuin knows full well that another invasion will only exacerbate these tensions. What the president needs now is to diffuse the situation, first by withdrawing America's military presence in Iraq; second, by committing America to a fossil-free future. Without one there cannot be the other, but the republican president is stuck in a catch-22—he cannot announce his intentions until after the election at risk of losing the financial support of his base, yet with each passing day the problems seem to be growing worse.

The question is whether the world can sit around and wait until November.

His thoughts are interrupted by his secretary's voice over the intercom. "Mr. President, it's two thirty."

"Thank you, Sophia." Straightening his tie, McKuin exits through his secretary's office and enters the Cabinet room.

Already seated at the conference table are his chief of staff, the directors of the CIA and Homeland Security, the Secretaries of Energy and Defense, and McKuin's vice president, Ellis Prescott. All rise as he enters to take his place at the open middle seat, his back to the bulletproof windows.

"Good afternoon. Hope everyone's keeping warm. As you know, King Sultan and I spent several hours together this morning discussing the situation in the Persian Gulf. The king assured me the recent unrest in Riyadh was an isolated incident and that tensions have dissipated. Unfortunately for the king, he's not a very good liar."

The vice president forces a smile. "Mr. President, what was Sultan's reply to our offer?"

"The Saudis have agreed to increase oil production by 1 million barrels per day, beginning March 1."

Applause and smiles around the table.

The president nods. "It'll be a nice boost for the economy and no doubt our poll numbers, but, as usual, it comes with a price. On the one hand, Sultan claims civil unrest is of no great concern; on the other, he wants to utilize our resources to contain this new rebel movement, the Ashraf. The king claims Al-Qaeda is behind the group and wants the NSA's help in identifying and hunting down its leaders."

CIA director David Schall smirks. "If Sultan's so worried about Al-Qaedea, why does he continue to allow their funds to pass through his banking system? As for Ashraf, we covered the group's activities in a daily briefing about six weeks ago. It's not a radical Islamic movement. In fact it's a civilian-based democratic movement coming out of Jiddah, one gaining popularity among the foreign workers that run the Saudi oil fields. So far, they've focused their attacks solely on Saudi Aramco sites."

"Which makes them a threat to our interests," states Howard Lowe, the Homeland Security director.

"No argument," Schall responds, "however, this is not Al-Qaeda nor is it part of a Bedouin influence. We're dealing with a group that traces its descendants directly back to Muhammad. These are modern thinkers who oppose Wahhabi traditionalism as much as they do the Saudi monarchy. The movement receives financial support from Prince Alwaleed bin Talal, who's been openly critical of the House of Saud and Saudi Aramco for years. The prince tends to be pro-American, though he's alienated himself in the past by speaking out for the Palestinians. Bachelor's degree from Menlo College. Completed his master's at Syracuse. In the past he's stayed clear of Saudi politics, focusing his energies on building a large international business called the Kingdom Holding Company. They're heavily invested in Apple, AOL, and Motorola and hold large stakes in a dozen major hotels. Forbes recently listed Bin Talal as the fourth richest man in the world . . . behind King Sultan, of course. It was his donation following 9/11 that Guliani turned down, but he's consistently contributed to many American institutions. If he's a radical, it's only in the context of opposing the House of Saud."

"Bin Talal's also invested heavily in entertainment conglomerates, including Rupert Murdoch's News Corp.," Director Lowe retorts. "That gives him a venue to spew whatever message he chooses across the globe."

"And what message is that? Human rights?" The president looks around the room. "Sounds to me like this Ashraf movement is one we should find ways to support."

"With all due respect, Mr. President," Vice President Prescott counters, "that's incredibly risky. Iran's already favoring oil exports to China. If King Sultan learned we were supporting his enemies—"

"Sultan's supporting *our* enemies," Benjamin Simon retorts. The Filipino-American chief of staff looks across the table at Prescott. "You read last week's PDB. The majority of Al-Qaeda's funding, as well as funding for other radical Islamic regimes, comes from corporations controlled directly by the House of Saud or from accounts originating from their central bank."

"Yes," the vice president responds, "as a counterweight to policies favoring the United States. The Saudis fear retribution. But if Sultan's inviting us in to take out this Ashraf movement, maybe we can use the opportunity to position nuclear warheads on our Saudi bases . . . counter the Iranian threat. Wouldn't you agree, Secretary Kendle?"

"I would." Joseph Kendle, McKuin's secretary of defense runs a thick palm across his short-cropped reddish-brown hair. "We can't just sit on our hands while the Iranians aim their nuclear missiles at our military bases. If taking out a few Ashraf leaders allows us to accomplish that, I say do it."

"No." The president registers the acid reflux broiling in his gut. "Placing ballistic missiles in Saudi Arabia is extremely dangerous. It will be perceived by the Muslims as a prelude to Jihad. As for helping Sultan wipe out his enemies, here we finally have a group that might lead to a sea change in morality in Saudi Arabia, and our first response is to stamp them out? What are we promoting here, people? If the oil's really there then someone's bound to sell it to us. Why not let it be a group that might finally institute some reform? Isn't that what Iraq was supposed to be about?"

After a moment, Patricia Moreau, the secretary of energy, speaks out. "It's certainly worth considering, Mr. President. At the same time, revolution means change, and change takes time. The Ashraf inhabit Saudi Arabia's west coast, but it's the Islamists who control the east, and that's where the big oil fields lie. With the way things are shaping up in Iraq and Iran, with the situations in Venezuela and Nigeria, can we really afford uncertainty in the Saudi kingdom at this juncture? The House of Saud has been in power a long time, and they're backed by the Islamists. I doubt the Ashraf will ever control the Red Sea cities, let alone the entire country. And if there really is a revolution, that door swings both ways. Anarchy presents the Iranians with an opportunity to gain a stronger foothold in the region. Toppling the Royals now could lead to an Islamic onslaught."

"Bin Talal is a royal, Secretary Moreau."

"Yes, sir. One voice among thousands. Maybe there are other princes willing to join him under the right circumstances, but it's unlikely. Let's face it, these Royals are pampered billionaires who have been known to kill their own. Bin Talal may support a revolution from a distance, but we've seen no indication he's interested in fighting for the crown."

A few nods of agreement.

The president is not ready to back down quite yet. "Tell me, what should the United States do if the streets of Saudi Arabia erupt in demonstrations shouting for democracy? What should our response be if the Ashraf take Mecca and Medina? Keep in mind that the Muslim hatred toward the House of Saud rivals their hatred for the West. The climate in Saudi Arabia is percolating. How much longer can we afford to prop up these Royals?"

"With all due respect, Mr. President," the vice president responds, "the House of Saud won't fall, not with our undivided support."

"Yes, Ellis. And Nixon and Carter said the same thing about the Shah of Iran." McKuin checks his watch. "I've got a call with the prime minister, so we'll table this for now."

The cabinet members stand to leave. As the chamber empties, the president grabs his CIA director. "David, can I see you for a quick moment?"

"Yes, sir."

Alone with the president, Schall closes the door. "An interesting meeting, Mr. President. You toss bait quite well. Something's clearly going on."

"Plans within plans. Sultan was prepped."

"What do you need from me?"

"Pat Moreau's right, the last thing we need right now is Saudi Arabia caught in a power vacuum, but the extent of that threat is weighted by how much oil is really left in usable reserves. What I need is information . . . hard data, not the stuff coming from the DOE."

"Agreed. Ghawar and the undeveloped Empty Quarter hold the key."

"How do we find out what's down there? Who would know?"

"No one we can get to. However . . . I do know of someone who could help."

"Who is he?"

"I met him several years ago at a cocktail party. His wife introduced us. Name's Ace Futrell. Works for PetroConsultants, at least he did until he went off the deep end at the Energy Hearings."

"Have your people reach out to him."

"Sir, it's . . . complicated. His wife was Kelli Doyle."

"Aw, hell."

"To make matters worse, Homeland Security opened a file on Futrell hours after Doyle was killed. If I back them off—"

"—it'll send up warning flags to our Neocon friends."

"Yes, sir."

The president mulls it over. "Handle it. Personally."

"When you're drowning, you don't say, 'I would be incredibly pleased if someone would have the foresight to notice me drowning and come and help me,' you just scream."

—JOHN LENNON

"It is clear the U.S. authorities did little or nothing to pre-empt the events of 9/11. It is known that at least 11 countries provided advance warning to the U.S. of the 9/11 attacks. Two senior Mossad experts were sent to Washington in August 2001 to alert the CIA and FBI . . . The list they provided included the names of four of the 9/11 hijackers, none of whom was arrested."

—MICHAEL MEACHER, MP,
U.K. Environmental Minister (1997–2003),
from "The War on Terrorism is Bogus,"
The Guardian,
September 6, 2003

CHAPTER 11

GARY LEE SCHAFER, DIRECTOR
RADICAL FUNDAMENTALIST UNIT
COUNTER-TERRORISM AND MIDDLE EAST SECTION
FBI–HQ
DECEMBER 29, 2011

Director Schafer:

This e-mail will serve as a follow-up to communications originating from FBI–Chicago between 12/14/11 and 12/27/11. FBI–Chicago has confirmed suspect Jamal al-Yussuf has received deposits totaling $112,210 from a Cayman Island account. Suspect Omar Kamel Radi has received deposits totaling $117,540. Over the last three weeks both suspects have purged their bank accounts of all monies. Neither suspect has been seen since.

We have received confirmation from the Strategic Support Branch (SSB) in Iran that indicates both suspects may have been recruited into Iran's Qods Force (Islamic Revolutionary Guard) sometime between December 2007 and April 2008. Photo surveillance confirms suspect Jamal al-Yussuf at Imam Ali Training base, located north of Tehran (Alborz Kouh Street), between April 2007 and December 2009. An SSB informant places suspect Omar Kamel Radi at Bahonar Training Base near Karaj Dam in Tehran (Chalous Highway) between June 2007 and December 2009.

Immigration confirms suspect Jamal al-Yussuf arrived in the United States (New York) in February 2011. Suspect Omar Kamel Radi followed two months later (April 2011). Both suspects met up in late September in Aurora, Illinois.

With this new information we are requesting:

• Electronic surveillance to relocate suspects.

• FBI monitoring of suspects' activities.

• NSA surveillance of suspects' cell phone activities.

Respectfully,

Adrian Paul Neary, Director
FBI–Chicago

Director Schafer re-reads the e-mail transmission a third time, his pulse racing.

◆ ◆ ◆

Originally trained as a computer systems engineer, Gary Lee Schafer was recruited straight out of college by the Federal Bureau of Investigation to work in the National Security Division at FBI Headquarters. After completing his training at Quantico, Virginia, he reported to New York City to focus on criminal and intelligence investigations where he designed programs aimed at countering domestic terrorism and preventing the use of weapons of mass destruction against the nation's population and critical infrastructure.

What looked like a promising career would be sidetracked in 1993.

On February 26, a 1,200-pound bomb detonated in the parking garage beneath the World Trade Center. The explosion killed six people and injured more than a thousand. Had the van transporting the bomb been parked a few feet closer to a main support pillar, the entire tower might have collapsed.

The FBI wasted little time in apprehending a suspect, Mohammad Salameh, who had foolishly been trying to collect a $400 deposit for the rented van. More plotters were quickly captured in what appeared to be a high-water mark for the FBI.

In reality, the FBI had failed to follow clues from an earlier case that could have prevented the attack. And it was their young, rookie agent, Gary Schafer, who would blow the whistle.

Back on November 5, 1990, Rabbi Meir Kahane, founder of the radical Jewish Defense League, was giving an anti-Arab speech at a New York hotel when El Sayyid Nosair, a thirty-six-year-old Egyptian immigrant, fatally shot the rabbi in the neck. Nosair was part of a cabal of Muslims that despised both Israel and Egyptian leader Hosni Mubarak. When Nosair's residence was searched, the police discovered paramilitary manuals, maps, and diagrams of buildings, including the World Trade Center.

Agent Schafer believed the evidence indicated that Kahane's assassination had been planned by a Muslim terrorist cell and that more attacks were on the horizon. Unfortunately, Schafer's supervisors were loathe to expand their investigation, looking instead for a quick conviction.

As Nosair's trial began, rioting took place outside the courthouse, with death threats made against the judge and lawyers. In an attempt to learn more about the Muslims, the FBI hired an informant, Emad Salem, a forty-three-year-old former Egyptian military officer, to assimilate himself within the group. Salem eventually became the bodyguard for Sheik Abdul Rahman, a radical Muslim cleric. Rahman had been heavily subsidized in the late 1980s by the CIA while in Pakistan to recruit Muslims to fight the Soviets in Afghanistan.

Incredibly, the jury found Nosair not guilty on the murder charge but guilty of possessing a firearm (the murder weapon that killed Kahane). Meanwhile, Salem continued his work as an FBI informant, sending information directly to Agent Schafer, for which he was paid $500 a week.

During the summer of 1992, Salem warned that the Muslim group was planning a major bombing in New York City. Agent Schafer reported Salem's information, but the FBI supervisors were convinced the informant was lying to save his job and decided to fire him.

Six months later, the World Trade Center was bombed.

After the attack, the FBI rehired Salem and promised him a million dollars to develop evidence of additional terrorist plots. Instead, Salem secretly recorded his conversations with FBI agents, which pointed the finger squarely back at Agent Schafer's bosses for failing to heed his earlier warnings. Many accused Schafer of instigating the tapings.

The FBI was doubly embarrassed when it was learned the contents taken from Nosair's apartment years earlier contained major clues that would have exposed the bombing plot.

Despite the fact that Muslim terrorists came close to killing thousands of Americans, there would be no congressional investigation of the FBI's failings. Director Louis Freeh was praised, and several agents received accommodations.

Agent Schafer, however, would suffer the fate shared by many whistle blowers, his promising career screeching to a halt.

Over the next sixteen years, Gary Schafer had repeatedly been passed over for promotion, forced to sit back and watch while far-less-accomplished agents had risen up the FBI ladder. Then, six months ago, Schafer "ran into" Jeff Anders, his old roommate at Quantico. Anders invited him on a diving trip in the Caymans, and soon the two were talking shop.

Like Shane Torrence and Marco Fatigo, Anders had been recruited by the Strategic Support Branch after serving three tours of duty in the Middle East. Anders told Schafer he had helped the SSB establish an intelligence network in Iran. A domestic surveillance operation was underway, one that required a trusted pair of eyes at FBI-HQ. If Schafer was interested, "arrangements" could be made.

Anders set up a meeting between Schafer and Graeme Turnbull, a retired colonel who had served in Iraq. Two months later the director of the FBI's Radical Fundamentalist Unit unexpectedly decided to retire, and Gary Lee Schafer was offered the position, along with a substantial raise in pay.

◆ ◆ ◆

Steadying his nerves, Schafer answers the e-mail.

Director Neary:

CIA and U.S. Military Intelligence now estimates Iranian Qods Force recruits more than thirty thousand foreign nationals per year, including non-mercenaries from Saudi Arabia, Bahrain, Afghanistan, Jordan, Iraq, and many Europan countries. At this juncture, the information your department has submitted to FBI-HQ does not justify the costly surveillance arrangements requested.

Continued monitoring of the suspects' bank transactions and use of identification should reestablish the subjects' new locations. Report progress immediately and directly to me.

G. L. Schafer, Director

Schafer re-reads his reply several times, then clicks Send. Shutting off his computer, he exits his office, informs his assistant he is grabbing a quick bite to eat, then catches an elevator down to the lobby floor.

A fifteen-minute drive brings him to the library phone booth. He dials the memorized number, allows the phone to ring three times, hangs up, and waits sixty seconds before calling back again.

"Speak."

"Chicago's on track."

"Understood."

The line goes dead.

"A man will be imprisoned in a room with a door that's unlocked and opens inwards; as long as it does not occur to him to pull rather than push."

—LUDWIG WITTGENSTEIN

"We shouldn't be making deals. If somebody wants to deal, we issue subpoenas. That's the deal!"

—MAX CLELAND,
Georgia senator and member of the 9/11 Kean Commission,
referring to a deal that was cut with the Bush White
House to allow a handpicked subset of commissioners
to be briefed on the Presidential Daily Briefings.
(Cleland later resigned from the Commission.)

CHAPTER 12

A WHITE FOG HANGS OVER MONTAUK beach, the result of an unseasonable warm front meeting the cold ocean. Ace, barefoot, dressed in shorts and a heavy mesh Georgia Bulldogs football practice jersey, tosses a football with his son, Sam. The eight-year-old, dressed in similar attire, insists on running deep post patterns. Each throw causes the former quarterback's surgically-repaired left knee to throb. He ignores the pain, enjoying the game of catch.

After twenty minutes, the boy tires out and heads back to the house to play video games.

Ace rejoins his daughter, Leigh, who has been watching from a sand dune, taking photos with her digital camera. "Get any good ones?"

"Not really. The light's terrible." She points to his left knee, the joint bearing two six-inch scars. "Does it hurt?"

"Nah."

"You were grimacing."

"Just stiff. It's fine."

"I bet it hurt when you tore it."

"Hell, yeah. This big three-hundred-pound defensive tackle blind-sided me and my cleat got caught in the turf. Knee bent backwards, but they said they could hear it pop in the cheap seats."

"Ever wish you could go back in time, you know . . . to play again?"

"Not really."

"Come on, Dad. To relive your college days, big man on campus—"

"That wasn't me."

"Mom told me stories, she said you were really good, that you would have been drafted if you hadn't gotten hurt."

"She exaggerates. I was just a flash in the pan."

"What's that mean?"

"It means I peaked and fell." He looks at Leigh's expression, unsatisfied. "When I played in high school I was a backup, so when I went to Georgia, I knew I really had no chance of making the team, let alone starting. But I continued working out on my own, and in the next two years I sort of grew into my body. Went from a 185-pound freshman to 230 pounds right before my junior year. I was in great shape; my arm strength really increased, and I caught the coaches' eyes during spring tryouts.

"Anyway, the first game comes along, and I'm listed as the third quarterback on the depth charts. Not too shabby for a big-time program. First quarter, first game and *bam* . . . our all-American quarterback goes down. Third quarter, we lose our backup. I see the coach looking around, and suddenly I'm in the game. The noise is so loud, everything happening so fast, and we're down. Our receivers couldn't get open, so finally I took off running. I ran so fast I nearly ran out of my cleats . . . probably was scared out of my mind. But things started happening after that play, and I tossed a few nice passes for touchdowns. We ended up coming from behind, and all of a sudden I'm the next Kurt Warner."

"Who's Kurt Warner?"

"He played for the St. Louis Rams. Went from a grocery store employee to the starting QB for the Super Bowl champs."

"Wow, Dad, so they could make a movie about you, huh?"

"Sorry, kiddo. Movies have happy endings. My career had . . . issues."

Leigh points to the narrow, white scars that cut lengthwise along the inside of her father's wrists. "Those issues?"

Ace forces a smile. "Yeah."

"How come?"

He looks out to the Atlantic, its dark surface still blanketed in fog. He has never spoken to his daughter about his suicide attempt, never felt it was the right time.

"It's hard to explain, it was a confusing time . . . everything happening so fast. You have to understand, I really wasn't that good . . . no, that's not true, I was good, I just lacked experience. When my coach put me in, no one expected much, but when we kept winning, the pressure kept building, and all of a sudden we're playing in the Orange Bowl, possibly for the National Championship. That's big time. College football in the South . . . it gets crazy. Websites like the Dawgvent—it's not a pastime with these fans, it's religion. I couldn't walk through campus without being mobbed. I couldn't study, I couldn't eat, I couldn't think, I had students and fans and reporters and boosters hounding me day and night, everyone wanting a piece of me, offering gifts, money, women . . . like I said, it was crazy. By kickoff time I was a bundle of nerves. My hands were shaking so hard with adrenaline that I could barely grip the ball. I fumbled the snap on the first play. Threw an interception on my second pass. The coach hung in there with me until halftime, then benched me. By that time the game was over."

Ace rubs at the scars on his right wrist. "Scholarship athletes tend to look down on us walk-ons, and I had replaced two popular teammates. It took all season to earn my teammates' respect, and I lost it in the first half of that game. The next few months were bad. I'd get threatening phone calls in the middle of the night, a few death threats . . . once someone even shot nails into my tires. Anyway, spring training comes along, and I'm still running with the starters. During our first scrimmage—non-contact for quarterbacks—my own defensive tackle pancakes me."

"That's how you hurt your knee?"

"Yeah. Guess they were sending a message."

"That's terrible."

"Coach cut the guy, and the trainers helped me rehab, but it really screwed with my head. That spring I started having panic attacks. I'd lay down to go to sleep, and suddenly I couldn't breathe. The team doctor prescribed sleeping pills. Then the attacks started happening during the day."

"Where was mom during all this?"

"Busy with lacrosse. Whenever I mentioned the panic attacks, she'd just slap me upside the head and tell me to cheer up. You know your mom. We were young, immortal. The things I had to work so hard on . . . they came natural to her. Big-time athletes didn't have anxiety attacks. She just couldn't relate."

"So what happened? Did you play football your senior year?"

"I tried, but the panic attacks kept getting worse, it was like . . . like being trapped in your own skin. I guess it was fear. The fear of failing. The fear of letting everyone down again. I handled it wrong; I know that now.

I should have talked to someone . . . gotten on an antidepressant. One night I just couldn't handle it anymore, so I decided to open a few veins and take a long hot bath."

Tears well up in Leigh's eyes. "Who found you?"

"Tet. Mark Tetreault. He was our tight end, my best friend. He saved my life."

"Tet? Is he the one who died?"

"Yeah. He worked on one of the upper floors for a securities company. They lost a lot of people. The heat from the jet fuel . . . they say it was so hot, the flesh was probably melting. People were jumping from windows, but not Tet . . . he hung in there, no doubt trying to guide his coworkers to safety, only there was nowhere for them to go." Ace clears the emotion from his voice.

"Dad . . ."

"It was a long time ago, Leigh. You don't have to worry."

She snuggles closer. He puts his arm around her, squeezing her tight. For several minutes they listen to the sounds of the pounding surf.

Ace turns to his right. Tenses as he spots the man standing by the water thirty yards down the beach. "Leigh, go back to the house. I'll be along soon."

She turns and sees the stranger. "Who is it?"

"No one important. Go on."

She trudges over the dune, following a narrow boardwalk that cuts through the saw grass.

Ace pulls on his sweatshirt and approaches the figure, who is dressed in a black windbreaker, dress slacks, and matching shoes.

"Hello, Ace. Let's walk." David Schall follows the shoreline east. "I want you to know I'm sincerely sorry about Kelli. She was more than a colleague; she was a friend."

"Who killed her?"

"Honestly, I don't know."

"You're the head of the CIA. Find out."

"Let's talk about you. Why did you spout off at last month's Senate hearings?"

"I don't know. Maybe I was tired of rehashing the same old crap."

"The president thinks you know a lot more than you're letting on."

Ace stops walking. "Is that what this meeting's about? Here I thought you were going to tell me why Homeland Security's got their collective heads crammed up my ass."

"I can get you back into the game."

"And what game is that?"

David continues walking. "The president needs to know how much oil's left in the Saudi reserves. Assuming you had unlimited resources, could you find out?"

"By unlimited resources, you mean—"

"Unlimited."

"What's in it for me?"

"Your job back at PetroConsultants, with a raise. Two pay grades."

"Pass."

"And Homeland Security off your back."

Ace stops. "Are they your doing?"

"No. But your wife was making a lot of people nervous about something. Care to venture a guess?"

A wave breaks close to shore, washing over Ace's bare feet, soaking the CIA director's dress shoes and socks. "Damn it!"

"Okay, David, you want the Saudi info, I can get it for you, but here are my terms, and they're non-negotiable. I want Kelli's assassin. I want his name and where to find him. Get me that and you'll get your information."

"I can't do that."

"Of course you can, you're the freakin' CIA. You start wars. And David, next time you instruct my attorney to meet me at the beach, at least wear sandals and jeans, huh? You look ridiculous."

"Not only did [FBI Supervisory Special Agent] Dave Frasca not share the information about Moussaoui to other appropriate intelligence/law enforcement authorities, he also never disclosed to the Minneapolis agents that the Phoenix Division had, only three weeks earlier, warned of al Qaeda operatives in flight schools seeking flight training for terrorists purposes! It is impossible to believe that Dave Frasca acted on his own, sitting on this information and not doing anything with it, unless ordered to do so. The Minneapolis FBI agents even tried to do an end run around Dave Frasca and notified the CIA's Counter Terrorist Center. The end result was that FBI Headquarters personnel (Frasca and unnamed higher ups) 'actually chastised the Minneapolis agents for making the direct notification without their approval.' Going even further, Frasca 'undercut' the search warrant application by not adding information on Moussaoui's foreign power connections which he had promised Minneapolis agents would be included. He also made damaging changes to the text provided by Minneapolis agents thereby, according to one Minneapolis agent, 'setting this up for failure.'"

—Steve Moore,
from "9/11: Foreknowledge or Deception?"
Global Outlook,
Issue No. 2
(Supervisory Special Agent Dave Frasca was later promoted to
Assistant Section Chief of the International
Terrorism Operations, Section I.)

"They [Islamic Radicals] are using our laws against us, they are using our democracy against us, and they know exactly what they are doing."

—Brigitte Gabriel,
Founder of www.AmericanCongressForTruth.com

CHAPTER 13

THE WHITE VAN CRUISES JUST BELOW the speed limit as it continues east on Main Street before turning south, entering a residential neighborhood. Magnetic signs on the vehicle identify it as belonging to a home improvement company in Decatur, Illinois.

Mike Tursi checks the time. He is forty minutes early, giving him ample opportunity to check out the neighborhood before making his delivery.

♦ ♦ ♦

Michael Tursi was twenty-one when he arrived at Sheppard Air Force Base in Witchita Falls, Texas, to begin training as a Ballistic Missile Analyst Technician—BMAT, for short. After fourteen months of intense training, the Turk knew every working part of an ICBM, inside out. Upon graduating, he was ordered to take a thirty-day leave before reporting to Vandenburg Air Force Base in Santa Maria, California, for his course work and training in working with nuclear warheads.

Tursi's introduction at Vandenberg began with the viewing of classified films detailing the effects of thermonuclear radiation. The Turk and his classmates were horrified to witness the demise of American soldiers in the 1950s who, acting as "lab rats," had been stationed too close to the nuclear blasts. The lucky ones had been vaporized upon detonation. The rest had died slow, agonizing deaths from radiation poisoning.

With their minds now properly set, the training began. Simulations rehearsed every possible accident scenario, including the launch and retrieval of a real missile shot over the Pacific.

Following his graduation at Vandenberg, Tursi finally received his first official assignment: Little Rock Air Force Base in Arkansas. It was 1983, the height of the Cold War, and tensions among members of the "God Squad" were running high.

Little Rock was the real deal, home to dozens of ICBM silos containing Titan II nuclear missiles. After arriving at the base, Tursi was assigned a room and a silo crew. Each member of the Turk's team had to know the job of every other member in case a launch was required and a crewman was injured or dead or had "flipped out" at the prospect of firing a weapon designed to kill millions of people. Training simulators were used to grade each individual and team, and the Turk's crew always graded out HQ (Highly Qualified).

Most nerve-wracking were alerts. Going on alert meant awakening at 4:00 a.m., arriving at squadron headquarters by 5:30 a.m., and going through intelligence briefings before coding in. Each underground missile silo has a connecting subterranean site where the crews are stationed; in order to enter, a crewman had to call into the team already locked inside with the correct password and emergency code (the latter, in the event something went wrong). Crewmen heading out on alert were heavily armed. Even the police had no authority over a BMAT on alert.

Arriving at the subterranean entrance, a solitary crewman would be allowed inside the outside portal to code in. Once inside, the replacement crew would complete a DSV (Daily Shift Verification) which meant physically going into the missile silo and inspecting critical parts of the ICBM, including the warhead. Working inside the silo, Tursi could actually feel the heat radiating from the nuclear warhead, and as he moved deeper in to the silo, the smell of fuel and oxidizer was overpowering.

While on alert a BMAT crew would be sealed inside the missile bunker for a minimum of twenty-four hours. On one occasion, the cooling towers in Tursi's silo shut down, raising temperatures to critical levels, forcing his team to stay with the ICBM for ninety-six straight hours before the system could be fixed. On that occasion, an accident was avoided.

The Turk's crew would not always be so lucky.

ICBMs require maintenance. Propellent Transfer Service (PTS) was a routine that required a crew to change out the fuel and oxidizer from every stage of the missile. It was a dangerous procedure, for ICBMs possess very thin skins that can easily be punctured. Large, two-pound socket wrenches, attached by cords to the technicians' utility belts, are required to loosen the umbilicals of the Titan II missile. As is usually the case, it is the smallest detail missed that often leads to the biggest accident.

Tursi's team was completing a PTS when a crewmen who had failed to attach his ratchet accidently dropped the heavy tool, which fell into the silo, banked off the wall, and smashed into the ICBM, puncturing the missile's lower stage tank. Fuel gushed out of the Titan II, pooling at the bottom of the silo. Michael Tursi knew an explosion was imminent, but he stayed with the warhead, quickly disconnecting electronics in the hopes of preventing the nuclear device from detonating when the fuel ignited.

As the Air Force Base went into lock down and red alert, the emergency reached a critical stage, forcing Tursi's crew to evacuate the silo. Michael waited until the last possible moment, then sped away in an awaiting jeep. Minutes after he cleared the perimeter area the silo exploded, the detonation blowing the twenty-ton silo door half a mile away. Smoke and debris covered the area for miles in every direction, but the nuclear warhead didn't detonate.

Had it gone off, a substantial section of central Arkansas would have been vaporized and contaminated.

No press were allowed within ten miles of the base. Personnel living within the security ring either stayed inside their homes or were arrested on sight. By sunrise, the warhead had been found, its casing wrecked but the nuclear device still intact.

No medals were handed out, the story spun, the real cause of the incident kept under wraps. Within the next five years the Cold War would end, the unstable Titan IIs phased out, pushing Michael Tursi out of a job. But his cool head had been duly noted by military intelligence.

Two days after leaving Little Rock, Arkansas, the Turk was recruited by the U.S. Intelligence Community, his first assignment, the CIA.

◆ ◆ ◆

Michael Tursi drives past the street three times, circling back on different routes before finally following the road until it dead-ends at the cul-de-sac. The van is a rental, its Maryland license plate assigned to a vehicle owned by Dubai Ports World in Baltimore, the United Arab Emirates company that took over the six largest ports in the United States less than four months following the 2008 presidential election.

Tursi slows the van, approaching a three-bedroom, single-story, brick ranch house located on an irregular lot. A concrete driveway leads back to a three-car, winterized garage, which the occupant uses as a workshop. The backyard is heavily wooded, part of the Shawnee National Forest. The brown-green waters of Deer Lake can be seen in the distance.

The home belongs to Professor Eric Mingjuan Bi.

◆ ◆ ◆

An expert in nuclear fission, now a tenured faculty member at Southern Illinois University, Professor Bi was born sixty-two years ago in Qingdao, China. He relocated with his parents to the United States when he was ten. Eric Bi's father was full-blooded Chinese, a civil engineer who worked on many of China's hydroelectric dam projects. Bi's mother, Adzumi, was Japanese, her family hailing from Urakami, a suburb of Nagaskai, located on Kyushu, the southernmost of Japan's four mainland islands. Adzumi's father and uncles ran an import-export business at the harbor while she was growing up. Their clan had been "recruited" by the emperor's navy to organize supply ships during World War II.

On August 6, 1945, the Japanese empire was felled to its knees when the city of Hiroshima was scorched from a "fire in the sky." Following the Americans' atomic attack, Adzumi's father immediately arranged passage for his wife and children to leave the island.

Three days later, at 11:02 a.m. on August 9, a more powerful nuclear bomb, code-named "Fat Boy," was dropped on Nagasaki. The primary target had been Kokura, but cloud cover had obscured the bomber pilot's vision. The weapon exploded directly above Urakami, vaporizing the town, along with the northern end of Nagasaki. Thirty-nine thousand people were wiped out in the blink of an eye, twice that many lingered on for weeks from lethal radiation poisoning, Adzumi's father and uncles among them.

Adzumi was seventeen and resettled in China when Japan finally surrendered to the Allies and thirty-one when her husband moved their family to the States to study earthquake engineering. An only child, Eric grew up listening to his mother's retelling of those last, horrifying days of the war—stories that enticed the boy to learn how to harness such incredible power. After earning a master's and a doctorate degree in physics, Eric spent three years at the DOE's Los Alamos Nuclear Laboratory in New Mexico. He was mentored by Wen Ho Lee, a nuclear scientist who was later accused of stealing military secrets for China from tips sent in by anonymous officials.

Wen Ho Lee would later be exonerated, the suspicion of espionage now redirected at Professor Eric Mingjuan Bi.

◆ ◆ ◆

Tursi backs the van slowly up the driveway, parking within five feet of the closed garage doors. The Turk exits his vehicle, carrying a small cardboard box.

Professor Bi exits from his kitchen, pulling on an overcoat. "You're early."

Tursi nods. "Let's talk inside."

Eric Bi keys open the side entrance to the garage, leading the Strategic Support Branch agent inside. A black Ford Explorer is parked in the middle space. A riding lawn mower and snow blower occupy another. Assorted tools hang along one wall. Nothing out of the ordinary, other than the garage is heated and insulated.

Tursi hands him the cardboard box. The professor wipes humidity from his wire-rimmed glasses, then tears open the container—

—removing the plastic-sealed packs of $100 bills.

"Two hundred thousand?"

"It's all there, you can count it later. You'll get the balance when I take final delivery. Let's see the colex."

Bi returns the packs of money to the cardboard box, then leads Tursi to a storage closet. He removes a wheelbarrow, then rolls back the dirty carpet, exposing a wooden floor. Using a crowbar hanging behind the door, he pries loose three floorboards, revealing concrete steps that lead down into a basement.

The Chinese professor enters first to turn on the lights, Tursi following him below.

The room is almost a thousand square feet, its twelve-foot ceiling and windowless walls lined in lead-board, a lead-lined drywall. A 16,000-watt, propane-fed generator occupies one corner of the room, a lead container the size of a small washing machine positioned along a far wall, next to a similar-sized plastic container. A biohazard suit is laid out across several folding chairs.

Occupying the center of the basement is an immense object—a rectangular tank, six feet high and deep, ten feet long, composed of iron. Thirty baseball-size holes cover the left side of the tank, each hole bearing a rubberized doughnut housing. The top of the tank has been removed, revealing an internal metal sheath that divides the tank in half. The sheath is porous, bearing quarter-size holes. At the bottom of the tank is a series of heating elements, their insulated electrical wires running out of the tank, connecting with the generator.

A pipe feeds out of the right side of the tank into two eight-foot-high centrifuges, one feeding into the other.

Michael Tursi peers inside the tank, looking confused. "I don't know, Bi, you sure this thing will work?"

"It will work. I guarantee it will work!"

"Okay, easy, just give me the Readers Digest explanation."

"What you have here is a colex—a column exchange unit designed to convert, or enrich, uranium-235 to uranium-238." Professor Bi points to the left side of the tank. "The U-235 fuel rods stolen from the Iranian reactor will be positioned in these holes, feeding unenriched uranium into the tank. The tank will contain the heavy water, along with a mixture of nitric acid, ammonium hydroxide, hydrofluoric acid, and fluorine. Heating elements will heat the water to precisely 250 degrees Fahrenheit, creating a chemical reaction, converting U-235 into uranium hexafluoride, or UF-6."

The physicist points to the two tall centrifuges positioned outside the main tank. "This first centrifuge will draw the UF-6 through the porous wall, separating enriched U-238 from the depleted U-235. This second centrifuge has two outtakes. The enriched uranium-238 will rise and be taken from this upper outtake and stored in a lead tank until there's enough to cook. The depleted U-235 will be drawn out of this bottom outtake and stored in a separate cache. The process is repeated until there's enough enriched uranium to create our two packages."

"How long to do the job?"

"Each fuel rod should yield a gram of enriched uranium a day. Thirty fuel rods, thirty grams a day, figure about six months. How soon will you be delivering the fuel rods?"

"Soon enough."

"I need to stay on schedule."

"Just make sure everything else is ready."

Bi nods nervously, wishing the dangerous man was gone. "Come, I'll show you where to run the hose."

Tursi follows the professor back up the steps into the garage. Bi unbolts a four-inch rectangular cap situated along the bottom of the garage door. "Feed the hose through here."

The Turk exits the garage. Using his electronic key chain, he unlocks the van and opens its rear double doors.

Mounted to the floorboards is a 1,000-gallon polyethylene storage container filled with heavy water smuggled out of the Canadian power plant. Attached to the bottom of the container's faucet is two hundred feet of hose.

Tursi takes the free end of the hose and feeds it through the hole along the bottom of the garage. Inside the garage, Professor Bi takes up the slack. Several minutes pass, then Bi taps on the garage window, indicating he's ready.

The Turk turns on the valve, releasing the heavy water. Leaning back against the van, he lights a cigarette, never realizing his every movement is being recorded.

◆ ◆ ◆

In the two-story home situated directly across the street, FBI Special Agent Elliott Green works at a makeshift desk in the master suite on the second floor, the windows of which face Professor Bi's home. Green, in his early forties, has spent the last two years assigned to a desk job at the CAC (Crimes Against Children) division at Springfield, Illinois. The agent's goal has always been to work in counter-terrorism, but openings at FBI–Chicago are few and far between. Knowing his young agent was desperate for a change, Green's supervisor, a former cop named Charles Jones, had offered him an assignment in the field—a job originating out of the Department of Energy. Green had gladly accepted.

The "field work" turned out to be running surveillance on Professor Eric Mingjuan Bi.

Elliott Green has occupied the house across the street from the Asian-American nuclear physicist for two months, purchasing it through a bogus Florida corporation from its original owner, an eighty-two-year-old widower. To sweeten the deal and hasten her departure into a local seniors facility, the company had agreed to buy the home with all its furnishings.

As much as Green enjoys his new "status," he also misses seeing his wife and six-year-old son. He hates the "old people" smell that lingers in the air. and he refuses to sit in any furniture or use any of the dishes collecting dust in the peeling sunflower-yellow kitchen cabinets. He lives exclusively out of the master bedroom, made fresh with a coat of white paint, new carpeting, bedroom suite, and home entertainment center, its flat-screen television linked to the closed-circuit cameras monitoring activities across the street.

After two steady months of surveillance, the FBI agent knows when Professor Bi awakens every morning, what he eats for breakfast, what time he teaches class at the university, where he takes his lunch, and to whom he speaks at school. So far, there has been nothing out of the ordinary to report, other than Bi spending long hours in his three-car garage, which doubles as a hobby room—

—until tonight.

Green watches the scene as it records and plays on his monitor. He zooms in on the short, stocky man's face as he reaches inside his van. Seconds later, the home improvement delivery truck's rear doors slam shut, the driver climbing back into the vehicle.

A few minutes later the van drives off—

— leaving Agent Green to his work.

"U.S. military sources have given the FBI information that suggests five of the alleged hijackers of the planes that were used in Tuesday's terror attacks received training at secure U.S. military installations in the 1990s. [Mohammed Atta] may have been trained in strategy and tactics at the Air War College in Montgomery, Alabama, said another high-ranking Pentagon official."

—*Newsweek,*
September 15, 2001

"You've just got to trust us. We are honorable men."

—Richard Helms,
CIA Director (1971)

Book Excerpt:
To the Brink of Hell: An Apology to the Survivors
by Kelli Doyle,
White House National Security Staff Advisor
(2006-2010)

The next 9/11 event will be a nuclear attack. In one hellish instant of inhumanity, millions of innocent Americans
will be vaporized into dust. Worse off will be those who
escape the initial blast. Blind, their flesh scorched to the
bone, they will lie in wait for hours and days, lingering in
agony as they pray for the Angel of Death to take them.

If you happen to be living in a targeted city, then your
days may already be numbered. Traveling on business? Visiting
relatives? Life is a crap-shoot; take it from one who knows.
Some of us get rich, others get cancer, and if that's God's
will, so be it. But the events of September 11, 2001 and the
more devastating attack(s) to occur have nothing to do with
the Almighty . . . no, these deaths are part of a premedi-
tated grand scheme being planned and financed by a moral
minority convinced that they alone have been blessed to carry
out God's work.

I cannot give you the exact date of the attack, nor can I
give you its location, but I can present you with the circumstances that have lead us down this path of destruction . . .
and what you can do to stop it.

* * *

To understand how we got to this point, we begin with a
brief history lesson—call it the rise and fall of Petroleum
Man. Petroleum, of course, is oil, and we're using it faster
than we can pump it out of the ground. Oil fuels the economy,
the economy fuels the military, and it was a combination of

all three that gave birth to the three groups vying for control of the Middle East: The House of Saud, the Neoconservatives, and the Islamic extremists. All three played a part in the events of 9/11, and all three will be involved when a nuclear detonation wipes out an American city.

Let's begin with the House of Saud.

King Sultan bin Abdul Aziz, the (anticipated) seventh ruler of Saudi Arabia, is the last surviving member of the "Sudairi Seven," the seven sons born to Hassa bin Ahmad Sudairi, the favorite wife of King Abdul Aziz bin Abdul Rahman al-Saud, better known as Ibn Saud. History books depict Ibn Saud, founder of the Kingdom of Saudi Arabia, as a natural-born leader, a man devoted to his faith, and a wise visionary who unified the Arabian Peninsula and used his nation's resources to benefit his people.

Ibn Saud was neither a unifier nor a wise man, nor was he even a descendant of royalty. Ibn Saud was a murderous brute whose family's rise to power came only because of a fortuitous relationship with an outside power: his wealth—an unearned find that bought him absolute power and fragmented a nation.

The history of the Arabian Peninsula dates back more than five thousand years to several distinct Semitic tribes—ancestors of the Akkadians, Assyrians, Hebrews, and Arabs. Back then, religion among the Arabian tribes followed different forms of paganism, although many Arabs eventually converted to Judaism and Christianity. Then, in AD 622, a man named Muhammad, born to the Banu Omar family, began preaching a new monotheistic religion that adhered to the teachings of Abraham and rejected idolatry. Forced to leave his home in Mecca, Muhammad and his followers consolidated their power base in Medina, and eight years later the Muslims returned in force to capture the city. Muhammad would die two years later, succeeded by his father-in-law, Abu Bakr.

Buoyed by Muslim conquests, Islam spread rapidly, with Mecca evolving into Islam's spiritual capitol and Medina, the religion's administrative and intellectual center. Over the next thousand years, different Muslim sects would battle for control of Arabia, all yielding to the rise of the Mongols and eventually the Ottoman Empire, which controlled the region into the fifteenth century.

In 1745, an upstart named Muhammad bin Saud, emir of the town of Dariya in the Nejd (central Arabia) joined forces with a spiritual leader named Muhammad ibn 'Abd al–Wahhab, who preached a violent puritanical interpretation of Islam. Over the next seventy years the "Wahhabi" movement and the House of Saud would wage a jihad (holy war) across Arabia . . . only to be driven back in 1818 by the Ottoman Turks and their Egyptian allies.

The Sauds and Wahhabis retreated to Riyadh, which became their capital. In 1890, the House of Saud's puppet ruler, Abdul Rahman bin Faisal, was driven out of Riyadh, and the Saud family was forced into exile in Kuwait.

In 1901, Abdul Rahman's twenty–one–year–old son, Ibn Saud, succeeded his father and set out to reclaim his family's land. A year later, Saud's army of twenty recaptured Riyadh by assassinating the Rashidi governor. Over the next several years, Ibn Saud conquered half of the Nejd, only to be turned back once more when the Ottoman Empire aided his sworn enemy, the House of Rashidi.

The outbreak of World War I would change Ibn Saud's fortunes, and with it, the destiny of the modern world.

British interests in the Arabian Peninsula had been growing since the late 1800s. By the eve of the First World War, Britain's leaders felt it necessary to deputize one of the four ruling Arab families in the hopes of gaining control of the region from the Turks.

Ibn Saud was neither educated nor linked to the descendants of Muhammad, making him the perfect puppet to fulfill the United Kingdom's needs. From 1911 to 1914, Ibn Saud used his new pipeline of British money and arms to turn his Ikhwan brotherhood—a sect of Wahhabi Bedouin—into a bloodthirsty mob. While rival Arab leaders attempted to modernize their people through farming and trade, the House of Saud practiced the ghazzu—violent raids on neighboring tribes. Encouraged by the British, Saud's ruthless followers burned thousands of people to death and beheaded others, displaying their spiked skulls at the gates of the city. Women were enslaved by the hundreds and were often given away to allies as gifts.

Working as England's exclusive enforcers, Ibn Saud invaded western Arabia, attacking the Hashemites and the other families. He captured the Jebel Shammar in 1921, Mecca in 1924, and Medina in 1925. Along the way, his Ikhwan followers ransacked entire towns, slaughtering adults and children while murdering any religious leader who did not share in their strict Wahhabi beliefs. In an attempt to gain legitimacy, Ibn Saud went so far as to hire an Egyptian religious sheik to fabricate a family tree linking the Saud lineage to the Prophet Muhammad. In 1932, he formally named his newly conquered region Saudi Arabia and declared himself its king.

The Wahhabi Ikhwan were fanatics who served to keep the House of Saud in power. A cruel and backwards sect, they had no tolerance for twentieth-century innovations or the presence of non-Muslims in Saudi Arabia. Eager to force reform on others, the Ikhwan committed massacres that slaughtered upwards of half a million people.

Though he would call himself a uniter, Ibn Saud had no interest in uniting the Arab people. Unorganized, lacking a formal education, King Ibn Saud ruled his nation from a tent and spread his seed among thirty other tribes. He had dozens of wives, even more concubines and slaves, and often bragged that he had deflowered virgins by the hundreds.

The House of Saud ruled Saudi Arabia with an iron fist and kept the power among themselves. Provinces were run by members of the family, no outsiders were allowed to rule. To control the more advanced cities in the Hijaz, Ibn Saud founded CAVES—the Committee for the Advancement of Virtue and Elimination of Sin, enforced by his Wahhabi brutes. People were flogged in public for wearing perfume, jewelry, or western apparel, and all men were required to grow beards. If a CAVES member wanted a woman for marriage, he couldn't be denied. The Hijaz legal system was abandoned, tribal law of the Wahhabi sect ruling the day. Backed by the Wahhabi clerics, British arms, and a monthly stipend, Ibn Saud continued to rule over his Bedouin police state.

And then, in 1933, everything changed.

Geologists had long suspected that the eastern Arabian Peninsula possessed oil, but no one knew how much. Ibn Saud had granted the first oil concession to Britain in 1923, but little had been done with it. By 1928 the deal had been nullified, and Standard Oil of California (SOCAL) entered the picture, purchasing the expired concession for a mere $250,000.

Eastern Saudi Arabia's oil caches are located in flatlands at very shallow depths, making them less costly to access, and the close proximity to waterways provided SOCAL with a ready-made means to bring the fuel to market. With SOCAL's foot in the door, Harold Ickes, the U.S. secretary of the interior, began "lobbying" Ibn Saud with grant monies and other financial contributions, all of which went directly into the king's personal pocket.

In 1936, SOCAL assigned its concession to its subsidiary, California Arabian Standard Oil Company (CASOC), a Saudi Arabia operating venture that eventually became the Arabian American Oil Company (ARAMCO). By the end of World War II, ARAMCO was producing three hundred thousand barrels of crude a day, and the United States had officially replaced Britain as Ibn Saud's sponsor. But unlike Britain, which often dictated to its foreign oil suppliers how profits should be reinvested into the nation's economy and educational system, the United States made no such demands on the House of Saud. Of the $400 million received between 1946 and 1953, Ibn Saud gave almost nothing back to the common Saudi. Tens of millions of dollars were spent on lavish palaces. Expensive cars were driven until they ran out of gas, then left on the roadside to be replaced rather than refueled. Family members received huge monthly stipends, and bribery became the means to all ends.

The rich got richer, the poor, oppressed.

Always wary of his neighbors, Ibn Saud used oil profits to entice other countries to wage wars. Egypt was coerced into feuding with Syria; Syria, with Iraq. It would be a practice continued over the next seven decades, designed to keep Saudi Arabia's influence over the region supreme.

Ibn Saud died at the age of fifty-two, leaving behind one hundred wives, forty-two sons, fifteen hundred princes, a country with no infrastructure, built totally on nepotism, and a legacy of immorality. Under his "leadership" Saudi Arabia's citizens remained poor, uneducated, medically unfit, and under constant threat by their Wahhabi clerics.

The man who anointed himself king was succeeded by his eldest living son, Saud, a simpleton whose moral corruption surpassed even that of his father. Saud married more times than Ibn, had an insatiable appetite for the ridiculous, and was known to appease his sexual desires with young boys. He was finally replaced after being caught in a botched attempt to assassinate Egypt's President Nasser, who was gaining popularity in the region.

For their third king, the Royal House turned to Ibn Saud's second eldest son, Faisal, who, being more clever than Saud, knew better how to hide his reign's immorality from the public eye. Faisal bribed Arab newspapers to run phony stories about his accomplishments, then, backed by the United States, he used the country's wealth to encourage Yemen to oppose Nasser in Egypt, earning points with the Muslims.

Faisal's domestic policies continued to crush the will of his own people. Under the guise of reducing stipends to the royals, he confiscated nearly 95 percent of all public lands, giving huge parcels away to family members, including an estimated $2 billion worth of tracts to his wife, Iffat. Faisal also encouraged members of his House to go into business for themselves, using oil to fund their corporations. To this day, Saudi government contracts cannot be won without a prince as a partner.

The United States knew full well about the unjust policies of the House of Saud, but America's newfound dependence on oil imports "encouraged" its leaders to look the other way. For his part, Faisal understood the delicate balance of maintaining both an Arab and Muslim identity while keeping the Middle East divided. After Egypt attacked Israel in 1973 and was beaten back once more, the king briefly won Arab support by shutting off oil supplies to the West. Faisal's own reign ended two years later when he was assassinated by a nephew, who was avenging his own brother's death (an execution ordered by the king for "religious reasons"). He was replaced by Crown Prince Khalid, whose first act as king was to appoint three of the remaining Sudeiri Seven: Nayef, Sultan, and Fahd (the latter deemed Crown Prince) to key ministerial positions. Relatives not of the Sudeiri lineage were denied posts. It was a coup among the House of Saud royals, and it created more bad blood within the family.

In 1982, Khalid suffered a fatal heart attack and Crown Prince Fahd took over as king. Among western statesmen and foreign diplomats, Fahd had earned a reputation as being lazy and poorly educated. He was known to go on wild drinking and gambling binges, and his personal excesses remained unparalleled, even for the House of Saud. His palace cost $3 billion, he had a fleet of twenty-five Rolls Royces and five Boeing 747s, and his entourage traveled with two hundred tons of luggage. His frequent trips to Spain cost up to $5 million a day, and he once gambled away $8 million in a single night in Monte Carlo. Under his reign, the House of Saud's top princes received payments of $100 million a year, with lesser family members taking in $4 million apiece. Fahd had more than one hundred wives, countless prostitutes, and on one trip to Los Angeles, he and his party spent tens of thousands of dollars on Viagra. Under Fahd's rule, and despite the influx of hundreds of billions of petroleum dollars, the Saudi government ran massive federal deficits.

To counter these expenses, King Fahd created a new scheme to allow the Royals to siphon off billions more from their country's resources. Under the guise of "protecting its borders" Saudi Arabia began importing weapons, each arms deal filling the coffers of its western sellers and lining the pockets of the prince assigned to the deal as its broker or "fixer." Commissions routinely ran from the tens of millions into the billions of dollars yet, from a sense of practicality, were a waste of resources. The Saudi military lacked both personnel and the training necessary to handle this diverse cache of hardware, which, imported from the United States, France, and Britain, were often incompatible.

In the wake of the First Gulf War, the House of Saud purchased over $100 billion in weapons, many of these sales arranged through (and profited by) the Minister of Defense and future king, Crown Prince Sultan. Skimming enough money to earn himself the title of "world's richest man," Sultan's purchases included American F-15 fighter jets, British Tornados, Bradley Fighting vehicles, and Chinese long-range ground-to-ground missiles. Sultan also commissioned the construction (through the Bin Laden family) of military cities and bases that, to this day, remain virtually empty. More than two hundred naval vessels were purchased for the Royal Saudi Navy, including eight submarines, a half dozen frigates, nine Peterson patrol boats, and four corvettes, yet the navy's entire personnel would only amount to an average of twenty-one people per boat! Hundreds of military vehicles were delivered, then left to rot in the desert.

The hypocrisy of both King Fahd and King Sultan's military buildup was that neither ruler had any intention of creating a strong national military presence. While Saudi Arabia remains a country surrounded by potential enemies, it is the enemies within its borders—the oppressed Saudi people—that have always been the greatest threat to the House of Saud's monopoly on power. Despite the hundreds of billions of petroleum dollars that have rolled into the country, unemployment has reached 30 percent, the social security system remains unfunded, and the public works, including the electricity and phone companies, are always in jeopardy of shutting down. As the economy moves closer to collapse, the Royals get richer, and the people grow more rebellious.

But revolution in Saudi Arabia is not an easy conquest. Thousands of family members occupy key governmental positions, including posts in the air force as well as the ministries of defense. Because of the Royals' fear of being hijacked, only a prince or a close family member can become a pilot. And while the House of Saud continues to profit from the billions spent on the military, the Royal Family has always been loathe to build an army capable of overthrowing its own regime, preferring to place its sophisticated weapons in the hands of its thirty-five-thousand-strong Bedouin Wahhabi National Guardsmen, overseen by the Crown Prince. The Saudi army, with its smaller numbers, remains stationed along the outskirts of the country's major cities, further discouraging a revolt.

When revolt does occur, the Saudi reprisals are swift and abominable. Accused conspirators have been publicly beheaded, tortured, and even tossed out of planes. Those who strike for better wages have been imprisoned. Religious leaders have been executed. Journalists who report anything considered an anti-government sentiment simply disappear. Anyone can be arrested at any time for simply acting "suspicious." Requests by human rights organizations to visit detainees or investigate brutalities have been denied. Reports of prisoners having their fingernails and toenails torn off and other graphic descriptions of torture have been well documented.

Yet the United States refuses to act, for as long as Saudi

Arabia provides America with cheap oil, the House of Saud will remain in power. But America's military presence in the Gulf is a double-edged sword. Radical Islamic fundamentalism forbids a foreign presence in Saudi Arabia, bringing the House of Saud in direct conflict with their own Wahhabis National Guard. To appease the ulema, the Sauds have funded the madrassas—schools that teach radical fundamentalism and the hatred of Americans, Jews, and Christians. Radical Islam is thriving, and not just in Saudi Arabia. Iran remains the biggest threat in the region, with fundamentalists gaining footholds in Jordan, Kuwait, the Sudan, Egypt, Morocco, but especially, in Iraq.

And so it goes, this wheel of insanity:

Addicted to oil, the West continues to use its might to keep the House of Saud in power.

To stay in power, the House of Saud continues to support Islamic radicals or risk becoming their target.

To gain support for their movement, Islamic radicals have sworn to destroy the West . . . targeting Iraq and its Shi'ite population, while Saudi Arabia's own population, long kept under the thumb of its theocratic oppressors, cannot bring true democracy to the region as long as the House of Saud receives the support of the United States.

For decades this wheel of conflicting interests has continued to turn, grinding over human rights and innocent lives as it rolls on, fueled by greed, driven by politicians empowered by an industrial world that uses a ledger sheet to determine civil rights from social wrongs. Add to this equation the estimated $850 billion the Saudis have invested in American corporations, and you have a powerful foreign leverage on the U.S. economy.

But what does the addict do when there are no more drugs to be had? What does the pusher do when the addict is no longer bound? The final pieces of the board are in play—a pawn, disguised as a king, being led into his final move by an unseen chess master—

—checkmating the end of civilization.

"The first hijacking was suspected at no later than 8:20 a.m., and the last hijacked aircraft crashed in Pennsylvania at 10:06 a.m. Not a single fighter plane was scrambled to investigate from U.S. Andrews Air Force Base, just 10 miles from Washington, DC, until after the third plane hit the Pentagon at 9:38 a.m. Why not? There were standard FAA intercept procedures for hijacked aircraft before 9/11. Between September 2000 and June 2001 the U.S. military launched fighter aircraft on sixty-seven occasions to chase suspicious aircraft. It is a U.S. legal requirement that once an aircraft has moved significantly off its flight plan, fighter planes are sent up to investigate. Was this inaction simply the result of key people disregarding, or being ignorant of the evidence? Or could U.S. air security operations have been deliberately stood down on September Eleventh?"

—MICHAEL MEACHER,
Former British Environmental Minister,
from "The War on Terrorism is Bogus,"
The Guardian,
September 6, 2003

"Bin Laden has been under surveillance for years: every telephone call was monitored and al Qaeda has been penetrated by American intelligence, Pakistani intelligence, Saudi intelligence, Egyptian intelligence. They could not have kept secret an operation that required such a degree of organization and sophistication."

—MOHAMMED HEIKAL,
Former Egyptian Foreign Minister

CHAPTER 14

Manhattan, New York
January 7, 2012
12:14 pm EST

The Upper West Side high-rise is located on 72nd street, offering most of its tenants an unobstructed view of Central Park. Jennifer Wienner's apartment is on one of the upper stories, a two-bedroom dwelling with hardwood floors, fireplace, and balcony, carrying a $6,000 monthly rental.

The former GOP political strategist is dressed in sweat clothes, seated on the floor of her master bedroom's walk-in closet, squeezed in between three large cardboard moving boxes. She has already filled two of the boxes with purses and shoes and is humbled by the amount of footwear and accessories she has accumulated over the years . . . and she hasn't even started packing her collection of boots. "That seals it, I'm definitely moving to Florida. From now on, it's strictly sandals."

The ringing doorbell signals yet another interruption. Cursing aloud, she makes her way back through the maze of boxes cluttering her bedroom and hallway, cringing at the pile of china that still awaits her attention on the dining room table.

Jennifer looks through the peephole. Opens the door. "Ace, what are you doing here?"

"I had a few errands in the city, thought maybe we could talk. Can I . . . ?"

"Yeah, sure." She lets him in, suddenly conscious of her attire. "Give me a minute to change."

"You're fine."

"Are you kidding? I haven't even brushed my hair. Sit, I'll be right out." She hustles back to the bedroom.

Ace enters the living room. Manages to locate the four home entertainment center remote controls but quickly gives up trying to figure out which device works the television. He powers on the flat-screen by hand, the channel preset to CNN.

"*. . . the Avian Flu virus continuing its deadly spread throughout parts of Southeast Asia. On the political front, the Iowa Caucuses are set for later this week, followed by the New Hampshire Primary, yet it's still hard to predict which democratic candidate will emerge from the field of eight to challenge President McKuin. Many consider Senator Clinton as the early favorite, but her campaign may still be feeling the effects of attacks by the GOP during the controversial 2008 election. Hoping for a good showing in Iowa is Governor Mitch Friedenthal, who would certainly carry his home state of Pennsylvania, one of four pivotal states in this election, but he is not as strong as Clinton in Ohio and is expected to falter in the south to Senator Joe Mulligan of Delaware. Of the five remaining candidates, only . . .*"

Jennifer returns, her ebony hair pulled back, her face revealing a touch of makeup. "Okay, now I feel human. So what's up?"

"Quick question—"Ace points to the television. "If you were hired to run a presidential campaign, say for a Democrat who supported alternative energy, how would you do it?"

"I wouldn't."

"It's purely hypothetical."

"So's a Dem winning back the White House, and I don't have time for Politics 101."

"Then be brief."

She recognizes the tenacious look in his eyes. Grabbing a hand-woven Chamarras wool blanket, she curls up on the couch opposite him. "Elections, like everything else in this life, essentially come down to money. Money buys message. Message gets candidates elected. Not truth, not policies, not resumes or war medals . . . message. When it comes to casting their vote, the majority of Americans go to the ballot box believing they are voting for the candidate who best shares their own values or secures their needs. Topping those values are taxes and abortion—also known as God, gays, and guns . . . not the environment."

"Why not? Global warming is a hot topic. Look what Al Gore has accomplished."

"Gore's made the public aware. He's instituted some local developments. Economists back his plan for a carbon emission tax . . . but they're not running for office. Democrats talk tough about the environment, but they never do anything, not since they got their asses handed to them for the BTU tax during Clinton's first term. That's how they lost control of Congress."

"Maybe times have changed. There's a new sense of urgency to be rid of fossil fuels."

"Ace, twenty-seven House Democrats represent states that are considered coal regions. You think they're going to make up those votes on the GOP side of the aisle?"

"So, despite all the evidence of climate changes, despite rising gas prices, despite air pollution and respiratory problems . . . despite the fact that the world is running out of oil and we're ill prepared for what will happen next—nothing will change?"

"Not in Washington. Ace, it's not about the problem, it's all about the message. Most candidates' policies run counter to their own voters' interests. They get elected on sound bites and staying on message. Repeat the biggest lie often enough, and the public will accept it as truth. Give me enough money to blitz the media, and I could get Elmer Fudd elected, assuming he occasionally went to church and could lose the lisp."

"Explain Bill Clinton."

"Clinton didn't have the first Bush's money, but he had a clear message: 'The economy, stupid.' Plus the guy knew how to deliver. Ironically, '41' lost his reelection bid against Clinton because he raised taxes. It was actually the right thing to do for the economy, just a dumb move if you're trying to get reelected."

"And the 2006 midterms?"

"The Dems didn't so much as win the House and Senate as the GOP lost it. Why are you asking me all these questions?"

"What if one of the candidates, say, this Senator Mulligan, based his entire campaign message on a radical plan to replace fossil fuels. Before you say no, imagine an economy based on clean energy. No dependence on the Middle East, no more war on terror. Eliminate oil from the equation, and you eliminate 90 percent of the causes for them hating the West. Think about how many Americans have died in Iraq."

"Doesn't matter."

"Of course it matters. The public hates the war."

Jennifer shrugs. "Okay, Ace, if that's true, how did McKuin, a Republican, get elected after eight years of Bush and Cheney? By your logic, the Dems should have swept the 2008 elections just like they did in 2006. Didn't happen. Know why? Money and the Republican Media Message Machine."

"What? Limbaugh and those cable news stations?"

"They're part of it, yes. You begin with the message, something you can sell. Doesn't matter if it's true. Then you spend a billion dollars in ads hammering it into the American psyche. There were two major democratic challengers in '08, Hillary and Obama. Rove and his merry men fueled their attacks against one another in the primaries like the Reagan administration fueled the Iranians against the Iraqis in the 1980s. Divide and conquer—a brilliant play—and the blood between the two camps grew so bad that the there was no way the Dems could heal the rift. The machine creates the message, the money fuels the media, and the media pounds it home every day until your mind subconsciously associates message with candidate. It's the Pavlov dog syndrome: ring the same bell over and over, and the swing voters eventually salivate."

Ace shakes his head. "So substance means nothing."

"Correct. Perceived substance, however, means everything. Take the invasion. Rove's primary mantra, besides WMDs, was that Iraqi oil would pay for the entire cost of the war. Andrew Natsios, the administrator of the U.S. Agency for International Development, actually appeared on *Nightline* saying that invading Iraq would cost the American taxpayers a maximum of $1.7 billion. That same message and dollar amount was repeated, over and over, until even Congress believed it. Here we are, ten years later, and we just passed a trillion dollars in spending! Billions in cash were redirected to Sunni insurgent groups, Al-Qaeda among them. Who's accountable? Maintain power and the answer is no one. As long as you control the White House, even the worst indictments get washed clean through a presidential pardon."

"And that's all there is to it? Money, message, and attacking your opponent . . . that's how you take power?"

"That's how you hold power, especially if you're aligned with big business. That trillion dollars of taxpayer money spent in Iraq . . . you don't really believe it went to building schools, do you? You think those American military bases just built themselves? And who builds military bases? The same corporations that benefit from controlling the number three oil-producing nation in the world? Haliburton, Brown, and Root, and the six sisters of oil. They collect billions and kick back millions in donations . . . and that's how you ensure no-bid contracts. For every Duke Cunningham, there are two dozen more politicians, from both parties, who don't get caught with their hand in the cookie jar. As for Mulligan, the Democrats' base simply can't compete when it comes to raising money."

"McKuin wasn't a Neocon."

"True, but he only took the nomination because he made nice with Pat Robertson and his religious cohorts, and he only won the White House because he added Prescott to the ticket, and Prescott brought in the war machine. Fear sells. The Dems tried to act tough, but what they should have been doing was attacking the message. They did the same thing in 2007 when they controlled Congress. Bush wanted war funding, and they caved in, afraid of public perception. Only the public's perception was that they were a bunch of pussies. That's why I worked with the GOP. They may be liars, but at least they play to win."

"If things were so good, why did you leave?"

She breaks eye contact. "Absolute power breeds arrogance, and arrogance gets people indicted. It was time to get out."

So you quit . . . instead of making a stand. You pulled a Clark Kent . . .

Ace walks over to the balcony and looks out onto Central Park, its paths and bridges camouflaged beneath a fresh blanket of snow. From his vantage, he can approximate the spot where his wife was shot. Her words come back to him now, as if the message were intended for the moment: *the only way we change course is with a radical change . . .*

"It's the reason I'm moving," Jennifer says, misinterpreting his expression. "I can't bear to look out there anymore."

He turns to face her, momentarily startled. In the light, and for the briefest of seconds, Jennifer is his wife's twin, albeit a dark-haired version . . . before Kelli's chemo.

"Ace, you okay?"

"The night Kelli died, she was trying to warn me about something. She said bad things were going to happen."

"Did you tell this to Homeland Security?"

"Before or after they tasered me? No, Jen, it didn't come up. For all I know, they could have been the ones who sanctioned her death."

"Easy."

"Did you know she was writing a book?"

"What kind of book?"

"A tell-all. She never showed it to me, but I imagine there's a bunch of people in Washington who weren't thrilled about it."

"And you think that's why she was killed? Come on, Ace, dozens of former cabinet members and generals write tell-all books every year. None of them are sanctioned, as you put it."

"Kelli said there was going to be another attack—something far worse than 9/11, dealing with Neocons and Islamic radicals. She wanted my help. She wanted to expose the plot."

"How?"

"She said it was all tied to oil. For the last three years my PetroConsultant teams had been compiling new data about world oil reserves. Last month I told a bunch of Senators that we may run out in five to seven years. But what if I'm wrong? What if the end's much closer than we think?"

"You're overreaching."

"Am I? Kelli worked for the national security advisor as liaison to the Persian Gulf. She made hundreds of contacts over the years. She was ready to go public with the evidence."

"Again, what evidence?"

"I don't know. But remember back in 2000 when Dick Cheney began conducting all those secret energy meetings? Kelli was in those meetings. What if 9/11 and the entire Iraqi invasion had to do with dying oil reserves?"

"Not another conspiracy theory?"

"Just hear me out—"

"Honestly, Ace, I gave you more credit than—"

She jumps in her chair as he kicks over a box, sending books flying everywhere. "For once, Jennifer, just once, can you close your mouth and listen with an open mind!"

Jennifer grips the blanket, unsure. She's well aware of Ace's past, how he had snapped under pressure back in college. *Kelli's murder. Losing his job. The arrest. In his state of mind, he's capable of anything.*

Ace takes a deep breath, calming himself. "My best friend died in the North Tower. He worked in one of the investment firms on the upper floors. Left behind a wife and three kids."

"I'm sorry."

"While he and his co-workers burned to death, the foreign investors who knew about the attacks made a nice little profit from insider trading. That's why he was in so early that day. He was trying to catch up on all the paperwork from the night before. I don't believe in conspiracy theories,

Jennifer, but the crap Washington fed us made no sense either. Remember golfer Payne Stewart? How is it that his private plane was intercepted by Air Force jets within ten minutes of wandering off course, yet a commercial jetliner, ninety minutes after three others were hijacked, was allowed to circle Washington, DC, repeatedly without a single fighter intercepting it before it smashed into the Pentagon? My friend's dead because a lot of people failed to act—or were instructed not to act—and now my wife's dead because of what she knew. You just got done telling me that the people in power will do anything to stay in power."

"I never said anything about killing people."

"Killing people is what happens when you invade another country under false pretenses. Your cousin died believing it's going to happen again, and all of a sudden I believe her."

"I think you should go. I'm serious, Ace. Please leave."

"Fine." He heads for the door. "By the way, you're wrong about one thing. Not everything in this life comes down to money. It took cancer for Kelli to figure that one out."

He leaves—

—Jennifer slamming the door behind him.

"The contractor is not required to perform perfectly to be entitled to reimbursement."

—RHONDA JAMES,
Spokesperson for the U.S. Army Corps of Engineers,
referring to Halliburton receiving nearly all of its costs on a disputed
$2.41 billion no-bid contract to deliver fuel and repair oil equipment
in Iraq.

"President Bush has named Barbara Bodine the director of Central Iraq. Many in government are upset about the appointment because of her blocking of the *USS Cole* investigation, which some say could have uncovered the 9/11 plot. She failed to admit she was wrong or apologize."

—WASHINGTON TIMES,
April 10, 2003
(Bodine was later fired for doing a poor job.)

"If Democrats were capable of handling the war of terror, then I ought to be singing on American Idol."

—VICE PRESIDENT DICK CHENEY,
March 24, 2006

"Then the fourth angel blew his trumpet, and one-third of the sun was struck, and one-third of the moon, and one-third of the stars, and they became dark. And one-third of the day was dark, and one-third of the night also."

—REVELATION 8:12

CHAPTER 15

THE RESIDENTIAL AREA OF THE MADISON Square–Oliver section of east-central Baltimore is thirty-two blocks of brick row-homes situated on narrow streets and alleyways that date back to the early nineteenth century. It is primarily an African-American neighborhood, interspersed with schools, firehouses, the occasional stone church, and a few small businesses. It is an area teetering between urban blight and reconstruction.

Jamal al-Yussuf exits the corner convenience store carrying two plastic bags of groceries. He can feel the eyes of the locals telling him he does not belong. A harsh winter wind cuts through his fleece jacket, reminding him of the same.

A siren, wailing in the distance, sends his thoughts returning to Baghdad.

♦ ♦ ♦

Jamal was born into hardship. Iraq's war with Iran had been long and violent, stealing a cousin and two uncles, wiping out an entire generation of people. The American threat in 1991 had brought the terror home, followed by a decade of living on bare essentials.

But nothing could prepare Jamal for the violence to come.

Jamal was nineteen when Bush (the son) began openly challenging Saddam. Jamal was a Shi'ite who had no interest in fighting for the regime, but the military officers he was assigned to threatened to shoot anyone who would not stand up to the foreign invaders. Given a uniform and rifle, he had been sent to Safwan Hill, a military observation post several kilometers across the border. There were few professional soldiers among their ranks, the Sunni guardsmen kept closer to Baghdad.

When the first American planes appeared, Jamal grew very nervous, but there were no bombs, only a flurry of white papers dropping from the sky. The leaflets warned the Iraqi army not to fight, that Saddam would be defeated, that it was better just to surrender.

Jamal didn't want to fight, but no one trusted the Americans. Bush's father had put Saddam in power yet later had led the fight to oust the dictator. It was no secret the Americans were coming to dominate the region and take Iraq's oil. Most Iraqis hated Saddam, but they didn't want the Americans there either. They simply wanted to run their own country themselves, free of outside interference.

Jamal was on duty one night when a deafening barrage shook the outpost—the United States Marines were opening fire with their 155mm howitzer guns. Jamal dropped his weapon and fled. Moments later, the observation post exploded in a huge fireball.

The night erupted into a living hell as American helicopter gunships swept in low to fire their missiles. Bombs exploded for hours on end, fires blazing everywhere. Jamal ran through streets covered in charred corpses and smoldering burned-out trucks, the soldiers' bodies having literally melted in the blasts.

This was not a fight, this was a massacre, and Jamal wanted no part in it. Shedding the remains of his uniform, he stole a motorcycle and rode back to Baghdad as machine-gun fire ripped holes in the air and columns of oily black smoke rose from decimated buildings, the survivors staggering into the streets, waving white flags.

Jamal returned to his family's house by dawn, but the war had followed him home. An exploding bomb had collapsed the roof, the debris crushing and killing his father. Jamal's mother was screaming. His younger brother was badly wounded, his gut torn open. Jamal picked him up and raced through battle-torn streets to the hospital, his hand all that was keeping the boy's organs inside his body. His brother would die before Jamal could get him medical treatment.

The next few days were a blur, the American planes always coming, the bombs always exploding in a world gone mad. There was no electricity, no water, barely enough food, and chaos everywhere. When the bombing would move off, Jamal and his cousins would take to the streets, looting stores like starving rats.

By the end of the week, the occupiers had arrived.

Iraq is a sectarian nation composed of Arab Shi'ites, Sunnis, and the Kurds, who are Sunni but are from a different ethnic background. Under

Saddam's reign, the Sunni elite had run the country, even though the Shi'ites represented 60 percent of the population. The United States invasion upended that arrangement, and the Shi'ites moved quickly to try to gain power with their numerical superiority.

Compounding the chaos were Shi'ite insurgents from Iran, who saw an opportunity to inject their own fundamentalist influence in neighboring Iraq. Stability was further disrupted by Abu Mousab al-Zarqawi, Al-Qaeda's leader in Iraq, himself a Sunni extremist. Then there were the wild cards—radical clerics like Muqtada al-Sadr, who ruled his Mahdi, an army of Shi'ites possessing a penchant for violence. As the United States military fought to maintain order in this maelstrom of competing national and international factions, the Iraq populace struggled to survive.

As Shi'ites, Jamal and his family were members of Iraq's poor working class. Talk of an American invasion had actually been welcome—until the opening hours of the attack when U.S. bombs had killed three of their household. Devastated by these losses, Jamal and his family tried to cope in a city overrun by vandals, their new existence void of security and the simplest of comforts.

Months after the invasion, Baghdad's residents were finally placed on energy schedules that provided a scant two hours a day of electricity. On hot days, temperatures could reach a broiling 120 degrees. For those with generators, finding fuel became an even bigger problem. In a country possessing the second-largest oil reserves in the Middle East, people were forced to wait in long gasoline lines just to fill up. Yet the American militia and the government's elite always seemed to have fuel. Occasionally, Jamal and his friends were able to purchase gasoline on the black market, paying upwards of 1,250 Iraqi dinars for a liter, twenty times the cost from the days of Saddam.

The Americans instituted a 6:00 p.m. curfew, along with a driving curfew. Lacking electricity, Jamal's mother resorted to cooking meals on the kerosene heater. Baths were taken cold, the Al-Yussuf home having no power to warm the water. Dinners were consumed by candlelight, and afterward Jamal would read to his younger siblings and cousins, then arise at four thirty in the morning to join his friends in gas station fuel lines, which were often a kilometer long. It was always extremely cold, and many times the station would run out of gasoline before their turn.

On good days they would ride over in Jamal's cousin's car, but on most days they had to walk.

Waiting in line, Jamal would hear rumors about the insurgency. Some were convinced the entire fuel shortage had been created by the Americans to limit the number of vehicles on the roads. Others believed local candidates running for political office were simply positioning themselves for the upcoming elections so they could supply gasoline at a later date and look like heroes.

Always present was the lure of Iranian insurgents who were offering upwards of $500 a month for local Shi'ites to target police cars and American tanks with their rocket-propelled grenades. Jamal was tempted but wary of their offers.

As the months turned into years, life in Baghdad showed sporadic signs of improvement, yet there always remained a palpable sense of anxiety in the air, residents knowing that their momentary semblance of normalcy could be shattered the next minute by an explosion. One day Jamal's family were walking down a trash-strewn road when they came upon a metal object protruding in the dirt. Two American soldiers took notice and within minutes the area had been cordoned off. As a crowd gathered, a demolition crew arrived, referring to the object as an IED (Improvised Explosive Device). Soldiers moved civilians back several hundred yards, and then the loudest blast Jamal had ever heard rocked their Baghdad neighborhood. Windows shattered, children screamed. But as the dust settled, Jamal could see that everyone was all right. As they passed the smoldering crater in the road, Jamal nodded thanks to two of the soldiers.

The elections brought a new kind of apprehension. Candidate lists were composed of people who were either affiliated with the Americans, led by the despised Ahmad Chalabi, or were tribal sheikhs whose sudden appearance in Iraqi politics threatened to turn the secular nation into one bordering on religious fanaticism. Adding to the Iraqis' apprehension was that each election list had to be confirmed by Ali al-Sistani, an Iranian-born ayatollah.

Being confined within a city under the constant siege of armed foreigners who do not speak your language creates an uneasy feeling among locals. Many Iraqis believed that if an explosion didn't wound or kill them, the Americans or Iraqi security forces would. And there was always the dreaded fear of being dragged off to Abu Ghraib as a suspected jihadist. Despite reported conflicts, Sunnis and Shi'ites had co-existed peacefully in Iraq throughout their shared history, often intermarrying. But when the government is unstable and security is lacking, racial and religious groups tend to gravitate toward one another for protection, even if it means congregating with the extreme elements of a sect.

The lack of security always seemed to keep life teetering between the promise of democracy and the expectancy of chaos. One could take pride in witnessing the construction of new shops and residential areas, yet just as prominent were government structures that remained bombed-out hulks.

Jamal's psyche was teetering as well, his thoughts dominated by the fear of losing more family members. As time passed, his outlook brightened. His cousins took to the streets to sell their wares and began earning a decent living, and Jamal even managed to get a construction job laying pipe for a new sewage project. Fuel lines gradually shortened, and electricity remained on longer . . . life seemed to actually be improving.

Then, in late February of 2006, foreign jihadists, dressed like Iraqi police commandos, set off explosives inside the Shi'ite mosque of Al-Askari. The golden-domed shrine was one of Shi'ite Islam's holiest sites, and its destruction set off a frenzy of reprisals against Sunni mosques. Amid the violence, a group of Baghdad youths fired upon a U.S. Bradley fighting vehicle, disabling it. As children got caught up in the cheers, an American helicopter swooped in on the scene and fired, killing some of the celebrating youth.

Two of Jamal's nieces were among the dead, and Jamal had borne witness to the carnage. It was a reality-shattering moment, even worse than when he had carried his dying brother in his arms. Saddam's reign was oppressive, but it had held a tide of anarchy in check. Now the dam was breaking, the blood of innocent children was on everyone's hands, and Jamal al-Yussuf could no longer stand to be in his own skin.

He had to lash out, he had to do something . . .

Two days later, he found himself in Tehran.

◆　◆　◆

Four blocks north and two blocks east, and he is back at the brownstone row home with the dented black aluminum door hood. Trudging up the snow-covered cement steps, he keys in.

Jamal enters the kitchen and leaves the groceries on the chipped lino-leum counter, where he finds the note.

Tonight, 7:30 p.m.
Dundalk Marine Terminal
2700 Broening Highway

"Man argues; nature acts."

—Voltaire

"By 2012 we will need on the order of an additional 50 million barrels [of oil] a day."

—Vice President Dick Cheney
(Fifty million barrels is equivalent to more than six times the current daily rate of oil produced by Saudi Arabia in 2006.)

"I'll admit it was . . . mixed signals."

—President George W. Bush, referring to his 2006 budget, which cut $28 million in funding for renewable fuel research . . . after his 2006 State of the Union address called for a greater emphasis on alternative energy resources. Conversely, a single tax break in the Interior Department's 2006 budget awarded oil companies an estimated $7 billion reduction in rent paid to drill on public lands.

CHAPTER 16

ACE PULLS HIMSELF UP THE STAIRCASE, his left knee sore from an earlier workout, his lower back stiff with arthritis. From the landing he can hear the girls giggling in Leigh's room. He heads for Sam's room and pushes open the door.

His son is asleep in the lower bunk, the lights out, the TV on. Hockey gear, ripe with sweat from tonight's two-hour practice, is strewn across the floor.

Better clean this up before Kelli . . .

Ace catches himself. He does that a lot, his mind not fully conditioned to his new reality—single parent. There is a part of him that still expects to see his wife emerge from their bedroom in her favorite sweat clothes or to hear her voice complaining that 'no one picks up after themselves around here,' or to hear her laughter as she converses with friends on the phone.

He looks down at Sam, fast asleep from an exhausting day, and sees Kelli's features in the boy's face. While Leigh takes after Ace—quiet, her world more internalized, Sam is outgoing like his mother, her personality living on in his. Both comforted and saddened by the thought, Ace covers the child with a blanket, turns the television off, and slips out of the room.

Following the giggles, he heads down the hall to Leigh's bedroom. He peeks in on his daughter and her two friends. They are huddled around her new computer, laughing as they instant message another group of teens.

"Leigh?"

"It's all right, Dad, we know who they are."

"They're boys from our class, Mr. Futrell," pipes in Leigh's best friend, Adeena.

"Fine. Just remember what we talked about." Ace closes the door, grateful for the distraction provided by his daughter's friends. Leigh is internalizing her sorrow about the loss of her mother, and time has not begun to heal the wound. It is her peers that have become the stabilizing force in her life.

He heads for his office. Turns on the television, catching the Iowa Caucus results on CNN.

". . . with 91 percent of precincts reporting, 47 percent of convention delegates have cast their support for Senator Clinton, 37 percent going to Senator Mulligan of Delaware, and a disappointing 11 percent to the governor of Pennsylvania. We are joined by our political analyst, Kira Gillean. Kira, Hillary Clinton takes Iowa, but with far less a majority than anticipated. What happened?"

"John, Senator Clinton tapped into the issues that really affect Iowans: out-of-control medical costs, the sagging economy, education, and, of course, the ongoing campaign in Iraq. But I think it was the recent rash of attack ads that hurt Clinton's numbers."

"Let's be clear, Kira. These attack ads were not sponsored by the GOP or the other Democrats."

"Correct. The groups responsible were 527s—tax-exempt organizations, created under Section 527 of the Internal Revenue Code, which are not regulated by federal or state election commissions. Specifically, there were two different special interest groups that made their presence known in Iowa. The first, Mothers for a Better America, sounds benign enough, but it's actually a conservative republican organization drawing from the same players who were involved in the Parents in Defense of Marriage attacks back in the 2008 election and the Swift Boat Veterans for Truth against John Kerry in 2004. Even harder hitting were ads sponsored by a second group, Christians for a Better Tomorrow, an anti-abortion organization that attacked Senator Clinton for supporting legislation to increase school funding for contraceptives and the morning-after pill."

"Kira, here's a clip from that ad."

Ace watches the commercial, which graphically interplays a fetus being aborted with a Jesus-on-the-crucifix, the statue seemingly watching from the operating room wall.

He shakes his head, incredulous. *Schools underfunded, seniors starving themselves to pay for prescription meds, American soldiers forever stuck in the quagmire of the Middle East . . . and all these idiots want to debate is gay marriage and abortion. It's the same old shell game . . . distract the dupe with a sleight of hand while the ball slips out of sight.*

"Kira, will we see more of these smear campaigns as we move closer to November?"

"Absolutely. Another conservative group, Progress for America, has already purchased saturation buys for the upcoming Nevada, South Carolina, and New Hampshire primaries. These commercials play the terrorism card, using images of the collapse of the World Trade Center and the foiled airline plots in the United Kingdom. It's an ad the group ran upwards of thirty thousand times throughout ten swing states during the final weeks of the 2008 election. The fact that these groups are already targeting Senator Clinton means they expect her to win the democratic nomination."

"Stand by, we have Senator Clinton's response to these attacks."

The taped interview takes place on the streets of Iowa. ". . . and no one, including myself, has ever encouraged abortion, which I've always said should be safe, legal, and rare. But with 66 percent of teens under the age of eighteen sexually active, there has to be a common sense approach to unplanned pregnancies. What happens to a young mother and her child after she gives birth? Where will she live? How will she afford any kind of safe housing? Who pays for her education, or her medical insurance? Can she get a decent-paying job or even maternity leave? Studies show most women turn to abortion mainly for financial reasons, knowing they lack the means and education to support a child. What really irks me is that these radical groups never seem to want to discuss those issues. It's as if they love the fetus but hate the child. Meanwhile, Republicans on Capitol Hill continue to slash programs vital to these young mothers, while a handful of commissioners at the FDA are still waging an internal war over the morning-after pill, casting it as another method of abortion when, in fact, it's an emergency contraceptive that would prevent abortions. This propaganda is not only harmful, it's scientifically false, and it's being trotted out simply to rattle emotions during an election year."

The office phone rings. Ace checks the caller ID: Jeffrey Gordon.

"Hey, man, what's up?"

"I have a craving for ice cream." Jeffrey says. "You in?"

Ace sits up, his adrenaline pumping. "Yeah, sure."

"Pick you up in fifteen minutes."

Living under the Homeland Security microscope, his phones tapped, his e-mail monitored, Ace has been forced to resort to code words, phrases, and his own "sleight of hand" in order to conduct business out of the specter of the federal eye.

Grabbing an old, ivory-colored windbreaker from a hook on the back of his door, Ace leaves his office, heads down the hall, and pokes his head in Leigh's bedroom. "Honey, Sam's asleep. I'm just running out with Uncle Jeff for a few minutes."

"Dad, what are you wearing?"

"What? It's comfortable."

"It's white. You're not a hundred. Wear the leather coat mom bought you."

"Sure. Be back soon. Keep an eye on things, okay?"

Ignoring his daughter's fashion tip, he heads downstairs, zips up the lined windbreaker, and waits outside for his friend to pick him up.

◆ ◆ ◆

Four hundred and twenty-two miles directly overhead, moving in a stationary orbit high above Long Island, is the ONYX spy satellite. Operated by the National Reconnaissance Office (NRO), one of sixteen agencies that make up the United States Intelligence Community (USIC), the satellite is as large as a bus and weighs upwards of fifteen tons. The spy satellite possesses a 150-foot solar panel wingspan and wire-mesh radar antenna, all housed around its synthetic aperture radar (SAR), a pulse system that creates its own illumination, allowing images to be processed in day or night and in the worst weather conditions. Part of a highly classified stealth satellite program known collectively as the Future Imagery Architecture (FIA), ONYX was severely criticized by members of the Senate Select Committee on Intelligence for its extraordinary price tag ($40 billion) and its inability to penetrate underground bunkers where Iran and North Korea house their nuclear facilities. Despite these objections, the program was funded by the GOP-controlled House and Senate appropriations committees.

◆ ◆ ◆

From his Sat-Lab at NRO headquarters, located in Chantilly, Virginia, tech officer Garret Matsuura watches a real-time video image of his subject, one Ashley "Ace" Futrell. The fourth-generation Japanese-American NRO employee had been assigned to Ace just over a month ago, and has been coordinating the subject's activities with his opposite number at Homeland Security. Matsuura has no idea why his deputy director is so interested in the former PetroConsultant field manager, nor why this particular case has been classified as UMBRA, an unusually high top-secret designation for domestic surveillance of an American citizen.

Matsuura finishes off the remains of his dinner as his subject climbs in the passenger side of a Chevy Astrovan leased to Mrs. Gay Gordon, wife of the New York attorney who is a close friend of the subject. The computer identifies the driver as Jeffrey Gordon, the man who had contacted Futrell by phone twenty minutes earlier.

Satellite reconnaissance stays with the vehicle as it pulls into the parking lot of an ice cream parlor. The two men remain in sight by the store's side window and proceed to place their orders.

Matsuura yawns. *Ordinary people living boring lives. Skip the hot fudge sundaes and hit a strip joint or something, fellas; you guys are killing me.*

As if on command, the two men return to the van with their desserts. After several minutes the driver pulls out of the lot and proceeds north for three blocks, then turns into a mini-mart. While Gordon pumps gas, Futrell walks around to the side of the building to use the restroom.

◆　◆　◆

Ace yanks open the rusty metal door and enters the men's bathroom. The CIA director is already inside. David Schall locks the door behind him and hands Ace a manila envelope.

Ace removes the contents. There are three photos, all black and white, taken from a telescopic lens. With trembling hands he stares hard at the face of his wife's assassin.

"His name is Scott Santa, spelled S-A-N-T-A but pronounced 'Shanta.' It's Russian. Moved to the States as a teenager, served in the Coast Guard as a radioman/crypto/morse code operator before being promoted as a boarding officer where he held top secret clearance. Served on two ships, a 210-foot medium-endurance cutter out of New Bedford and a 180-foot Buoy tender out of Homer, Alaska. The tender was the first vessel on the scene during the Exxon Valdez spill."

"Get to the important stuff."

"Twelve years ago, he left the Coast Guard and took a job with the Vinnell Corporation. He was assigned to train the Saudi National Guard."

"Vinnell? Wait . . . Vinnell's a CIA front."

Schall nods, partly from embarrassment. "You can imagine how this has piqued my own interests, and before you say anything, no, the CIA did not have your wife sanctioned."

"But someone obviously did. Where is he now?"

"We're not sure, though we suspect he returned to Saudi Arabia . . . after New York. What we do know is that he left Vinnell eight months ago. He does a lot of business in Jiddah and Riyadh. Small arms, that sort of thing."

Ace removes his windbreaker, unzipping a hidden compartment in the lining. He tucks the envelope into the space, zips it closed, then slips the jacket back on. "I suspect our paths may cross while I'm in Saudi Arabia."

"That's your business; let's discuss mine."

Ace reaches into his front pants pocket and removes several typed pages of notes. He hands it to Schall, who quickly reads through it.

"You're kidding, right? This is nothing short of a major military operation."

"Yeah, well, they don't call it the Empty Quarter for nothing. The Rub al-Khali covers 250,000 square miles, did you think we were just going to set off a few firecrackers and take a reading? It's also nasty out there, a trackless expanse of shifting sand dunes that gets downright frigid at night, often near zero."

"Isn't there a way to refine the search?"

"I did refine it. We're focusing only on the southernmost Saudi corner, close to the Kidan, Shaybah, and Ramalah fields. We're also sneaking a peak at what's left in the Ghawar, the largest oil field in the world. From those geological readings I should be able to compile a fairly accurate assessment of what's really left in the Saudi reserves."

The CIA director pockets the information. "You realize it'll take me months to have everything in place."

"I figured mid-April." Ace unlocks the bathroom door to leave, but Schall grabs his arm.

"You're not quite getting it, are you, fella? The president needs this information now, not in three months."

"Then tell the president to ask King Sultan. Better yet, get Prescott to do it, I hear the two of them are old pals. Meanwhile, get Homeland Security off my back like you promised, or there's no deal."

Twisting his arm free, Ace pushes open the door, exiting into the night.

"The main obstacles to investigate Islamic terrorism were U.S. oil's corporate interests and the role played by Saudi Arabia in it. All the answers, everything needed to dismantle Osama bin Laden's organization can be found in Saudi Arabia."

—JOHN O'NEILL,
FBI counter-terrorism expert
(O'Neill was killed in the World Trade Center attacks on 9/11.)

"Although Bush administration officials have frequently lashed out at Syria and Iran for helping the insurgents and militias who attack U.S. troops and civilians in Iraq, the largest number of foreign fighters and suicide bombers in Iraq comes from a third next-door neighbor, Saudi Arabia, according to a senior U.S. military officer and Iraqi lawmakers."

—NED PARKER
Los Angeles Times
July 16, 2007

"A senior administration official confirmed to CNN on Saturday that the United States is developing a proposed $20 billion, 10-year arms sales package for Saudi Arabia aimed at giving the Saudi military an upgraded capability to counter Iranian aggression in the Persian Gulf region. One of the most potentially controversial portions of the proposed sale will be the first sale to the Saudis of satellite-guided bombs known as JADMs. The sale may include both a 500-pound and 2,000-pound version of the aerial bomb. Other elements of the sale include new naval vessels, an advanced version of air-to-air missiles already used by the United States and advanced Patriot missiles."

—CNN.COM,
July 28, 2007

CHAPTER 17

SITUATED ON FORTY-FIVE MILES OF WATERFRONT on the Patapsco River
Basin, the Port of Baltimore dates back to the early 1700s, when it became
the official port of entry for England's tobacco trade with the colonists.
Baltimore Harbor is now one of the United State's largest deep-water ports,
its ninety-four piers loading and discharging up to 175 ships a day.

Jamal al-Yussuf works perimeter security at the Dundalk terminal
main gate, checking identification and work orders of truck drivers making
pickups and deliveries. By day, he divides his prayer time between several
local mosques, asking Allah for strength. He has joined a neighborhood
gym and works out three times a week. He has made a few friends but, as
per his training at Qods, will not allow himself to become close. Within
three months, he expects to receive his first promotion, enabling him to
check cargo containers from foreign ports.

Until then, he bides his time, making sure he is always punctual and
respectful to his bosses.

It is nearly eight thirty in the morning when he clocks out from his
night shift, a long weekend ahead. He arrives home by bus forty minutes
later, the white van with the home improvement sign already parked outside his apartment building.

Omar Kamel Radi is in the driver's seat, dressed in overalls and a
flannel jacket.

"Good morning, dog."

"What did you call me?"

"Dog. Among men of color, it is a term of endearment."

"It is an insult coming from the mouth of a Sunni. Do not address me in this manner again."

Jamal climbs in the passenger side. He attempts to recline the seat all the way back so he can sleep, but the two large storage containers anchored directly behind him make it impossible. Curling up against the door, he pulls his wool cap down over his eyes. "Do not wake me, Sunni dog, or I will cut you so your own mother does not recognize you."

Omar rolls his eyes and starts the van. He has a long drive ahead.

◆ ◆ ◆

Omar Kamel Radi was born in Haditha, a farming town of ninety thousand, located on the Euphrates River, 140 miles northwest of Baghdad. While the Iraqi capitol and its fortified green zone had paved the way to a new constitution, Haditha had been transformed into an insurgent stronghold. Here, it was the mujahideen who decide who got paid, what clothing people were allowed to wear, what music they could listen to, and, ultimately, who lived and who died.

At dawn, the Iranian insurgents would carry out public executions at the town entrance on the Haqlania bridge, nicknamed "Agents' Bridge," a mortuary reference relative to the number of American agents who were beheaded. Small crowds would gather, each decapitation or disembowelment filmed, the DVDs distributed later that day in the Souk market.

That Haditha, once part of the Sunni triangle, had fallen to Shi'ite insurgents became one of the biggest failings of the American invasion. It was here that the Tawhid al-Jihad, the Iraqi chapter of Al-Qaeda, remained virtually unchallenged, and to even be suspected of aiding the Americans was to invite death. Like most people living in Haditha, Omar and his family were Sunni, and while they did not oppose the insurgents, they did not support them either.

On November 19, 2005, all that changed.

It was just after 7:15 in the morning. Four humvees carrying United States Marines of Kilo Company were patrolling the residential area when a bomb went off, killing twenty-year-old Lance Corporal Miguel Terrazas. Five suspects—occupants of a taxi—took off running.

Perhaps it was the stress of dealing with an impossible situation, the seemingly endless tours of duty, or the repeated exposure to so much senseless bloodshed, but the killing of Miguel Terrazas caused the moral compass of the American soldiers to snap. Opening fire, the Marines gunned down the suspects and inexplicably went on a rampage, moving from house to house, breaking in and destroying furniture while lining up men, women, and children for execution. When the killing spree was over, twenty-four Iraqis lay dead, nineteen of whom had been woken from their sleep at gunpoint. Among the victims were several young children and Omar's pregnant wife.

The truth about the massacre would be hidden from the American public for months, though it incited riots in Haditha that would spread throughout Iraq. Sadly, shockingly, as horrific as the attack had been, it was all-too-quickly swallowed by the continued, daily bloodbath of suicide bombers, beheadings, kidnappings, and unchecked violence that was claiming five hundred Iraqis every week.

But for Omar Kamel Radi, his world had shattered beyond repair. Weeks of grieving eventually settled into a cold, hard rage.

One day, he ran into an old friend from school who introduced him to Islam. Omar rejected the ideals at first but soon found comfort in the society's rules. After three weeks of study, he recited the *Shahadah*, completing the process of reversion, his "submission to God."

Becoming a Muslim does not convert one into a terrorist (far from it), but Islam is a religion struggling between two identities: moderation and extremism. And in Iraq, it is Radical Islam that has joined the fight against American imperialism.

It was a fight Omar welcomed—to make the American people feel his pain, to make them taste what their government was force-feeding his people. Three months after his wife and unborn child were laid to rest, Omar Kamel Radi joined Qods, an Iranian-based terror camp.

JIDDAH, SAUDI ARABIA
JANUARY 11, 2012
12:37 PM LOCAL TIME

THE PORT CITY OF JIDDAH IS located along the Red Sea in western Saudi Arabia, in an area known as the Hijaz. More than three centuries old, once surrounded by high mud walls that secured its population, Jiddah is now a modern commercial center, complete with an international airport and major roadways connecting it with other Saudi cities.

Many of the Hijazi who inhabit Jiddah are Ashraf Muslim—direct descendants of Muhammad. Each year, tens of thousands of these pilgrims travel Jiddah's roadways on their journey to the holy city of Mecca. Living off the sea and working as merchants and traders, theirs is a lifestyle more westernized than their Bedouin cousins.

The tribal communities known as the Bedouin are scattered farther east in the Najd, an arid region of Saudi Arabia that contains Riyadh, the Saudi capital. Continue south by southeast and you'll eventually arrive in an uninhabited desert known as Rub al-Khali—the Empty Quarter, home to the world's largest oil field: the Ghawar.

◆　◆　◆

The Red Sea Palace is a seven-story hotel located in Jiddah's commercial district. Scott Santa exits the hotel elevator and strolls through the grand lobby out into the Arabian sun. Following a concrete walkway, he makes his way to the pool, every so often glancing at the digital display on his Casio watch.

Twelve thirty-nine . . .

The tall Russian-American locates an empty lounge chair in the shade, angling his view so he can watch two Asian women in matching blue and white striped bikinis sitting by the whirlpool. He orders a drink from a waiter and checks his watch again.

Twelve forty-two.

Santa removes the cell phone from his pants pocket. Powers on the device.

Twelve forty-four.

The phone rings once. "Go."

The American voice in his earpiece is amazingly clear, considering it is coming from half a world away. "He's coming. First week in April."

"Why the delay?"

"Unavoidable."

"It reduces our timetable considerably."

"Deal with it."

Santa smiles at the Asian women. One giggles. The other smiles back.

"Okay, I'll be waiting."

SPRING
2012

"The waves of a new Islamic Revolution will soon spread to the entire world."

—IRANIAN PRESIDENT MAHMOUD AHMADINEJAD,
2006

"We shouldn't fear the future, because we intend to shape the future."

—PRESIDENT GEORGE W. BUSH,
2006

CHAPTER 18

Iran Arms Radar-dodging Missiles with Nuclear Warheads

Associated Press: April 19, 2012

TEHRAN—Iran's military announced today that it has loaded nine of its Fajr-3 radar-dodging missiles with nuclear warheads. Each ballistic missile is capable of traveling 1,200 miles while avoiding anti-missile missiles. General Hossein Salami, the air force chief of Iran's elite Revolutionary Guards, was quoted as saying, "At the first sign of attack, the great nation of Islam will strike back against its sworn enemies, flattening Zionist cities and hostile western military bases in Iraq and Saudi Arabia. Allahu akbar, God is great."

Press secretary Kris Hamilton, himself a former officer in the U.S. Navy, was firm in the McKuin administration's response. "The president takes these latest threats very seriously. While it has never been the United States' intention to attack Iran, we will never hesitate to come to the aid of our allies in the region, nor shall we rule out the use of tactical nuclear weapons if we perceive a serious threat."

The UN Security Council issued warnings that Iranian aggression in the region would not be tolerated but, again, stopped short of sanctions.

Montauk, New York
April 21, 2012
9:37 am EST

"Dad, the airport limo's here!"

"Coming!" Ace shoves two more T-shirts inside the overstuffed suitcase and forcibly zips it closed.

Leigh hands him his passport. "Don't lose this."

"I won't. I'll only be gone eight days. Aunt Jen'll be here."

"Just do what you have to do, we'll be fine."

"Dad, the limo's—"

"Sam, I'm coming!" Ace gives Leigh a hug, then heads downstairs where Jennifer and Sam are waiting. He passes his suitcase to the limo driver. "I'll be right out."

His son gives him a quick hug. "Where are you going again?"

"Abu Dhabi."

"That's not a real place."

"It's in the United Arab Emirates. Look it up."

"Bring me back something?"

"For another hug."

The boy complies, then heads upstairs to play video games, leaving Ace alone with Jennifer. "Don't worry," she says.

"I always do." He hugs her. "Jen, listen—"

"We're family, Ace. Now go, before you miss your plane."

He leans in and kisses her on the lips, then pulls away, embarrassed. "Jeez, I'm sorry . . . force of habit."

She sees the confusion in his eyes and smiles as he half-trips out the door, hustling to the awaiting car.

Carbondale, Illinois

The tank sits in the concrete bunker, humming softly. Protruding from the left side of the rectangular iron casing are thirty uranium fuel rods, taken from Iran's nuclear reactor.

Professor Eric Bi, sealed within a somewhat antiquated environmental suit, carefully draws a wet, powdery, coffee-colored paste from the outtake located atop the second centrifuge. Gently, he empties the cache of enriched uranium into the large, lead container in the far corner of the basement.

So delicate. So powerful. A force of nature, harnessed by man . . .

The physics professor returns the cache to the outtake, then empties the smaller outtake along the bottom containing depleted uranium into the plastic container for disposal.

Thirty fuel rods, each yielding a gram of enriched U-238 a day. Three hours of work a day, tops, multiplied over six months time . . .

Eric Bi returns to the lead containment cache, using his tools to knead the enriched U-235 residue into a thick paste—a paste he will eventually heat and solidify.

One hundred and eighty days, three hours a day . . . that's five hundred and forty hours of work . . . divided by $2 million . . . that comes out to $3,700 an hour. Not bad for a part-time job.

The paste becomes moldable like wet clay. Bi works it into one of the two golf ball–sized enriched uranium deposits he has collected, losing himself in thought.

Got to start working on the triggering mechanism. They want it wired into a cell phone . . . easy enough. Solder the wires from the phone's capacitor to the blasting cap, that should be enough to set off the C-4.

Bi's eyes glisten as he sets to work on the second deposit.

Sixty-seven years since Nagasaki. The last bomb ended a world war; the next will begin one. What would mother say if she were alive? Would she be proud of her only child, or ashamed? But this isn't about the past or revenge, Mother, it's about the future. This is to stop western domination. The lives of a billion and a half people are at stake . . .

No, Mother, what I do now isn't for Japan . . . this is for China!

◆ ◆ ◆

Across the street, FBI Agent Elliot Green reads the morning paper as he finishes off his coffee and buttered raisin toast. The image of Professor Bi's garage remains a constant on the flat-screen television, just as it has every morning for the last fourteen weeks.

The ringing cell phone shatters his morning routine. "Yes?"

"Mr. Green, are you available for Mr. Jones?"

Elliott tosses the paper aside. "Yes, of course."

A moment later, Chuck Jones, director of the FBI's Springfield office, comes on the line. "Elliott, sorry we haven't relieved you yet, but we've had a shortage of man power."

"I understand."

"More important—the computer produced a positive match on one of our friend's visitors. I'm sending the file over to you now. I'll also be pursuing the matter with our friends in DC. Let me know if there's any further contact."

DC? Green's heart races as he grabs his laptop.

The "visitors" had been three employees of a Decatur home improvement company. The "supervisor" who had arrived on the night of January 3 had sent two workmen back to Bi's residence two weeks later in the same white van. They had unloaded sheets of drywall along with a pair of heavy-looking wooden crates marked "Shelves." Everything had been hauled inside the garage, the professor making a great show to the taller man where he wanted the work to be done.

The work had taken two hours . . . all of it concealed behind the closed garage door. When the men left, they had taken with them the old drywall garbage, including the pair of now-empty crates.

After the work had been completed, Elliott had waited until Professor Bi had left for the university the following morning before peering in the garage window. A quick visual check had verified the interior walls had indeed been replaced by fresh drywall, along with a row of new cabinets. At the time, he'd assumed the heavy cartoons had simply contained the latter.

Green had sent the images of all three men's faces to FBI–Springfield for identification. After all this time, he had actually forgotten about the inquiry.

He opens Chuck Jones' e-mail and downloads the encrypted file.

Nothing on the two workers, but the foreman's face appears on screen, along with his identification:

Subject name: Michael Tursi

Graduated with honors: Ballistic Missile Analyst Technician, Sheppard Air Force Base.

Graduated with honors: BMAT—Advanced Training, Vandenburg Air Force Base.

Assigned: Little Rock, Arkansas: Titan II nuclear missiles.

Honorary discharge: August 1986

Current Whereabouts: UMBRA

Elliott Green stares at the information. That Michael Tursi had extensive training in nuclear missiles was not as bothersome as the UMBRA classification—Above Top-Secret.

Whatever Professor Bi was working on in that garage, he had the support of at least one member of a branch in the intelligence service.

UCLA MAIN CAMPUS
LOS ANGELES, CALIFORNIA

OMAR KAMEL RADI WALKS THROUGH THE south part of the UCLA campus, heading for the Student Activities Center. Although he occasionally attends lectures, he is not a student. He thinks often about enrolling, especially when he watches the varsity soccer team practice. He imagines himself playing goalie, and he daydreams about walking arm in arm with one of those blonde American cheerleaders.

Omar's studio apartment is located within walking distance of the campus. He is amazed that students can afford such rents—an amount that would surpass three months salary in Iraq. He could never afford the apartment based on his current job—working evening maintenance at the U.S. Bank Tower in downtown Los Angeles. But money is no longer a concern.

Days are easy for Omar, the campus offering a sense of peace he could never experience back in Nasiriyah. It is the night that tears at his soul, the time when his dreams return him crashing back to earth.

Walking east on Manning Avenue, he pauses at a small gym to watch an aerobics class in session. The instructor, an athletic blonde in her mid-thirties, leads a group of nine women and two men through a series of punches and kicks.

The class ends a few minutes later.

Omar enters the gym. He waits until the students leave, then approaches the woman. "You are very good. How much, please . . . if I wish to train with you?"

The aerobics instructor towels herself off, her eyes taking in the tall Middle Easterner. "Classes are twenty dollars a session, but you have to join the gym. Is it just for you, or your wife too?"

"My wife . . ." Omar's eyes tear up. "She died six years ago. An automobile accident."

"Oh, gosh . . . I'm so sorry." She holds out her hand. "Susan Campbell."

"Omar al-Saddat."

"Saddat? Are you related to that Egyptian fellow?"

"You have heard of my great uncle, Anwar?"

"Wasn't he assassinated?"

"Yes."

"Wow. Well, listen, I hope you join, I teach class every morning from 7:30 to 10:30, Monday through Friday."

"Thank you, Susan Campbell. I will see you tomorrow."

She offers him a good-bye smile, grabs her gym bag, and heads out the door.

Omar's heart seems to swell as he watches her go. He will spend the next six hours in the mall, shopping for workout gear, dress clothes . . . and new sheets and comforter for his bed.

"There is enough oil [in the Gulf of Mexico] to fuel almost 85 million cars for 30 years."

—BARNEY BISHOP,
Oil lobbyist

"Their predictive track record has been awful. In the land of the blind, reliable OPEC data is either untrusted or nonexistent. OPEC should provide field-by-field production and well-by-well data, budget details and third party engineering reports. The entire world assumes Saudi Arabia can carry everyone's energy needs on its back cheaply. If this turns out not to work there is no Plan B. Global spare capacity is now all Saudi Arabia."

—MATTHEW R. SIMMONS,
President of Simmons and Company International,
a specialized energy investment banking firm,
2006

SAUDI ARABIA OIL FIELDS

CHAPTER 19

Abu Dhabi, UAE
Middle East
April 23, 2012
7:56 pm Local Time

The landmass of Saudi Arabia dominates the Arabian Peninsula, its western shores stretching to the banks of the Red Sea, its eastern coastline meeting the Persian Gulf. While Iraq and Jordan border the kingdom's northern region, three smaller Arab nations form a "boot" around the Saudi southern border, separating it from the Arabian Sea: Yemen, Oman, and the United Arab Emirates (UAE).

The United Arab Emirates is located at the mouth of the Persian Gulf, wedged along the instep of the Saudi "boot." Considered one of the most modernized and liberal of all the Arab nations, the UAE is made up of seven independent states: Abu Dhabi, Dubai, Ajman, Fujairah, Ras al-Khaimah, Sharjah, and Umm al-Qaiwain. A Supreme Council of Rulers, composed of the states' seven ruling emirs, appoint the UAE's prime minister and cabinet.

Abu Dhabi is the capital and largest of the seven emirates, its landmass, (which includes almost two hundred islands) constituting nearly 80 percent of the UAE. Oil was discovered here in the 1950s, and by 1962 Abu Dhabi had become the first of the seven emirates to export its black gold. Yet unlike Saudi Arabia, Iraq, and Iran, Sheikh Zayed, president of the UAE, reinvested his nation's wealth back into the development of the seven emirates, transforming Abu Dhabi and its sister city, Al-Ain, into vibrant westernized areas featuring sleek skylines, parks and gardens, superb roadways, and a modern international airport. The emirate of Dubai, meanwhile, has become an entertainment and resort mecca, attracting celebrities the world over.

◆ ◆ ◆

It is dusk when Ace Futrell exits the air-conditioned lobby of the Baynunah Hilton Tower in downtown Abu Dhabi, carrying his leather briefcase. By the time he reaches the curb, the humidity has adhered his long-sleeved, denim shirt to his back.

A line of taxis occupy the entryway. Ace heads for the last vehicle, its driver leaning on the hood of the car, reading an Arab newspaper.

"I need a cab."

"There are others available. I am on break."

"I'm heading for the racetrack, and I'm in a rush."

The cab driver never looks up. "I have a tip for the fourth race. You would place a bet?"

"Agreed." Ace climbs in back, the Arab spewing expletives at other drivers as he hurls the taxi into traffic.

◆ ◆ ◆

An hour later, the skyline fades against a golden-pink horizon as they motor west along the Abu Dhabi-Tarif coastal highway. On Ace's right is the Persian Gulf, its shoreline containing shallow lagoons that drain with each tide. Patches of coral are covered with pockets of mangrove, along with vast black mats of algae that resemble oil pollution.

On Ace's left, running inland, are the salt flats known as the *sabkha*. Beyond the salt flats are vast expanses of sand dunes that roll like cream-colored waves toward the southeast, driven by the prevailing northwest winds.

The sun disappears, yielding to a velvety night sky and cooler temperatures. In the distance, Ace can see patches of glowing lights marking oil refineries in Saudi Arabia. A road marker indicates that the Saudi/Qatar border is twelve kilometers ahead. The highway is empty; other vehicles are few and far between.

Without warning, the driver stops the taxi in the middle of the road and turns around in his seat to face Ace. "Get out."

"Here? In the middle of nowhere?"

The gun appears, its barrel pointed at his face. A wave of fear sets his skin tingling. "Cross the *sabkha* to the dunes." The Arab motions with the gun. "Move!"

Ace grabs his briefcase and climbs out. The taxi immediately executes a tight U-turn across the tarmac and races away—

—leaving its passenger stranded in the middle of an empty desert highway.

A cold wind blows in from the sea, churning memories of Montauk's shoreline and his children. *Get moving, pal. You're about a million miles from home.*

Zipping his windbreaker and adjusting his collar, he jogs across the empty highway, crossing onto the salt flats.

It takes him fifteen minutes to reach the first set of dunes. He begins climbing, cursing aloud as the coarse sand fills his shoes, the effort of managing the shifting incline registering in his surgically-repaired knee. Gusts of wind whip at his back and howl in his ears, the sand tearing into his exposed flesh like shards of glass.

Reaching the summit, he looks out onto a desert that stretches as far as the eye can see. In the distance is a small oasis of light—the Abqaiq Oil Refinery, the largest oil and gas stabilization plant in the world. Located twenty-five miles inland from the Persian Gulf, Abqaiq can process up to 13 million barrels of crude oil a day. Ace knows current production runs at only half that figure, which represents 80 percent of Saudi Arabia's daily oil production, much of it coming from the supergiant known as Ghawar.

Spanning a thousand square miles, the Ghawar oil field contains thirty pumping stations powered by six generators that transport crude oil through a network of pipelines to Abqaiq's Gas Oil Separation Plants. These "GOSPs" take the sour oil (crude, containing hydrogen sulfide and carbon dioxide) and filters out the impurities. Once "sweetened," the crude oil is pumped to Ras Tanura, the main refinery and oil port on the Persian Gulf, where it is readied for export. Besides being a refinery, Abqaiq functions as a small town, its population of 2,200 consisting of Americans, Saudis, and other nationalities. The compound is surrounded by a heavily guarded security fence, and only upper-level Aramco personnel and their dependents are permitted to live inside.

Ace tears his eyes away from Abqaiq, focusing on the vast expanse of dark desert that lies before him. Somewhere out there is Ghawar, its secrets holding the entire world hostage.

Movement below catches his eye. Ace looks down.

Resting in a gully like a giant black scorpion is the AH64-D Longbow Apache helicopter.

"At the current rate of growth in demand, China alone will consume 100 percent of the world's currently available exports in ten years."

—ANONYMOUS OIL OFFICIAL,
October 2005

"My father rode a camel, I drive a Rolls Royce, my son flies a jet airplane, and his son will ride a camel."

—ARABIAN PROVERB

CHAPTER 20

Driven by its twin 1,700-horsepower turbo shaft engines, the Apache helicopter soars twenty feet above an endless flow of dunes, its nose down and tail high, flying like a wasp. The pilot, Lieutenant Master D. L. Garst, is seated in the elevated rear cockpit, his "smart" helmet, adorned with night vision sensors, linked to a rotating turret situated on top of the Apache's nose. As Garst moves his head, so moves the turret, its optical sensors transmitting the live video feed to a monocular lens positioned in front of the pilot's right eye. With his left, the pilot scans his interior display panels, which include a radar signal processor linked to a dome located on the mast above the airship's main rotor blades. The radar dome transmits millimeter radio waves in all directions, identifying and targeting any objects within range of the Apache warship.

As the military chopper races inland, the dunes turn a deep red-brown and begin rising like mountains. The dark color is a result of the sand's thin, gray coating of clay, which oxidizes within the arid climate.

Adjusting his swash plate, the pilot alters the blade's tilt, increasing his altitude while continuing his "nap-of-the-earth" flying. "We're approaching the northeastern tip of the Empty Quarter. How you doing up there?"

Ace Futrell is seated in the forward gunner's cockpit, surrounded by enough weaponry to wipe out a small city. "Good . . . fine. What happens if we run into the bad guys?"

"We avoid them."

". . . because I could fire a hellfire missile."

"That won't be necessary, sir."

"What about the Bedouin? They've been known to fire on aircraft."

"Sir, we're armored with Kevlar, thick enough to stop a 12.7mm round. Just relax and enjoy the ride."

In the distance, Ace can make out pinpoints of light—pumping stations situated around Ghawar, the largest reservoir of oil ever to have existed on the planet.

♦ ♦ ♦

The origins of hydrocarbons that make up oil and natural gas began as algae, organic matter, and plankton that formed in the warm seas of the Jurassic period tens of millions of years ago. This biomass slowly accumulated in stagnant sink holes, eventually settling in sedimentary rock. Through chemical reactions this bio-mass was converted into kerogen, a solid, waxy, organic substance.

Temperatures underground increase by fourteen degrees Fahrenheit for every thousand feet of depth, and it was at six thousand to fifteen thousand feet (the oil window) where kerogen-containing sediments, cooked over millions of years, "cracked" into oil. Natural gas, requiring greater heat and pressure, is often found in the same source rock deposits, only at greater depths.

Reservoirs of oil were formed and remain under tremendous pressure until tapped. As a well bore punctures the cache, the pressure allows the crude to flow upwards through pipes to the surface, the lighter oil flowing easier than the heavier viscous oil. As oil is depleted, the pressure naturally eases, requiring water or gas to be injected into a reservoir to maintain production. Natural surface seepages can also occur, the LaBrea tar pits in Los Angeles, aided by tectonic activity from the San Andreas fault, being a prime example.

Of all the oil fields in the world, only four have ever produced more than 1 million barrels of crude a day: The Cantarell field in Mexico, Da Qing in China, Burgan in Kuwait (substantially downgraded in 2005), and the Ghawar in Saudi Arabia, which produces more than the other three giants *combined*. Discovered in 1948, this mega-supergiant, the largest of six fields that account for all of Arabia's production, is located in the southeastern quadrant of the Saudi Kingdom near the Empty Quarter, close to the Persian Gulf. Shaped like an elongated stocking running north-south, the reservoir is 174 miles long and twelve to eighteen miles wide, its tank consisting of two sub-parallel structural crests, separated by an oval-shaped saddle. Although it is a single field, it is divided into six sections. From north to south, the sections are Fazran, Ain Dar, Shedgum, Uthmaniyah, Haradh, and Hawiyah.

Ghawar's production, which began in 1951, actually peaked in 1981 at 5.7 million barrels per day, a production figure later restrained for "market reasons." Since then, Aramco, the Saudi national energy company, has been forced to inject more and more seawater into the reservoir to force out more crude. This "water cut" surpassed 55 percent in 2004, meaning more than half the outflow from the supergiant is now saltwater. It is estimated that Ghawar, a field responsible for 60 percent of all the oil ever produced in Saudi Arabia, is being depleted at a rate of 8 percent every year.

◆ ◆ ◆

The Apache sets down behind a quadrant of rocky escarpments and sand dunes, the natural barrier serving as cover for two camouflaged tents and an Armored Medical Treatment Vehicle (AMTV). The AMTV is a heavy battalion truck designed to treat injured soldiers under the protection of armor. Painted on its desert-camouflaged hull is a red cross. Anchored to its roof is a satellite dish.

Ace climbs out of the forward cockpit, assisted by a corpsman dressed in desert fatigues. "Sir, Lieutenant Commander Watkin is waiting for you in Ops."

He is led inside the main tent, which houses two portable generators that feed power to a series of computer stations. An Army technician sits at one post, tracking the approach of a low Earth orbiting satellite, while another tech keeps a vigil on his radar screen. Dominating the Central Command is a computerized GPS map of Saudi Arabia, guarded by a tall man in a khakis uniform, sporting a grayish-brown crew cut.

Lieutenant Commander Matthew "Swatkin" Watkin began his career in the United States Army in 1994 as a combat engineer. The Virginia native has spent the last two decades in Kuwait, Afghanistan, Iraq, and Saudi Arabia, coordinating military ground operations for the Strategic Support Branch with Kellogg, Brown, & Root. The commander's attention is focused on the map and the walkie-talkie pressed to his ear, his eyes diverted from the main board as Ace enters the command post.

"Stand by, he just arrived." The lieutenant commander wipes his palm across his khakis, ignoring Ace's extended hand. "You Futrell?"

"Yes, sir."

"Watkin, Matthew J. Congratulations, Futrell, you now occupy the bird's nest position atop my personal hit list. Been my displeasure to have spent the last three months coordinating this little covert adventure of yours, most of the time operating on nothing but a swag."

"Swag?"

"Scientific Wild-Ass Guess. You have any idea what you've put me through? Got a hundred and fifty men spread out over three thousand miles of desert, two dozen predator drones, and a GPS satellite circling somewhere over this godforsaken desert, all so you can collect a bunch of data. Three locations, seven hundred explosives, all set to detonate at ten second intervals . . . do I look like the choreographer of the freakin' Arabian Olympics?"

Anger courses through the blood vessels in Ace's neck. "This isn't a piss-hole we're peeking under, Commander, it's a reservoir, biggest in the world. Cut the explosives in half, and you need twice as many receivers. So if you've got a better *swag* on how to accomplish what I've been ordered to accomplish without starting a jihad, my ears are open Watkin, Matthew J."

"Still a pistol." The commander's face breaks into a broad smile. "Don't remember me, do you? South Carolina game. I sacked your scrawny ass twice on that final drive before you scored the winning touchdown on a naked bootleg. Practically spiked the ball on my friggin' head, you little prick."

Ace grins. "Watkin . . . Swatkin Watkin, weakside linebacker, number 57. Nastiest cheap-shot artist in the Southeastern Conference. That last sack was an illegal hit, you practically drove your helmet through my sternum and out my ass. Still hurts every night when I get up to pee."

"Long as I made an impression." Watkin extends his hand. "Welcome to the magic kingdom, Ace, land of the crazies. Run by a Mickey Mouse ruler and his royal family of rodents. We've got about twelve minutes before our satellite makes its pass, just enough time for you to explain this whole setup."

Watkin leads him to the computerized map of Saudi Arabia's southeastern region. The Ghawar oil field appears olive green against the black desert, its profile ringed by darkened red pinpoints of light. Two more immense olive-green areas—irregular and oval shaped—occupy the Empty Quarter farther to the south.

"Everything's in place as per your instructions; two hundred explosives at the Empty Quarter sites, three hundred more at Ghawar. Deploying

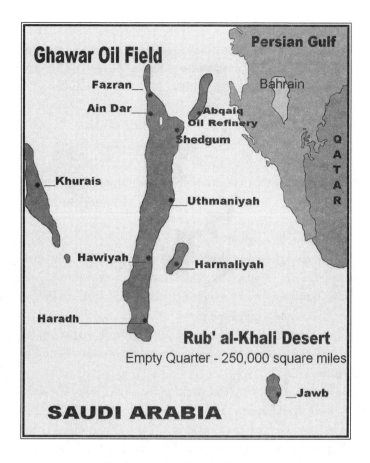

GHAWAR OIL FIELD

our teams over the Ghawar field figured to be the more difficult maneu-ver, but it turned out to be the easier of the two. We ended up disguising our guys in Aramco uniforms, most of the blue-collar stiffs working the fields are expatriates anyway, so who can tell? We stole two of their heavy utility trucks and dropped each man off at his post the moment it got dark. Had the charges planted and the geophones in place in under two hours. The Empty Quarter sites . . . they were hell."

"You sure the locations are set at the right intervals?"

"Every location was triangulated using predator drones, verified with GPS. Now, maybe you'd like to explain how this whole damn thing's supposed to work."

"It's called reflection seismic survey. Essentially we're using the explosives to create a three-dimensional CAT scan of the geology using echolocation. The geophones measure the travel time of the seismic energy released by the surface detonations, sort of like tossing a stone into a pond and tracking the ripples. Seismic energy is refracted or bent in the subsurface, then reflected. The reflection produces an image of the subsurface geology, creating a three-dimensional image. Data will be recorded by the seismographs, uploaded to the GPS satellite, and downloaded to the main computer . . . which reminds me, I'd better set up my interface."

Opening his briefcase, Ace removes his laptop. He powers up the device and plugs his board into the larger mainframe using several high-speed cables.

"And this'll tell us what's down there?"

"Assuming all goes well. My laptop will process the data, cross-checking the downloaded seismology with Ghawar's flow pressures, oil production, and oil and water ratios—information my team gathered over the last year. That should give us a pretty accurate assessment of how much crude Ghawar's got left in her tank. As for the Empty Quarter, either there's a vast reservoir of oil down there or there's not. Either way, we'll finally know."

The corpsman tracking the satellite calls out, "Two minutes."

"Acknowledged." Commander Watkin pulls Ace aside. "The geophones are rigged to detonate two minutes after the array has been completed. We'll leave behind a bunch of outhouse-sized craters, not much else. However, it's possible our command center may experience some blowback."

"What kind of blowback?"

"From the good guys. Few years ago, when Al-Qaeda starting launching attacks on Aramco's refineries, the DoD decided to position a dozen of their SSB hit squads in the Saudi Eastern Province. Once the fireworks start, the Strategic Service boys'll be on Ghawar like bees to honey. Our presence can be justified, but the Saudis know who you are; they'll quickly put two and two together. My orders are to wait until you upload your report to our friends in Washington, then get you the hell out of dodge."

"Sixty seconds."

"What exactly are these SSB hit squads packing?"

"Enough SAMs to bring down an airfield of 747s. They'll shoot first with extreme prejudice, then check the ID badges later."

"Nothing like working on the same team."

"Thirty seconds."

"Commander, all units are clear of their targets and report a go."

"Tracking's a go."

"Radar's still clear."

"Ten seconds. Nine . . . eight . . . seven . . ."

Ace moves to the computerized board, his heart pounding.

"Five . . . four . . . three . . . two—"

On the "one" count, a pair of red lights flash "On" along the computer map's three target sites—

—another pair, one to the east and west of the first pair, flash "On" ten seconds later . . . the sequence repeating itself every ten seconds, each successive explosion igniting a seismic wavefront that causes the reflected subsections of the three subterranean geologies to glow green on the main computer board.

"Radar?"

"Still all clear, sir."

Raw data streams onto Ace's computer monitor while three separate images begin materializing like a slowly evolving MRI on the big screen. The detonations quickly complete the twelve-mile northern width of the Ghawar and continue as they make their way south down the field's respective eastern and western flanks.

"Commander, I'm detecting activity at Abqaiq. Two helicopters, both Aramco."

Ace wipes a trickle of sweat from his forehead.

The Empty Quarter detonations continue circling their targets, the Ghawar field, with a third more explosives, materializing far slower on the computer board.

"Aramco choppers are circling Ghawar, Commander. Forty miles out and closing."

The commander winks at Ace. "No worries, just mouseketeers. It's the guys converging on us that we can't see that'll do us the real harm."

"Two minutes."

The two Empty Quarter targets complete their seismic surveys simultaneously, the Ghawar explosives still moving south. Quickly, Ace types in a series of commands, running an analysis of the raw data being downloaded from the main frame.

The last pair of Ghawar explosions converge upon one another, racing to meet at the southernmost tip of the field.

"Ace?"

"Got the first two images, Commander, just waiting for the big boy to finish."

"Saudi choppers closing fast! Fifteen miles."

The last set of explosives detonate along the Ghawar.

"Corpsman, is our pilot standing by?"

"Yes, sir."

"Mr. Futrell, the blitz is coming—"

"Data's in. Computer's analyzing it now."

"Saudi choppers have closed to eight miles."

"Got it!" Ace hurriedly scans the completed report.

Ghawar Field

Tank: 277 billion barrels
Estimated recoverable: 75 percent
Total: 208 billion barrels

Empty Quarter

Tank: 310 billion barrels
Estimated recoverable: 65 percent
Total: 201 billion barrels
Combined proven reserves: 409 billion barrels

Commander Watkin hovers over his shoulder. "So what's the verdict? Do I need to invest in a windmill, or can I continue to enjoy my nudie channels on the satellite dish?"

Ace stares at the data, dumbfounded. "The Saudis . . . they weren't lying. The reserves are strong."

"Terrific," Watkin says, the sarcasm dripping, "another twenty years in the desert, watching these towel heads spend our money. Upload your report, then let's get you out of here, A-sap."

Ace quickly encodes the information, transferring it to a secured file before he e-mails the report to David Schall at CIA headquarters. He unplugs his laptop, stows it in his briefcase, and hustles after the commander to the awaiting Apache.

Watkin slaps him hard on the back as he climbs into the open forward cockpit. "Nice seein' you, fella. Remember me the next time you get up to pee."

Ace turns to respond, but the commander is gone.

Seconds later, the Apache lifts off, racing southeast over the desert dunes.

Ace lays his head back, closing his eyes. *After all these years, how could I have been so wrong? The Empty Quarter . . . sure, it was always an unknown variable, but the Ghawar? Saudi Aramco's been injecting 500 million barrels of seawater into the carbonate reservoir since 2004 just to maintain enough pressure to draw out half that in crude. That seepage has to be flowing west, yet it's barely registering on the seismic survey. The original oil column was 1300 feet thick; six years ago it was less than 150 feet. How the hell can Ghawar possibly contain—*

Alarms sound within the cockpit, chasing Ace's thoughts as the Apache pulls a steep vertical climb.

"Surface missile, fired at close range! Hang on!" The pilot activates the Longbow's jammer, its varying infrared frequencies confusing the inbound heat-seeking missile, buying them precious seconds as they soar east, then dive back to earth.

Ace grabs for the console—

—as two more missiles appear on his screen.

The Apache goes vertical, the sudden G-force pinning Ace to the back of his seat, the vomit rising as his stomach is squeezed in a vise—

—releasing him as they barrel roll and dive again, everything spinning in his vision, the dunes lunging at them like waves on an ocean, alarms renting the air, console lights flashing death knolls.

". . . no good, gotta ditch! Hang on!"

He braces himself, his insides jumping as the Apache swoops low, skims a sand dune, then spins and smashes sideways into an immovable object, the impact jolting reality into blackness as the Kevlar canopy crumples around Ace Furell like a crushed aluminum can.

"When you engage in actual fighting, if victory is long in coming, the men's weapons will grow dull and their ardor will be dampened. If you lay siege to a town, you will exhaust your strength, and if the campaign is protracted, the resources of the state will not be equal to the strain. Never forget: when your weapons are dulled, your ardor dampened, your strength exhausted, and your treasure spent, other chieftains will spring up to take advantage of your extremity. Then no man, however wise, will be able to avert the consequences that must ensue."

—Sun Tzu,
from *The Art of War*,
sixth century BC

"When you ignore what people are saying on a daily basis, calling for the annihilation of your country, you are ignoring them at your own risk."

—Caroline Glick,
Senior Fellow,
Center for Security Policy

"Then I looked up. And I heard a single eagle crying loudly as it flew through the air, 'Terror, terror, terror to all who belong to this world because of what will happen when the last three angels blow their trumpets.' "

—Revelation 8:13

Book Excerpt:
To the Brink of Hell: An Apology to the Survivors
by Kelli Doyle,
White House National Security Staff Advisor
(2006 – 2010)

The next major terrorist attack will be a nuclear detonation. Can the death of millions of innocent people and
another war in the Middle East be averted? To answer that,
we have to understand how our roll in the politics of the
Persian Gulf has changed.

Prior to the Bush–Cheney–Rumsfeld doctrine, America's
policy in the Middle East had always been about fostering stability to allow the oil to flow unimpeded. Stability required
maintaining a balance of power between the Arabs and Muslims while the West and former USSR pulled at their proxy's
strings. The Communists had Egypt and Syria, while Israel,
being the lone democracy in the Middle East, became America's
muscle in the region, Saudi Arabia, our OPEC enforcer.

Storm clouds first appeared on the horizon when Egypt and
Syria, equipped with Soviet weapons, attacked Israel on Yom
Kippur in 1973. Initially caught off guard, the Israeli forces
fought back, driving both invaders beyond the 1967 borders.
It was a stunning defeat for the Arab world, and it placed the
Saudis in a tenuous position among their Arab peers. To save
face, the Saudis agreed to an American oil embargo.

Though the '73 oil crisis was artificially created, its
effects staggered the U.S. economy. Long lines at the pumps
forced Americans to consider alternative fuel sources. Solar
panels were placed on the White House roof, gas mileage
improvements were enforced, and conservation was encouraged
by the Carter administration. It was a turning-point event

that could have changed the course of the world, but alas, the movement died when the Reagan–Bush administration took office and the Saudis released a glut of cheap oil upon the market.

It was about this time that the CIA's puppet ruler in Iran—the Shah—was overthrown and replaced by Ayatollah Khomeini. Iran's Islamic fundamentalist movement changed the balance of power in the Middle East, encouraging other Muslim groups to revolt against the West . . . a direct threat to the Saudis.

Iran, with its theocratic Islamic fundamentalist regime, has always been enemies with Iraq, a secular Arab nation-state. Iraq was ruled by the heavy-handed Saddam Hussein and his pan-Arabist Ba'ath Party. Encouraged by the Carter administration, backed by secret financial agreements with Saudi Arabia, Saddam launched an attack on Iran. The resulting war pitted the second-largest oil producer in the world against the third-largest. As oil production declined, the House of Saud stepped up their own production, keeping prices down, prolonging the war.

Enter the Reagan–Bush administration. The White House was torn over which side to support: Iran, whose fundamentalists had kidnaped American citizens; or Iraq and its brutal dictator. A prolonged war would serve to weaken both countries, but Reagan, who had publicly taken a stand to fight the Islamists, could not be perceived as aiding Iran. And so a covert strategy was devised, one that would allow the Reagan–Bush administration to both funnel weapons to Iran through Israel and overthrow the left-wing government of Nicaragua by supporting the right-wing rebels, known as the Contras.

To fund this strategy, the CIA began trafficking drugs.

The U.S. House of Representatives had already voted 411 to 0 to prohibit any funding to the Contras, and the DoD and CIA were, by law, prevented from getting involved in any covert Contra operations. To circumvent this ban, the Reagan administration used the National Security Council to "raise funding" for the Contras. These arrangements were overseen by Colonel Oliver North, who had established a working relationship with Manuel Noriega, Panama's drug baron. Over the next decade the CIA transferred twenty-eight C-130 Hercules transport planes from the Department of Defense to the U.S.

Forest Service, and from there into the hands of "private contractors" to move massive quantities of cocaine from Columbia, Mexico, Panama, and other drug-producing countries into the United States. Billions of dollars worth of cocaine found its way into urban American neighborhoods like Los Angeles, the profits from which poured into the Contras . . . the victims of these immoral policies mostly Black and Hispanic kids.

Complicating this illegal arrangement was Saudi Arabia's King Fahd, who wanted to be paid off for his part of the equation with hundreds of Stinger missiles. Once more bypassing Congress, the Reagan administration invoked "emergency measures" to settle their debt with the House of Saud.

To make these illegal payoffs, the CIA turned to the Bank of Credit and Commerce International (BCCI). Founded by a Pakistani banker, Agha Hasan Abedi, BCCI was an elaborate multinational corporation made up of an impenetrable series of holding companies, subsidiaries, banks-within-banks, and affiliates that managed to avoid audits and regulators. It had offices in more than fifty third-world countries, held key contacts with everyone from prime ministers and presidents to their wives and mistresses, and operated free of government control. In 1977, BCCI had begun exerting its influence in U.S. politics by purchasing the National Bank of Georgia from its CEO, Bert Lance, a close friend of President Carter. Using these fronts and shell corporations, BCCI covertly funneled money and arms. The bank had its own intelligence agency and even its own paramilitary wing, known as the "Black Network." BCCI could provide the phony documents and letters of credit needed to purchase weapons, and it was through this international network of terror that the Reagan White House funded the Contras and escalated the Iran-Iraq War.

But there was one other covert operation that would make its impact felt in the Middle East and in the rest of the world . . .

In July of 1979, President Carter had begun a secret campaign to provide military aid to the Mujahideen—Afghan rebels who were fighting the Soviets in Kabul. The Soviets took the bait and crossed the border into Afghanistan, and suddenly the USSR had its own Vietnam War. The House of Saud embraced this guerilla action, for it supported both Islam and the West against the atheist Soviets. When the Reagan administration took office, the White House increased aid to these "freedom fighters," causing the Soviets to expend even more resources into the conflict.

The leader of these Afghan rebels? Osama bin Laden.

By 1983 things were not going well for Saddam and Iraq, whose army had resorted to using chemical weapons purchased from western firms against the Iranians. To maintain balance and prolong the war, the Reagan administration secretly began supplying Saddam's regime with helicopters, bombs, and howitzers—all in direct violation of the Arms Export Control Act. They also gave Saddam nuclear, biological and chemical warfare suits, sophisticated guidance systems, and components for their chemical plants. As a result, by 1985 the war tilted back in favor of Iraq, causing the White House to respond in kind, this time selling more than five hundred TOW missiles to Iran.

In time the pendulum swung, and again the White House reacted.

In February 1986, the Reagan administration arranged for the House of Saud to secretly sell Saddam British fighter planes along with fifteen-hundred MK–84 bombs, each containing two thousand-pound payloads. But the Iraqis were ill-prepared to use their new gift, so the White House dispatched Vice President George H. W. Bush to the Middle East on a "mission of peace." The former CIA director (and future president) left for Jordan with two objectives: first, to supply military intelligence to Saddam so that he would use his air force to attack Iranian targets; second, to get Iran to release American hostages in exchange for four thousand missiles. Within forty-eight hours he succeeded on both counts, and the Iran-Iraq war reached new levels of mass destruction.

Meanwhile, the House of Saud continued supporting the White House's covert operations. The Royal Family, whose oil revenues had surpassed $115 billion a year, had on deposit more than $100 billion in U.S. financial institutions. America's banks were using this newfound leverage to lend money to other Third World banks. U.S. businesses soon took advantage, with companies such as AT&T, Proctor and Gamble, and IBM borrowing hundreds of millions of dollars. The arms trade between the two countries heated up, and the House of

Saud purchased F–15s, Stinger missiles, and C–130 transport planes—each sale yielding tens of millions in commissions to the Saudi princes overseeing the deal. The rich were getting richer, the Iranians and Iraqis were dying, and the Saudi people were building up their hatred for the Royal Family . . . and their American co-sponsors.

In March of 1988, Saddam dropped chemical bombs from U.S. helicopters on Halabja, an Iraqi town in Iranian-held territory, killing more than five thousand Kurds. It was not the first time chemical weapons had been used, but this time the Iranians rushed reporters to the scene, and the world finally reacted. By August, there was a cease-fire, and five months later, George H. Walker Bush took office.

The Iran-Iraq War had ended in a stalemate but left Saddam with a million-man army, backed by sophisticated U.S. weaponry. President Bush continued using BCCI to fund the Iraqi dictator, allowing him to initiate a chemical, biological, and nuclear weapons program. In 1990, Saddam boasted that he had enough chemical weapons to consume half of Israel, a bold statement that finally forced Washington to react. After providing Saddam with more than $5 billion in military aid, the puppet had become too powerful, and now it was necessary to bring him down a few pegs. Kuwait would be the bait.

Within days of the end of the Iran-Iraq War (and in direct violation of OPEC quotas), Kuwait began releasing more oil onto the market. The price of oil dropped, directly affecting Saddam, whose country desperately needed the money to rebuild its infrastructure. To compound matters, Kuwait was pumping the oil from the Rumailla fields, an area partially located in Iraq. Though it didn't need the money, Kuwait suddenly demanded Iraq repay an $8 billion loan Saddam had made during the war . . . all the while openly conducting ongoing meetings with the Iranian Foreign Minister and members of the CIA.

Saddam had no means to repay the loan, so Kuwait sold the debt notes at a huge discount, preventing Iraq from borrowing money on the international market. For the next sixteen months, Iraqi officials attempted to settle their border dispute, but the Saudis refused to allow an Arab conference to convene. It was an old-fashioned squeeze play, forcing Saddam to turn to his one-time ally, the United States.

As Iraqi troops amassed along the Kuwaiti border, President Bush sent April Glaspie, the U.S. ambassador, to Iraq to meet with Saddam on July 25, 1990. Glaspie gave Saddam America's blessing to raise the price of oil, causing an inter-Arab dispute. When she asked the dictator what else he wanted, Saddam replied that his country's aim was to reclaim the Shatt al-Arab, a region of Iraq that was now part of Kuwait. Glaspie's response was that "the Kuwait issue is not associated with America." In essence, the United States had just given Saddam a green light to invade Kuwait.

On August 2, 1990 Iraq invaded Kuwait. In response, King Hussein of Jordan called a meeting of the Arab heads of state, hoping to avoid another war. Saddam agreed to withdraw twenty thousand Iraqi troops from Kuwait, and it seemed a peaceful solution was at hand.

Enter U.S. secretary of defense Dick Cheney. On August 6, Cheney and his entourage met with King Fahd and his ministers, providing them with doctored satellite photos from the CIA and NSC that showed two hundred thousand Iraqi troops poised to attack Saudi Arabia. Cheney asked the king to allow American troops to land in his country. When Crown Prince Abdullah became alarmed, Cheney insisted Saudi Arabia was in danger of falling to an Iraqi-Yemeni-PLO invasion.

Four days later, the Arab heads of state, led by King Fahd and President Mubarrak of Egypt, mysteriously voted against mediating the Iraq-Kuwait dispute. The UN resolutions that followed only backed Saddam deeper into a corner.

Kuwait is far from a democracy, it is an oil-rich, oligarchical Islamic regime run by the Al-Sabah royal family, who, like the House of Saud, routinely violates the rights of its own citizens. Knowing that the American public would never support a U.S.-led invasion force to liberate another repressive regime, the Bush administration turned to the public relations firm of Hill & Knowlton, who were paid $10.7 million by an organization calling itself Citizens for a Free Kuwait. Craig Fuller, the firm's president and chief operating officer, had been George Bush's chief of staff when he was vice president to Ronald Reagan. After several failed attempts to register a blip with the American public, the firm fabricated a news story about how Iraqi soldiers had removed 312 babies from their incubators and left them to die on a hospital floor in Kuwait City. The firm even produced an eyewitness—a fifteen-year-old Kuwaiti girl, who testified at the October 10th Congressional Human Rights Caucus. This "eyewitness" was actually the daughter of Saud al-Sabah, Kuwait's ambassador to the United States.

Over the next five weeks, President Bush used the baby incubator story no less than a half-dozen times in his speeches. The deceived American public changed its tune.

On January 16, 1991, President Bush unleashed Operation Desert Storm, a war designed to "liberate" the monarchy of Kuwait.

Saddam surrendered on February 27. George Bush got what he wanted—Iraq had been removed as a threat to the House of Saud. But the president had stopped short of invading Iraq, a move that irked many neoconservative members of his party, among them, Dick Cheney, Donald Rumsfeld, and Paul Wolfowitz.

Meanwhile, Osama bin Laden had used America's annual $700 million stipend in military assistance to build a vast training facility in eastern Afghanistan. Bin Laden's army had swelled to twenty-five thousand strong, representing Islamic extremists from more than a dozen countries. Weakening Iraq, the most powerful secular nation in the region, created a vacuum that was quickly filled by Bin Laden's Islamic fundamentalists, who opposed a western presence in Saudi Arabia.

The United States' own foreign policy had indirectly given birth to Al-Qaeda—the base.

"Royal Dutch Shell shocked investors when it unexpectedly announced that it was slashing its estimate of proven reserves by 20 percent."

—*WASHINGTON MONTHLY,*
June 2005

"According to a restricted report issued by the authoritative industry newsletter Petroleum Intelligence Weekly (PIW), internal Kuwaiti records reveal that the nation's oil reserves are far below the officially stated amount of 99 billion barrels. The PIW report claims that Kuwait's remaining proven and nonproven oil reserves total about 48 billion barrels, or 51 billion fewer barrels than previously advertised. Another way of stating the matter is that the amount of estimated world oil reserves just fell by 5 percent . . . the equivalent of almost 20 months worth of total cumulative worldwide oil production and consumption, based on the current world oil use of about 84 million barrels per day."

—BYRON W. KING,
Energy Bulletin,
January 25, 2006

CHAPTER 21

Paralysis. The kind that prevents movement yet still allows pain to seep into the nerves.

Blindness. A heavy darkness . . . filtered by shards of lunar light.

Silence. Unnatural . . . overpowered by the noise in his head, a terminal buzz, yielding to . . .

Blackness.

AFTERNOON

ACE BLINKS HIS EYES OPEN. GINGERLY moves his arms. He is in the Georgia locker room, lying on the training table, the team physician checking his vital signs, his head coach hovering close by.

"You all right, son? That was some hit you took."

"Got his bell rung good, coach. He's done."

"No . . . I'm okay, coach, I can play! Put me back in!"

"Put you back in? Son, haven't you caused enough damage?" The two men laugh, the sound echoing in his brain.

♦ ♦ ♦

"Huh!" Ace opens his eyes. He is in a subterranean room, lying on a bare mattress. Shards of sunlight filter through floorboards above his head, providing a dim, gray light. Relief floods into his psyche as he moves his arms—

—until he realizes they are shackled to the concrete floor.

His head has been bandaged. A dull ache greets him as he sits up. His eyes focus on his Arab guard, seated in a folding chair. A machine gun rests across his lap, a cooler by his feet. The man offers a blank stare. Reaching behind him, he knocks on the closed door at his back.

Moments later, another Arab enters the room, dressed in a traditional white silk *thobe*. He is short and slender, with dark black hair and eyes and an olive complexion.

"How are you feeling?" The English is smooth and eloquent, belying a western education.

"Who are you?"

Reaching into a cooler, the man removes a bottled water and tosses it to Ace. "You have a concussion and some minor bruises. The pilot broke his arm and was treated for secondary burns. He is being kept sedated in another room."

"What do you want with me?"

"That, Mr. Ace Futrell, really depends upon you." The Arab smiles at Ace's surprise. "Yes, I know who you are. I also know about your wife and children, your home in Long Island, your glory days in college, and your recent trouble at PetroConsultants. Your first reaction will be to assume I am with an intelligence agency, and I was, but my information comes to me firsthand, from a very trusted friend."

The Arab crosses the room and removes a blanket from a piece of furniture that turns out to be a combination television and VCR. He presses play. An image moves into focus.

It's his wife! From Kelli's appearance, the video must have been taken within the last eighteen months, the chemo having just started to rob her of her hair and twenty pounds of muscle. She is seated in a living room—*their* living room—and the Arab is seated next to her, dressed in a sweater and jeans.

"Hi, hon. If you're watching this, well then there's a good chance that . . . that something bad happened to me and I'm no longer around. Before you jump to any wild conclusions or lose that famous temper of yours, let me introduce you to a friend of mine . . . a trusted friend. This is Ramzi Iskander Karim. Ramzi's family comes from Egypt, though he was educated in the States. Ramzi and I first met at Camp Peary; he joined the Company about the same time I did. That's right, he's CIA . . . sorry, ex-CIA. In a few moments, Ramzi's going to share some very important information with you. I need you to trust him, Ace."

Kelli nods to Ramzi on the video, who takes his cue and leaves the room, offering her privacy.

The live Ramzi occupies himself in another section of the basement.

Kelli stares at Ace from the television screen. "This is hard. You live your life, you wish you could turn back the clock, undo certain things . . . make amends. I'm sorry, Ace. I'm sorry for not being there for you our senior year at Georgia when you were going through hell. I'm sorry for not being there now, for leaving you to raise Leigh and Sammy alone. Most of all, hon, I'm sorry I have to involve you in all this. If . . . if you had been in another profession, a football coach, a teacher . . . but the simple fact is, your business deals directly with everything that's been going on, and in order to stop something terrible from happening, I need your help. There are only a few people I trust these days, Ace, and Ramzi is one of them. Please listen to what he has to say and help him, if not for me, then for the kids."

She pauses, turning from the camera to wipe away tears.

Ace's eyes well up too.

"I've been involved in some bad things. The world can be an ugly place . . . sometimes you get swept up in that ugliness. You don't know how often I wish we had married right out of college. Things would have been so different. There's so much I regret, Ace, things that have festered in my gut the last six years . . . it's no wonder the cancer started there."

She chokes out a laugh. "You're probably saying to yourself, who is this woman and what did she do with my wife? Cancer and Kaballah have given me a new perspective on life. I know you like to tease me about my Kaballah classes, but it's what finally made me take a hard look at myself. Kaballah says it's our negative energy that separates us from God. What you went through at Georgia, the stress, the fear . . . it probably felt like you were in prison. I know my own choices imprisoned me. I believe now that each one of us are destined to accomplish great things . . . things that positively affect others. That's the key to escaping our prisons, Ace, to do godly things. Everything we say and do matters, and every positive and negative action we do affects others. Kaballah teaches us that God is the light, darkness, the result of ego—the desire to receive for the self alone, and we're either moving into the light or moving toward darkness.

"I've been involved in some bad things, and now I need to make them right. Ace, the world's moving down a very dangerous path. On one side, you've got a growing sect of radical Islamists competing for the attention of the Arab world. On the other side, you've got a group of radical hawks—capitalists who believe the only way to bring about change is through the barrel of a gun. Ego, greed, and self-righteousness . . . each side pushing the other, each side pointing the finger as they inch the world toward Armageddon. I know that sounds melodramatic, but I was a part of it, and now I want to do everything I can to change it."

She moves closer to the camera.

"Something bad's going to happen, sweetheart, unless we expose it and cripple the machine that feeds it. I've been actively working on solutions. Ramzi's a part of that. He needs your help. I told him you could do it. I told him how strong you are. You are strong, Ace, never doubt that. Things are going to get bad, but under every rock of discomfort is concealed an opportunity. All of us are God's vessels, Ace. We can do godly things. It's the fight of your life, but I'll be with you every moment. I love you, Ace."

The image goes blank.

Ace stares at the dark screen, emotionally drained. He wipes away tears, his insides trembling.

Ramzi returns and powers off the television. "She left her memoirs on a CD-ROM. You'll need to read it here. It's far too dangerous to keep with you while you travel. I'm sorry. I know this must be hard for you."

"Hard?" The words catch on the lump in his throat. "Why was Kelli killed? Who gave the orders? What the hell were you two working on?"

"The prevention of Armageddon." Ramzi rattles a command in Arabic to the guard. The man unlocks Ace's shackles and leaves the room.

"Ace, have you ever heard the term, '*shihadah*'?"

"No."

"*Shihadah* means to die for the sake of God, it comes from the true meaning of jihad, which translates to 'enjoin good and forbid evil.' Muslims are raised to do God's work, but it is the zealots of Islam that have bastardized the word of the Prophet Muhammad, in the same manner the more extreme elements of the Christian faith have warped the teachings of Jesus Christ.

"When I studied in the States, I remember reading an account of the Hatfields and McCoys, two families whose rivalry turned into a violent feud. In many ways, this rivalry reminded me of the Sunni-Shi'ite conflict—two sides sharing so much in common, at war not as much because of internal strife as external, exacerbated by a history of extremist violence. The Middle East remains divided by this strife, and the rest of the world chooses sides based on which nation supplies them with the most crude oil."

"And where do you stand?"

"I stand with the innocent majority, who seek merely to live in peace."

Ramzi opens a bottle of water. Drains half of it. "My family was originally from Aswan, Egypt's most beautiful city, a small community set upon the southern banks of the Nile. My father owned a floating restaurant. Each day, tourists in sailboats would arrive to dine on fresh fish and listen to Nubian music as the sun set. When I was nine, a group of radicals set fire to our barge, destroying everything we owned. One of my sisters was badly burned. My father's brother was a physician living in Mecca. He invited us to move in with him while he treated my sister, and so we left Egypt and took up residence in the kingdom ruled by Al-Saud.

"My father was a devout Muslim. His family were part of the Al-Hashem tribe, direct descendants of the Prophet Muhammad. These tribes are known collectively as *Ashraf*, and individuals like my father are called *Shareef*. My father was a powerful businessman, but he was ill prepared for what awaited us in Saudi Arabia.

"Despite western opinion, most Muslims are peaceful, like any nation or religion; it is the radical elements that foster bad reputations. Through-out their history, the Wahhabi element of Islam has fiercely opposed any-thing they viewed as *bida*, a derogatory term that refers to any behavior that deviates from the fundamental teachings of the Koran. This puritanical view condemns anything considered western, including television, telephones, music, and movies. Yet it was this neoconservative religious sect that was instrumental in creating the Saudi monarchy. It is their strong-arm tactics that keep Saudi citizens under control.

"What exists today in Saudi Arabia is an Arab identity held hostage by the hypocrisies of the Royals, who maintain dominance through the fanatical brutality of their Wahhabi clerics, who themselves have looked the other way while the Royal Family has trampled upon the Koran—behind their palace walls, drinking, gambling and woman-izing. Control remains the key to power for extremists. This is why, instead of teaching the word of God, religious schools and mosques now teach hatred. In Palestine and Lebanon, in Iran and Iraq, the Jew is the devil personified, the United States, his minion. Arab children are brainwashed from an early age. Hatred is the government's necessary ingredient to allow these oppressive regimes to maintain power within a closed society. This psychosis of violence is a distraction meant to temper the people's desire for freedom.

"After my sister recovered, my father, desiring to be close to the water, opened a restaurant in Jiddah. One day, a Saudi prince visited our establishment, a man who had earned a reputation for deflowering virgins. The prince took notice of my twelve-year-old sister and sent one of his entourage to negotiate a price with my father. My father spit on the messenger and ordered the others to leave. A few hours later our restaurant was visited by the 'mutawa,' the Wahhabi religious police. My father was beaten, arrested, and taken to prison. To bring him home, my sister offered herself to the prince, who kept her in his palace for six months. My father was eventually released, having been abused by the Saudi torturer, Ali Shams, for nearly a year. He would live out his days bound to a wheelchair.

"When I was seventeen, I joined the *Rai al-Nas*, an underground press that spoke out against the atrocities of the House of Saud. To be caught working for the paper meant certain death. Fearing his only son's beheading, my father arranged for my education in the States."

"So you joined the CIA to fight the Saudis?"

"I joined because I believed I could make a difference. I was wrong. The CIA is merely another tool of the West that enables the Royal Family to maintain control as stewards of cheap oil. That stewardship will soon come to an end, bringing the world to a crossroads. Without oil the House of Saud will collapse. The question is—who will fill the void? The rise of radical Islam terrifies the Royals, but rather than stand up to its threat, they have chosen to bribe its leaders, enabling them with money and weapons. Radical ideologies spread because the middle class has lost the will to quash them or because the people are forced to choose between the lesser of two evils. To the common Arab, American fascism is far worse than Islamic fascism; everyone knows the western invaders care only about stealing our oil. By invading Iraq, the United States chased the very people who would have stood up to Islamic fascism into their camp. And so the cancer spreads, from Iraq into Egypt and Jordan, from Saudi Arabia into Syria and Lebanon.

"Iran is the wolf at the door. While they would never challenge the United States or Israel in a conventional war, a new strategy appeared with the success of Al-Qaeda and the *intifada*. The strength of the Americans and the Israelis is also their weakness—they cherish life, while the terrorists do not. Hezbollah launches attacks while hidden among women and children, taunting the Israelis to attack so they may exploit the bloodshed to gain sympathy to their cause—which is not peace but the violent eradication of every Jew and every non-Muslim in the Middle East. Meanwhile,

Al-Qaeda plots their next act of terror, sending a message to the world that Islam can fell a superpower with a small band of warriors using cardboard cutters and common household items.

"All that is about to change. Iran's decision to enrich its uranium opens a Pandora's box. There is a growing fear among intelligence agencies in Washington that Islamic extremists, supplied by Iran, will use suitcase bombs to unleash a nuclear holocaust in U.S. cities. Your wife was involved in a radical contingency plan—a preemptive nuclear strike whereby an American city would be wiped out by a terrorist cell, their success, an excuse to crush the Islamic movement in Iran."

"Crazy bastards . . ."

"Kelli helped set the contingency plan in motion, then she got sick. As she just relayed to you, her illness gave her a newfound perspective on the situation—a new means to quell the storm."

Ace watches as Ramzi rolls back a Persian rug. Using two razor-thin metal hinges, he works loose a slab of concrete from the floor and lifts it up, revealing a high-tech safe buried in the foundation. Rotating the safe's retinal eye scan into place, he enters a combination, then presses his forehead to the device, submitting to the blue laser scan.

The safe verifies his identification and clicks open.

"We have two terror fronts that must be derailed in order to avert a nuclear holocaust. My role was to offer the Arab people a third choice—a true democracy, one that comes from within—in essence, a revolution. The *Ashraf* movement is that revolution—a true movement of the middle class and the poor, but it can only succeed by gaining control of the Royals' true weapons of power: Saudi oil and the fortunes they stole from the Saudi people."

The former CIA operative opens the lid of the safe and removes what appears to be a black CD-ROM case. "Are you familiar with a program called Promis?"

"No."

"Promis is the eye that sees everything. Its original creator was an American named Bill Hamilton. Many years ago, Hamilton developed a computerized dictionary for the NSA that translated Vietnamese into English. Later, he decided to create a new program—something different, something that could track the movements of people around the world. He would fulfill this dream when he left the NSA and bought out a company called Inslaw, a non-profit entity that developed software designed to cross-reference legal cases and court actions with potential witnesses and their families. By 1981, Hamilton had enhanced the system so that it could tap into virtually any computer network, searching utilities, telephone companies, airlines, and other services to track the location of a target by cross-referencing activities of a subject, their friends, relatives, and associates. Hamilton attempted to lease the program—Promis—to the Justice Department, but without much success.

"What Hamilton never knew was that the Justice Department had secretly made copies of Promis and had distributed them to the U.S. Intelligence Community. The CIA saw Promis as a means of tracking Mafia money-laundering schemes, as well as using it as a tool to spy on Columbian drug barons. A copy of the program eventually ended up in the hands of Earl Brian, a man who had worked under Reagan when he was governor of California. Brian had contacts with Israel's Mossad—at the time Mossad was deeply embroiled over the first Palestinian *Intifada*. Brian was introduced to Rafi Eitan, an Israeli businessman who eventually took the Promis design to a far greater level. The new Promis became a disk that could be used in a personal computer, correlating data at far greater speeds. More ingenious, Eitan had a colleague equip Promis with a secret trapdoor—a built-in chip that, undetected by the user, would allow Israeli Intelligence to monitor all ongoing activities of its user host.

"Earl Brian's company, Hadron, was setup to sell the security program to foreign governments. Jordan was first to take the bait. Once installed at the military headquarters in Amman, Promis wired itself into a French-manufactured tracking system that the Jordanians were using to follow the activities of the PLO. Thanks to Promis, the Israelis could now track the PLO's leaders, which helped Mossad combat the *Intifada*.

"The potential usages for the Promis spy network were enormous, but Eitan and Brian's resources were limited. Enter Robert Maxwell, CEO of Degem Computers in Tel Aviv. Using the company's offices in South America, Maxwell began selling Promis to foreign governments and heads of state, including PLO Chairman Yasser Arafat. Almost overnight, Promis gave the Israeli and American Intelligence communities access into everything from Soviet-bloc military intelligence to the movements of thousands of terror suspects . . . to monetary activities involving banking and financial institutions across the world."

"What about Bin Laden?"

"Ah yes . . . Bin Laden. An FBI agent, Robert Hanssen, had used his Russian contacts to sell Al-Qaeda the Promis program. Promis gave us access to bin Laden's movements and activities, but Promis also gave Al-Qaeda the ability to monitor our own investigations, as well as a financial tool to access their own money. Hanssen was later convicted as a spy, but the damage was already done."

"Then 9/11 . . . the White House must have known about the plot."

"Of course they knew, as many people already suspect, but the lies go far beyond the events of that day. Promis gave its owners access to all computer programs, as well as the means to alter data. All computers, Ace."

The blood drains from Ace's face. "The presidential elections . . ."

Ramzi nods. "Voting machines tallied and controlled by computers, manufactured by companies that exclusively endorsed GOP candidates. Florida in 2000, Ohio in 2004, Virginia and Pennsylvania in 2008. Ever wonder why these same swing states still refuse to mandate paper ballot receipts, despite the repeated controversies? The powers-that-be, in an attempt to maintain an edge, consistently block any and all election checks-and-balances, their decisions backed by judges appointed by the same regime. Democracy, it seems, has become an illusion."

Ace lies down on the mattress, feeling dizzy. "If Promis gave Kelli access to everything . . . would that include Saudi Aramco's data?"

"Not just Aramco, but nearly every oil company and third world national energy conglomerate, revealing the planet's true remaining oil reserves. Cheney knew back in 2000. It's the reason he refuses to release details of his energy meetings. Of course, the CIA already knew Iraqi reserves had peaked long ago, Iranian reserves as well. Iran's posturing about going nuclear could have been derailed long ago, initially it was a reaction to the United States covertly building military bases in Iraq. It's a prime example how one extremist reaction births an equal but opposite reaction."

Ace sits up. "When you found me in the desert, I had just completed a seismic survey. My data indicated Ghawar still has strong oil reserves. The untapped Empty Quarter too."

"Whose data? Who performed the tests?"

"The military."

"Which branch?"

"Strategic Support Branch."

"SSB is an organization established by Donald Rumsfeld and used by the Neocons to keep things from the prying eyes and ears of the other intelligence agencies. Tell me, how were the surveys conducted?"

"It was a massive military operation, involving hundreds of men, seven hundred controlled explosions. I don't see how—"

"You saw these men? You witnessed the explosions?"

Ace feels queasy. "No. All I saw were lights on a damn computer board . . . Bastards, they set me up! There never were any explosions, were there? Just a bunch of rigged data they wanted me to send to DC."

"And having sent it, you became expendable. Fortunately, the Bedouin are not as competent with their SAMs as their American counterparts. Who sent you to Arabia to gather data?"

"Schall, the CIA director, but the request originated from McKuin, at least that's what I've been told. The president wants to initiate a new alternative energy policy, something with teeth. First, he needed accurate data on the Saudi reserves."

"Instead, the puppet-masters led you to file a report that indicates the crude is plentiful. Who would benefit from such a fabrication?"

"The usual suspects. Oil companies. The Saudi Royals."

"Yes, but you are missing the true devil. There's another faction pulling the strings, the same group responsible for manipulating the events of September Eleventh."

"The Neocons? What would they have to gain?"

"Control. Once Iran falls under U.S. domination, the remaining nations that harbor Islamic radicals will be next in line, beginning with the country that controls the only significant oil reserves left in the world—"

"—Saudi Arabia." Ace shakes his head, overwhelmed by everything he is hearing. "Large Saudi reserves would justify funding an invasion . . . assuming the Royals were linked to this contingency plan."

Ramzi nods. "The threat from Iran has forced the House of Saud to trust the Neocons. Kelli believed the preemptive strike would occur shortly before the next presidential election, allowing the Republicans to once again use fear as their trump card."

"Where will the bombs go off? What are the target cities?"

"We don't know. Nor do we know how the weapons will be smuggled into the country."

"Why must they be smuggled at all? If these Neocons have access to—"

"The Neoconservatives are not the ones pulling the trigger. Unlike the events of September Eleventh, this is a very small, covert operation. Two Islamic radicals have been chosen as mules—puppets whose strings will lead back to Iran. The nuclear residue will be the key evidence—enriched uranium residue can be traced back to its original source, in this case fuel rods used by Iran's nuclear reactor. Kelli was kept out of the loop as to how this might be accomplished."

"Okay, so we go to the FBI, have them seal the ports."

"There are 317 ports of entry into the United States. Homeland Security inspects a mere 7 percent of the cargo, and those are only the official ports. Yachts, cruise ships, private jets . . . even with Promis, it's impossible to pinpoint where and how the nukes will enter the country."

Ace feels the blood vessels in his left arm constricting from stress. "Okay, so what's the plan? While you're out trying to instigate a revolution, how do we stop these nut jobs from taking out an American city?"

"Two ways. First, we expose the plot using Kelli's memoir. We blanket the internet and media, force it to become an election issue."

"Won't the GOP's election machine just spin it as more conspiracy theory, churned out by the liberal media? Based on the last election, the Democrats will be too afraid of any potential backblow to touch it."

"We have to try. It may cause certain individuals involved in the plot to back off."

"That's true. What's the second course of action my wife had in mind?"

"That . . . is a bit more tricky. We collapse the financial infrastructure of both the terrorists and the Neocons."

"How?"

"By using Promis. The program can tap into any computer, including those of financial institutions. Kelli used Promis to track the dirty money used by terrorist organizations. Days prior to September Eleventh and right up until the moment the first World Trade Tower fell, traders had been placing put calls on stocks against companies involved in the attacks. You are aware of this, yes?"

"My best friend, Mark . . . he died servicing those transactions."

"Kelli used Promis to trace the activity. Almost $15 billion of blood money eventually found its way into the bank accounts of major corporations, financial institutions, Saudi Royals, Afghani druglords, lobbyists, even politicians. The combined assets of the guilty total more than a trillion dollars." Ramzi holds up the CD-ROM case. "Promis can access every penny in every account—that was Kelli's plan—to use these funds to finance the revolution. The data is stored on this Promis disc. Kelli said you had the means to set the plan in motion—a former teammate, I believe; one who had the level of sophistication necessary to access, harbor, and redirect the funds."

Ace shakes his head, another piece of his wife's puzzle dropping into place. "Yeah, a former teammate. One she helped parole. For someone battling for her life against cancer, she sure managed to pull a lot of strings."

"Kelli was indeed a force of nature, but do not let your guard down. What your wife has outlined is extremely dangerous. Kelli's former contacts in the SSB have already targeted you and your family. You cannot have Promis on you when you travel; arrangements will have to be made to send it ahead to your contact in the States. Will you help us?"

Ace rubs the tension from his eyes. *Is this contingency plan of Kelli's really happening? Even if it's not, terrorists won't hesitate to use nuclear weapons. Either way, this is life and death on a massive scale, yet getting involved means placing the kids at risk. I'm already under scrutiny . . . the attack on the Apache means I've been deemed expendable. If I choose to be proactive, then maybe I can help derail things . . . if I do nothing, who's to say that one day they won't execute me, just like they did Kelli?*

"Before I agree to go through with this, there's something I want from you. There's a former CIA operative, a man named Scott Santa, Russian-American. He worked for Vinnell—I'm guessing he's still in the Persian Gulf. I want you to find him for me."

"Kelli's assassin?" Ramzi shakes his head. "This is very dangerous. It's better we handle him ourselves."

"No! It has to be me. I want to look the devil in his eyes as I take from him what he took from me."

"Ace, the man you seek is a trained killer, supported by various intelligence agencies. It is far too risky. Kelli would not approve."

"I wasn't asking her."

Ramzi sees the look in Ace's eyes. "Very well. But you must understand, the neocon machine . . . they also have Promis. You'll be watched and tracked every moment. You have children; they remain your Achilles' heel. You will need to make arrangements to keep them safe. You cannot know where they will be taken. Do you understand what I am telling you? If you're caught, these people know how to acquire information."

Ace nods, his pulse pounding in his throat as he recalls Kelli's video-taped warning.

The fight of your life . . .

"If a nation expects to be ignorant and free, it expects what never was and never will be. The People cannot be safe without information."

—THOMAS JEFFERSON

"Therefore, every Muslim and every honorable man who is not a Muslim must stand against the Americans, English, and Israelis and endanger their interests wherever they may be."

—AYATOLLAH AHMAD JANNATI,
Secretary Guardian Council,
Iran

"Last year, (Ion Sancho, head of Leon County, FL. elections) discovered the supposedly impossible—that Diebold Election Systems touch screens and optical scanning machines had serious security flaws. Sancho challenged hackers to break into his voting machines four times. They always succeeded. Sancho raised alarms. Florida secretary of state Sue Cobb, a Jeb Bush appointee, ignored him. And then they took away a $564,000 federal grant for disabled-accessible voting machinery."

—HOWARD GOODMAN,
Fort Lauderdale Sun-Sentinel,
March 26, 2006

CHAPTER 22

GARY LEE SCHAFER, DIRECTOR
RADICAL FUNDAMENTALIST UNIT
COUNTER-TERRORISM AND MIDDLE EAST SECTION
FBI–HQ
APRIL 24, 2012

Director Schafer:

I am forwarding surveillance footage submitted by Special Agent Elliott Green (155-16533-17) that confirms DOE subject Professor Eric Mingjuan Bi (file # 112-11292-377) came in contact with an UMBRA-classified subject (Tursi, Michael R.) on 3 January 2012. The nature of this meeting appears to be the delivery and installation of drywall and garage shelving, most likely a cover story for transporting the contents of two large unidentifiable packing crates into suspect Bi's garage several weeks later. Keeping in mind subject Bi is a professor of nuclear physics associated with two separate incidents of nuclear secrets espionage, I hereby request permission to conduct a FISA search of the subject's garage.

Charles Jones, Director, FBI: Springfield, Illinois (155-63775-17).

Gary Schafer curses to himself. He re-reads the e-mail a third time before hitting Reply.

Director Jones:

Thank you for forwarding the surveillance footage. As you know, UMBRA requires special clearance, far and above your current status. I will investigate the matter and take the appropriate measures. Please continue your diligent surveillance of subject Bi and report any and all new developments directly to me.

—G. L. Schafer, Director

Schafer hits Send. He contemplates erasing the message, thinks better of it, and prints a hard copy to be filed in Eric Bi's folder. Then he picks up the phone and dials the extension of his assistant, Jim Leary.

"Jim, do me a favor and pull the file of Special Agent Elliott Green. I believe he's based in Springfield, Illinois."

BRIDGEVIEW, ILLINOIS
APRIL 25, 2012
8:44 AM CST

THE VILLAGE OF BRIDGEVIEW IS LOCATED just west of Chicago, its 3.6 square miles supporting an urban population of just over fifteen thousand. Included among its populace is an active Muslim community.

Most of these families are simply seeking to maintain an Islamic identity. They send their children to school at a local *Madrassah*, where boys and girls are segregated while studying the Koran. Older girls must wear the *hijib*, a traditional head scarf that runs below the knees, even while participating in sports.

The struggle to remain moderate Muslims becomes challenging during worship at the Bridgeview mosque. Over the years, the mosque has attracted larger numbers of Palestinian-Americans, along with members of the Muslim Brotherhood, a militant group who have condemned American culture, praised suicide bombers, and prefer a more fundamentalist interpretation of Islam. The Brotherhood, whose members helped found the terrorist organization, Hamas, disguise their true intentions by running local charities and organizing peaceful political demonstrations.

More vocal and proactive than their moderate contemporaries, the Brotherhood began a fund-raising campaign several years ago, asking

Arab governments to help them "prevent the undoing of Islamic society at the hands of the West." More than a million dollars poured in from Kuwait, the Saudi government, and the religious ministry of the United Arab Emirates. In addition, Jordan's religious affairs ministry sent over Masoud Ali Masoud, a fifty-seven-year-old Palestinian, to work to at the Bridgeview mosque as an assistant prayer leader. Soon, a strict interpretation of Islam infiltrated the mosque, women ordered to cover their hair, segregated from their men during social events.

While there are over fifty other mosques in the Chicago area, few are as popular as the Bridgeview mosque, whose radical teachings draw more than two thousand congregants for Friday prayer.

◆ ◆ ◆

The 2009 Chevy Trail Blazer is parked outside the bank, its occupant, Jamal al-Yussuf, reading from the Koran . . . waiting.

A second vehicle parks nearby. Omar Kamel Radi knocks on the truck's passenger window. Jamal unlocks the door, allowing his fellow Iraqi entry. The two men exchange a quick embrace. "I can't believe I'm saying it, but it is actually good to see you. How are things in Los Angeles?"

"Good. The weather is beautiful."

"You are not smiling about the weather."

Omar nods. "I met someone, an aerobics instructor. She is blonde and so beautiful. I told her I am a foreign exchange student from Cairo, studying engineering. I bought several textbooks; I even attend classes."

"This is very dangerous. If your sponsor knew—"

"My sponsor is a lazy dog. He leaves me notes on occasion, but I never see him."

◆ ◆ ◆

Parked in a van across the street from the bank are Shane Torrence and Marco Fatigo. The two Strategic Support Branch "handlers" have been eavesdropping on their subjects since the Iraqis first entered the United States nine months earlier.

"Hear that, Marco? Your boy thinks you're a lazy dog."

"Maybe I should send him a copy of the videotape I took of him banging that peroxide blonde so he can watch himself do her from behind. Better yet, I'll do her and send him a tape."

"You're a cruel man. My guy would never think of looking at an American woman. Too religious. Prays every night."

"Either that or he's a sausage smuggler."

The side door of the van is yanked open. Michael Tursi hands each man a coffee and bag of doughnuts, saving himself the one in the cardboard carrier. "I see I missed our Muslims' happy reunion."

"Arabs," Torrence corrects, taking a bite out of a chocolate creme doughnut. "You've got your Arabs and your Muslims. These two are Arabs."

"You can be both, moron."

"Turk's right." Marco says, draining his coffee. "Now your guy, Shane, he's Shi'ite, definitely a Muslim. Omar, the kid I'm babysitting . . . Sunni Arab. Saddam was Sunni, and he hated the Muslims. Turned out the whole reason he was posturing so much about weapons of mass destruction was because of Iran, not the U.S. He was more afraid of a Shi'ite invasion than anything we were going to do."

"Shut the hell up." Tursi snaps a fresh clip into his gun. "Read the damn dossier, Marco; your Sunni converted to Islam. Far as I'm concerned, they're all bomb-toting towel-heads. Stay here, I'm taking a walk." He exits the van, slamming the side door closed.

Marco digs through his bag of doughnuts. "What's he so edgy about?"

"FBI caught him on surveillance tape back in January at Bi's house."

"Hell. Where was Schafer?"

"He didn't know. It was a DOE operation—nothing to do with counter-terrorism. But you know the Turk; he won't sleep until he cleans up the mess."

♦ ♦ ♦

Back in the Chevy Trail Blazer, Omar's good mood has festered into frustration. "You wouldn't understand, Jamal. You are Shi'ite. You are a simple desert people, disobedient to God. You are unbelievers who worship the teachings of Ali, the Prophet Muhammad's nephew. No Shi'ite will ever rule Iraq."

"And you are a Sunni dog," Jamal retorts. "Was Iraq better with Saddam?"

"Saddam was excessive in his cruelty, I'll admit, but Iraqis remain united only by the rule of the sword. And I didn't always despise your people. It was the Americans who divided us. The army they trained were all Shia and Kurd. No Sunni was permitted an officer's rank, as if we'd bring Saddam back from the dead."

"If you believe what you say, then why are you here?"

Omar stares out the passenger window at the bank. "The occupation won't last forever. When the Americans leave, the Iranians will move in. I refuse to see my country ruled by Islamic clerics."

"Yet you joined the Islamic Revolutionary Guard."

"What choice did I have? Haditha, Anna, Qaim, Rawa, Ramadi . . . all had fallen to Islamic rebels worse than the Taliban. The Americans have no idea who they are even fighting, so the bastards shoot everyone. If it were not for the money being sent to my family, I would not be here."

"Is that the only reason you are here? Money?"

Omar turns to Jamal. "At first I wanted revenge, but now I want something better for my family. Is that so bad? With the money I send, they could leave Iraq."

"Not me. If I die *shahid*, I will go to a place in heaven near God's other messengers. Is there a greater glory?"

Omar snorts a laugh. "You think Allah will let you enter heaven after slaughtering innocent women and children? You will not die *shahid*. You seek revenge for your father and brother, for your younger cousins. Revenge is not part of Islamic law, nor is martyrdom, no matter what Al-Qaeda preaches."

"The cleric who recruited me in Tehran, he said this assignment would strike a blow to the West's military agenda. For that I am prepared to die."

"Jamal, this does not have to be a suicide mission."

"*Shahid* is not suicide. Has your blonde American made you a fool and a coward?"

"Cease your tongue and listen. When I was in Tehran I heard rumors that many of the Magnificent Nineteen were still alive. Mohamed Atta and Salem al-Hazni—"

"And Saeed Alghamdi, and the two Alshehris, yes, I heard this too! At Qods many asked about Atta's behavior, questioning whether he was truly a devout Muslim. We had read stories about his drinking, about visiting bars and strippers the night before the attacks. Our trainer confided to us. He told us Atta and the other planners . . . that these men were never even onboard the planes. They had been traveling on false passports, instructed the night before the attacks to get publicly intoxicated and to scream insults at the infidels so as to attract attention to themselves. We were told these men were no one's fools, that they had purposely allowed their driver's licenses to be photocopied, that they even used public library computers to send e-mail using unencrypted messages, all to leave false trails to the FBI."

"It's true!" Omar jumps in. "Their apartments . . . why would they leave behind ridiculous information about stealing planes, as if they wished to be caught? The American Press reported it, and the infidels swallowed every falsehood."

"Omar, our sponsors . . . they instructed us to leave behind our own false trail."

"The laptop. Yes, I have thought about that too. And why must we drive two days to this town, just to wire money home to our families?"

Jamal checks his watch. The bank has opened. Do you wish to go first, or should I?"

"Go on, Shi'ite. Martyrs before rebels. I still have something to live for."

American Hospital
Dubai, UAE
April 26, 2012
6:13 am Local Time

Starlight. It blinds . . . then fades. Blinds, then fades . . .

"He's coming to."

Ace blinks open his eyes. Through blurred vision he can make out a gray room and a tall figure, hovering close by, checking his pulse.

"Ah, there we go. Good morning, my friend. My name is Gary Groves. I'm a physician here at the American hospital."

"I'm in the States?"

"Sorry, no, you're in Dubai. Nurse, bring the lights up please."

The room brightens, forcing Ace to squint.

"The local police found you wandering close to the highway. Heat exhaustion, dementia, no identification. Can you tell us your name?"

"Futrell. Ashley Futrell."

"Well, Mr. Futrell, you've got a nasty head injury. Looks to be about a day old. You must have been wandering around out there for quite some time. Can you remember what happened?"

"I was . . . in a taxi. At night. I was heading to . . . to Aqua Dunya, to see the *Desert Pearl* cruise ship. I accidently left my wallet at my hotel."

"What hotel?" A Dubai police officer enters the room.

"The Baynunah Hilton."

"Continue."

"The driver got mad because I had no money. He pulled over to the side of the road, we were out in the middle of nowhere. He demanded I give him my laptop. When I refused, we got into a fight. I don't remember much after that."

"What is your business in the Arab Emirates?"

"I'm a petroleum geologist, recently out of work. I came here seeking employment."

"I am sorry you had these troubles," the officer says. "Before you are discharged, I need you to fill out a police report."

"Yeah, sure. Then I think I'd just like to go home."

"In the aftermath of the Dubai ports dispute, the Bush administration is hiring a Hong Kong conglomerate to help detect nuclear materials inside cargo passing through the Bahamas to the United States and elsewhere. The administration acknowledges the no-bid contract with Hutchison Whampoa Ltd., represents the first time a foreign company will be involved in running a sophisticated U.S. radiation detector at an overseas port without American customs agents present. A U.S. military intelligence report, once marked 'secret,' cited Hutchison in 1999 as a potential risk for smuggling arms and other prohibited materials into the United States from the Bahamas."

—ASSOCIATED PRESS,
March 23, 2006

"I see the White House is like a subway, you have to put in coins to open the gates."

—JOHNNY CHUNG,
Chinese lobbyist

CHAPTER 23

Operated by the Port Authorities of New York and New Jersey, John F. Kennedy International Airport (JFK) is located in the southeastern section of Queens County, New York City, on Jamaica Bay on 4,930 acres. The airport processes more passengers and air cargo than any port in the United States and handles the most international arrivals, between 150 and 160 aircraft a day. JFK's Contraband Enforcement Team processes 6 million parcels annually, confiscating huge quantities of counterfeit consumer products, undeclared currency, and illegal narcotics, averaging close to eight hundred drug seizures a week.

Like herded sheep, Ace and the other passengers from Emirates Airlines Flight 201 file through customs, everyone weary from the fourteen-hour trip. Guessing at which domestic line is moving quickest, Ace takes his place behind a dozen other Americans . . . and waits.

Ramzi had set Ace free on a stretch of highway close to Dubai. They had gone over his story a dozen times, one they felt offered the best chance of avoiding an official U.S. inquiry. The Apache pilot would be taken to another medical facility two days after Ace's arrival in New York, and released.

The line moves forward as a family of five is led behind a Red Cross curtain.

Ace rubs his left arm, registering stress-induced, catheter-like pain in his veins. *They wanted me dead . . . what happens now? Will the CIA believe I walked miles in the desert after the crash? Did Schall have anything to do with it? Will he simply accept my report on the oil fields, or does he plan on parading me in front of the Senate as a witness? Do they suspect Promis is being smuggled into the country?*

"Next."

Ace hands the female customs officer his passport.

"Anything to declare?"

"No."

She stamps his passport. "Second curtain is open. Remove your jacket and roll up your sleeves."

"What for?"

"Bird Flu inoculation. Next."

"Wait, why do I need—"

She points to a sign, giving him the tired look of someone who has answered the same question repeatedly for forty hours a week.

Every person entering the U.S. is required to be inoculated for Avian Bird Flu prior to entering the country.

"Next in line."

Ace moves to the second of six curtains displaying the Red Cross emblem. A nurse, identified by her badge as Beth Newman, directs him to an empty chair. "Afternoon. Where do you want it, arm or cheek?" She holds up a large hypodermic needle.

"Don't you have a pill?"

"Homeland Security says they're working on it. Sure would make my life easier."

"What's in that thing? How do I know it's safe?"

She hands him a flyer. "That'll explain everything. Now unless you want to go back to wherever you flew in from, I'd take the shot. Arm or butt cheek?"

"As a symbolic salute to Homeland Security, stick me in the ass." Unbuckling his belt, he drops his trousers and ceremoniously flashes Nurse Newman his left butt cheek.

She jabs him with the needle.

"Ouch! How bad is this flu threat anyway? They've been talking about a pandemic for years."

"Potentially, really bad. We've heard about a dozen recent outbreaks in Asia and Europe, worst one was a small community in France. Killed about half the people infected. Tonight when you go to bed, you ought to thank God for the American pharmaceutical industry."

Ace buckles his pants and limps away, suddenly feeling uneasy.

CARBONDALE, ILLINOIS
3:47 PM CST

THE ABRUPT KNOCK STARTLES ELLIOTT GREEN from an afternoon nap. The FBI agent checks his watch, verifying Professor Bi will not be returning from his bowling league for another hour. Then he heads downstairs, his gun tucked in the back of his blue jeans.

The television repairman is an olive-skinned Italian with dark hair and a five-o'clock shadow.

Green opens the door. "Can I help you?"

Shane Torrence flashes the falsified FBI identification. "Only if you're Agent Green. Jerry Bobo, I'm your relief." He enters the house and looks around. "Smells like old people."

"Tell me about it." Green shuts the door behind him. "I wasn't expecting you until next Tuesday."

"I can leave."

"No, no, I'm more than ready." Green leads him upstairs to the master suite, the bedroom, an oasis of electronics and dunes of dirty laundry. "Sorry about the mess, like I said—"

"No worries." The SSB officer scans the room and sees the CD-ROM files. "Bet you're eager to get home."

"You have no idea."

"Bring me up to speed, and we'll get you on the road."

MONTAUK, NEW YORK
11:47 PM EST

THE KIDS ARE IN BED ASLEEP, having survived their father's hugs and inquisitions about school. Now it is just Ace and Jennifer, alone in the family room.

"It's a nice night. Want to take a walk by the water?"

She smiles. "I would have thought you'd be tired of the sand by now. Just let me grab my coat."

♦ ♦ ♦

The moon is three-quarters and high, its glow filtered behind a haze of clouds. For a brief moment Ace is back on the Saudi desert, alone on the empty stretch of highway. His life, once a set routine of work, travel, and little-league hockey games now seems to be leaping forward in quantum episodes of chaos, everything stemming from his wife's murder.

Four and a half months since Kelli died . . . is that even possible? Everything since the funeral . . . like some bad dream. When will I wake up? How can I even move past the grief when she's reaching out for me from beyond the grave, putting me on a road to who-knows-where? How do I know this nuclear scheme is even true? Because she said so on tape? Because some former colleague of hers showed me a CD-ROM, spinning it into some unverifiable tale of conspiracy? So maybe we are running out of oil, and yes, there is the possibility of a nuclear terrorist attack, but would Iran really have the balls to arm these guys? Is it really necessary to risk my life, to make Leigh and Sammy orphans? This mission of hers sounds like suicide.

Suicide.

The word shakes him to the core. Years ago, after the attempt, Ace had woken in a hospital room, his wrists bandaged, his arms strapped to the bed rails. He had bawled his eyes out, feeling alone and humiliated. Kelli was on a road trip, but Tet was by his side, always supportive, never judging. "Okay, Ace, so you screwed up. Forget about it. Just figure things out and move on. Remember what coach always yells when one of us goofs up: 'Bring 'em in, huddle 'em up, and focus on the next play.' "

Suicide . . .

Suicide was about dealing with fear and pain . . . it was a choice— the anguish of having to go on versus a less-painful alternative. Life and death. Now he was being asked to choose again . . . this time to risk his life and all he cherished to prevent the unthinkable.

"Ace, you okay? You haven't said a word."

He turns to Jennifer, who is staring at him. "Yeah, fine. Actually, I did want to talk to you, but—" he looks around, the two of them alone on the beach, exposed on the deserted shoreline. "Let's sit back here, by the dunes."

"Oh-kay." She follows him to the crest and sits next to him, their silhouettes now hidden behind sand and sawgrass. "So? What did you want to tell me?"

"This has to stay between us. What I'm going to say may upset you. I don't want you to react. Just hear me out."

He tells her everything . . . from his meeting with the CIA director to why he was really in the Persian Gulf. He describes Kelli's video and Promis, and the future attack being orchestrated by the Neocons. She remains stoic through it all, her jaw muscles knotted behind clenched teeth.

When he's through, she continues staring at the ocean.

"Jen?"

"What is it you want from me?"

"Your opinion, for one. You worked with Kelli—Butch and Sundance. Is there any truth to what I've just told you?"

She chokes out a chuckle, wiping strands of dark hair and tears from her eyes. "I am such an ass. Here I am, thinking that maybe you wanted to be alone with me . . . you know, for other reasons. Instead we're back to more of your conspiracy theories."

"You mean? Oh wow, I wasn't, I mean I could be—"

"Just forget it."

"No, Jen, listen, it's just my head's so screwed up right now and—"

"Shut up, just—" She looks away. "To answer your question, yes, there's some truth to it, but it's not what you think. Some of the more radical elements of the Bush administration, Rummy's people, had talked with Kelli about it years ago. They asked her to identify key population zones in both Iran and Saudi Arabia. But it was just the usual war game stuff, nothing more."

"Targets for what?"

"Biological and chemical weapons, mostly. Something that would wipe out a population—"

"—and leave the infrastructure intact." Ace feels his left arm tighten again.

"It was just conversation, Ace, it happens all the time in the Pentagon. As for Kelli's video, remember your wife wasn't exactly stable these last few years. Dealing with cancer, the thought of dying, leaving you and the kids, and that whole Kabbalah thing . . . suddenly everything made her feel guilty about something. McKuin's in office now, and he's anything but a Neocon. A lot of the nut-jobs from the Bush regime were pardoned, but I seriously doubt they'd want to risk their freedom by being accused of treason. Just let it go, okay? Iran knows it's suicide to arm a terrorist organization with enriched uranium. As for this whole oil deal, it will work itself out."

"Work itself out? You still don't get it yet, do you? This isn't about long lines at the gas pump or ten-dollar-a-gallon prices. This is about going dry. We're not ready for this. There is no substitute in place for oil. Zero, nothing. We should have committed to a different path a decade ago—probably two decades ago—but we didn't, so now we're screwed. Without oil you can't grow enough food to feed the masses, let alone get the goods to market. You can't heat your home or drive your car. Without oil, our entire economy collapses. If the last tanker stopped shipping oil tomorrow, within months a million people would starve to death or die of medical complications in New York City alone. Transportation, electricity, the economy . . . the military. Your Neocon pals knew; Jen, most of them worked in the industry. Oil filled a need, gave them an excuse to invade. Since then, they've managed to steal two elections, regain control of both Houses, the Judiciary, and the White House while invading Afghanistan and Iraq, all while making a fortune in the process. Problem is, they took their eye off the real enemy, and now they want to get back into the game by staging a small nuclear attack . . . leading to response that will kill 70 million Iranians. Still, it's far fewer than the number of those who may eventually die after we run out of oil, which will tally in the billions. Call it ledger-sheet logic. To these heartless bastards, it was a no-brainer."

"Stop! What you're saying . . . it's too preposterous. And President McKuin would never allow any of this to happen."

"He won't be around. You watch. He'll be sacrificed, just like Kelli and Tet. Just like the Americans who died in those planes and in those buildings. Prescott's McKuin's Brutus; even he must know it."

She walks away, following the path back to the house, leaving him alone with conspiracy theories that even he doesn't believe.

Way to go, schmuck. All she wanted was a little affection. Instead, you gave her the end of the world.

"They think they are absolutely right. That's one of the characteristics of fundamentalism—'I think I am right because I am close to God, and anybody who disagrees with me is inherently wrong and therefore inferior.' "

—PRESIDENT JIMMY CARTER,
on the fundamentalist Christian right

"Halliburton has pulled off the impossible. They have actually done a worse job under its second Iraq oil contract than it did under the original no-bid contract."

—REPRESENTATIVE HENRY A. WAXMAN,
on a fifteen-page report by auditors citing that
Halliburton intentionally overcharged, using hidden calculations to bill the U.S. government
in costs it never incurred.
House Committee on Government Reform,
March 29, 2006.

"It's not the people who vote that counts; It's the people who count the votes."

—JOSEPH STALIN

CHAPTER 24

Christina Jordan, President McKuin's campaign manager, hovers over her boss as his makeup artist applies fresh base beneath his eyes. "It's important we maintain a presence, Mr. President. The Democrats may be down to three candidates, but they're still getting around-the-clock media attention. We can't appear to be a lame duck while they continue their attack."

The president nods, his eyes closed, eyelids fluttering.

Christina pulls the makeup woman aside. "Roxanne, he looks washed out, like he just had chemo. Can't you fix that?"

Roxanne Dunlap, herself an ovarian cancer survivor, shoots Christina a nasty look. "He's sweating. I'm doing my best."

"It's the lights," the president retorts weakly.

"He was sick earlier," chimes in Mario Childress, the president's six-foot, three-inch 240-pound Secret Service bodyguard. "Said he had a bad headache."

"I'll be fine."

"Of course you will," Christina says, fixing her dishwater blonde hair in the mirror. "The gym's packed, and the TV crews are set. A quick speech, and we're in the limo and back on Air Force One in less than two hours."

"I don't know, Tina," Roxanne adds. "He didn't look so good before the makeup."

"There are twenty-seven district delegates from the Indiana State Republican Convention expecting to see him, pale or not. This is a key swing state, Mr. President."

McKuin nods. His pulse is racing, his skin, cool and clammy, and the dull ache is building again in his head.

"—at which time you'll be introduced by Luke Messer. He's the executive director of Indiana's Republican Party. He's represents the 57th district. Luke's a sixth generation Hoosier, so I slipped in a few football references on your teleprompter."

"Basketball," Agent Childress mumbles.

"Really? Anyway, Shelbyville's also the home of Thomas Hicks. He was the twenty-first vice president of the United States, under Grover Cleveland and . . . Mr. President?"

"Oh, hell—" Roxanne grabs McKuin's head as it flops backward, his mouth choking up a bloody bile. In one motion, the Secret Service man swoops in and catches the president in his left palm while simultaneously activating an alert switch on his shoulder with his right hand. Pushing the makeup artist aside, he scoops the president up in both arms, gently lowering him to the floor—

—as a dozen more agents rush the room, sweeping along with them the president's medical team.

Atlantic City Expressway
New Jersey
5:07 pm EST

The navy-blue Chevy Astrovan weaves its way through a convergence of lanes near the Haddonfield exit as it merges onto Route 42–South. Ace glances at the mile marker, his adrenaline pumping. *Eight more miles. He'd better be there.*

He had begun his journey earlier that morning—a seemingly innocent trip to the dry cleaners, followed by a stop at the shopping mall. He had parked in an underground garage, visited the sporting goods store to pick up a hockey pad for Sammy, grabbed a quick cup of coffee and a doughnut, and had returned to the garage—

—to Jeffrey Gordon's car, the keys hidden behind the front passenger tire. While his friend drove out of the garage in Ace's Corvette, Ace had waited another fifteen minutes before departing the mall lot in the Gordon family van.

He had headed south, paralleling the New Jersey Turnpike before catching Interstate 95, continuing south through Philadelphia. The detour had added an extra hour, but he had no choice, knowing the turnpike's tollbooth's fast-pass sensors would register Jeff's car, the information potentially received by Homeland Security.

◆ ◆ ◆

Ramzi's plan, to avert the next 9/11 by exposing it to the masses, was not sitting well with Ace. If there was anything the Neocons had proven, it was that by controlling key factions of the government and media one could get away with even the most outrageous violations of code, conduct, and American law. The Constitution could be trampled upon with no repercussions. Bribery and ethics charges could be swept under the rug. Elections could be falsified, whistle-blowers, ridiculed. The vice president could even shoot a man in the face without having to submit to a police inquiry at the scene. And when someone finally did go to jail, the president, upon leaving office, would simply issue his "get out of jail free" pardon, proclaiming the violator had "served his country faithfully and had found the error of his ways with Jesus."

It was Promis's ability to track and move the bad guys' money that had ultimately committed Ace to the mission. With Kelli's data and Promis's access, Ace could play a global game of Robin Hood, using the world's dirty money to fund clean, alternative energy resources that might ultimately avert the Big Rollover. For once, the guilty and greedy would have to pay for their crimes—in every sense of the word.

He owed that to Mark.

◆ ◆ ◆

Ace slows as he passes mile marker 37. *There . . . up ahead.* He blinks his lights at a car parked along the side of the road. A heavyset, bearded man in beige cutoff shorts and a midnight-green Philadelphia Eagles jersey steps out from behind the raised hood and waves at him for assistance.

Ace pulls over. "Need some help?"

"What was your first clue?" Kenneth Franklin Keene Jr. climbs inside the van, punching his former teammate on the shoulder. "Good to see you, asswipe."

Ace drives off, the scent of tobacco and sweat is pungent. "Life must be good. You really let yourself go."

"I was in prison, douche bag."

"I watch TV. Don't prisoners have access to weight rooms or barbells in the yard or something? You're supposed to be an athlete."

"That was twenty years ago, dog meat, and I was the friggin' kicker. And who are you to talk? At least I'm chillin'. You look like you ate stress for breakfast."

"You've got that right. Hey, put the cigarette away; it's not my car."

"You send me the freakin' neocon version of Frankenstein's monster, and I can't even smoke?"

"You sound frazzled."

"Frazzled? Dude, I passed frazzled a week ago. The only reason we're even speaking is because your old lady arranged my release."

"And here I thought you'd be salivating at the chance to make a big score."

"Money's fine if you're alive to spend it. Kelli was playing with fire. She must have tracked every drug deal, covert weapons sale, and money laundering scheme the Feds have dipped their wick in since '82. Heroin flowing out of Afghanistan, SAM missiles sold to the Sauds—name a terrorist organization, and I'll show you how they got funded, what they bought, the trail of bank accounts the money passed through, and which Richie Rich the transaction made richer. This thing's a friggin' global spider's web of the nasty and powerful. You go public with it and they'll eat you for lunch."

"And my plan?"

Keene grins. "You mean to steal their money?"

"Blood money. We'd just be re-appropriating it."

"Re-appropriating, good word. A lot of my cell mates were in for the same thing. Look dude, I'm a hacker. There's nothing to hack here; Kelli did that for us. But even with Promis, you can't just move a trillion dollars, not without sending off a million warning bells and whistles. This has to be done on the sly. Bleed it quietly over weeks—even months—every transaction masked, every money trail erased. Plus you've got to set-up bogus trails. Create histories . . . everything to mask the money before you can move it into legitimate accounts without sending up any red flags. It takes a real artist to do that, an expert in COBOL."

"What's COBOL?"

"It's an acronym, stands for Common Business Oriented Language, the premier high-level computer programming dialogue of our time. Banks used to write all their code in COBOL, most financial institutions still do, especially in third-world nations where a lot of this dough is stashed. COBOL was also the first programming language mandated by the Department of Defense."

"I take it you have someone in mind?"

Keene smiles. "Oh, yeah. The COBOL queen. Her name's—"

"Don't tell me—it's better I don't know. Can she do the job?"

"Dude, she's a python. Back when the Y2K deal was going on, she made a fortune writing code to protect systems. With Kelli's info and Promis as a delivery system, she'll create a COBOL worm that'll hack into every account and electronically transfer the funds through a matrix so complex that Magellan couldn't find his way home. Once downloaded into the mainframe at the National Commercial Bank in Saudi Arabia, we'll be able to—"

"Whoa . . . this has to be downloaded from a Saudi bank?"

"It's the perfect insertion point. The NCB's the biggest bank in the Middle East. At some stage, almost every dirty dollar either originated there or passed through on its way to another financial institution. It's the central hub in almost every Al-Qaeda transaction funded by a Saudi prince and ol' King what's-his-puss, and we're talking hundreds of billions. Download the worm and it'll flow outward like the big bang—a million tentacles reaching into a million financial institutions, and we'll withdraw every dirty dollar . . . eventually."

"Eventually?"

"Again, steady progression. Just enough to keep the auditors busy without alerting the Feds."

"How do you plan to enter a Saudi bank and download the worm?"

"That's your end, Mister Hero Quarterback, not mine."

"You expect me to walk inside the biggest financial institution in Saudi Arabia, find my way to a computer terminal, and download a program?"

"It's our only real option. Maybe your old lady was going to do that, I dunno. You'll need at least twenty minutes on the terminal, thirty tops. Once the worm's in the system, there's no stopping it. Everything'll be time released, with domestic monies staying in the States and foreign investments remaining overseas. That way we don't start collapsing economies . . . except, of course, in the states that sponsor terrorism. Those we'll flush like turds."

"What's in it for you?"

"Kelli allocated $15 million, but my associate and I expect double that fee or no deal."

"Thirty million? For a programming job?"

"Do you have any idea what this entails? We're talking tens of thousands of man hours. I'll need to set up an entire organization—a legitimate company of illegitimate computer geeks that can be trusted to keep their mouths shut, not that we'll give them any clue as to what they're actually working on. But the reward still has to justify the risks, and the risks are death. Once the powers-that-be figure out they're being systematically robbed, they'll come after us, guns blazing."

"What about seed money? You'll need to rent office space, purchase computers . . . I can probably get you twenty grand."

"See, dude, this is what I'm talking about. Move anything more than a few hundred bucks out of your account, and the Feds'll be all over your ass. No, the money we'll use is already in a safe, hidden beneath the tiles under your clothes dryer. Combination is the day of the month you, Leigh, and Sammy were born, in that chronological order."

Ace looks at Keene, dumbfounded.

"Kelli told me about it the day I was paroled. She didn't say how much, and I knew better than to ask, but she was obviously planning this for quite a while."

"Obviously."

"So where's all this blood money going, Robin Hood? Do you have a list?"

Ace reaches into his pocket and withdraws a hard diskette and hands it to Keene. "The first $700 million needs to be dispersed into a series of 527 accounts, accessible only to Kelli's cousin Jennifer. The next chunk of change gets invested into alternative energy companies. After that, educational programs and charities across the board. I earmarked $4 billion for Lance Armstrong's Cancer Foundation."

"Damn. That should buy a lot of wristbands, huh?"

"It used to drive Kelli crazy, even before she got sick, that the Pentagon could spend $70 billion every budget on Iraq while hundreds of thousands of Americans were dying each year of cancer. Armstrong lobbied the Bush White House for a billion dollars and received pennies. Pennies for people, dollars for war."

"This'll be like friggin' Christmas."

"The 9/11 Family Fund gets a nice deposit as well."

"I'm sure Mark's family will appreciate that."

"You'll see one more familiar name on the list. It sets aside $5 million in an account registered to Mitch Wagner. Make sure he can get to the funds without any hassle."

"Wagner? As in Wags, our old Left Tackle? What're you cutting him in for?"

"Wags doesn't know it yet, but he and his wife are going to be taking in my kids."

"Oh." For the first time Keene feels the weight of the conversation.

They pass mile marker 26, along with a sign indicating another five miles until the Frank S. Farley Service Plaza.

"Ace, there's something else. Kelli left you an encoded message."

"What kind of message? What did it say?"

"It was a map, some out-of-the-way place way up in Canada. She was pretty insistent you go."

"Go to Canada? What for?"

"She wanted you to find someone named Casper."

"Casper? This is a joke, right?"

"I don't think so. She used the term, 'on the souls of our children.' "

"This is nuts. Homeland Security's all over my ass. How did she expect me to cross the border without getting caught?"

"She, uh, left you a fake passport and drivers licence. I printed and laminated everything . . . Stephen."

"Stephen?"

"Stephen Murphy. That's your new identity. You're a Canadian living in Melbourne, Australia, in the oil and gas safety business." Keene digs into his pants pocket, retrieving a plastic freezer bag containing the forged documents. "Your wife, she was really something, huh?"

"Unbelievable."

Ace follows the far left lane into the rest stop. "K.J., I'm really counting on you here; if we do this thing, you can't screw it up."

"Hey, Cochese, I'm ice water."

"You weren't against Tennessee."

"Screw you! It was a bad snap, and I still hit the goalpost from forty-eight yards. And who the hell are you to talk, Mr. Three Interceptions and a Fumble in the Orange Bowl. Just worry about how you're going to make it into that Saudi bank."

Ace parks. The two former teammates exit the car without informal good-byes, playing out their roles for any prying eyes. Keene heads for the gas station, and Ace walks toward the main building to use the restroom.

A crowd has gathered around a television, their stunned expressions telling all.

"*. . . again, if you're just joining us, President David Francis McKuin was airlifted to an Indiana hospital earlier this afternoon after suffering what doctors say was a massive stroke. The president was pronounced dead on arrival. Vice President Ellis Prescott has been sworn in as the forty-fifth president of the United States. We are told he will be addressing the nation later this evening.*"

Ace stares at the monitor, the blood rushing from his face.

Those bastards . . . it's really begun.

"I would like to call on the Arab world to enter into the world of peaceful use of nuclear energy with all speed and momentum."

—AMR MOUSSA,
Arab League leader,
March 29, 2006

"Today, a remarkable goal of the Islamic Republic of Iran's defense forces was realized with the successful test-firing of a new missile with greater technical and tactical capabilities than those previously produced."

—GENERAL HOSSEIN SALAMI,
Air Force chief in Iran's Elite Revolutionary Guards,
on the test-firing of a new multi-warhead missile not detectable by radar, capable of reaching Israel and U.S. bases in the Middle East.
April 1, 2006

CHAPTER 25

Ace guides the Corvette through the dark streets of his neighborhood. He turns left down his cul-de-sac, his pulse pounding as he spots the black sedan parked in his driveway. *Bastards, they must've caught K.J. What if they made him a deal? Turn me in, and he walks. Guy's on probation, I never should have trusted him!*

He slows, driving down the left side of the street. Lowering his window, he positions the plastic baggy holding the fake passport and driver's license in his left hand. Approaching a neighbor's mailbox, he yanks it open and shoves the contents inside, all without braking.

Circling the cul-de-sac, he swerves around the sedan and parks in his driveway, his high beams momentarily blinding the CIA director, who is already approaching from the stone path that leads to the Futrells' front door.

Ace's mind dials back to a distant memory—Kelli teaching him about facial expressions, body language, and eye contact. *Head position tells a lot. Don't tilt, and don't raise your chin. Look straight at your interrogator, and never look away, no matter what he throws at you.*

He keeps the headlights on a moment longer just to annoy David Schall, then climbs out of the low-slung sports car. Glancing up, he notices Jennifer looking out from behind the curtain of an upstairs window. Watching everything.

"Director Schall, don't you ever sleep?"

"Where were you today, Ace?"

"Gay pride parade, communist rally, the usual thing."

"Answer the question!"

Ace returns the man's glare. "Atlantic City. There's a sub shop on Arctic Avenue. You'd like it, it's called the White House. Unlike the place in DC, these guys actually provide a public service."

"You expect me to believe you took your friend's car on a six-hour jaunt just to get a sandwich?"

"Cheesesteak, and they're the best on the planet, rolls are brought in fresh every hour." Ace reaches inside the passenger side open window and pulls out a heavy, brown paper bag, a half-dozen two-foot-long hoagies and steak sandwiches protruding out the top. "I'd offer you one, but I really don't like you."

"You took Gordon's car."

"Still tracking my whereabouts? I thought we had a deal." Ace moves closer, looking Schall straight in the eye. "Not that it's any of your business, but Jeff was entertaining an important client and was stuck with his wife's car, so I let him borrow mine."

"You're playing a dangerous game."

"Game? What game? I ran your little errand and almost got myself killed. Much to my surprise, it turns out there's plenty of oil in Saudi Arabia. Who knows, maybe I'll start working for Saudi Aramco."

"How'd you manage to cross sixty miles of desert?"

"I didn't. The chopper crashed, next thing I know I'm in a Dubai hospital. Someone obviously pulled me from the wreckage. I assumed it was one of your guys."

"Ramzi Karim?"

"Who?" *Lock eyes, don't look away.*

"You're a bad liar, Ace. Karim's ex-CIA, he's stirring up a lot of trouble in the Persian Gulf. By now, you know he was friends with your wife. Close friends. The kind that spent a lot of late nights together, or so I've heard."

"Screw you and your mind games." Ace pushes him aside and heads for the house.

"They found the Apache pilot, Ace. He was dead. Shot once in the heart."

Ace freezes.

"You're in way over your head, my friend. I'm offering you free advice, be wise and take it. Find yourself another job, love on your kids, and walk away from this mess before someone else you care about gets hurt."

Ace swallows back the bile rising up his clenched throat. He remains silent, the adrenaline coursing through his body causing every nerve and muscle to tremble. He refuses to move, waiting in silence as the sedan backs out of his driveway and pulls away.

CARBONDALE, ILLINOIS
MAY 7, 2012
10:12 AM CST

ELLIOTT GREEN DRIVES SLOWLY PAST PROFESSOR Bi's home and parks his Subaru two doors down from the residence he has spent the last six months living in. Climbing out of the car, he removes his sport coat, handing it to his wife. "I'll only be a minute."

"Elliott, if we're late for the ceremony, my sister will never speak to me again, which makes you a dead man walking." Carol Green tilts the rearview mirror toward her, applying a fresh layer of lipstick.

"It was my grandfather's Swiss Army knife; I can't just leave it. Besides, I know my guy's routine. He won't be home for hours."

Green walks briskly past the neighbor's home and cuts across the front yard of the stakeout house. He knocks on the door several times. Waits. Glances across the street at Eric Bi's home.

Something's different.

He knocks again. Then he locates the spare key under the planter and lets himself in.

"Hello?" No response. *Maybe he's sleeping?*

He hurries upstairs into the master suite, the bedroom door open. Bed, linens—

—no surveillance equipment . . . everything gone!

He races back down the stairs and out the front door. He dodges a car as he sprints across the street to Professor Bi's garage and looks in the window.

No cars. No tools. Empty!

Cursing aloud, he crosses the driveway to the side door leading into the kitchen. He peers inside and sees nothing.

Walking quickly back to his car, Green yanks open his wife's door, popping open the glove compartment.

"Elliott, what are you doing?"

"Stay here." A quick search produces the pick—a long, thin piece of metal that curves up at the end like a dentist's instrument. He locates the thin flathead screwdriver, pockets it, and grabs his gun.

"Elliott, don't do this! Remember what happened six years ago."

Ignoring her, he hustles back across the street, his dress shirt already tinged with sweat. He tries the kitchen door, verifies it's locked, and inserts the screwdriver into the keyhole. Applying torque, he offsets the lock's plug from its housing, opening a slight ledge that allows him access with the pick. Gently, he feels his way in, prodding and lifting each pin pair completely into the lock housing, listening for the familiar *click* of the upper pin as it falls into place on the ledge in the shaft—

—popping open the lock.

Green enters, gun drawn. "Hello?" He moves from room to empty room, his pulse quickening.

The front door bashes open, Green greeting the blinding swath of daylight with the business end of his revolver. "Freeze!"

"Ahh!" Startled, Denice "Daisy" Webb spills droplets of scalding-hot Starbucks coffee across her bare arm, adding a voluminous breath to her already ear-piercing scream.

"Where's Bi?"

"Don't shoot!"

"Professor Bi, the guy who lives here. Where is he?"

"I swear I don't know. My husband, Ken . . . he bought the house a week ago from a realtor. Please, mister—"

Sold the house . . . Bi's gone! You blew it, schmuck. Green smacks himself in the forehead and lowers his gun. Looks around. "Okay, this realtor of yours, where can I—"

He screams as the hot coffee catches him flush in the face. Green drops the gun, panting in agony, then looks up in time to see the two hundred–pound half-Italian, half-Choctaw Indian charge him like a bad-tempered Rhino.

"FBI! I'm FBI!" He fumbles for his ID, then covers up as the irate woman delivers several body blows and a kneecap to his face.

FLAGSTAFF, ARIZONA

LOCATED AT A 7,000–FOOT ELEVATION, THE Northern Arizona community of Flagstaff is a small town surrounded by desert, nestled between Ponderosa Pine forests and the snow-capped peaks of the San Francisco Volcanic Field. At the center of town is historic Flagstaff, a grid of art galleries and restaurants, inns and country stores made popular by an annual influx of tourists. The majority of Flagstaff's year-round population is settled within the borders of Interstates 17 and 40, the latter more commonly known as Historic Route 66.

The free-standing cinder block building is located on the east side of Flagstaff, not far from the Econolodge, the General Motors Auto Plaza, and a half dozen fast food joints. Once a transmission shop, the facility has recently been leased to a private firm out of Tampa, Florida, though one would hardly know it based upon its boarded-up frontage and a dozen No Trespassing signs.

A lone vehicle occupies the lot—a white van that has been parked around back every day for the last week. A magnetic sign identifies the owner's company as Smith Heating and Air Conditioning. The worker, an Asian man in his sixties, has been seen coming in and out of the building, occasionally picking up takeout food at the local diner. The only visible sign of a tenant preparing to move in are the brand-new security cameras mounted above the two locked entrances.

Professor Eric Bi is inside, working in one of the auto pits in a full radiation suit. The ceiling of the pit, once open to accommodate the lift, has been sealed at its floor level with half-inch-thick lead sheeting. Two dehumidifiers are plugged into the pit's far wall, sucking moisture from the cool air. The trunk of a 1967 Buick Electra has been lined with lead, fashioned into a makeshift storage box.

Situated on a workbench before the nuclear physicist is a three-foot plexiglass cube with built-in rubber gloves. Held upright within this cube is a putty-like ten-kilogram sphere, approximately the size of a large grapefruit. Over the next few months Professor Bi will use his tools to shape and smooth the ball of enriched uranium-235 and its twin, preparing the fissile material for its final destination among the rest of the components of the Mk-54 Special Atomic Demolition Munition suitcase bomb—

—and their inception into the darkest chapter in the history of modern man.

SUMMER
2012

"As the details of the [9/11] plan are not yet fully known, it cannot be determined if Moussaoui has sufficient knowledge of the 747-400 to attempt to execute the seizure of such an aircraft."

—HARRY M. SAMIT,
Minnesota FBI Agent,
futilely urging his FBI supervisor to act quickly
against Zacarias Moussaoui, one of the planners of
the September 11, 2001 terrorist attacks

"FBI Supervisory special agent Michael Maltbie, who removed information from the Minnesota FBI's application to get the search warrant for Moussaoui, was promoted to field supervisor."

—SALON,
March 3, 2003

"Pasquale D'Amuro, the FBI's counter-terrorism chief in New York City before 9/11, was promoted to the bureau's top counter-terrorism post."

—TIME MAGAZINE,
December 30, 2002

CHAPTER 26

Lake George, a thirty-two-mile-long waterway located in the northeast section of New York State, was created at the end of the last Ice Age when glacial deposits dammed up two ancient rivers that flowed north to south through the Adirondack Valley. Ten thousand years later, the Queen of the American Lakes would serve as strategic real estate in the battles between the Algonquin and Iroquois Indians, the French and Indians, and the British and Colonialists during the American Revolution. Where blood was once shed, vacationers now roam, with families enjoying the area's hiking trails, museums, beaches, waterslide parks, and personal watercraft rentals.

The Futrell family had been vacationing at Lake George ever since Leigh was just an infant, the prior summer's stay interrupted by Kelli's radiation treatments. With his wife gone, Ace had been hesitant to re-book the log cabin, concerned about how Leigh and Sam would handle their first family vacation without their mom. In the end he had relented but decided upon a cabin along the shoreline rather than their usual rental on one of the lake's 245 islands. Leigh had lobbied to bring along a girl-friend, but Ace said no, opting to invite his in-laws instead.

Of course, Ace had apprized Bruce and Sharon Doyle of his plans weeks earlier. Convinced Ace had lost his faculties because of their daughter's murder, it was all they could do to keep from hiring a lawyer and demanding custody of their grandchildren. Jennifer had stepped in to reassure them that it was best just to humor him, and in the end they agreed, but only because they refused to take a chance with the kid's safety . . . just in case there really was something to their son-in-law's dementia.

As for Jennifer, her sudden change of heart regarding Ace's conspiracy theories had more to do, she claimed, with innuendo surrounding President McKuin's last month in office. Confidential sources revealed that subtle security changes had been discreetly made in the White House's residential quarters, including a recent hiring within the pharmaceutical staff that oversaw McKuin's blood pressure medication. The First Lady had insisted on an autopsy, but in the end relented to "internal pressures."

Newly appointed President Ellis Prescott had wasted little time in making wholesale cabinet changes, swapping centrist McKuin loyalists for advisors sharing a more neoconservative viewpoint. On his recommendation Vanessa Shannen-Anderson, a former oil executive, was brought in to serve as vice president and 2012 running mate, and within days, the fossil fuel lobby began kicking in record-setting donations to see the new ticket take the White House in November.

♦ ♦ ♦

It is the end of another busy day of activities at Lake George, the family's ninth together at the resort, and the lump Ace Futrell has been registering in his throat all week has only gotten worse. Whether it was the boating and fishing or the three-hour hot air balloon ride, it has taken all his effort to maintain his emotions around his children. At one point, Leigh had noticed her father tearing up, but he had covered himself with an anecdote about the family's first visit to the lake.

That night, they had cooked the day's catch—fresh trout—followed by roasted s'mores by the campfire. Ace trembled when he hugged his son and daughter good-night, then excused himself to read while they fell asleep in the cabin's loft.

Now it is quiet, just after eleven at night, and Ace finds himself standing on a mental precipice. Circumstances beyond his control seem to be forcing him to take the plunge—an act that potentially could prevent him from ever seeing his kids again. He continues to debate the matter internally, even as the ticking wall clock demands he make a decision, even as he carries his sneakers outside to the darkened front porch where Bruce and Sharon are waiting. His mother-in-law gives him a cold hug before returning inside.

Bruce waits by the porch steps while Ace slips on his shoes. "I parked the rental by the side of the road like you asked. Your travel bag is in the trunk."

"Thank you. Give the kids a few hours before you wake them. Make sure you remember the letter and money. Jen will get the word out like we agreed when things are safe. As far as my friend, just tell the kids he's a second cousin on my side of the family. Give him a three-hour head start, then you and Sharon disappear, and I mean really disappear, someplace you've never been . . . never even mentioned. Be sure to mail your credit cards and licenses to that Post Office Box like we talked about. Once you're on the road, use only your new IDs and—"

"—and no e-mail or phone calls, we know. Can you at least give us a clue where you're going?"

"I can't. If all goes well, I'll be back in about ten days. But if things go bad—"

"If what goes bad?" Leigh is standing in the doorway behind the closed porch screen door in her robe. She steps outside, the rusty hinges creaking. "Dad, are you going somewhere?"

Ace breaks out in a cold sweat. "Honey, it's just a business trip."

"You're leaving now, in the middle of the night, without saying good-bye? Where are you going?"

"Shh, don't wake your brother. I can't go into detail right now, but—"

"You said if things go bad. What can go bad? Is this why you've been acting so weird?"

Bruce slips his arm around her. "Grandmom and I will explain everything. Come on back inside—"

"No!" She pushes him away. "Daddy, you're scaring me. Where are you going, and don't lie. Does this have anything to do with what happened to Mom?"

"Come here." Ace hugs his daughter, the words burning in his throat. "You have to trust me, okay? There are some things you're better off not knowing. Grandpop's going to tell you what he can. I want you to listen to him and do what he says, okay?"

She's sobbing now, afraid she'll never see him again. "You're coming back, right? You're not going to leave us?"

"I'm coming back, Leigh, I promise." He squeezes her tight, then kisses her twice on the cheek. "Watch out for Sammy, okay?"

"Okay." She hugs him again, then heads inside.

Bruce squeezes Ace's shoulder. "They'll be okay. Do whatever it is you have to do."

The two men embrace.

Ace steps off the porch and disappears into the forest, cloaked by the night.

Elsmere, Delaware
August 7, 2012
9:08 am EST

Jennifer drives the rental car off the lot at the Philadelphia airport, following the signs leading her south onto Interstate 95.

At her request, the meeting had been scheduled at an off-site location, away from pollsters, volunteers, and the ever-watchful eyes of the television news crews. After a forty-minute ride into Delaware, she exits on Route 141 through the town of Elsmere. Following the faxed directions, she heads north on Kirkwood Highway, looking for a building with dark blue awnings. Five minutes later, she arrives, parking in the private lot belonging to the law offices of Doroshow, Pasquale, Krawitz, and Bhaya.

The building is a half-century-old home renovated into office space. She leaves her name at the reception desk and finds a seat by an old stone fireplace in the waiting area.

"Ms. Wienner?" A spry Italian gentleman in his early fifties greets her with a warm smile. "Bob Pasquale. Did you have any trouble finding us?"

"No." She shakes his hand.

"Elsmere's a small community, but our clients prefer the location over downtown Wilmington. Everyone's upstairs in my office, if you'll follow me."

The law firm's founding partner leads her up a flight of steps, the second floor landing guarded by two plain-clothes Secret Service agents. One searches her belongings while the other checks her for weapons, using a sophisticated metal detector. Satisfied, they allow her entry into Robert Pasquale's private office.

Senator Joseph B. Mulligan, the democratic nominee for president of the United States, is seated on a leather sofa, his tie loose, shirt sleeves rolled up. He is listening to a large man with a shaved head, goatee, and Georgia accent rattle off figures about the southern Baptist vote. Two other 'suits' and a lone woman feign interest as they feed off the remains of a breakfast platter.

The woman—Suzie Perlman—beams a huge smile as Jennifer enters the office. "Well, hallelujah, the cavalry's arrived. Senator Mulligan, this is Jennifer Wienner, although we always called her Sundance."

The Senator stands to shake her hand. "Thanks for flying in. This is our campaign manager, Silas T. Whitener," the bald man grips her hand with excessive force, "Cesar Diaz, our regional director—"

"—yes, we met at the convention in '08."

"—my chief of staff, Aaron Coombs," another big man with a kinder grip, "and you know our gal Suzie. So?"

"So, we were a bit surprised when you called," Whitener says, motioning her to an empty chair. "Not sure we really need your help, but we'll be happy to listen."

Senator Mulligan chides him with a look. "What Silas means is we feel pretty good going into the convention. Guess no one expected us to take the nomination from Senator Clinton."

"Sorry to rain on your parade, fellas, but the only reason you won the nomination was because the GOP wanted you to win. Their aim was always to drive Hillary and the other front-runners out of the race. Like it or not, you won by default. And here's another reality check, just in case you don't read the papers: Prescott has three times your war chest and a 7 percent lead in the latest poll. Your campaign's floundering; unless you pull a rabbit out of the hat at the convention, you'll be dead as McKuin come November."

Whitener begins to retort, but Mulligan signals refrain. "Fair enough. But if we're in such dire shape, why the sudden interest? I've never heard of a born-again liberal."

Jennifer smiles. "I'm not a liberal, I'm a realist. We're entering dangerous geopolitical waters, and the Neocons prefer force where tact is needed. America needs to steer the western world onto a new course, the question is whether you have the balls to see it through."

"I'm listening."

"The mistake all Democrats make is moving to the center to try to win votes. Americans need a clear choice, not Republican-lite. You need to carry a new message of hope to the American people, and that message is no more oil. 'In '13 we go green.' "

Mulligan glances at the negative responses from his staff. "An entire campaign on the environment? I don't know—"

"Not just the environment—energy. Your platform will radically wean us off oil. If Brazil can do it, so can we. No more oil means creating a new infrastructure, one that produces good jobs that will remain in this country. New jobs mean a new tax base that will help clean up the deficit. They ask you about Iraq, and you tell them we went in for oil, but since we won't be needing oil anymore, our boys and girls can come home, and anyone who refuses to allow our kids home is obviously not a patriot or a parent. Every time the Rove Rats toss another God, gays, or guns grenade at you, you'll repeat this exact phrase: 'This election's far too important to the future of our country to be caught up in the usual republican horseshit."

Senator Mulligan looks around the room. "Horseshit? You really want me to use that word?"

"Yeah, I do."

Cesar Diaz shakes his head. "You'll lose the Christian right."

"You never had the Christian right. Let the American public see you as the no-nonsense guy you are, not the wimp these middle-of-the-roaders have turned you into. Speak your mind, but stay on message. When they ask you about Kyoto, you say we'll sign, even if China refuses. Then you force the Chinese to stand alone. They'll cave, believe me. They can barely breathe in their big cities. When the media corners you on abortion, you look them straight in the eye and say, 'I'm all for outlawing abortion, but only if we start doing a better job educating our teenagers about having unprotected sex.' When they ask you about the war on terror, you go back to the energy message, and how it's America's addiction to fossil fuels—an addiction fueled by oil pushers like Ellis Prescott and his new running mate—that helped hijack our foreign policy. Simple message: No more addiction. We create a twelve-step program to wean us on green. In '13 we take our country back from the pushers. You repeat that every day in every interview, in every debate, on every bumper sticker, and you'll win the White House."

Suzie Perlman claps.

Cesar Diaz is not as enthused. "What about money? You start targeting big oil and the military suppliers and—"

"And what? You think the scraps they're tossing you now are meant to feed you? Wake up, Amigo! Those funds are designed to keep you in line. Stick to your message, and the money will come—big money— because the majority of Americans actually feels the same way you do, only they've been waiting for a democratic candidate with a set of testicles who can rally the troops while not looking like some staged, gun-toting dork. Bill Clinton may have dipped his wick in the Oval Office, but his poll numbers never dipped; that's because America likes a man in the White House who has something hanging between his legs, not some prissy Ivy Leaguer who spends his weekends sailing. And no photo shoots with Hollywood celebrities! You think Jack and Jill Average American can relate to these people? You graciously accept their contributions and tell them we'll see 'em at the inauguration ball. Until then, just sign the check, and stay the hell off the TV."

Jennifer looks around the room, the men dumbfounded, Suzie grinning. "Any questions?"

Senator Mulligan smiles. "When can you start?"

"Those who expect to reap the blessing of freedom must, like men, undergo the fatigue of supporting it."

—Thomas Paine

"The Clean Air Act amendments of 1990 were thirteen years in the making. Bush undid all that good in one sweep of the pen."

—Anonymous congressman

"When unexpected things happen . . . rise to your feet and go ahead."

—Mikhail Gorbachev

CHAPTER 27

LAKE GEORGE/QUEBEC/
NEWFOUNDLAND/HOPEDALE
AUGUST 7, 2012

IT HAD BEEN A LONG NIGHT.

With heavy heart and force of will, Ace had left his children, only the uncertainty of whether he would ever see them again outweighing the trepidation he felt about what lay ahead. Distracted emotionally, he quickly became lost as the cabin's lights were swallowed by the density and darkness of the forest. Eventually, he did find the trail, but it was the wrong one, and it left him out on the main road a good half mile from where his father-in-law had parked the rental car. By the time he had located the vehicle and had driven off the resort grounds onto Interstate 87 it was nearly one in the morning.

He drove in silence for the next several hours, traveling north on the Adirondack Freeway, the Canadian border looming somewhere up ahead. At random moments, his anger at his predicament became overwhelming, and his body shook with rage as he punched the steering wheel. He forced himself to regain control when he reached the Canadian border. Showing his phony license, he stepped out of his car when commanded for the vehicle search, the patrolmen using mirrors attached to long poles to see beneath the chassis. After a few benign security questions, he was allowed to proceed through the checkpoint and onto Quebec's Autoroute 15, where he continued driving north to Montréal. He arrived at the airport at daybreak, giving him a three-hour reprieve before the Air Canada flight departed for Halifax en route to St. Johns, Newfoundland.

◆ ◆ ◆

Designated one of the four corners of the world by the Flat Earth Society, Canada's northeastern coastline has two distinct landmasses—

the island of Newfoundland, located in the Atlantic Ocean at the mouth of the St. Lawrence River, and its rugged coastal mainland, known as the Labrador Province.

Forming the eastern edge of Canada's "shield," Labrador is a 250,000-square-mile composite of granite heaved upwards from sea and earth some 800 million years ago. Its dramatic coastline, covering more than 10,000 square miles, has been shaped by a succession of ice masses that have torn long finger-shaped gouges from its rocky mass. Continue inland and Labrador becomes an unfettered landscape of lakes, fjords, and deep valleys—one of the last great wildernesses on the planet. Three great mountain ranges cut across its expanse: the volcanic Kaumajet, the Kiglapait, and the mighty Torngat—the highest mountain range east of the Rockies. Boreal forests hold enough game to feed a small city. Farther to the north, the tree line ends, yielding to a vast wasteland known as the tundra—a place few humans have ever seen photos of, let alone ventured.

That civilization has avoided this region is no surprise, for the weather is brutal, with extended winters escorted by coastal ice sheets and sub-arctic temperatures. The few people that do populate the area reside in six communities located on the harsh northeast coast, yet none of these outposts are linked by roadway, forcing travelers to rely on boats and planes in summer, snowmobiles and dogsleds in winter. Despite these brutal conditions, Labrador's population is the oldest in all of North America, their arrival predating Columbus by more than four thousand years.

These aborigines are known collectively as the Innu. Nomadic tribes that migrated across the Bering Strait from Asia, the Innu eventually settled in Arctic North America and Greenland. The term Inuit means "real people," Innu translating as "human being," and both native words are preferred over the more commonly used Eskimo or Indian references. Despite the diffusion of their population across the Canadian Arctic, the Inuit traditions have stood the test of time, with tribes still living off the land, tracking caribou in the winter, and returning to the sea in summer months to fish and hunt seals and whales. Migrating Innu reside in ice igloos or tents made of walrus and sealskin, their permanent winter homes constructed of stone or driftwood, framed in whalebone and covered with sod or moss. Adaptation into western cultures has been slow, but for the Innu living in Labrador, a need to have a say in their own future has forced them to acclimate into Canadian culture, with modern settlements established in Sheshatshiu, at the mouth of Goose Bay, and Natuashish, located on the northern coastline near Hopedale.

◆ ◆ ◆

It was after three in the afternoon by the time Ace's plane touched down in St. John's, the largest and oldest city in Newfoundland. From here, Kelli's instructions were to fly on to Hopedale, a remote village located some five hundred miles as the crow flies up the northern Labrador coast. Exhausted from not having slept the last thirty hours, Ace booked passage on a 10:20 a.m. charter, then checked himself into a hotel for the night.

◆ ◆ ◆

Ace lays in bed, staring at the clock: 8:35. The scent of cheap carpeting and musty bedding magnifies his despair. He yearns to speak with his kids, wishing he could reassure them that everything will be all right, but by his own design he has no way of knowing where they are or how to reach them. His eyelids flutter from exhaustion and his body aches, yet despite his overwhelming fatigue he cannot fall asleep, his mind refusing to cease its endless chatter.

What am I doing here? Kelli's dead, my life turned inside out as I chase shadows. What if Schall is right, what if you are being set up? What if it wasn't even Kelli on that tape? And what kind of father leaves his kids with total strangers eight months after their mother was murdered?

What if, what if, what if! This is insane; you're insane. You'll never make it into the Saudi bank, let alone download the Promis worm. The Saudis will arrest you, lock you away, torture you until you confess or die, whatever comes first. You'll simply disappear, but Leigh and Sam, they'll carry the burden of your bravado the rest of their lives.

I miss them so much, but I can't go home, not with Homeland Security just looking for a reason to arrest me or worse . . . not with what's potentially coming down the pike. And who's this Casper guy in Hopedale? Why is it so important that I find him? Does he know about the nuclear attack? Can he help stop it?

Go home to your family, Ace. Stop living the insanity that was Kelli's life—

—you are the insanity.

"Shut up! Shut up, shut up, shut up!"

Ace tosses the pillow and claws at his hair, the room growing smaller, the walls closing in, "Get out, gotta get out . . . can't breathe!"

He's dressed and outside in less than a minute, gasping lungfuls of the cold night air. Down the metal stairwell and onto the street. He walks by the harbor, but it's way too cold, so he cuts through an alleyway, an inclined walkway leading to a pub, the Duke of Duckworth. Desperate, he enters, only it's a wall of people inside, strangers with lingering eyes, friends he'll never meet.

No good, keep moving . . .

Back into the night, trekking east again through downtown St. Johns, unable to escape the overwhelming feeling of emptiness. He turns down Military Road, his bearings nonexistent, the hotel a figment in his exhausted state of mind. He is Alice fallen down the rabbit hole, swallowed by a strange city, a refugee in a bizarre land, his identity falsified, his soul diminishing with every painful step.

The church looms before him, stone and Roman Catholic. He staggers toward its three sealed portals, his mind frantic from exhaustion.

Locked.

Locked.

The last door creaks open, beckoning him entry into the house of worship. Ace has not been a believer for years, but there are no atheists in foxholes, and he is in it up to his ears.

The cathedral is empty, the lit candles rapidly diminishing.

He kneels by a bench. Lowers his head to his hands. Chokes out the words, "give me strength," before collapsing face-first onto a pew.

◆   ◆   ◆

Son?

Ace opens his eyes. Morning light filters through stained glass windows. He sits up, having slept the last ten hours on the polished wooden bench.

The priest's face is tanned flush and weathered. "Son, you can't stay here. There's a mission . . . it's down the road."

"I know, Father. I'm on my way."

SPRINGFIELD, ILLINOIS

IT IS ALMOST NOON BY THE time Elliott Green arrives home from his meeting with Charles Jones, the Springfield FBI director. His wife, Carol, opens the door before he has a chance to key in.

"That was fast. Good or bad?"

He rolls his eyes as he pushes past her. "It's not enough I have to walk through that building listening to snickers about the broken nose and bruised ribs; what's worse was having to witness Chuck get reamed on speaker phone by Adrian Neary."

"The Chicago director? Why's he involved?"

"He heads up counter-terrorism in Illinois. Frickin' Gary Schafer at HQ chewed his ass out yesterday, so naturally he tore a piece out of Chuck's hide."

"Wait . . . I thought Chuck sent a memo to Schafer about the UMBRO guy? How can they blame you for—"

"Crap flows downhill, Carol. The Department of Energy's pissed, Schafer's covering his ass, and Chicago's blaming Springfield for me being duped by whoever was posing as my field replacement. The long and short of it is HQ's officially taken charge of the Bi file, and I'm off the case. Oh yeah, I also received an official reprimand, which goes into my file, for allowing the suspect to flee."

He heads for the kitchen.

She follows him in. "If you remember, I was the one who told you not to break inside that house. If you had listened to me, your record would still be clean, and I wouldn't have missed my sister's wedding!"

"You don't get it, do you? Bi's gone. He told the university his brother passed away, took a sabbatical to spend time with the family in Beijing. One problem: Bi has no siblings. Records show he never even left the country, which means whatever he was working on, he's still working on it, only now we've lost him . . . I lost him. Plus he's got a spook with UMBRA clearance riding shotgun."

"He'll turn up."

"These guys are experts in nuclear explosives, Carol. Bi's mother's entire family bought the farm in Nagasaki, and I suspect he holds a grudge. If a dirty bomb goes off in some mall, guess who becomes the FBI poster boy for screw-ups."

"Okay, so find him."

"Didn't you hear me? I'm off the case."

"Then take a leave of absence, and find him on your own. You're good at tracking people down. Remember that pedophile, the one who set up shop as a child psychiatrist? He ran too, but you found him in Vancouver. Took you six weeks, but you nailed him."

"Eight, and I had the Bureau's assistance. This time I'm shut out."

"Shut out by who? Chuck Jones? Adrian Neary?"

"No, this one's coming from Director Schafer. The big cheese."

"And why would the head of the FBI's counter-terrorism division give a rat's ass about you . . . unless he was afraid you might expose something he was involved in."

Elliott's eyes widen. "Yeah . . . that's true."

"Uh-huh." She heads into the living room. "I'll take that as a thank you."

ST. JOHNS/NEWFOUNDLAND COAST/
LABRADOR COAST/HOPEDALE

THE TWIN-ENGINE CHARTER BOUNCES TWICE BEFORE gaining lift off the Torbay Airport runway, the easternmost airport in North America. Ace is one of only three passengers onboard, seated on the left side of the tiny aircraft, which looks like it has been flying since the days when Newfoundland was still a British colony.

His back is sore from having slept on the Church bench, but the night's sleep has done his psyche a world of good. He is no longer worried about his children. He knows they are safe. His mind is now focused on the mission at hand.

The plane climbs to two thousand feet, then turns north, following the breathtaking coastline of Newfoundland on its way to Labrador and the village of Hopedale. Directly below is the Old Battery, a small community of weathered homes that seem to climb the sheer cliff face that rises out of the sea like a mountain. Moments later, they are over Harbour Grace and Conception Bay, its blue waters teeming with sailboats. Farther east, the sea picks up a newfound fury as it crashes into Cape Bonavista, a plateau of rock that guards its lighthouse.

The plane climbs higher as the wind howls along its aluminum wings. Above the clouds, the occasional unobstructed view reveals a landmass carpeted in Pine as they pass over L'Anse aux Meadows, the northernmost community in Newfoundland, an area once settled by the Vikings.

The coast of Labrador greets them at Henley Harbour, a waterway that sports icebergs in cooler months. By the time they are over St. Lewis, the cliff faces have noticeably flattened, the forests gone, the land still rocky but suddenly bare. Georges Cove, Bateau Harbor, Grady Island, Cutthroat Island . . . each territory takes them closer to the tundra as they continue their journey north.

The populace is also shrinking. Once home to thriving fishing communities, the northern coastal towns were cut to the quick back in 1992 with the cod moratorium. Smaller independent vessels have been replaced by larger corporate fleets capable of traveling hundreds of miles offshore in search of shrimp and crab. As a result, these once populated "outports" have become obsolete.

Ace tightens his seatbelt as the plane begins its turbulent descent. Somewhere in the distance is Hopedale.

◆ ◆ ◆

Located in Northern Labrador where large coastal bays open to the Labrador Sea, Hopedale was founded in 1782 as an Inuit settlement. Originally named Agvituk, an Innu-aimun term meaning "a place where there are whales," the name was later changed to Hopedale by Moravian missionaries arriving from Germany. Today the population numbers less than 650, 90 percent of which is Inuit, English being their predominant language. The Innu call their Hopedale community Natuashish, which means beautiful. It is one of only two organized Inuit communities in Labrador, the other being Sheshatshiu, located farther inland and to the south at Goose Bay, home to the largest air force base in North America.

Ace grips his armrests as the plane's wheels skid across a small, 2,500-foot gravel runway that seems to be diminishing all too fast. Miraculously, the plane stops before it meets sea, and moments later the outer door opens, venting the cabin with a blast of Arctic air that rocks the aircraft on its landing gear. Ace zips his leather coat and climbs down the steps, greeted by the low rumble of water riding against rock. The Labrador Sea sparkles before him beneath a cloudless blue sky.

The pilot empties luggage and mail from the hold. Ace grabs his bag, slings it over his shoulder, and heads out to the main road, a dirt path that winds around a rock-strewn field leading to Hopedale, a good mile in the distance. There are no cabs or cars, just two teens on bicycles, both Innuit females, possessing the familiar Eskimo-Asian eyes, jet-black hair, cherub cheeks, and warm smiles. Attached to each bike is a small sidecar.

"You are going to Hopedale, sir?" asks the younger teen, who looks about Leigh's age. "My sister could give you a ride. Maybe you will give her a nice tip?"

Ace inspects the rusty sidecar, unsure. "You sure this thing will hold me?"

"Of course, sir. Very safe."

He climbs in, the sidecar sagging beneath his weight. The older sister struggles to gain inertia until finally they are cruising down a gentle slope toward Hopedale.

"Maybe you can earn a bigger tip. I'm looking for someone. The name is Casper."

The teen continues smiling and pumping the peddles but says nothing.

"It's a strange name, I know. Ever heard of him?"

Still no reply.

They reach the outskirts of a community whose dwellings appear to be straight off the set of a spaghetti western. They ride past whitewashed wooden homes, spread sparsely apart, and a church with a white picket fence. Situated on a boulder-strewn acreage is a modular schoolhouse resembling a series of warehouses. Ace can hear school children playing outside, their voices carrying over the flat expanse. The men follow the sea, its rocky embankments supporting a colony of dingy, one-room wooden shacks, some built so close to the water that their single occupants could fish out an open window.

Inuit are everywhere—some men repairing fishing lines or nets, others bringing in the morning catch from their small boats. Children play close to home while their mothers clean fish and skin seals. Some glance Ace's way, a few even wave.

But there are other Native Americans in Hopedale who are not so preoccupied with chores. A few lay on stoops, passed out drunk, while others congregate in small groups, drinking and smoking. Some are teens, others are middle-aged men and women. They gaze at him with vacant eyes . . . lost souls.

His young driver brakes in front of a large, two-story building, a sign identifying it as the Amaguk Inn. "This okay? Ten dollars, please."

Ace climbs out of the side car, drops his bag on the dirt road, and pulls out his billfold. He hands her a ten-dollar bill, then shows her a twenty. "For you, if you can tell me who might know where I can find my friend Casper."

"Ask the chief. He knows everything." She snatches the twenty-dollar bill and rides off, kicking up clouds of dust. "*Qujannamiik!*"

"Yeah, thanks . . . thanks a million. Not even a receipt, huh?" Bag in hand, he trudges up four wooden steps, crossing a porch to the inn's entrance.

It is more hunting lodge than hotel, the wood-paneled walls covered in framed scenes of dog teams, hunting parties, and fishing trips. The innkeeper, part Innu, part caucasian, is seated by a work bench, tinkering with a portable stove. Ace approaches.

The man never bothers looking up. "I'm guessing you're our Australian guest. Frank Nasuti, proprietor."

"Murphy. Stephen Murphy. From Canada originally."

"That right? What brings you home?"

"Home's Quebec, but a close friend spent some time in these parts, bragged about it being the best damn salmon fishing he ever experienced. I was in St. John's on business, thought I'd fly up and hire his guide. Goes by the name of Casper."

"Don't know any Casper, but we can set you up nicely. How long you staying?"

"Not sure. Maybe a few days."

"Need a room?"

"That would be great."

"That's too bad, I only have twelve rooms, all occupied. Next time call ahead. What about food? You hungry?"

"Hungry? Sure."

"Dining room's open, but it's only for guests. Try Sylvia's Takeout, down the road on the left. There's also the Big Land Grocery."

"Any other hotels in town?"

"No. But I have a friend whose wife died last winter. He'd probably share a bed with you."

"That's a tempting offer, but—"

"Think about it while you eat. You can leave your bag in the lounge."

Ace peaks inside the lounge where several older men are seated around a color television set. "Thanks, no, but I think I will grab a sandwich. Down the road, huh?"

"On the left."

Ace waves his way out the door—

—and steps into a sea of children, fourteen in all, ages eight down to three. Two women herd them away, smiling and apologizing, their words drowned out by the sonic boom of a squadron of fighter jets passing overhead, returning to the NATO base at Goose Bay.

The contrast in cultures is not lost on Ace, the new world overpowering the old, its influence gradually evaporating thousands of years of traditions. And yet soon, he knows, the pendulum may swing the other way, and it may be the ancient culture that survives.

Sylvia's Takeout is a small eatery with a few tables set up inside for summer hours. Ace orders a plate of fried chicken from a local girl working the counter and takes the corner table, feigning interest in some of the brochures tacked to a bulletin board.

The man entering the premises is in his late fifties, tall, thin, and Caucasian, his gray-white hair pulled back into a ponytail, his beard and mustache grown heavy over a tan complexion. The maroon sweatshirt is so stained with grease that the college insignia is no longer readable. He doesn't enter the eatery as much as invade it, every step in his dust-covered army boots shaking the floorboards, every syllable rending the air.

"Duke, the usual! Chop, chop, son, I'm in a hurry. Make sure it's the fresh stuff too. You know I can tell the difference. Save that old crappola you've got frozen out back for the *takungartut*." His gaze swings around to Ace, his eyes narrowing as if looking right through him. "Well, well, look what the cat dragged in. Fresh meat."

He saunters over. Kicks out a chair from beneath the table and sits on it backwards. "Richard Lawrence, friend's call me Dick. Mechanic by trade, loner by choice. So who be you, *Gringo*?"

"Stephen Murphy. I'm in oil, the safety end of things. Decided to take a few days and see if the fishing's as good as they say."

"It's better. Got a forty-foot coastal with twelve hundred–horsepower that sleeps five. Taking 'er out as soon as I get my grub. You're welcome to join me; don't get to speak with the white man too often these days."

"I'd like that, but I sort of promised a friend I'd use his personal guide. Maybe you know him? Goes by the name Casper."

"Casper, as in the ghost? Sure I know him, only Casper's what the Americans call him. He's Inuit-Metis, part Aborigine, part European. Spends a lot of time up near Nain, the next community to the north. The man hunts whales and seals all summer, then heads inland to track caribou when the weather turns. Crazy mother, lives in igloos half the year. Not sure he'll have time to take you out fishing, unless you're after mammal."

"No, but just the same, I'd love to meet him."

"Consider it done. Hey, Duke, wrap my friend's stuff to go, he's coming with me!"

"Thanks. By the way, that word you used earlier—"

"*Takungartut*. Means stranger. No worries, these people treat everyone like a friend. We're the ones that screwed 'em up. Forced 'em to join the twenty-first century. Canadian provincial government made 'em political orphans. Started regulating their game, restricting their culture. Hell, these people were here long before our ancestors ever built their first boat. Took us a while, but we finally ruined 'em. Rob a people of their culture, and you steal their soul. Introduce new gadgets and widgets, and you give them the tools to hang themselves. Literally. Natuashish's not as bad, being a fairly new community, but Sheshatshiu, down by the air force base, now there they've got some serious challenges. Bad unemployment led to a feeling of being powerlessness. Innu aren't used to feeling useless, and there's nothing that attracts a fallen soul when he's down more than booze. We're talking major alcohol addictions. Kids see their parents losing it, and they get depressed and start sniffing gasoline. Lethal habit. Suicide rates among the Innu are some of the highest in the world. Things are gradually getting better, but it takes time . . . everything takes time, like our friggin' food! Hey, Duke, how about it? Before the sun sets this fall!"

◆ ◆ ◆

The Wellcraft 360 coastal offshore cruiser seats three plus the helmsman within its open cockpit, another six in the transom. Below decks is a full-service galley, a master suite, loft area, head, and engine room, which services the boat's twin Cummins Tw six hundred–horsepower engines.

Ace unties the bow and stern lines then climbs aboard as Dick Lawrence pulls away from the dock, heading north along the Labrador coast. The bow bounces across a three-foot chop, the frigid sea spray catching Ace, chasing him to one of the cushioned pedestal seats next to his host.

"So," yells Lawrence, "what part of Canada you from?"

"Quebec. South side of Montréal."

"Know it well. Spend any time in Little Italy?"

Ace's pulse increases. "Not much over the last nine years."

"What do the French call it again?"

"Couldn't say. My family's English, we never *parle-vous'd* much, if you know what I mean."

"I hear ya."

Ace looks astern, the shoreline disappearing rapidly. "I thought we were following the coast up to Nain?"

"Casper never returns home until late. Thought we'd do some fishing. I know a great spot not far from here. You know, if we stayed on this heading, in a few hours we'd hit Greenland."

Ace smiles and nods, while alarm bells blare in his head. He holds on as the swells increase in size, bouncing the boat three quarters of the way out of the water.

"You think this chop is bad, you should be out here in winter. Huge waves, icebergs, and the cold . . . unbelievable. I've served time on freighters. Ice builds up on the exterior of the ship, and I mean thick ice, sheets of it. Conforms to everything, makes the vessel dangerously top heavy, not a good thing in rough seas. My first time out, the captain hands us these heavy, wooden mallets and tells us to start clearing ice. Imagine being out on deck in below freezing conditions, the wind howling, the swells twenty feet, and you have to smash apart tons of ice covering the bulkheads while your ass is slipping and sliding across the deck."

"Anyone ever go in?"

"Once in a while. Water's so cold it starts shutting down your organs in less than two minutes. One guy went overboard, took us a few minutes to get back around to find him. By the time we fished him out, he was gone."

"What about in summer? How cold's the water now?"

"Good question." Lawrence slows the boat, then idles the engines, keeping the bow pointed at the incoming swells.

"This the spot?"

"This is it. Wait here, I'll grab the gear." Lawrence goes below.

Ace holds on as the never-ending swells rock the boat harder. *Kelli, what have you gotten me into now?*

Dick Lawrence returns, holding a length of heavy rope—

—and a shotgun.

"What the hell are you doing?"

"You're a bad liar, son. I've got questions but not a whole lotta time, so here's how it's gonna be. You're gonna strip naked, tie this rope around you, and get in the drink while I ask you a few questions. Once you tell me what I need to know, you can get out. I figure you've got three to five minutes tops before you turn into bait."

"You're insane."

The shotgun blast echoes across the water as its payload kicks up sea. "You can take a dip with a bullet hole in you or without. Your choice."

Ace stares down the gun's smoking barrel, then unzips his coat and removes it. He kicks his shoes off slowly, his muscles quivering from adrenaline and the cold. The Arctic air bites into his exposed flesh as he strips off his socks and pants, peeling off his underwear and shirt.

Lawrence tosses him one of the ends of the rope. "Secure it tightly around your waist, I'd hate to lose you to a killer whale."

Ace loops the cord around his waist and below his armpits, hyperventilating as he ties the knot. His mind races, trying to prepare for the sudden shock.

"Okay, get in. Now!"

Ace moves to the rail. Swings one leg over the side, then the next. He hesitates a long second, eyeballs the gun still aimed at his head . . . and jumps—

The frigid sea jolts his body in spasms, driving the air from his lungs in a primordial yell as he fights to tread water a mere thirty-eight degrees Fahrenheit, his blood feeling as if it's curdling to lead as the agony of a thousand piercing needles courses through his scorching flesh.

"First question: what's your real name?"

"Accccee Fuutrelll." His fingers and toes burn in excruciating pain, as if Neptune is soldering them with a blow torch.

"Who sent you looking for Casper?"

"Mmmy wiffffe. Ke . . . Kelli Doyle."

"Where's your wife now, Mr. Futrell?"

"Deaddd. Mur . . . mur . . . dered." The blood flow to his extremities slows, his limbs moving in slow motion, his body sinking.

Lawrence tugs on the rope. "That was two minutes. It'll get easier as you go numb." Looking away, he scans the horizon, almost bored.

Ace's eyes grow wide, his teeth involuntarily chattering. "Isss thaaat it?"

"Who murdered your wife? Who do you suspect?"

"Agent." Ace is no longer certain his body is moving.

"You mean like a federal agent? Domestic or foreign?"

"Ff . . . foreign." His wheezing lungs can barely power his voice box.

"How do you know?"

"Long . . . story."

"Yeah, I bet it is." Lawrence checks his watch. "Six minutes. You're strong. Most people would have passed out at the three minute mark. Thirty seconds."

Thirty seconds? Lawrence's voice echoes in his brain. *Thirty seconds. Thirty seconds. Okay, boys, time for two plays, three if we can get out of bounds. Come on, Dawgs, come on! Ace breaks the huddle. Stands over center.*

What's the play? Dope, you forgot the play! Screw it, just find the open man. Snap count? Can't . . . think. Hut . . . hut . . . hut . . .

Dick Lawrence hauls Ace out of the water, his skin mottled and gray. He half-carries him below, where hot steam is pouring from the open bathroom door. Carefully, he lays the naked man on the shower floor, allowing the warm water to slowly revive him.

"Within the next half-century, it will be essential for the human species to have fully operational a flexibly designed, broadly equitable, and internationally coordinated set of initiatives focused on reducing the then-current world population by at least 80 percent."

—J. Kenneth Smail,
Professor of Anthropology,
from *Confronting The 21st Century's Hidden Crisis: Reducing Human Numbers by 80 Percent,*
May 1995

"The nations of the world must develop a plan to reduce global population from nearly 6 billion to about 2 billion."

—David and Marcia Pimental,
Professors of Ecology and Agricultural Science,
from "Food, Energy, and Society,"
2000

"The human population is living far beyond its means and inflicting damage to the environment that could pass points of no return, according to a major report issued by the United Nations. Climate change, the rate of extinction of species, and the challenge of feeding a growing population are putting humanity at risk."

—James Kanter,
The New York Times,
October 27, 2007

CHAPTER 28

Hopedale, Labrador Coast
August 9, 2012
7:23 pm ADT

"Here, drink this."

Ace takes the mug of cocoa from Dick Lawrence with both hands, his limbs still not fully his to control. He is dressed again, still shivering despite being wrapped under several wool blankets.

Lawrence had piloted the boat on to Nain, anchoring in a secluded cove. It is after seven in the evening, but the sun remains fixed above the horizon—Labrador's version of a summer Arctic night.

"Acute hypothermia. Condition becomes critical if the body's core temperature drops below ninety degrees. Body shuts down, dementia sets in. If I had to go, that's the way I'd do it."

"Don't let me hold you back."

Lawrence offers a half smile. "There are reasons I did what I did. First, I needed to find out what you knew. Second, and more important, there's a microscopic tracking device floating through your bloodstream. I needed to shut it down."

"Tracking device? What the hell are you talking about?"

"The Federal Government's latest gimmick for violating our civil rights. Every citizen accounted for, every foreigner tracked. Americans too, if they make the White House hit list, which you obviously made."

"This is crazy, there's no tracking device on me!"

"Yeah, there is. They injected you with it when you went through customs at Kennedy International."

"Injected? No, that was a vaccine to prevent—"

"—Avian Bird Flu, sure it was. And you know this because you had the elixir analyzed, right? For someone who was married to a former spook, you really are naïve." Lawrence takes the empty mug from him. "Total Information Awareness—TIA, for short—another program brought to you courtesy of DARPA and the Evil Empire. Used to be a time when the Constitution actually protected the privacy rights of its citizens—of course, that was before the Patriot Act. But the Feds weren't satisfied with just being able to monitor your finances, internet, e-mail, phone calls, and travel plans. No, they wanted to be able to actually get *inside* our biology. Enter the *Mu* chip, a tiny invader the size of a grain of sand. *Mu* allows the government to scan you, track you, and determine what hazardous materials you've come in contact with. The next generation *Mu* will enable Washington to eavesdrop on our very thought process. Exciting, huh?"

"The cold water . . . disabled it?"

"Yep. The chip's designed to embed itself within the wall of an artery. It's powered by your core body heat. Drop the core temperature below ninety-three degrees, and you short-circuit the device. The Feds have been tracking you for months. They were using you to lead them to me. I'm Casper, by the way. The name was your old lady's idea. And I'm sincerely sorry for your loss; your wife was a good soul. If not for her, I wouldn't be alive."

Ace lays his head back against the cushioned bench, exhausted physically, overwhelmed mentally. "Okay, Casper, I'll bite. Who are you?"

"Who I am is no matter. What I was, however . . ." Lawrence crosses the cabin to the bar and pours himself a drink. "I'd offer you one, but it's a fallacy that alcohol raises core temperature."

"Just answer the question."

"I was a microbiologist. I ran a lab specializing in anti-viral vaccines. In 1997 we began extensive field work on Avian influenza, an infection that occurs naturally among birds. Wild birds carry the viruses in their intestines, and infected birds shed the influenza virus in their saliva, feces, and nasal secretions. There are more than a dozen different subtypes of influenza, but the virus had never seriously infected people. Type-A influenza, however, is constantly evolving, and in 1997 we began receiving confirmed cases of human infection. The culprit was H5N1, a subtype that had crossed the species barrier to kill off 70 percent of those infected, the majority being once-healthy children and young adults. Scary stuff. Were H5N1 virus to suddenly gain the ability to spread easily from person to person, we'd be facing an influenza pandemic.

"Any hoot, in March of 2000 my research team was taken over by ARPA, the Advanced Research Projects Agency, a DoD initiative responsible for, and I quote, 'the direction or performance of such advanced projects in the field of research and development as the secretary of defense shall, from time to time, designate by individual project or by category,' unquote. ARPA, sometimes known as DARPA, depending upon whose ass sits in the Oval Office, decided they wanted my team to evolve the H5N1 virus. In essence, they wanted a strain that could actually cause the pandemic."

"What the hell for?"

"DARPA claimed it would assist us in finding a cure, should the need arise, but in a more evil sense, it also gave them the capacity to play God. Still, working with lethal strains is nothing new, and we certainly had ample facilities to contain the virus, but coming from the DoD the request still sent shivers down our spines. Then, about a year later, our paranoia turned into real fear when microbiologists around the world began turning up dead."

"From the disease?"

"No, no, this was murder, targeted sanctions. The first one happened on October 4, 2001, less than a month after the 9/11 attacks. Air Sibir Flight 1812 left Israel, en route to Novosibirsk, Siberia, only the plane was shot down by what was later called an errant surface-to-air missile—the missile errant by about one hundred miles. Everyone on board was killed, including five of the world's top microbiologists. About that same time, two more Israeli scientists were murdered, supposedly by Arab terrorists.

"Eight days later, Benito Que, a cell biologist at the University of Miami, was found dead outside his hematology department. Police called it a mugging, even though Que didn't have his wallet on him at the time. Four days later, Donald C. Wiley, one of the world's leading microbiologists and winner of the 1995 Albert Lasker Basic Medical Research Award for his work on anti-viral vaccines, was reported missing after attending a dinner at the Peabody Hotel in Memphis. His dead body was later found snagged on a tree near the Hernando de Soto Bridge. Investigators ruled it a car accident, even though his rental had been abandoned on the bridge, with no structural damage."

"Jeez . . ."

"Oh, it gets better. On November 23, Vladimir Pasechnik, a Soviet defector and expert on DNA sequencing, turned up dead outside his home. One day later, another airliner crashed, this one a Swissair flight. Onboard was Avishai Berkman, Amiram Eldor, and Yaacov Matzner—directors of the hematology department at the Ichilov Hospital in Israel, the Hebrew University School of Medicine, and the Tel Aviv Public Health Department. Two weeks later, on December 10, Robert Schwartz, founding member of the Virginia Biotechnology Association and the executive director of research and development at Virginia's Center for Innovative Technology was found murdered in his home. Not even twenty-four hours later, Dr. Set Van Nguyen got his. Nguyen supposedly died after entering a refrigerated storage facility in Geelong, Australia, unaware that there just happened to be a toxic leak of liquid nitrogen inside. Feel free to Google any of these names . . . tell me I'm wrong."

"I think I get the picture."

"I'm far from done!" Lawrence snaps. "February 8, Victor Korshunov, head of the microbiology sub-facility at the Russian State Medical University, suffered a lethal cranial injury. Three days later, it's Ian Langford's turn. British Police claim they found nothing suspicious about the death, even though Langford's body was discovered crammed under a chair, his home ransacked, blood everywhere. Tanya Holzmayer was shot dead in Mountain View, California, on the twenty-seventh, when she answered the door for a pizza delivery boy. That same night, in another part of California, microbiologist Guyang Huang was shot in the head while jogging in a park in Foster City. Nineteen dead scientists in four months— all experts in the field of viruses. No arrests, everything kept out of the news and conveniently swept under the carpet. Coincidence or conspiracy theory, you tell me. Ah, but here's another coincidence: it turns out many of these biowarfare experts all worked for research facilities that received grants from—drum roll please—the Howard Hughes Medical Institute, a group long suspected of 'allegedly' funding black ops biomedical research for the CIA. And everything happening right after 9/11 . . . about the time militarized anthrax turned up missing at the biowarfare facility at Fort Detrick, Maryland, a complex whose security makes Fort Knox look like a 7-Eleven. If you remember, it was about that time the Bush administration was trying to ramrod the Patriot Act down Congress's throat, only the Dems controlled the Senate by one vote, thanks to Jim Jeffords switching from Republican to Independent. There were two influential Democrats poised to thwart the Patriot Act—Tom Daschle and Patrick Leahy—and they were the only ones on Capitol Hill to receive packages of anthrax. The anthrax used in those packages was traced back to the Ames strain taken from Fort Detrick, yet John Ashcroft refused to follow up on that little piece of evidence—a strong-arm tactic so blatant you would have thought the Mafia conceived it. But forgive me, after all, I'm just a conspiracy theorist."

"How does Kelli figure into all this?"

"Your wife found out about the Neocons' little plot, which is essentially a radical contingency plan to deal with the 'Big Rollover,' the end of oil. I know I'm preaching to the choir, but the Big Rollover is essentially a math problem. See, even with oil, the planet only has a feeding and energy capacity for about 2 billion people. We manage now because 4 billion of our fellow human beings are slowly starving to death in Africa and Asia. That leaves about a billion or so of us lucky ones who get to lead the charmed life, only the rules change when the pumps run dry. Divide 6 billion into what little food and fuel resources are left after the Big Rollover, and you come up with approximately 500 million people, give or take a few hundred thousand. No substitute for oil, no problem, we'll just sit back and systematically starve 5.5 billion people. Ah, but civilized folk, they don't just lay down with their kids and grandmas and friends to die, first they go crazy. Anarchy's a definite problem to the haves of this world, so we needed a contingency plan . . . just in case we really do screw the pooch. When it comes to thinning the herd, you can't just drop a few dozen nukes or start a conventional war, not without gasoline, so what's the solution to global chaos? You guessed it—pandemic. Brought to you courtesy of DARPA—makers of the new and improved H5N1 virus."

Ace swallows the vomit rising from his gut. "The dead scientists?"

"Yep, they were the ones who would have found a cure. See, when you go to all the trouble to start a pandemic, the last thing you want are the Jonas Salks of the world running around curing your disease, so it's best you kill them off first. Kelli got to me just in time. Saved a few of my colleagues as well. Gave us new identities and kept us alive. If and when the pandemic finally strikes, a few chosen pharmaceutical companies will pocket another $500 billion, and the powers-that-be will dole out the antidote . . . oh, but not all Americans will be saved. If you're a heterosexual, God-fearing Caucasian Christian who believes in Jesus—congratulations, your future looks bright. Black and Hispanic . . . not so good. Jew? For now, but only because the New Testament says we need Israel around to complete Revelations. Homosexual? Sorry, Brucie. According to Jesus' earthly disciple, Pat Robertson, God wants you dead, only God, in this case, is some sick, neoconservative, capitalistic grim reaper who passed a law allowing him to inject you with a microchip designed to regulate your personal biochemistry. Ah, but in the end, guess who gets the last laugh. Yep, it's the man upstairs Himself, the Lord Almighty. See, those religious hypocrites who preach Jesus and 'love the fetus, but hate stem cell research' are still going to need fuel, and you don't think they'll be tapping into wind or solar do you? Nah, they'll use coal. Got to keep the wheels of commerce turning. One slight problem: coal increases carbon dioxide levels, and despite George Dubya and the fossil fuel lobbyists' claims to the contrary, Earth's atmosphere really has been teetering on the catastrophic fence when it comes to lethal levels of greenhouse gases. Add more coal, and the planet surpasses its critical absorption limit. Global warming becomes a runaway train, Arctic ice melts like it was in a micro-wave, and all that fresh water inundates the North Atlantic current, effec-tively shutting down the oceans' heat exchange system. North America and Europe become winter wonderlands, and we say bye-bye to the white man, but hey, no worries—the human race will go on, thanks to people like the Inuit and the Maya, aborigines cultures that always respected the land and never needed electricity anyway. Poetic justice, huh? The white man steals the land from the Indians and exploits their resources, and modern man's reign ends in ignorance and self-destruction. What was it Jesus said? 'And the meek shall inherit the earth.' Smart guy."

Ace pushes Dick Lawrence aside, barely making it to the toilet as he purges his lunch.

"The Army Corps of Engineers, rushing to meet President Bush's promise to protect New Orleans by the start of the 2006 hurricane season, installed defective flood-control pumps despite warnings from its own expert that the equipment would fail in a storm. The drainage-canal pumps were custom-designed and built under a $26.6 million contract awarded after competitive bidding to Moving Water Industries Corp. of Deerfield Beach, Florida. MWI is owned by J. David Eller and his sons. Eller was once a business partner of former Florida Governor Jeb Bush in a venture called Bush-El that marketed MWI pumps. Eller has donated about $128,000 to politicians, the vast majority of it to the Republican Party, according to the Center for Responsive Politics."

—CAIN BUREAU,
Associated Press,
March 14, 2007

"Remember JFK? When John F. Kennedy ran for president he had to convince the American public he would leave his [Catholic] religion in the pew. Today, politicians have to wear their religion on their sleeves . . . because 'Jesus knows who he wants to nuke.' "

—RANDI RHODES,
The Randi Rhodes Show,
June 6, 2007

"The Islamic fascists hate our freedom, they hate everything about us! How do you propose we deal with Iran?! You can't deal rationally with a religious group hell-bent on our destruction!"

—TODD SCHNITT,
The Schnitt Show,
June 6, 2007

CHAPTER 29

IT SITS ON FIFTY-TWO ACRES IN downtown New Orleans, a concrete and steel palace that, seven years earlier, had served as a refuge to thousands of people fleeing Hurricane Katrina. Now, beneath the repaired ten-acre dome that had nearly blown off in 140-mile-per-hour winds, tens of thousands of democratic delegates and constituents congregate as one. The arena buzzes with excitement and anxiety as they await their candidate, hoping and praying he delivers the home run their presidential campaign desperately needs in what most agree will be the most important speech of his political life.

From her perch in one of the press boxes, Jennifer Wienner opens her laptop, ready to chart Senator Mulligan's speech on a real-time polling program.

"My fellow Americans, I give you Senator Joseph Bryan Mulligan, the next president of the United States!"

Senator Mulligan steps out from behind the curtain, waving to his audience. He shakes hands with the VIPs on stage, then steps to the podium, allowing the applause to die down before he begins.

"The eighteenth-century English poet Edward Young wrote, 'All men think all men mortal but themselves.' Ladies and gentlemen, this election isn't about religious preferences or challenging abortion. It's not about gun rights or gay rights, which candidate goes to church more often or who has the best smile for TV. It's not about living in a red state or blue state. It's not even about living in the United States. This election is about one thing: survival. Our survival as a species, and the world we want to leave our children. There are two choices that lie before us; two paths, two destinies . . . and one way or the other, your vote is going to make a major impact on deciding which course humankind ventures down. One choice leads to hope, the other, to oblivion. One leads to an independent, clean, thriving economy, the other to a planet teetering on global warming, foreign dependence, and unforeseen chaos.

"Our country, founded on the principles of liberty and independence, has been hijacked by a group of self-serving politicians and businessmen who have used their influence to trample upon our civil liberties and sell our freedom. For three presidential elections, we the people, caretakers of the present and guardians of the future, have remained all-too-silent while the unbridled power of the few have combined with the greed of the many to steal our hopes and dreams. Corporations, not voters, now shape our policies, the needs of a nation ignored. Members of Congress, entrusted and appointed by the American people to enact laws that protect our families, have time and again voted in their own self-serving interests. Hard-working, dedicated Americans have watched in shock and disgust as the pirates of Wall Street have been allowed to pillage companies and steal pension funds that belong to you. Pharmaceutical companies have lobbied Capitol Hill to enact legislation that has allowed them to feast in windfall profits, while our sick and elderly must starve themselves just to afford their monthly medication. Twelve years ago, our country was an economic bedrock, swelling with jobs and holding a surplus in our treasury. Now, three republican administrations later, we are generations in debt, our jobs outsourced, our retirement funds stolen, our nation bogged down in a war that maims and kills our sons and daughters while making its puppet masters richer. Tonight I stand here before you, and I say enough!"

A crescendo of applause.

Jennifer watches the Pollster lines spike on her laptop. She types in a few notes.

"Back in 1973, the Arab world gave us a taste of what it means to be dependent on another nation or group of nations in order to fuel our cars and feed our masses, to power our homes and drive our economy. Instead of seizing the moment, instead of investing our resources in technologies that would have led us to clean, cheap, home-grown energies, our leaders let the moment pass, the oil addiction to manifest. If we could turn back the clock and take that high road, today there would be no war in the Middle East nor threats of terrorism. Today there would be no deficit, no global warming. Having sown our seeds in a new, green infrastructure, we would be reaping a fruitful harvest instead of maneuvering our armies in the desert to suck up the last remaining drops of Persian Gulf crude.

"For a moment, let us imagine the world that could have been, the changes I intend to enact as your next president. By law, all cars will be fueled by E85, a clean-burning brand of ethanol made from grain alcohol. By investing in E85, we not only reduce our dependence on foreign oil and lower CO_2 emissions but also pump new blood into our farming sector, stimulating a key component of our economy. But that's only the beginning. Imagine driving along our vast coastlines and seeing millions of brand-new, high-tech retractable windmills—windmills that will harness nature's unlimited fury to power our homes and businesses with cheap, affordable, clean electricity. Windmills whose aluminum and steel is forged by American workers, windmills whose turbines are constructed by American technicians, erected by American construction firms. And when my administration enacts laws that require all new construction to use solar panels, it will be the American worker who will assemble those photovoltaic cells, and it will be the American family who will benefit from clean, cheap, electricity. It takes leadership to turn this dream into a reality, and it takes a real commitment to change our infrastructure from a dependent, carbon-based economy into a lean, clean, and green society, and that is why I am here!"

Thunderous applause shakes the Superdome.

"My fellow Americans, vision is not enough. For you have heard the rhetoric before, but the intent was hollow, the action nonexistent. It's not enough to talk the talk; we have to roll up our sleeves and make it happen. To change the world, we must first change directions, and to change directions, we must first purge our nation's capitol of all those elected officials who would stand in our way, all those beholden to the fossil fuel industry, all those whose candidacies are funded by the blood of our children. Over the next seventy-five days, our campaign will identify those politicians who stand with us and those individuals who stand with the oil companies, and there will be no blue or red—only green!"

Raucous applause. Jennifer smiles in satisfaction as the polling data spikes again.

"We know where Ellis Prescott and his cronies stand. We know where his campaign funds come from, which oil companies dole out the checks, which zealots fuel the vicious attacks broadcast by 527 organizations—organizations whose only strategy is to make up outrageous lies and repeat them over and over and over again until they blur the lines of truth. Do not allow their message of hatred to be the message of this election. Do not take your eye off the ball, ladies and gentlemen, when my opponent trots out the same old rhetoric of fear. This election is not about God, gays, or guns. Do not allow yourselves to be deceived by the devil who will steal your vote as quickly as he will steal your pension fund. Prepare yourself now for a war of words, for as the election draws closer, my opponent will become more desperate, and each of you must know the difference between what is truth and the snake oil being sold as truth.

"To those of you who are amateur golfers, you know what a mulligan is." The Senator grins at the smattering of applause. "To those who don't, 'mulligan' is a term that means I screwed up and would like a do-over. My fellow Americans, as a nation, we screwed up. The Democrats screwed up because we weren't as strong and decisive as we needed to be, and the Republicans screwed up because they allowed their grand ole party to be taken over by radical elements of the right. All of us screwed up when we trusted that our leaders would not engage this country in a war under false pretenses. We screwed up when we trusted our government to build levees that would last and protect us in times of natural disasters. Now we must trust our hearts to decide which path leads to glory and which path leads to more lies and deceit, more pain and anguish, more dependence on third-world countries that do not especially like us. On election night, your vote becomes the catalyst for change. No more red states, no more blue. Tonight, I accept this nomination on behalf of all Americans who believe our leaders must be held accountable."

The senator pauses, waiting for the applause to die down.

"Every election, the environment gets placed on the back burner as we are told by candidates and the media that our focus should be on war or abortion, on gays and guns. That our economy is far more important than the quality of the air we breathe or the food we eat. That taxes will affect our families more than global warming . . . which some members of the Republican Party and their fossil fuel backers still dispute. Yet a sea-change in how we derive energy from our planet can douse the flames of hatred coming from the Middle East. A commitment to clean energy sources will open up new job markets that will lift our economy, and placing a green energy agenda at the top of our priority list will improve everyone's lives. Of course, we have heard the words before and nothing happened. We have listened to the State of the Union speeches preaching about the need to wean us off foreign oil, followed by more inaction, or worse, by policies that put more funds into the hands of those 'struggling' oil companies. Five decades ago, President John Kennedy challenged our nation to put a man on the moon and bring him home safely. President Kennedy's challenge brought out the best of America. We need to set goals that all of us can rally around, but a goal without an action plan has no chance of succeeding, just as a policy lacking votes in the House and Senate cannot become a law. So tonight, I offer the American people an action plan; tonight, I announce my acceptance as leader of the Green Party, a political party made up of Democrats, Republicans, and Independents who promise, upon being elected, that they will support a sweeping agenda to end our dependence on fossil fuels and fund a new clean energy program!"

Raucous applause, the network cameras focusing on recognizable faces in the crowd who are talking rapidly among themselves, caught off guard perhaps by their candidate's surprise announcement.

"Any candidate running for office who is committed to supporting a green agenda must declare himself a Green candidate by September 15. In this way, we shall hold our politicians accountable to abide by the will of the American conscious. Make no mistake, each of you must be held accountable too, for every eligible voter must vote. Inaction is inexcusable when the future of our existence is at stake. As Americans we love our country, and if you truly do love this great nation, then on November 8 you have one chance—one vote to make things right. Together we can correct our mistakes; we can do it over the right way. My fellow Americans, let me be your Mulligan!"

The three colored needles on Jennifer's monitor hit the upper reaches of the graph as the arena rocks beneath thunderous applause and the music of The Who's *I Won't Be Fooled Again* jump starts the Democratic Party.

ATLANTIC OCEAN
TWELVE NAUTICAL MILES NORTHEAST OF PORTLAND, MAINE
AUGUST 26, 2012
4:28 AM EST

THE MOON'S REFLECTION SPLAYS ACROSS TWO-FOOT swells, rippling in the boat's bow wake. Ace stretches in the pilot's chair, grateful for the calm.

They have been at sea a solid two weeks, following the Labrador coastline south through the Strait of Belle Isle, down past Quebec and through the Cabot Strait before hitting rough seas along the coast of Nova Scotia.

Dick Lawrence had used the time, elements, and Ace's subsequent seasickness into his training regiment. "When I dunked you, you were too focused on relieving the pain. It was too easy to extract the information."

"I had no reason to hide it."

"And if the Saudis capture you? If this plan of yours is to succeed, you have to believe in your alibi and hold out as long as possible."

"And how do I do that?"

"You have to train yourself to tuck your mind inside a place where they cannot reach you. You must dissociate your mind from the physical torture."

"The torture . . . what kind of things have you heard?"

"I won't lie, if these guys capture you, death may be your best option. The Chilean military, trained and financed by the United States, used to do barbaric things to their victims before they died. Electric shock or acid to the genitals; bayonets rammed into the anus; various body parts mutilated or punctured; toes, tongues, and ears cut off. Female prisoners were raped while members of their family were forced to watch, rats placed in their vaginas and into their mouths—"

"Stop!"

"I'm telling you these things to prepare you. You came to me with a cover story filled with holes. Your accent was wrong, your basic knowledge, nonexistent. You need to study, Ace. You need to know your new identity inside out. If someone yells 'Ace' from across the room, you have to be conditioned not to look. You have to become this new person. Because if they see through the ruse, the pain they'll inflict will be excruciating. They'll keep you alive, at least until they get what they want from you, which is why we need to prepare you. Beg to live, and you're as good as dead. But if they see you want to die, they won't kill you. It's simple reverse psychology, but it tends to hold true."

The fear tactics had worked. Ace had studied, creating memories for his new persona, rehearsing what he would do at customs, how he would enter the Saudi bank, what he would say, how he would react. Knowing his false identity would never hold up under interrogation. He and Lawrence had come up with a legitimate reason why Ace would be seeking the help of a Saudi banker under false pretenses. The new alibi was stronger, and the training gave him confidence, just as it had twenty years ago on the football field. After two weeks, he felt ready for his "bowl game."

◆　◆　◆

The horizon bleeds red as the sun moves closer to dawn. Gulls caw in the distance, the shoreline becoming visible again. They will arrive in Gloucester, Massachusetts, before noon, giving Ace ample time to catch a taxi to Boston's Logan Airport. The reservation is under Stephen Murphy—a round-trip ticket to France. A hotel has been booked in Paris, where he will stay for two days. Dick Lawrence's associates in Paris have scheduled a meeting for Ace with a French businessman who knows one of the branch managers at the National Commercial Bank in Riyadh. A meeting with be set.

In five days, Ace Futrell will return to the Kingdom of Al-Saud to kick off the biggest game of his life.

"A federal investigation into the bank accounts of the Saudi Embassy in Washington has identified more than $27 million in 'suspicious' transactions—including hundreds of thousands of dollars paid to Muslim charities and to clerics and Saudi students who are being scrutinized for possible links to terrorist activity. The probe also has uncovered large wire transfers overseas by the Saudi ambassador to the United States, Prince Bandar bin Sultan. The transactions recently prompted the Saudi Embassy's longtime bank, the Riggs Bank of Washington, DC (PNC), to drop the Saudis as a client after embassy officials were 'unable to provide an explanation that was satisfying,' says a source familiar with the discussions."

—*Newsweek*,
April 12, 2006

"The Saudis are active at every level of the terror chain, from planners to financiers, from cadre to foot soldier, from ideologist to cheerleader. Saudi Arabia supports our enemies and attacks our allies."

—Laurent Murawiec,
Analyst,
Rand Corporation

CHAPTER 30

Iran Threatens Retaliation through Hezbollah

Associated Press: August 28, 2012

As tensions in the Middle East continue to increase between the United States and Iran, Homeland Security experts have voiced growing concerns that Iran's newfound nuclear weapons capability could lead to an attack on American soil.

"We know Iran supports (Lebanon-based) Hezbollah, which has cells in the United States, as well as Al-Qaeda," said Patrick Blanchard, Homeland Security assistant director of counter-terrorism. "The Iranian government views the Islamic Jihad as an extension of their own state policies. Unlike the attacks of September Eleventh, one- or two-man operational teams armed with a nuclear device could be deployed without much preparation."

President Prescott addressed these concerns in his speech yesterday in Cleveland. "We live in dangerous times. I think the American public understands and appreciates the fact that the last two republican administrations were always tough on terrorism, and now is no time to back down. There is nothing more important to me than protecting our homeland, and for my opponent [Senator Mulligan] to focus all his attention on energy issues is a big mistake. While I too believe in investing in alternative energy resources, you don't get a mulligan when a nuclear weapon or a dirty bomb goes off. Come November, I believe most Americans will want a leader in the White House who best protects their family, not a man building windmills."

WASHINGTON, DC
AUGUST 29, 2012

FBI DIRECTOR GARY SCHAFER PULLS INTO the donut shop parking lot, checks his watch to verify he is still early, and heads inside.

A half-block away, Elliott Green parks his car curbside. The suspended FBI agent has been shadowing Schafer's movements for the last eleven days. Today marks the first time the director has left his office during working hours, and Green doubts it's because of a sugar craving.

Minutes later, Schafer emerges from the donut shop with a coffee. Instead of returning to his car, he heads for the pay phone mounted on the building's exterior brick facing.

Bingo. Green's heart races as he aims a handheld parabolic dish the size of a small frisbee out his open passenger window. The electronic surveillance device amplifies the collected sounds, concentrating them to the center of the dish, where they are picked up by a sensitive microphone. Positioning padded headphones over his ears, Elliott simultaneously eavesdrops and records Gary Lee Schafer's call:

"It's me. What's your status?" (Pause)

Green grabs his camera with his free hand and adjusts the telephoto lens. He snaps a few quick pictures.

"Why the delay?" (Pause) "Yes, well now it does matter. The powers-that-be are debating moving up the date." (Pause) "Because our friend is trailing in the polls, or don't you read the newspapers?" (Long pause) "Six weeks, nine at the most. Just be ready to mobilize. I'll call you next week with their decision."

Green gathers in his equipment as Schafer climbs back into his car and drives off the parking lot. He waits another thirty seconds before jogging over to the pay phone. Dials a number.

"Green, Elliott. Identification number 155-16533-17. I need the phone number and location of the last number dialed out from this pay phone."

RIYADH KING KHALED INTERNATIONAL AIRPORT
RIYADH, SAUDI ARABIA
SEPTEMBER 1, 2012

THE AIR FRANCE COMMERCIAL JET DESCENDS over endless brown desert, the steep escarpments of the Tuwaiq highlands rising along the periphery.

In the distance is King Khalid International Airport, an oasis of concrete and glass spread out over eighty-seven miles of flatland.

Once a remote desert town, Riyadh has been transformed into the largest city in Saudi Arabia. The nation's capital boasts two of the country's largest universities: King Sa'ud University and Iman Muhammad Ibn Sa'ud Islamic University, as well as the most sophisticated medical center in the kingdom. Riyadh is also home to the Saudi Arabian Monetary Agency (SAMA), which functions as the country's central bank and investment authority.

The plane touches down, then taxis to its designated terminal. Removing his briefcase from an overhead bin, Ace follows his fellow passengers through a carpeted air bridge and down an escalator into the terminal leading to customs and immigration. Sunlight streams in through a great tiered roof composed of seventy-two curved, triangular panels. Water cascades down tiled banks into a collection pool, and fig trees grow out of garden courtyards. Upwards of seven hundred fifty thousand plants and three hundred varieties of trees, shrubs, and flowers have been imported to fill the airport's terminals, malls, and pavilions, as well as a mosque that can hold five thousand worshipers, and the Garden of Eden effect is dazzling.

"Are you here on business or pleasure, Mr. Murphy?"

"Hopefully both."

The passport is stamped, the customs official sending Ace off to collect his belongings. The limo driver is waiting at baggage claim, holding a sign that reads Stephen Murphy.

Twenty minutes later, they are on the highway, heading for downtown Riyadh.

◆　◆　◆

"Why the hell are you calling me?"

Scott Santa feels satisfaction at having tweaked David Schall's blood pressure. "Our boy just arrived in Riyadh. I thought you'd want to know."

"What? Hold on . . . stay on the line." Santa hears the CIA director relocate to another room for privacy. "Are you certain?"

"You forget, I still employ people in customs. He's traveling under an alias, using a Canadian passport. The new security cameras scanned his face, and the markers came up positive for an alert I had placed back in March. I told my contact to allow him through."

"What the hell for?"

"If he insists on hunting me, better I know where he is."

"He's a loose cannon! I suggest you—"

The Russian-American snaps his cell phone shut, cutting off the irate intelligence director. Seated in the lobby of the Intercontinental Hotel on Maazar Street, Santa watches with perverse amusement as Ace Futrell checks in at the front desk.

◆ ◆ ◆

"Welcome to the Hotel Continental, Mr. Murphy. We have you on the seventh floor. Your room charges have already been taken care of. Is there anything else I can do for you?"

"Yes, I was expecting a package."

The clerk searches under his desk, emerging with the Federal Express package containing the Promis worm CD-ROM. "There you are, sir. Have a good stay."

GARY, INDIANA
SEPTEMBER 1, 2012

LOCATED ON THE SOUTHERN BANKS OF Lake Michigan, twenty-seven miles from downtown Chicago, is Gary, Indiana, a city named after Elbert H. Gary, the chairman of U.S. Steel, though it is better known as the hometown of the musical Jackson family.

Mitchell Wagner, Ace's former teammate, is the vice president of operations for the Gary Southshore Railcats, a minor-league baseball team competing in the Northern League, which operates in the Midwestern United States and the Canadian provinces of Manitoba and Alberta. Wagner escorts Leigh and Sammy Futrell into his office, his bay window overlooking right field of the U.S. Steel Yard, the Railcats' six-thousand-seat facility.

"I know it's not Yankee Stadium, but we still have a lot of fun. You can watch the games from here or from our reserved seats behind home plate. What do you think, Sam? Maybe I can even put you to work as a ball boy."

"I wanna go home."

Leigh hugs her younger brother. "When can we go home?"

"Now we've been through this. As soon as your dad feels good about things, I'll have you on the next plane to New York. Until then, let's all just make the best of it."

"What about school? We're supposed to start school in a couple of weeks."

"We'll hire a tutor. I'm sure your dad will be home soon and—"

"And what if he's not?" Leigh's eyes cut into Wagner, who has been wavering himself of late about the legal guardian position Ace dropped on him out of the blue. "What if something bad happens? What if he never comes back?"

Sam tears up again. "I'm supposed to play peewee football. Me and Matthew Cubit already signed up."

"The Bears! I've got season tickets to the Bears." Wagner searches his top desk drawer for an envelope of tickets. "Sam, you and I could go, how about that? And Leigh, Mrs. Wagner could take you shopping. Have you ever been to Chicago? It's a great city, with cool museums and tons of malls. How about that?"

Sam wipes his face. "I don't like the Bears; I like the Jets."

"The Jets, huh?" Wagner looks frantically for his Chicago Bears schedule. "Hmm, we don't play the Jets this year. How about the Packers or the Vikings?"

The boy sniffles.

"Hold the phone, how about the Giants? Look-ee here, Bears versus the New York Giants, and it's a Monday night game. That's pretty cool, huh? By then you'll probably be back home with your dad, but let's plan to go, all four of us. We'll spend the day in the city, then it's Monday Night Football. You like the Giants, don't you, Sam?"

Sam looks at his sister, who nods.

"Beautiful." Wagner circles the date, wondering when the kids' father will ever get around to wiring the promised funds . . . or if he is even alive.

NATIONAL COMMERCIAL BANK
GHARNATA BRANCH, KHALID BIN WALEED STREET
RIYADH, SAUDI ARABIA
SEPTEMBER 3, 2012
10:27 AM LOCAL TIME

IT WAS THE FIRST BANK ESTABLISHED in Saudi Arabia, founded in 1953, pursuant to a Royal Decree made by the late King Abdulaziz bin Abdul

Rahman al-Saud. With nearly 270 branches and total capital exceeding $1.6 billion, it is the largest, most powerful financial institution in all the Middle East.

Like most NCB banks, the Riyadh branch is laid out in four distinct sections. The main area includes a lobby complete with electronic services for clients to make deposits and withdraws or to pay bills. The second section is specifically for private banking clients, known as *Al-Weesam*. The third section is for individual client services, and the last segregates its banking services for women.

Ace enters the heavily air-conditioned building, the back of his shirt already drenched in sweat beneath his tan business suit. He leaves Stephen Murphy's name at the reception desk and has a seat in the lobby, keeping his briefcase by his side. He is more excited than nervous.

Seventeen minutes pass before he is greeted by the branch's assistant manager, Mr. Ibrahim al-Kuwaiz. A stocky man with graying goatee and bushy eyebrows, Al-Kuwaiz leads Ace back to his private office.

Ace closes the door behind them, his eyes immediately targeting the computer terminal.

"So, Mr. Murphy, I understand you know our friend and client, Mr. Daniel Pernini."

"More of a business associate, but Mr. Pernini speaks very highly of your bank, which is why I recently opened business accounts at your Paris branch. My company plans on expanding our operations in the Persian Gulf, but first I had a few issues to discuss."

"Such as?"

"First, if you could pull up my new account on your computer." Ace hands him a blank business check, the banking codes and account numbers printed along the bottom.

Al-Kuwaiz enters his personal information into the computer to access the system; then he types in Ace's banking info. "Hmm. Yankee Clipper Products. What is it you sell, Mr. Murphy?"

"You've heard of the New York Yankee baseball team? Well, we do it all. Souvenirs, programs—$2 billion worth a year." Ace opens his briefcase and takes out a Yankees baseball cap. "For you."

"Most kind." The manager sets it aside.

"I have another gift; it's something very special. I want your opinion about it. It's very important. The bank manager in Paris tried it and loved it, but I find Saudi tastes to be different." Ace takes out a pack of chewing gum with a Yankee emblem. Removes a stick and hands it to Mr. Al-Kuwaiz. "This is a new flavor of gum. Chew it and tell me what you think."

"I am really not a gum chewer."

"But you are a businessman. A few quick chews and you'll have the freshest breath in the bank."

Al-Kuwaiz unwraps it. Hesitates, then pops the yellow rectangle into his mouth, his thick goatee twitching as he chews.

As Ace watches, Al-Kuwaiz's eyes grow heavy, his jaws ceasing mid-chew. The gum is laced with Burundanga, a soluble powder better known in Columbia as Zombie Dust. Made from the borrachera plant, Burundanga has been called the world's most dangerous drug as it leaves its victims in a virtual coma, preventing the brain from recording any and all memory until it wears off hours later.

"Mr. Al-Kuwaiz?"

No response.

Ace removes the CD-ROM from the *John Lennon's Greatest Hits* case, along with the Yankees' yearbook. Sliding his chair next to Al-Kuwaiz, he feigns reading the yearbook to the comatose manager as his eyes dart to the monitor. Casually, he leans under the desk, opening the computer hard drive's CD tray. He quickly positions the CD-ROM containing the Promis worm inside, then closes the drawer.

A command pops up in Arabic. Using the mouse, he double-clicks on the prompter, his heart pounding as the timer bar pops up, signaling that the worm is downloading.

Ace checks his watch: 10:38 a.m.

Referring again to the yearbook as if it is the Koran, Ace pretends to point out key passages to his Saudi Arabian zombie, silently urging the downloading bar to move faster—

—unaware that above his head, mounted in the ceiling behind a mirrored decoration, the bank's security camera is recording everything.

◆ ◆ ◆

Scott Santa enters the bank, wearing dark sunglasses and a beige Panama fedora. He smiles at the receptionist as he pretends to sign in, his eyes searching the registry, stopping at the name Stephen Murphy.

"May I help you, sir?"

"Yes, but first I must use the Internet."

The receptionist directs him to a vacant cubby along the far wall. "Help yourself."

◆ ◆ ◆

". . . and George Steinbrenner was finally forced to sell the team after he physically choked his manager following another tough loss to the Red Sox. Of course, that was also the last year we were in the playoffs, so naturally everyone wants King George back."

Ace checks his watch again: 11:14 a.m. His eyes remain glued to the bar code as it fills to 100 percent.

The monitor blinks off, then re-boots.

"Well, it's been fun, but I really must be going." Ace pops out the CD-ROM. He slips it into the pages of the yearbook, grabs his briefcase, and exits the office.

Every computer terminal in the bank has re-booted, inconveniencing personnel and customers alike. Ace forces himself to slow down as he reaches the lobby, then exits the bank—

—followed by his wife's assassin.

Ace leaves the bank entrance and turns right. He walks a block and rounds the corner as his fingers search the yearbook for the CD-ROM. Pausing, he forcibly steps on it, shattering it into a half dozen pieces. He picks up the shards and tosses all but one piece into a nearby trash receptacle, then hails a cab.

◆ ◆ ◆

He is back at the Intercontinental Hotel within twenty minutes, adrenaline coursing through his body. His bladder tingles as he crosses the lobby to the elevators. The car loads, stops to let off other passengers, and finally delivers him to the seventh floor. He keys open his room. Rushes to the bathroom to urinate, then changes out of the suit into casual clothes. Stuffs the suit into his bag, flings the remaining shard of CD-ROM out the open window and into the bushes below, then grabs his bags and exits the room.

There are no cabs in front of the hotel. He signals to an attendant and waits, reminding himself to heed Dick Lawrence's advice. *Don't rush. Blend in.*

A taxi pulls into the hotel driveway. Ace waits for a middle-aged couple to climb out, then slides in back and slams the door. "Airport, please."

The taxi enters traffic.

Flight leaves in two hours. Get through customs, grab a sandwich, board the plane. Three hour layover in Paris, then it's on to the good ole U.S. of A. No, thanks, I was already inoculated for Bird Flu, and I had an allergic reaction. Now if you don't mind, I want to see my kids.

You'll get to New York by three tomorrow afternoon, hopefully in time to phone in the ad to the New York Times personals: Game over, final score 7-3. *Wags will call the phone booth at seven thirty, Eastern. Don't forget the all-clear password. By Wednesday night, Leigh and Sammy will be back in my arms again . . . then it's payback time.*

He hums a Diana Ross oldie. *Back in my arms again . . . so satisfied—*

"Sir, what airline?"

"Air France."

The driver lets him off at the international terminal. He makes his way through the Garden of Eden lobby and waits at the end of a long line at customs.

Twenty-five minutes pass. He grows nervous.

What if they find the bank manager before the drug wears off? Maybe you should have flown out of Jiddah? Or crossed the border into Israel? No, too dangerous.

"Passport, please."

Ace hands the officer his passport.

"Thank you, sir. You've been randomly selected for a security check, please follow the officer to room six."

Random. Stay calm. Happens to me all the time.

He follows a customs officer into the brightly lit room.

It happens to Ace Futrell all the time—

—not to Stephen Murphy.

There are four of them. The Muttawa's beard is long, the religious cop's white *thobe,* five inches too short. The other three men are Saudi police officers.

He never sees the fifth man, who clubs him across the back of the skull.

"You steal our wealth and oil at paltry prices because of your international influence and military threats. This theft is indeed the biggest theft ever witnessed by mankind in the history of the world."

—OSAMA BIN LADEN,
"Letter to the American People"

"President Bush and Vice President Dick Cheney authorized Cheney's top aide (I. Lewis Libby) to launch a counterattack of leaks against administration critics on Iraq by feeding intelligence information to reporters, according to court papers citing the aide's testimony in the CIA leak case."

—ASSOCIATED PRESS,
April 6, 2006

"Extremism is so easy . . . when you go far enough to the right, you meet the same idiots coming around from the left."

—CLINT EASTWOOD

CHAPTER 31

PHILADELPHIA, PENNSYLVANIA
SEPTEMBER 4, 2012
4:27 PM EST

THE INDUSTRIAL PARK IS LOCATED OFF Grant Avenue, a main thorough-
fare that runs past the Northeast Philadelphia commuter airport. Like the
other office buildings in the complex, Unit 22 is a three-story affair, its
brown brick facing divided by the occasional narrow slit of rectangular
glass that serves as a window.

The entire upper floor of Unit 22 has been leased to an entity calling
itself the Johnston Foundation. Brochures describe the organization as a
"united global effort to end suffering among children." There is a photo
of a malnourished African child with a distended stomach on the front of
the brochure and an address on the back where interested parties can send
tax-deductible donations. The information lacks details about the size of
the fund or who the foundation has helped.

Charles Wallace, known to his employees as CW, patrols the "Bull-
pen," seven rows of computer terminals eight rows deep. Each station
is manned around the clock on eight-hour shifts, seven days a week,
by three rotating teams of computer technicians. "Starting pitchers" work the morning shift, creating new bank accounts in various
financial institutions located in non-red-flagged countries throughout
the world. "Middle relievers" work the afternoon shift, moving small
deposits of seed money in and out of these accounts to create a history
of activity. "Closing pitchers" work the night shift, stringing random
sequences of accounts together before passing them on to "clean-up
hitters" (located in another building), who eventually arrange "donations" to a final recipient.

Attached to the base of each computer hard drive is a small, black box the size of a cigarette pack. In the event of trouble, Wallace can press a preprogrammed number on his cell phone, instantly erasing every file within every computer's data base.

On the first floor of Unit 22, two floors below the Johnston Foundation, resides Brewer Travel. The agency handles just enough business to occupy its sole travel agent, Betti Fortier, a forty-year-old mother of four. Fortier enjoys the light hours and good pay, though she worries how long the owner can afford to keep the agency open. The slow business never seems to bother Lynn Brewer, who spends most of her time hunkered down in her private office at her computer, sipping diet vanilla Pepsi behind her closed Venetian blinds.

Brewer, a self-described "hyperactive, hard-rocking Irishwoman," is a former computer systems analyst who has spent the last decade bouncing between one missile defense contractor to another, always following the money. Over the last twenty years she has done everything from creating software programs to chasing hackers, but her specialty is banking systems. For twenty-three days, the "COBOL queen" has been monitoring Promis, waiting for the spy program's worm she designed to come online.

At precisely 4:53 p.m., her computer blinks.

"Well hello, gorgeous." She tosses aside the trashy novel she has been reading and rapidly types a series of passwords and commands.

The screen changes, revealing passages of streaming data.

Brewer smiles in satisfaction as she dials a number on her cell phone. "Mr. Keene? Lynn Brewer over at Brewer Travel. If you're still interested in booking that package to Maui you should do it soon, it looks like airfares are going up."

MABAHETH INTERROGATION CENTRE
RIYADH, SAUDI ARABIA

THE CELL IS WINDOWLESS. A BARE bulb hangs from the ceiling, centered above a wooden table and folding chairs. Ace sits upright, his arms pinned painfully behind his back, his wrists handcuffed. His head throbs where the baton had struck his skull, his hair caked with dried blood. His shoes and socks have been removed, his bare feet in shackles, propped up on the table.

A guard hovers behind Ace, leaning on a thick bamboo cane. The police interrogator continues to ask questions. "Who do you work for, Mr. Murphy?"

"I told you, I dabble in all sorts of ventures. Oil, a souvenir company."

"What was your business at the National Bank?"

"I'm starting a new product line in the Middle East. A friend recommended I move some of my assets into the bank. Is that a crime?"

"What did you do to the bank's assistant manager, Mr. Al-Kuwaiz?"

"Nothing. We were talking, then the guy sort of went dumb on me. Did he have a stroke or something?"

The interrogator nods.

The guard steps forward. Smiles at Ace—as he whacks the soft bottom of Ace's bare feet with the bamboo cane.

Ace jumps as he howls in pain, his body convulsing beneath him.

The investigator calmly continues. "You inserted a CD-ROM into the banker's computer. What was it?"

The bare bulb spins in Ace's blurred vision. "A video game, a sample of my wares. He . . . he asked to see it."

The guard pins Ace's legs to the table once more, the cane slamming repeatedly against the bottom of his feet. Ace screams as the bones in his toes nearly shatter and his arches swell, the pain nearly yanking him into unconsciousness.

"We call this the *Falanga*. What awaits you will make this look like a woman's loving embrace. I want to be very clear here, Mr. Murphy: you are being charged with espionage. You have no rights, no lawyers, and the American Embassy will be given no information about where we will take you. No one will intervene on your behalf. There will be no trial. The penalty for espionage is death by beheading. At this juncture, you have two choices: you can answer my questions now and spare yourself incredible human suffering, or you can continue to play the fool, in which case you will still give us the information we seek, only you will do it as you are being slowly dismembered."

Ace spits a mouthful of foamy saliva on the floor. "I am not . . . a spy."

The interrogator grabs Ace's hair and looks into his eyes. "Very well. This was heaven, Mr. Futrell. Now you are going to hell."

He nods to the guard. "Clean him up for transfer to Inakesh. I want him in Jiddah before dark."

♦ ♦ ♦

The ride lasts six hours. Ace sleeps through most of it on the van floor. They are heading west, following a two-lane highway across desert flatland. It is dark outside, darker in Ace's dreams.

Forcibly shaken awake, he sits up painfully in time to see the high walls of what looks like a palace. As they move closer, he can see the walls are cement, the palace a prison. Heavy steel gates retract, allowing the van to enter. Security lights cut through the desert night, escorting the vehicle as it makes its way around a circular drive to the front entrance of a rectangular three-story building.

Ace is dragged out of the van and led up granite steps to the front doors of a massive stone building. Heavily armed National Security guards strip off his clothing. He is tossed a stained prisoner's uniform, then led down a flight of fourteen concrete steps to a basement corridor. Bare bulbs light a long hallway reeking of human sweat and feces. There are cells to his right and left; he is unsure if they are occupied.

They stop at the second to the last door on his left. The guard opens the cell, revealing a four-foot-wide by six-foot-long room, the walls solid cement. A bare mattress is on the floor. There is a sink, its drain pipeless, aimed at a bare squat-hole in the floor. The scent of waste from the crude toilet is overpowering.

A large, metal ring is bolted ankle-high to one wall near the door. The guard, a dark-skinned Bedouin built like a professional wrestler, opens Ace's left handcuff, then re-cuffs it to the metal ring.

The Bedouin leaves, slamming the heavy cell door behind him.

Ace Futrell curls up in a ball on the mold-ridden mattress, fear causing his body to shake uncontrollably. He closes his eyes to the cold cell, illuminated by a single bare bulb dangling from the twenty-foot-high cement ceiling above his head.

Sound slowly seeps inside a heavy silence. Vermin claws scrape concrete somewhere close by. Insects buzz near his head. Whispers of Arabic filter through the barred, rectangular portal in his steel door. Sobs of the condemned mix with the wail of the justifiably insane.

Ace has entered purgatory—

—what awaits him is hell.

"We had very, very good intelligence of the general structure and strategies of the al Qaeda terrorist organization. We knew, and we warned, that al Qaeda was planning a major strike."

—James Pavitt,
CIA Deputy Director of Operations

"Osama bin Laden did not comprehend that his actions serve American interests . . . If one looks at the map of the big American bases created for the war, one is struck by the fact that they are completely identical to the route of the projected (Afghan) oil pipeline to the Indian Ocean. If I were a believer in conspiracy theory, I would think that bin Laden is an American agent. Not being one, I can only wonder at the coincidence."

—Uri Averny,
Former member of the Israeli Knesset, now a columnist for Ma'ariv,
February 14, 2002

Book Excerpt:
To the Brink of Hell: An Apology to the Survivors
by Kelli Doyle,
White House National Security Staff Advisor
(2006–2010)

The blueprint for 9/11, the Iraqi invasion of 2003, and the nuclear attack still to come all trace their roots back to two converging events: the coming oil crisis and the end of the First Gulf War.

In 1992, President George H. W. Bush was finishing up his first (and only) term in office when undersecretary of state Paul Wolfowitz, a young Neoconservative, oversaw the drafting of a new policy statement entitled the "Defense Planning Guidance" (DPG). Co-authored by I. Lewis "Scooter" Libby, the document essentially provided details of how America should increase its military advantage across the globe to preclude the rise of another great superpower. The plan found its way into the highest offices of the Pentagon and was eventually "leaked" to the press, forcing then secretary of defense Dick Cheney to "soften" parts of the document. Allies named in the paper as potential rivals were none too pleased, and Congress labeled it "over the top." With an election year upon him, President Bush refused to implement it.

Bill Clinton won the White House and the DPG was subsequently buried by the new administration, which preferred to cut defense spending following the collapse of the Soviet Union.

Over the next six years, intelligence reports submitted by my department in the CIA-Persian Gulf division would eventually bring me into the fold of a hardline group of Neoconservatives, headed by Dick Cheney, Paul Wolfowitz,

Richard Pearle, Jeb Bush, and Donald Rumsfeld, all members of an organization calling itself the Project for a New American Century (PNAC). Using the Defense Planning Guidance as its blueprint for America's future, the group created their own strategic military document, entitled "Rebuilding America's Defenses." Admonishing the Clinton administration for its adherence to the 1972 ABM Treaty and for cutting military spending, the plan outlined a grand strategy that sought to exploit America's newfound position as the world's lone superpower. In order to thwart any future challenges as well as reduce the threat from attack by the rogue nations of Iran, Iraq, and North Korea—years later referred to by President George W. Bush as the "Axis of Evil"—the report called for an immediate military buildup centering on upgrading and expanding our nuclear forces, developing space-based anti-ballistic missile defense platforms, repositioning our bases in the Persian Gulf, and increasing the battle-ready efficiency and sheer numbers of our deployed troops. According to the document, the United States should answer to no one, including NATO and the U.N., and had a responsibility to take a more permanent role in the security of the Persian Gulf.

Armed with their military agenda, the Neocons took aim at the 2000 presidential election, focusing their considerable influence and financial clout behind the candidacy of George W. Bush. Aided by brother Jeb's governorship in Florida and a conservative Supreme Court, the GOP wrestled the election loose from Al Gore and grabbed the White House.

Within months, Vice President Dick Cheney was organizing secret Energy Task Force meetings involving some of the biggest players (and donors) in the fossil fuel and nuclear industry. My role in these meetings was to supply maps of Iraqi oil and natural gas fields, as well as the locations of pipelines, refineries, and terminals. Of course not everything involved post-invasion plans. Enron's Ken Lay urged the administration to weaken power plant pollution regulations while oil executives divvied up the Arctic National Wildlife Refuge as if it belonged to them.

But the subject that concerned almost every participant at these secret meetings was the Caspian Basin.

Following the collapse of the Soviet Union in 1991, major U.S. oil companies, including Texaco, Unocal, BP Amoco, ExxonMobil,

Shell, and energy powerhouse Enron had doled out billions of dollars in investments (and bribes) to secure equity rights for oil and gas fields in the Central Asian nations of Turkmenistan, Uzbekistan, and Kazakhstan. The key to harvesting these yet-to-be quantified energy reserves, theorized to be worth upwards of $6 trillion, was to build and secure a pipeline across Afghanistan and Pakistan.

Afghanistan is a mountainous region, its chief export: heroin. At the time the country was controlled by drug warlords and the Taliban, which, aided by Saudi Arabia, took over the city of Kabul in 1996. Ten years earlier, Osama bin Laden and his guerilla regime had constructed a cave system throughout the mountains in order to battle the Soviets. The system was built by the Binladin Construction Group out of Saudi Arabia and funded in part by the CIA.

In December of 1997, Unocal officials met with Taliban representatives in Texas to finalize a $2 billion pipeline deal. One condition: the United States had to recognize the Taliban as the official government in Afghanistan. Despite the pleadings of Unocal's vice president, Congress refused, and a short time later Al-Qaeda bombed U.S. embassies in Tanzania and Kenya. The pipeline was quickly becoming a pipe dream.

Fast-forward to May of 2001: Vice President Cheney released his national energy plan, which stated that the United States had to seek "non-traditional supplies of oil" to meet our nation's growing needs . . . even in the face of foreign resistance. But drilling in the Caspian states was producing nothing near the projected oil and natural gas bounty U.S. companies had anticipated, while negotiations had completely broken down between Unocal and the Al-Qaeda-supported Taliban.

As referenced earlier, Afghanistan is the world's largest producer of the opium poppy used to make heroin. It is estimated that $500 billion flows from poppy fields annually, the drugs ending up on the streets of the United States and other western nations, the profits washed through banking systems across the globe.

Plain and simple: drugs finance cooked banking ledgers and the world's debt.

In early 2001, the Taliban decided to strike back at the economies of the West by destroying its own opium crop, and by late summer of 2001, the Dow Jones had plunged below 7,300. As the stock market fell, intelligence agencies the world over began warning of a pending Al-Qaeda attack on U.S. soil.

On August 2, 2001, Christina Rocca, the State Department's director of Asian affairs, met secretly with a Taliban ambassador but again failed to secure a pipeline deal. Thirty-five days later, planes struck the Pentagon and World Trade Center.

Afghanistan was invaded, and the Taliban regime fell within months. One of the first acts of the CIA was to "liberate" many of the opium warlords who agreed to "cooperate" with U.S. troops, who in turn were advised to "look the other way" as production of Afghani poppy fields came back online. Within a year, heroin exports rose from a low of 180 tons in 2001 to 3,700 tons in 2002. By 2003, record levels of opium were being harvested, bringing more money to Afghanistan than foreign aid had. Hamid Karzai, a former employee at Unocal, became president of Afghanistan, while another Unocal representative, Zalmay Khalizad, took over as the Bush administration's envoy to Afghanistan. Months later, George Bush and his Neocon advisors, using false evidence trails to connect the events of 9/11 to Saddam, ordered our military into Iraq.

FALL
2012

"Then the fifth angel blew his trumpet, and I saw a star that had fallen to earth from the sky, and he was given the key to the shaft of the bottomless pit. When he opened it, smoke poured out as though from a huge furnace, and the sunlight and air were darkened by the smoke."

—REVELATION 9:1–2

"We will work to help Afghanistan to develop an economy that can feed its people."

—PRESIDENT GEORGE W. BUSH,
April 2002
(The White House failed to fund Afghan reconstruction in its
January budget proposal [an oversight fixed by Congress]. The Bush
administration later cut the State Department's
$75 million request for continuing Afghan
anti-narcotics efforts to $40 million.)

"Afghanistan is as unstable as it was before the American coalition went in. Right now . . . there is very little to show that things are improving."

—TAMARA MAKARENKO,
Central Asian crime expert,
University of St. Andrews in Scotland

"Afghanistan produced dramatically more opium in 2006, increasing its yield by nearly 50 percent from a year earlier and pushing global opium production to a record high, according to a U.N. report. Early indications suggest Afghanistan could see a further increase in opium in 2007."

—VERONIKA OLEKSYN,
The Associated Press

CHAPTER 32

Paghman, Afghanistan
September 5, 2012

The town of Paghman is located in the hills outside of Kabul, its de factor ruler—Abdul Rabb al-Rasul Sayyaf—an ultra conservative Islamic fundamentalist with ties to extremist Saudi groups. Once a mujahedin leader who fought with the United States against the Taliban, Sayyaf has become a political force that is driving Afghani politics back into the Stone Age. To the West, he remains the key influence that led to a new constitution, in reality, it is his own lawlessness that is decimating the country. He has personally appointed most of Afghanistan's judiciary, while his sub-commanders run extortion and kidnaping cartels in and outside of Kabul. A kingpin whose rule intimidates even President Karzi, Sayyaf enforces a strict Wahhabi doctrine of Islam, keeping women under the same restrictions as the Taliban he helped remove from power. To western journalists he will often preach the virtues of democracy while his men disrupt weddings where music is played and assault locals for listening to cassette players. Like the Saudi Royals, he lives a life of hypocrisy, his wealth affording him mansions, servants, and SUVs.

All that is about to end.

Sayyaf stumbles through the garden of his gated home in a daze, one bloodied hand loosely gripping the pistol, the other tugging at his thick, black beard. The still-warm bodies of the dead and dying bleed in clusters throughout his estate, staining his Persian carpets, pooling on the white ceramic tile. Some are indentured servants who failed to escape his rage, others were sub-commanders whose loyalty he believed had been purchased long ago. Two of the dead are Pakistani—members of the ISI—dragged from their beds earlier in the day when news of the theft had first become known.

Everything gone—nearly $200 million, vanquished from bank accounts sworn to be untraceable. *Was it Karzi and the Americans? Was it the United Nations?*

He senses the military's presence before he hears the first jeep arrive. Within minutes, they have surround the house—they will attempt to take him alive.

Sayyaf scoffs at the notion as he pushes open the rusted iron gate and confronts the armed forces, aiming his gun at the first commando he sees—

—the movement seting off a chorus of gunfire, the air whistling with bullets. His flesh ripples as it's torn apart, his corpse dancing before collapsing in a bloody heap across his stone-paved driveway.

IJAMSVILLE, MARYLAND

LOCATED THIRTY-FIVE MILES NORTH OF WASHINGTON DC, the Whiskey Creek Golf Club is a par seventy-two championship course that offers its high-end clientele dramatic views of the Catoctin Mountains as they drive pine-forested fairways to picturesque elevated greens.

Scott Swan's guests include James Raue and his eldest son, Adam—CEOs of a steel plant in Grand Rapids, Michigan—and Jeffrey Allen, an insurance lobbyist from Mitchell, Nebraska. The foursome are playing the back nine, teeing up on the twelfth hole—a long 455-yard par four that doglegs left.

The senior Raue is given the honor to hit first, based on his prestige, not on his last hole. He takes an awkward chop, the ball slicing fifty yards before caroming off a tree. "Damn!"

"Take a mulligan," Scott offers. "You're entitled."

"Yeah, think I will. Doesn't make me a Democrat, does it?"

The others laugh.

Scott's cell phone vibrates. The Tech-Well Industry executive snatches it out of the golf cart, walking away from the group to answer. "Swan. This better be important."

"It's Brian Westly, over at the bank. Is there something going on I should know about?"

"Westly, I'm a little busy—"

"You transfer $448 million, and you're too busy to tell me about it?"

Swan's heart skips a beat. "What the hell are you talking about?"

"This morning's electronic transfer. If you're purchasing more 747s for your Arabian pals, you certainly didn't need to liquidate so much cash."

"Westly, what the—" He pauses. Smiles and waves at the group, then turns his back and lowers his voice. "What transfer? I never authorized a transfer—"

"Four Carlyle privately managed investment accounts. Your password and authorization codes moved the funds."

"I never authorized any damn transfer! Call Carlyle—"

"I did. They're not exactly saying, but it sounds like their accounts are hemorrhaging too."

"You better find that damn money, Westly—"

"The money's gone. We tracked it to a private account in Greenland, where it stayed about two nanoseconds before splitting off into cyberspace. You'd better get in here, Scott, this is serious."

JIDDAH, SAUDI ARABIA

THE GIRLS ARE ALL AMERICANS, SEVENTEEN in this particular lot. The majority are under twenty, the most precious barely twelve. Having been drugged on and off since their arrival by private jet, they have been dressed in revealing Arabian outfits—to be paraded in front of a select group of Saudi princes—the high-end slave buyers among the kingdom's elite.

While most nations have at one time or another participated in slavery, only Saudi Arabia and a handful of other Islamic countries continue the practice. Islam does not condemn it, nor has any Islamic leader. Despite publicly addressing the "evils of human trafficking," President Bush waived all financial sanctions on Saudi Arabia for failing to do enough to stop this modern-day slave trade, and President McKuin never broached the subject during his first term in office.

Yet the Saudi slave trade remains common knowledge around Washington power circles, a tolerated "look the other way" crime that has been going on since King Fahd and his sons first ran child sex rings from their private mansions in Beverly Hills. Through a network of pornographers and pimps, American girls (and occasionally boys) are "recruited" through bogus modeling agencies and newspaper ads looking to hire dancers or women to work in escort services. Videos are taken of the subjects and are sent to potential Saudi buyers. Selected teens are later invited to hotels for "tryouts," while others are targeted for kidnaping from shopping malls, video arcades, fast-food joints, and teen hangouts. The younger ones, bearing the higher price tags, must be lured away on their way home from school. Once taken, victims are hustled to airports and smuggled onto private Saudi jets (immune to searches) before the local police can even begin processing a missing persons' report.

Many anti–child abduction organizations have refused to admit the activity takes place for fear of losing their federal funding. On the rare occasion a Saudi prince or one of the king's nephews is caught in the act, a State Department official intervenes, releasing the Saudi national under terms of diplomatic immunity. If an international sex ring serving the Royals is busted, Washington allows those caught the freedom from criminal and civil prosecution by providing them with retroactive diplomatic immunity or State Department protection under the Foreign Sovereign Immunity Act. Parents of abducted children become flustered and frustrated by the endless gauntlets posed by the State Department, which control all Saudi investigations.

The "Sauduction" of Washington . . . yet another deal with the devil to keep the oil flowing.

◆ ◆ ◆

It takes less than an hour for the young ones to be selected by their new masters. The "lucky" among them will end up as wives, Islamic law allowing a man to marry his slaves. But first each prince must make settlement with "the bank."

The banker, a "Bagowi" foreigner hired by the Royals to do their dirty work, tallies the first prince's allotment, then accesses his bank account.

He accesses it a second time. Then a third. The banker turns pale.

The prince, a second cousin to King Sultan, loses his patience. "What?"

"Your Highness, I do not understand. Your funds . . . "

The prince stares at the screen. His account, which had earlier exceeded $782 million, has been drained to a zero balance. "Filthy son of a dog, what have you done with my money!"

"Your Highness . . . I swear I have done nothing!"

The enraged prince grabs a knife from one of the palace guards and stabs the banker repeatedly in the neck and chest, the shrieking man's blood splattering across the polished marble floors.

WEST PALM BEACH, FLORIDA

THE HIGH-RISE OFFICE BUILDING IS LOCATED in the downtown area of the city on a stretch of land situated between the Atlantic Ocean and Intercoastal waterway. The headquarters of "Citizens for a Green Society," a 527 political organization, occupies most of the thirteenth floor.

From her corner office Jennifer Wienner can see a haze of blue ocean in the distance. She rarely looks, her attention focused on the map of the United States stretched across one entire wall, its colored tacks representing congressmen and candidates running for election. Green tacks designate politicians who have committed themselves as members of Mulligan's new Green Party, blue are Democrats and Republicans who have yet to commit. Red tacks are the enemy—ultra-conservative right wingers beholden to the fossil fuel industry, or Democrats who fear being anything other than centrists.

Jennifer stares at the map as she has done every day since her lease began in mid-August. On her desk are sixteen two-page scripts, each a sixty-second commercial spot waiting to be filmed. Taped to her wall is a triage list of targeted cities and the rates of local television stations who will air her spots. On the shelf by the window is a framed picture, taken six years earlier, of her and Kelli.

Not a day goes by that she doesn't talk to that photo. Not an hour goes by that she doesn't think about Ace, wondering what happened to him, wondering if he is still alive.

She curses silently at her cousin and looks up as her assistant, Collin Bradley, knocks on her open door. Bradley is a former capitol police officer who she met years earlier when he was assigned to the Senate Chambers. Licensed to carry a firearm, Bradley doubles as her private security guard.

The big man is smiling. "The bank just called. They're receiving wire transfers. Hundreds of them."

Jennifer returns to her laptop and logs onto the Internet. She scans the company's bank account ledger.

The deposits are coming in rapidly, most in denominations between $20,000 and $50,000, though she counts at least eight in the six-figures. As she watches, the account balance surpasses $5 million.

"Contact Ken Ashe at Matchframe. Tell him to start shooting those spots. Then get me the Fox and ABC affiliates in Cleveland." She winks at Bradley. "Looks like the Green Party's in business."

"The U.S. does not authorize or condone torture and has not transported detainees from one country to another for the purpose of interrogation using torture."

—CONDOLEEZZA RICE,
U.S. Secretary of State

"There's no question in my mind where the philosophical guidance and the flexibility in order to do so originated—in the vice president of the United States' office. His implementer in this case was [Defense Secretary] Donald Rumsfeld and the Defense Department."

—RETIRED U.S. ARMY COLONEL LARRY WILKERSON,
Chief of staff to former secretary of state Colin Powell,
in regards to U.S. torture policy.
CNN.com,
November 20, 2005

"I can teach you about torture, but sooner or later you'll have to get involved. You'll have to lay on your hands and try it yourselves. . . . The precise pain, in the precise place, in the precise amount, for the desired effect."

—HEAD OF THE U.S. OFFICE OF
PUBLIC SAFETY (OPS) MISSION,
while teaching classes in the art of torture.
Uruguay,
1981

"Don't be afraid of what you are about to suffer. The devil will throw some of you into prison and put you to the test."

—REVELATION 2:10

CHAPTER 33

INAKESH PRISON, SAUDI ARABIA

His mind swims through feverish pools of delirium as the monsters continue to suckle and feed. He can feel their claws digging into the skin along his back, their weight pressing against his ravaged spine as their sharp rodent teeth tear off what little remains of his flesh . . .

◆ ◆ ◆

They had come for him in his dreams a dozen times before the two Bedouin guards keyed open his cell door. The smaller man had aimed his automatic weapon at Ace while the other had attached a set of leg shackles around his ankles, using a special tool to tighten the U-bolts. When he finished, the guard freed the handcuff connecting Ace's left wrist with the cell wall and motioned a command for him to dress in the prison garb he had been using as a blanket.

Ace pulled the long-sleeved nightshirt over his upper body, the heavy cloth material falling over his boxer shorts and down around his knees. Barefoot, he followed the two guards out of the cell.

Each step was cumbersome, the chain heavy, the slight slack in the metal cuffs digging into the flesh around his heels. As he limped past the row of cells, he caught glimpses of other prisoners looking back at him— dark, sunken, depraved eyes staring from behind the barred rectangular viewing holes in their doors.

Reaching the end of the corridor, Ace ascended the steps slowly, counting fourteen before he reached the ground floor. The bigger guard dragged him through the gated portal into blinding daylight while two Mutawa—religious police—glanced at him with vacant eyes. A hot gust of wind tantalized his flesh as he crossed the yard, entering another building.

A sand-dusted tiled hallway ended at a heavy oak door. One of the guards knocked, waited for a muffled reply in Arabic, and pushed Ace inside.

The chamber was the size of a small gymnasium, its concrete floor stained with sweat and blood. There was a garden hose connected to a faucet, and several grated drains. A stucco wall was adorned with leather whips and bamboo canes of varied lengths and thickness. An aluminum table held a tray filled with thin, metal skewers soaking in rubbing alcohol, bloody residue everywhere. There were two chairs in the room, both anchored to the floor. One, positioned by the aluminum table and an IV stand, had thick padded arms and legs that dangled velcro straps. The second chair was situated next to a series of car batteries and held one frightening feature—its seat had been cut out.

Laid out on a central work table was a series of bore needles used to inject fluids into body cavities. There was a pair of heavy pliers with flat ends—designed to remove fingernail—and a small stack of clean face towels. Assorted lengths of rope hung from hooks on another wall, along with a pair of wrist shackles that dangled from a pulley and winch rigged to the ceiling.

The sight of the torture chamber left Ace queasy. *Pre-game intimidation tactics. Don't even think about it.*

The guards pushed him through to another door, this one leading into the warden's air-conditioned office. Seated behind a cheap, metal desk was a man in a khaki uniform, his head cleanly shaved, his salt and pepper mustache thick and bushy.

Behind him and off to one side stood the woman.

She was in her early thirties, a dark-skinned Arabian beauty blessed with high cheekbones and full lips, her long, black hair hidden away behind a matching black scarf. Her physique, tall and trim, was cloaked in the traditional black burka worn by Saudi women. But it was her eyes that set her apart from anyone Ace had ever seen—fiery, hazel-green eyes rimmed in golden flecks—blazing animal eyes that seemed to possess an inner rage.

Those eyes followed him as the two guards pushed him to sit in a folding chair positioned in front of the uniformed man's desk.

It was she who spoke, her English like velvet ice, carrying the slightest hint of a British accent. "This is General Abdul Aziz. He is warden of Inakesh Prison. I am here to translate."

One of the guards wheeled a small aluminum table next to Ace's chair. From its single drawer he removed a lie detector kit. Rolling up Ace's right sleeve, he forcibly positioned a blood pressure cuff around Ace's biceps while his partner strapped two rubber pneumograph tubes into place, one around Ace's chest, the other tight against his abdomen. Two finger plates were clipped onto Ace's index and middle fingers, the galvanometers designed to measure perspiration.

Game time. Ace closed his eyes, willing himself to remain calm. No machine detects lies; a polygraph is simply a device that monitors significant involuntary physiological responses present in a person's body when that person is subjected to stress.

My name is Stephen Murphy. My name is Stephen Murphy. My name is Stephen Murphy—

The General rattled off a command in Arabic, ordering the woman to begin.

"Please state your name."

"Stephen Murphy."

"You are American?"

"Canadian."

"What is your occupation?"

"I'm in the oil business, among other ventures."

"Why were you in the National bank?"

"I was arranging the transfer of assets." The rehearsed answers flowed easily, fabricated around multiple threads of truth. *With any luck . . .*

"What was on the CD-ROM you downloaded onto the bank manager's computer?"

"It was a video game, an idea I've been developing, part of the reason I wanted to set up shop in the Middle East. The manager wanted to see the game, only it never downloaded. Apparently it wasn't compatible with his computer."

The smaller guard monitoring the polygraph test said something to the warden.

The general nodded.

Before he could react, a thick palm clenched Ace by his throat, dragging him backwards over his chair and into the torture chamber—

—as the second guard lowered the shackles from the ceiling pulley and snapped them into place around his wrists—

"Wait!"

—his prison garb and boxer shorts stripped from his body.

Naked to the world, he stood before the woman, his arms outstretched above his head, his face flushed with humiliation. The hazel eyes seemed to absorb everything, yet her expression remained callous and cold. "All prisoners must learn that lies are poison, that only the truth shall release you from the agony you are about to experience."

Heads turned as the torturer entered the chamber. He was a squat heavyset Bedouin in his late sixties, his long beard gray and curly, his eyes black and cold, like a shark. This was *his* chamber, and his very presence within its confines brought an air of danger, his every movement belying a performance that dated back decades.

He was the devil personified—a sadistic Arabian Grim Reaper—and even the guards seemed intimidated.

His piggish dark eyes darted over Ace's physique, evaluating him. Turning to the far wall, the maestro selected a thick, leather whip from its mount. Testing it with several expert flicks of his wrist, he ceremoniously removed his tunic, stripping down to a short-sleeved undergarment held tight around his paunch waist by an elastic band. Grabbing a towel, he wiped off the whip's handle, re-folded the cloth to his liking, placed it on the padded chair, then nodded to the guards.

The shackles lurched to life, releasing a tsunami of pain—incredulous as it was instantaneous—as Ace was violently hoisted off the floor by his wrists, the agony in his arms and shoulders forcing the breath from his lungs, his vertebrae crackling as the muscles around his back and scapulae contorted in violent spasms, threatening to tear ligament from bone.

Through tears and screams, he rasped, "Enough! I'll talk! I'll tell you everything!"

The death merchant moved closer, his rancid breath overpowering as he spun Ace slowly around until he was facing a back wall splattered in dried blood.

Oh, jeez . . . He sucked in quick breaths, his tortured muscles trembling with adrenaline.

The whipped cracked air and flesh—

—Ace's scream exploding out his windpipe, sweat bursting from every pore as the skin was peeled away from his lower back. His body jerked in mid-air as the second lash pummeled his overstretched latisimus dorsi, shredding the flesh from his ribcage.

No more screaming! I won't scream again!

"Ahh!" He danced on the chain like a slab of raw meat, his splattered blood redecorating the back wall as again and again the whip came down, his screams receding into grunts, the grunts into mere wheezes . . . until finally there was just the crack of the whip.

The butcher stopped. He toweled himself off, then spun his prize around to face the others.

Fully conscious, Ace's eyes rolled back into place, his brown irises locking onto those of his tormentor. "That the best you got, fat boy?"

The two guards looked at one another, incredulous. The warden, wide-eyed, turned to his flustered sadist, who was already grabbing for another whip on the wall.

Ace spun himself back around, anger and adrenaline now fueling his resolve in this newfound game of wills, his mind detaching itself from the pain, his ego refusing to allow himself to succumb to unconsciousness.

Whap!

The new whip, lighter, carried a far deadlier sting, bringing fresh tears to his eyes.

Whap! Whap! Whap!

Bring it on, you fat prick; you can't hurt me! I'm already dead!

Seventeen lashes later, he passed out—

—only to be forcibly awakened by the shocking burst of cold water.

The sadist flung the empty bucket against the far wall, cursing in Arabic. The two guards shirked away.

The woman spoke, her voice clearly shaken. "Your name?"

The pain shook Ace's body. Through diminishing tunnel vision he could see the shadow of death dancing along the periphery of his fading light.

"Your name!"

"Ashley Futrell." It was his voice—unrecognizable.

"You are American?"

A nod.

"What is your occupation?"

"Petroleum geologist."

"Why were you in the National Bank?"

"Money . . . the Feds . . . threatened to take everything."

"The CD-ROM?"

"Assets . . . transfer."

The General barked out a slew of Arabic.

"General Abdul Aziz says you are lying. He says you are a spy."

Ace stared at the warden through bulging eyes. "Tell the general he can go screw himself." The words sprung forth delirious fits of laugher—

—as the whip tore across his abdomen, barely missing his genitals. His body overtaken by convulsions, his mind fled the scene, repelling into blackness.

◆ ◆ ◆

Ace opens his eyes, chasing the monsters away.

He is back in his cell, dressed again in prison garb. His body is feverish and quivering. His stomach is nauseous, but he dare not vomit, dare not move, so afraid is he of disturbing the raw, open weight licking the wounds along his back like burning gasoline.

A wave of pain grips him again, dragging him under.

◆ ◆ ◆

"Drink this. It will soothe the fever."

The beautiful woman with the animal eyes is leaning over him, pouring the clear liquid into his mouth. Ace swallows and chokes, then drinks some more.

She removes a stethoscope from a concealed pocket in her burka. Checks his heart beat. "You are lucky to be alive. No prisoner has ever remained conscious after so many lashes. Your strength angered Ali Shams. I must clean your wounds. This is going to hurt."

Carefully, she peels away the blood-soaked cloth from his back, wincing as she sees the extent of his injuries.

"Let me die."

"If it is Allah's will. My orders are to keep you alive. If you die, I will take your place." From another pocket she removes a container of salve. Rubs some on her fingers.

His body convulses as she touches the cream to his back.

"I am sorry, but this must be done."

"Wait." Ace's fingers quiver as he positions his shirt sleeve inside his mouth and bites down.

The wave of pain jolts him off the floor and into a sea of blackness.

◆ ◆ ◆

Ace opens his eyes.

His head is resting in her lap. His upper body is wrapped in gauze, the rawness of the pain gone, replaced by a tremendous pressure, like a weight tugging against the open wound.

He sits up suddenly, crawls to the open hole in the floor, and pukes—over and again until the convulsions have been reduced to dry heaves.

Drained, Ace curls up in a ball atop the bare mattress, his body shaking uncontrollably.

She curls next to him, her back to his chest, draping his arm around her waist. "For warmth."

Pressing his face against the nape of her neck, he passes out.

♦ ♦ ♦

Ace stirs himself awake. Many hours have passed. His fever is gone, and so is the girl. The pain is tolerable if he doesn't move. Carefully, he inches the half-empty bottle of water closer, sipping its remains. His empty stomach aches.

He hears someone outside his cell door. Keys jiggle in the lock.

She enters. "You have been unconscious two days. No one believed you would last." She kneels to him and checks his pulse. "Good. Your heartbeat is more regular."

"Are you . . . a doctor?"

"No, but I have received some medical training. Do you think you might be able to tolerate food?"

"Not yet." He sips more water. "What's your name?"

"Nahir."

"You're a beautiful woman, Nahir." Ace lays back again on his side. Closes his eyes. "Why is such a beautiful woman in such an ugly place?"

"If I am beautiful, then it is a curse. For many years, my father was a chauffeur for one of the Royals, a prince. At first, the prince was generous to our family, paying my father enough to afford a good life . . . to send me away to school. For three years I attended Cambridge University, studying pre-med. The summer of my junior year I returned home to spend time with my ailing mother. When the prince saw me, he became enraptured and insisted I become his wife. The prince had dozens of wives and even more slave girls, and I had a fiancé back in London. I told my father I did not want to marry the prince. In response, the prince had my father beaten and taken away to prison. I agreed to marry the Prince only if he released him.

"Several years passed. The prince, who was very ambitious, decided to maneuver his way closer to the throne by poisoning his older brother. The assassination failed. As punishment, the Royals sentenced the prince to ten years in prison. Royals do not go to prison, Mr. Futrell. I was chosen to serve his time.

"When General Abdul Aziz learned I could speak English, he made me his official translator. That was three years ago. The warden has been most generous. I have a room next to the interrogation chamber to myself, and I am permitted free movement within the prison walls. On special occasions I may even take leave, as long as I am supervised."

"The guards leave you alone?"

The hazel eyes avert his gaze.

"And if I die, you die."

"Al Saud fears you for some reason. Why do they fear you, Mr. Futrell?"

Ace closes his eyes. "I really don't know."

"Over the course of two years [independent journalist Daniel] Hopsicker not only added information to what was known about [the 9/11 hijackers] military training, he established that some of the hijackers associated with wealthy Floridians had both intelligence and Bush family connections. Hopsicker also confirmed that within hours after the attacks, Florida Governor Jeb Bush had a military C-130 Hercules transport fly into the Venice [Florida] airport where a hastily loaded rental truck, filled with the records of Huffman Aviation—where Atta, Alshehri, and others had trained—was driven directly into the plane. The C-130 immediately took off for parts unknown."

—MICHAEL C. RUPPERT,
from *Crossing the Rubicon: The Decline of the American Empire at the End of the Age of Oil*

"Ask not about things which, made plain to you, may cause you trouble."

—THE KORAN

CHAPTER 34

THE FRENCH RIVIERA, LOCATED ON THE Mediterranean Sea along France's southeastern coast, is one of the most luxurious and expensive vacation spots in the world. Known for its azure shorelines, gorgeous women and topless beaches, mega-yachts and exclusive marinas, and a nightlife that encompasses five-star restaurants and glamorous casinos, the French Riviera has become the destination of the ultra-rich and super-famous, many of whom congregate to Cannes each spring for the world-famous film festival.

Scott Swan maneuvers past couples dressed in tuxedos and evening gowns as he hustles along the Promenade des Anglais, following the waterfront street to the Hotel Negresco. Built in 1912, the pink-domed palace still dominates the Bay of Angels, each suite individually decorated, reflecting the styles of the French Renaissance and Louis XIII.

The distressed CEO enters the grand lobby, passing beneath a monstrous chandelier originally designed for the Russian czar. Checking his watch, he opts for a quick pit stop and ducks inside the men's room.

September Eleventh . . . of all days to be meeting with these clowns.

The washroom is straight out of the Napoleonic era, the wall lights made from helmets, the sinks designed within officers' campaign trunks. He stares at a battle scene mural as he uses the urinal.

European decadence. Give me the Hawaiian Hilton any day.

Ignoring the attendant, he exits to the lobby and catches an elevator to the penthouse floor.

Swan is greeted by two members of the French National Police. One searches him for weapons while the other checks his passport, then verifies his appointment via house phone. He is led to the double doors at the end of the hall, one of the most expensive suites in the hotel.

A member of the Saudi National Guard escorts him inside to a greeting area decorated in seventeenth-century baroque. Swan follows him through doors leading into a formal dining area.

They are seated around an enormous cherrywood table lit by a ten-arm cognac-finish chandelier. The walls are papered in satin-red, a gold-framed painting of Napoleon dominating one entire wall.

King Sultan bin Abdul Aziz is seated at the head of the table, dressed in a dark business suit, his head adorned in a white ghotra. His son, Prince Bandar bin Sultan, the ambassador to the United States, is on his right, the Saudi finance minister to his left. Swan is shocked to see the finance minister's left hand is gone, the remains of his wrist wrapped in bloody bandages.

Filling in the rest of the chairs are three generals, all dressed in uniform. Swan slides into the empty chair opposite the king. The man's skin tone is a pasty gray, his expression causing beads of perspiration to break out across Swan's forehead. Swan's contacts at the Carlyle Group have been sending him daily updates of civil unrest in the Saudi kingdom, no doubt the reason the king has chosen the French Riviera to take an extended holiday.

"You are late, Mr. Swan. What have you to say?"

"My apologies. Our plane was delayed, extra security and all."

"About our money!"

Swan takes a measured breath. "The Carlyle Group is investigating the withdrawals. What complicates the matter is that all the appropriate passwords and codes were used, the monies routed into the Saudi National Bank before being dispersed. I realize $680 million is a lot of money, however—"

"Six hundred and eighty million! You think I'd waste my breath on such paltry sums!" Sultan turns to Prince Bandar. "Tell him!"

Bandar opens a folder, reading from a ledger sheet. "In the past twenty-two days, a total of $493 billion has been removed from Saudi accounts, a third of those funds from American institutions."

The blood drains from Scott Swan's face.

"Where is Mr. Baker? Where is Mr. Bush? Why are my calls being ignored? If I didn't know better, Mr. Swan, I'd say your country is preparing for an invasion."

"Your Excellency, please . . . I'm as shocked as you are by these circumstances. My own business accounts have been—"

"Do I look like a fool!" King Sultan stands, making his way slowly around the oval table toward his American guest. "In 2001, two days before September Eleventh, the Bush administration shared with us a twenty-seven-page top-secret document detailing battle plans for the invasion of Iraq. Does such a document exist for the invasion of Saudi Arabia?"

"No," Swan stammers.

"The thefts are having a measured affect on every financial institution in the kingdom," Prince Bandar states. "Saudi banks report losses approaching $500 billion. Seventy-three percent of these funds directly involve royals, eighteen percent affecting private corporations. The BinLaden Group declared bankruptcy six days ago after $27 billion was transferred out of its holding accounts. Our economy has all but collapsed. If this continues—"

King Sultan hovers over Swan. "Three-quarters of a trillion dollars stolen without a trace, Mr. Swan, yet the World Bank remains quiet, the United States says nothing, and why should they? Wall Street has not suffered, at least not yet. So here is my message to President Prescott: The United States Treasury and the Department of Defense will immediately employ their joint powers to stop the purging of our accounts, while guaranteeing the return of every missing dollar to the House of Saud, with interest. If these conditions are not met by October 15, OPEC will declare an oil embargo on the West, at which time we will demand the expulsion of all American troops from the Saudi kingdom, to be replaced with permanent military bases manned by the Chinese.

"If the House of Saud goes down, Mr. Swan, we will take you with us."

OVAL OFFICE, WHITE HOUSE
WASHINGTON, DC
SEPTEMBER 17, 2012

"THESE WERE NOT RANDOM ACCOUNTS THAT were targeted," states Leonard Snyder, the president's chief economic advisor. "At least half the monies taken originated from commissions skimmed by the House of Saud on arms contracts. Patriot Missiles, F-15s, AWACS, Canadian Halifax frigates, French Helec torpedo boats, the British Yamama sale . . . as well as off-the-book deals that can be traced as far back as the Reagan years. The worm also raided the accounts of Hamas and Hezbollah, as well the satellite networks used by the Muslims to spew their hatred of Israel and the West. Naturally, the French and the rest of the European Union were quick to accuse Israel of masterminding the plot. They only backed off when it became evident the Israeli banks had lost billions as well."

Homeland Security director Howard Lowe chimes in. "Funds have been stolen, even after banks transferred holdings into new accounts under new corporate IDs. Whatever this worm is, it has the ability to lock onto its target and trace it through any computer-operational system. CEOs in the defense industry have become so paranoid that they're cashing out whatever they have left—bonds, pension funds—and that's sending a shiver throughout the entire financial community."

"I don't understand," Prescott spits back. "How does a trillion dollars simply vanish?"

"It hasn't vanished," Snyder replies. "It's been electronically removed, its trail wiped clean, then redistributed into who-knows-where. Whoever set this up was very clever about it, when they stole from Peter to pay Paul, they kept the transactions balanced, which is why most financial institutions are still intact. This was a very complex, well-planned operation. Can the funds be relocated? Doubtful, at least at this juncture."

David Schall kneads the pounding pulse in his neck as his mind races. *Promis . . . Futrell . . . it has to be—*

Prescott glances at the CIA director. "Director Schall, you have something to add?"

"Sorry, Mr. President, I was just thinking . . . whoever these thieves are, they've managed to target accounts used by terrorist organizations and drug cartels to launder money. The Saudi situation aside, maybe we can spin this into a good thing."

"Are you saying that the Carlyle Group . . . that the Haliburtons and the Brown and Roots of the world are terrorist organizations?"

"No, sir, of course not. I only meant—"

"Leave us, Mr. Schall. I'll speak with you in private when we're through."

His face flushed, David Schall looks around the room, the stares confirming his lost status within the group. Without another word he exits the Oval Office.

Defense Secretary Kendle nods to Prescott as the others breathe sighs of relief. "Good call, Mr. President. I never trusted the man."

"His resignation will be tenured after the election. Let's get back to the problem at hand. Wall Street is taking a hit but seems to be rebounding, the big emergency looming ahead is this potential oil embargo. Vanni, how do we deal with the Saudis?" Prescott turns to his new vice president, a trusted friend since his first run for governor back in 1994. Though not a Neocon, Vanessa Shannen-Anderson is a fossil fuel insider firmly committed to seeding stability in the Middle East . . . by any means necessary.

"Saudi Arabia is facing two major threats, its economy is collapsing and the Royals are being threatened by their own populace. That leaves us two choices: we either negotiate a loan package or allow the inevitable to happen. Unless we catch these computer thieves, negotiating a loan package means nothing as the same thing could happen again. Allowing Saudi Arabia to collapse creates a dangerous power vacuum that will be contested by Islamic radicals, Iran, and the Ashraf. Since either situation leaves the Royals with the short end of the stick, we offer them an opportunity to remain in power as a puppet government while we stabilize their borders, inside and out."

"It'll never fly," Leonard Snyder says. "The House of Saud blames the United States for their losses."

"Let's at least negotiate the point," Prescott says, turning to Joseph Kendle. "A lot can happen in thirty days, wouldn't you agree?"

"Yes, sir, Mr. President," the secretary of defense concurs, "I would."

FLAGSTAFF, ARIZONA
10:23 PM MST

MICHAEL TURSI SNATCHES THE PAY PHONE off its hook after the first ring. "Speak."

"The patient's in labor."

"So soon?

"Her water broke early. Yes or no, is the doctor ready to deliver?"

"He's ready. I hear its twins. Which hospital?"

"St. Mary's."

"St. Mary's is expensive. Whose paying the hospital bill?"

"It'll be taken care of." The line goes dead.

The Turk exits the phone booth, his heart racing. "Damn . . ."

♦ ♦ ♦

"Damn . . ." The electronic surveillance records the man's final words as Elliott Green pulls the small dish back inside his car. The rogue FBI agent has been staking out the Flagstaff phone booth ever since he arrived in Arizona on September 2, and tonight was the big payoff.

Green snaps another close-up of Tursi's license plate with the telephoto lens as the car speeds away. He waits until the cloud of road dust settles before restarting his car, his mind replaying the conversation.

The patient's in labor . . . the attack must be imminent. "Haul ass, Elliott, don't lose this guy!"

He pulls out onto the road, accelerating after his suspect.

"Undercover investigators bought radioactive ingredients needed to make a dirty bomb and drove them into the USA past border security agents. When Homeland Security radiation detectors went off, the investigators gave Customs and Border Protection agents fake government licenses and receipts. Agents searched the cars, reviewed the documents and ultimately gave the undercover officers the OK to bring the material into the USA."

—*USA Today*,
March 28, 2006

"There are no permanent allies and no permanent enemies—just permanent interests."

—Lord Palmerston,
Nineteenth-century British leader

CHAPTER 35

THERE IS NO DAY AND NIGHT in solitary confinement, there is only pain and depression—a physical emptiness that can break a man more than any inflicted wound. For Ace Futrell, loneliness has become a vacuum of immeasurable time, and though the welts from his first beating have gradually thickened and healed, his spirit continues to weaken.

Through feverish bouts of sleep he dreams often of his children, each reunion shattered by violence . . . a roadside bomb wiping out the inside of a shopping mall, a tidal wave striking their private beach, a tornado exploding their home into shrapnel. Kelli's presence is always there, but only on the periphery and never as his wife, and whenever he would try to focus on her features, her face would morph into Jennifer's.

He would awaken disoriented, sometimes screaming, his senses in chaos, assaulted by the around-the-clock noise of prisoners yelling in Arabic, cussing and banging on their doors, or the constant scent of human feces, some of it caked and hardened in the grooves of his concrete walls. At times he would hear whispers, his mind always wandering, and yet part of him was grateful to be in the cell . . . at least here he was safe. At least here he wasn't being beaten.

They fed him once a day, a bowl of rice and some unrecognizable meat. He could barely tolerate it the first week, but gradually he forced himself to eat.

He did not see the woman again until the sixteenth day . . . the day they came for him.

♦　♦　♦

She was waiting for him in the torture chamber, her hazel eyes cold and penetrating like their first meeting. Once more the two guards stripped him naked, this time placing him in the chair with no bottom so that his genitalia dangled below. His ankles and wrists were strapped tight.

His Angel of Death spoke as the sadist she had called Ali Shams reached under Ace's chair between his legs and doused his testicles with a wet towel. "I am going to ask you a few questions regarding your business in the Saudi Kingdom, a truthful answer shall not be punished."

A wave of nausea shook him from his groin into his throat, sweat oozing from every pore on his body as the metal clamps were attached to his genitalia.

"A lie, Mr. Futrell, shall bring with it terrible pain."

The warden entered. He sat down next to Nahir, watching from a folding chair.

Focus! Stick with the story, you have to hold out! Do it for Leigh and Sam! Do it for—

"What is your name?"

"Ashley Futrell." He felt lightheaded, dizzy, unable to catch his breath.

"What was your business in the National Bank?"

"Transfer . . . I wanted to transfer my assets into—ahhhhhhh!" *Daggers . . . flames . . . genitals . . . on fire . . . searing pain . . . so deep . . . white-hot . . . can't breathe!*

Off.

"Ughhh!" Vomit spewed from Ace's mouth across the cement floor, then he flopped back in the chair, his sweat-soaked body sliding sideways within the restraints, his muscles in spasms, his nerves dancing uncontrollably.

He is jerked awake as the sadist drenches him with water from the garden hose.

Ace moans, rolling his aching head from side to side, his frayed nerve endings still smoldering, his twitching body causing his extremities to dance, his vision blinded by purple spots. *Stupid walk-on . . . they were toying with you . . . this is a man's game . . . you're just a child . . . you can't win; you can't fight back.*

"What is your name?"

His eyes flutter, the words chasing his mind through a feverish sea.

"What is your name?"

"Acefew . . . trell."

Your son, Sam, will be vaporized . . .

"Whuh?"

Leigh, too. We know where they live.

". . . your business in the National Bank?"

Sam and Leigh will die a horrible death.

His eyes snap open. "What did you say?"

She is taken back by his sudden ferocity. "I asked your business at the bank."

"You said something about my kids! What did you say?!"

"I said nothing—" She glances at the warden, unsure.

"Whore! What did you say!"

The General grabs her by the arm. Commands her in Arabic.

"Mr. Futrell, what was your business at—"

"Blow me! You know what that means? It means crawl under this chair and suck on my dick! Go ahead, translate that to your general!"

Her eyes widen in fear.

"Do it! Tell him!"

The punch to his face breaks his nose but clears the fog from his head. He turns to Ali Shams and spits blood on the Arab's clean shirt. "Game on, asshole! That's right, smile, you prick. You think you scare me? I'm not afraid anymore! Death doesn't scare me! Pain doesn't—"

Ace's body jumps off the chair, the restraints threatening to tear loose from his arms and legs as the voltage seems to pin him in mid-air—

—his mind caught in the roll of a great tidal wave, his being held under, unable to breath, his body tossed about as it's ripped to shreds against the points of a thousand needles.

Off.

He collapses back in the chair, more dead than alive.

This time the hose fails to revive him.

The general yells at the woman. She hurries to Ace. Checks his pupils. Feels his pulse. Shakes her head no.

Ali Shams pushes her aside and grabs a fistful of Ace's hair.

"*La!*" The warden instructs the enraged torturer to leave.

◆　◆　◆

The sea has calmed. He is floating on his back. The sun is bright, occasionally passing behind a cloud. He can feel its radiation warming his skin. Someone is speaking to him.

No . . . just let me float.

A wave tosses him, jerking him awake.

Ace opens his eyes.

He is back in his cell, lying on the mattress. His left wrist is hand-cuffed to the iron ring, his right arm is stretched out, palm up. The woman pins his forearm down with her bare foot as she inserts the IV needle. She tapes down the connection in his vein, anchors the intravenous bag to the sink, and starts the drip.

Too weak to object, he lies back, registering a cool, calming sensation that eases through his bloodstream. "What is that?"

"An electrolyte solution."

He closes his eyes. "Just let me die."

"You are not a man who seems ready to die. You are a bull, always ready to fight. You must back down, the next time Ali Shams will kill you."

"Good. Better to die up there than down in here."

"How many children do you have, Mr. Futrell?"

His eyes snap open, flashing a warning.

"I'm sorry, I meant nothing by it. I told you before, I too am a prisoner."

"It doesn't mean I trust you."

She stands over him, her hazel eyes portals of defiance. "When Ali Shams strips you in front of me, it humiliates you. I can see it in your eyes. Perhaps I can ease your embarrassment."

As he watches she removes her head scarf, allowing her long black hair to fall free. Loosening her burka, she steps out of her clothing, completely naked, her taut, shapely figure wrapped in velvet mocha skin, her breasts small but firm, her left hand covering her groin.

Ace sits up, his heart racing in his chest.

She backs a step away, then turns around slowly, revealing a swath of thick white scars criss crossing her back.

"We are kindred souls now, yes?"

"Yes." Muscles quivering, he lays back again as she redresses.

"I hate Al-Saud, Mr. Futrell. I hate what they have done to me, to my family, to my people. Why does Allah forbid us freedom? Why does he bless the evil ones with power?"

"I don't know. The same thing seems to be happening in my country. The rich become more powerful, the poor get trampled upon, and the masses accept it all in stride."

"You are not a spy."

"No."

"Why—"

He takes a deep breath, fighting to focus through the pain. "My expertise is in oil. I was hired to check on the Saudi Aramco reserves. The men who employed me are very well connected. If I don't return to the United States before the presidential election, these men will issue a public report stating the Saudi reserves will be tapped out within five years."

"But this is not true?"

"No," he lies. "The reserves are healthy for now."

"And the bank?"

"A risky side trip. I was to receive payment in laundered funds from an associate in the Middle East. The transfer didn't work. Now I remain unpaid and in prison."

"These men you work for . . . they are well-connected politically?"

"Yes."

"If I can get word to the American embassy, if I can get you out of Inakesh . . . you would take me with you?"

"Yes. Absolutely."

She pauses, debating the matter internally.

"Then I will help."

"Richard Bergendahl (55) fights the war on terrorism in Los Angeles for $19,000 a year, one of the legions of ill-trained, low-paid private security guards protecting tempting terrorist targets. Bergendahl, who protects the fifty-two-story high rise near the U.S. Bank Tower, said his training usually consists of a real estate manager reading security measures to him every few months. His building rarely has evacuation drills. Management's advice? 'Keep your coat buttoned. Keep your shoes shiny.' "

—LARRY MARGASAK,
Associated Press,
May 30, 2007

CHAPTER 36

U.S. Bank Tower
Los Angeles, CA
September 27, 2012
11:33 pm PST

Rising seventy-three stories above ground level, the U.S. Bank Tower, often referred to as the Library Tower, is the tallest North American skyscraper west of Chicago, and one of the top twenty-five in all the world. Years earlier, the public learned (after the fact) that the building had been one of the original infrastructures targeted by Al-Qaeda for the September 11, 2001 attacks, and was later a target of a foiled attempt in mid-2002. Security is tight for visitors entering the building, and businesses are advised to run background checks on all potential employees.

The maintenance company's security check on Omar Kamel Radi had been outsourced to a bogus corporation operated by Marco Fatiga's supervisor, Jeff Anders, at the Strategic Support Branch of the Department of Defense.

Omar changes out of his soiled uniform, inserts his time card to clock out, and heads up to the main lobby.

Susan Campbell is waiting. "How was work?"

"Work is work." He kisses the blonde aerobics instructor. "Perhaps I should shower before we go to dinner, yes?"

"Let's go back to my place. We can shower together." She takes his hand and they leave, strolling past Marco Fatiga, who has been watching everything.

INAKESH PRISON, SAUDI ARABIA
SEPTEMBER 28, 2012
7:45 AM LOCAL TIME

ACE AWAKENS TO THE CHAOS OF men ranting in the outer corridor. He scratches lice from his beard, then sits up painfully just as his cell door is keyed open. His guard, a large Bedouin named Hasan, unlocks his shackle, then tosses a pile of clothing at him—the business suit he had worn at the bank.

They're releasing me! Nahir did it!

He dresses quickly, his heart racing as he allows leg shackles to be placed over his slacks, his wrists handcuffed behind his back. But as he shuffles out of his cell, his moment of exhilaration is drowned in a wave of anxiety.

Three prisoners wait in the corridor, two men and a woman. All are dressed in street clothes, all on their knees, praying and begging their guards to allow them to return to their cells. The guards yell back, flogging them with bamboo canes as they drag them to their feet and herd them up the concrete steps.

Ace turns to the larger guard. Hasan is looking at him . . . grinning.

♦ ♦ ♦

Ace is led into the courtyard, the sun high in a cloudless blue sky, the heat stifling. The others have already been loaded into the back of an awaiting van. One of the guards cloaks Ace's head in a black *ghotra*, pulling it low on his face before fitting a blindfold tightly over his eyes.

Ace feels the strength seep from his body, forcing the guard to half carry, half drag him to the back of the van, shoving him roughly inside. Blind and on his knees, he uses his head to feel his way onto a bench, climbing up next to another prisoner as the vehicle accelerates out of the prison courtyard.

It is the female prisoner. She is sobbing, the men praying.

"*Marhaba.* Can anyone speak English?"

One of the men replies, "American?"

"Yes," Ace rasps. "Please, where are they taking us?"

"Today is Friday. Those selected on Fridays are taken to Jiddah for public execution. Today we are to die."

Ace slumps in his seat, each jolt from the uneven road banging his head against the van's aluminum interior. Tears run down his blindfold to his neck, not because he is afraid to die, but because he is sad for his children. After losing their mother, after abandoning them . . . and all for what? Emotions well in his gut as he remembers their last night together at Lake George, hugging his son good night, promising his daughter he'd be back in a few weeks.

That was forty days ago, maybe more!

You lied to her. You lied to yourself.

He slams the back of his head against the van's aluminum interior, grinding his teeth as he curses his existence. *I knew better. I never should have left them! Why did I listen to her? I hate you, Kelli, I hate you! I hate you! I hate you!*

◆ ◆ ◆

The van stops. After a moment the rear doors open. He waits until his guard drags him from the vehicle, joining their small procession as they walk past interested onlookers watching from the parking lot. The muscles in his legs shake as he stumbles blindly up a set of stone steps. From the direction of the noise, he can tell they are being taken to the center of a vast market place.

He recognizes General Abdul Aziz's voice bellow a command. His blindfold is removed, his *ghotra* pulled away from his eyes so he can see.

They are on a ten-foot rise situated in a crowded square. Across the street is a hotel, guests watching the festivities from private balconies. People are gathering quickly, joining the several hundred onlookers already present.

Twelve feet away, the executioner stands ready, his broad steel sword polished and glistening. He is a big man with a thick mustache and goatee and dark psychotic eyes. His khaki uniform is stained in sweat, the white *ghotra* atop his head drenched as well. By the way he plays to the crowd, it is obvious he enjoys his work a little too much.

Please, God, do with me what you will. Just take care of my kids—that's all I ask. With that, Ace closes his eyes, shutting down his thoughts as his body goes numb.

The general approaches, selecting the man seated on Ace's right. Two guards grab him by his arms, dragging him toward the executioner. The man falls to his knees as an Islamic judge—one of the Wahhabi clerics—uses a microphone to read the charges to the crowd.

The marketplace grows silent, the thick air heavy with an almost primordial bloodlust. People climb atop cars to see better.

The condemned man sobs, bowing his head to face Mecca.

Ace opens his eyes. He doesn't want to look, but he can't help himself.

The executioner raises the heavy sword high above his head, then in one powerful downward arc plunges the blade through the base of the man's neck.

The crowd swoons, the first few rows splattered with blood as the body falls to one side, the head rolling to another.

Ace gags and looks away, his insides wracked by spasms.

More charges are being read. The woman on his left sobs against his shoulder. The General drags her to her feet, shows her to the crowd, then shoots her twice in the head, spraying onlookers with a bloody mist.

The dead woman collapses in a heap by Ace's feet.

Chants rend the air. There are two prisoners left, and they want the American.

From his second-story balcony, Scott Santa reports the drama via cell phone to CIA director David Schall.

Ace is dragged off his feet. His body is lead as he is dropped onto his knees before the executioner. All sound ceases. His muscles quiver uncontrollably.

He hears the crowd cheering, and suddenly finds himself whispering a Georgia Bulldogs cheer, "What's that comin' down the tracks? Them good ole boys in red and black."

The executioner pauses, unsure.

Ace chants louder, "Ain't nothin' finer in the land than a drunk, obnoxious Georgia fan! Go Dawgs! Go Dawgs! Sic 'em!"

And then a woman's voice buzzes in his head. For a moment he imagines it to be Kelli, only the words are Arabic. In a daze he turns to his left.

Nahir is pointing at him, speaking rapidly to the general.

The executioner snaps out of his spell. He repositions Ace's skull. Shadows jump as the sword is raised overhead . . .

"I believe in God, but not as one thing, not as an old man in the sky. I believe that what people call God is something in all of us. I believe that what Jesus and Mohammed and Buddha and all the rest said was right. It's just that the translations have gone wrong."

—JOHN LENNON

"People who wear Christ on their sleeves and vote against helping people are the biggest hypocrites."

—CHARLIE MELANCON,
U.S. Representative (D-LA),
after the House rejected funding to repair
New Orleans's levees

CHAPTER 37

THE SCREAM SHATTERS THE NIGHT, STARTLING Mitchell Wagner from a deep sleep. It takes the big man two full minutes to drag himself out of bed and join his wife in the guest room. By that time, both Futrell kids are crying.

Yvonne is in the girl's bed, hugging Leigh tightly to her bosom. Sammy is crying because his sister is so upset.

"What happened?"

"She had a bad dream. Take Sam downstairs for some milk."

"What did you dream?"

"Sammy, go with Uncle Mitch. There's fresh brownies in the refrigerator."

"What was it, a nightmare?"

Yvonne scowls at her husband—a silent command for him to leave.

Leigh looks up, her eyes red with tears. "Daddy's dead."

JIDDAH, SAUDI ARABIA

NAHIR SITS ALONE IN THE BACK of the van, her arms pinned painfully behind her back by the handcuffs. Her black head scarf loosens and she shakes it free.

The rear doors open—

—Ace Futrell tossed inside.

She waits until the vehicle accelerates down the road before she goes to him. "Ashley?"

"Nahir?"

Kneeling, she turns her back to him and works the blindfold free from his face with her fingers.

Ace looks up at her, choking back tears. "You saved me."

"As you will save me."

He sits up painfully, twisting within his shackles. Nahir bends down to him until their cheeks collide and their lips taste one another, setting off a frenzied kiss driven not by passion but a primal need simply to feel.

The van turns suddenly, shaking them loose. She moves to him again, only Ace turns away. Torn from the brink of an accepted death, he is emotionally spent, the waves of nausea still settling inside him. "Nahir, I can't. I'm so very grateful, but all I can see and taste is death."

"I need to feel you, Ashley, even if only for a moment."

"I can't."

"Would you rather be dead?"

"I am dead. I'm dead to those who care."

"I care."

"I know . . . What did you say to the general?"

"I repeated what you had confided to me in your jail cell. I knew this would affect him. Some say a revolution is close at hand, others believe an invasion. Those who serve the House of Saud fear retribution. I am not certain what the general will do next but I am sure he will want answers. In the end, I may have done you a disservice. You may have been better off dead."

He moves closer, nuzzling her cheek. "I'm alive for now, and that's all that counts."

FLAGSTAFF, ARIZONA
OCTOBER 3, 2012
3:20 AM MST

THE TWO WHITE VANS ACCELERATE AWAY from the EconoLodge parking lot, Shane Torrence and Michael Tursi in one vehicle and Marco Fatiga driving the other.

Elliott Green waits thirty seconds before exiting his hotel room to tail the two vans in his rental car.

The matching vehicles head through town, making a circuitous route before finally turning into the deserted parking lot of the former auto repair center, its three bay doors boarded up. Michael Tursi hops out of the passenger side of his van and unlocks the left and middle bays, allowing the two vehicles to enter. The Turk looks around and sees no one. Satisfied, he walks inside the garage, closing the two bay doors behind him.

Elliott Green watches through night glasses from the twenty-four-hour Mart across the four-lane highway.

Inside the garage, Professor Eric Mingjuan Bi emerges from his self-contained underground bunker in the far right bay, awkwardly ascending the ladder in his biohazard suit. "You're early. You said four o'clock."

Tursi ignores the remark. "Where are the twins?"

Bi removes his hood and gloves and activates the right bay's lift. The lead plates that had sealed the subterranean hole have been removed, allowing the I-shaped lift to rise to ground level.

Strapped onto the iron support are three lead crates.

Torrence hesitates. "What about radiation? We're not wearing suits."

"The lead crates minimize the exposure. There's no danger," Bi states. "Give me a hand."

The four men pair up to remove the two 145-pound metal boxes and the third smaller box from the lift. The nuclear physicist releases the lids from the first two containers, revealing matching army-green metal cases, each about the size of a small footlocker. A ten-inch cell phone antenna protrudes from the matching bombs.

Professor Bi smiles proudly. "As promised, two Special Atomic Demolition Munitions—SADMs, for short."

Tursi drags one of the suitcases from its lead box and undoes the latches, revealing the bomb's contents for inspection.

Inside is a bell-shaped device, housing a smaller cylinder-shaped canister. Wires run from the head of this device to the back of a cell phone.

Professor Bi points. "The cell phone's battery connects to a blasting cap in the main cannister. When you dial the phone number, the ring will send a power surge to the blasting cap, setting off the C-4 inside the main cannister. That will blow one piece of the enriched uranium through another, starting a chain reaction that will end in a nuclear explosion."

Torrence looks worried. "What if we get a telemarketing call or a wrong number?"

"The cell phones remain off until you're ready to set the device. No one else has access to these numbers."

"Where's the cell phone numbers?" Tursi demands.

Professor Bi unzips his radiation suit, then removes an envelope from his pants pocket and hands it to Tursi. "My bank account and routing number. The moment my final payment hits the account, I'll call you with the cell phone numbers."

The Turk's face turns red with rage. "Why should we trust you?"

"The question is, why should I trust you? I've delivered the twins as asked, I've even included a third container of radioactive elements so you can leave your false trail. The success of this mission relies on both of us disappearing into the shadows. I want the mission to succeed. Remember, it was your people who wiped out mine. But I will not allow you to eradicate me, not if you want the twins to detonate." The Asian scientist's heart races, but he stands firm.

A tense moment passes as Tursi eyeballs the professor, contemplating. "Tomorrow by noon. I'd better have those numbers within two minutes of the transfer—"

"You will. Absolutely."

Tursi turns to Torrence and Fatiga. "Load up, we're out of here."

The four men carry the heavy cases to the vans, one SADM secured in the back of Fatiga's vehicle, the second suitcase nuke and the smaller container of radioactive parts in Torrence's van.

Tursi pulls Marco Fatiga aside. "I received confirmation from our people in Baghdad. They took out Omar's siblings this morning, the hit-men dressed as American soldiers. Word will be sent through the Muslim Brotherhood to your boy within a few days."

"That ought to teach him to fall in love in the middle of a mission."

Professor Bi tosses his radioactive suit into the right bay's hold. "I've rigged the pit with TNT and gasoline. I'll wait twenty minutes before detonating the evidence."

Tursi nods.

Torrence and Fatiga open the middle and left bay doors.

"One moment, please!" Professor Bi hurries over to Tursi as he opens the passenger door of Torrence's van. "The target cites . . . which ones are they?"

The Turk grins. Says nothing.

"At least tell me what day the twins will be birthed?"

Michael Tursi climbs in the vans and slams the door. Shane Torrence punches the gas, accelerating backwards out of the building, Marco Fatiga's van following seconds later.

INAKESH PRISON, SAUDI ARABIA

ACE FUTRELL'S EYES BULGE FROM THEIR sockets, the veins from his neck.

Nahir averts her hazel eyes. "General Abdul Aziz has spared your life. Now he wishes to know who your contact was in the Persian Gulf."

Ali Shams pulls the rope tighter. Encircling Ace's neck, the cord cuts through his flesh and wraps around his arms, which have been pinned awkwardly behind his back before feeding through the overhead pulley. A second cord has been secured around the head of Ace's penis, preventing him from urinating.

His bladder is ready to burst. His face is purple.

Ace grunts through clenched teeth.

The tension is released. He gasps a breath.

"Your contact's name?"

"Santa," he rasps. "Scott Santa. Russian-American, lives in Jiddah, works in Riyadh. Release my bonds . . . I'll tell you everything."

Nahir translates. The general nods.

He falls to his knees as the ropes are freed. With trembling fingers, he turns his back to Nahir as he claws loose the cord tied around the head of his penis, releasing a blood-tinged urine that pools across the concrete floor.

"The general is waiting."

"He's taller than me, Caucasian, dark hair, thick eyebrows. Last time we met was in New York, right before Christmas. He worked for the Vinnell Group, trained the Saudi guard. He's on his own now, probably freelances for the CIA. I know oil, Santa . . . he knows everything."

"When one does not have the truth, one is afraid of debates; when one does not have the truth, one is afraid of openness."

—Li Datong,
Editor of *Bingdian (Freezing Point),*
on the shutdown of his magazine by the Chinese authorities

"A bad government is elected by good people who do not vote in elections."

—Unknown

CHAPTER 38

McALISTER AUDITORIUM, TULANE UNIVERSITY
NEW ORLEANS, LOUISIANA
OCTOBER 3, 2012
8:04 PM EST

"GOOD EVENING FROM TULANE UNIVERSITY IN the revitalized city of New Orleans. I'm Katie Couric, host of the CBS Evening News, and I'd like to welcome you to the first of the 2012 presidential debates between President Ellis Prescott, the republican nominee, and Senator Joseph Mulligan, the democratic nominee, sponsored by the Commission on Presidential Debates. Tonight's debate will last ninety minutes, following the rules of engagement worked out earlier by representatives of the two candidates. Tonight's topics shall focus on foreign policy and homeland security. All questions posed come from me and have not been discussed with the two candidates. Each question allows for a two-minute response, a ninety-second rebuttal and, at my discretion, an extension of one minute for further discussion. As by rule, candidates may not direct a question to each other. The debate will end with two-minute closing statements. Senator Mulligan, since you won the coin toss, the first question goes to you.

"Senator, it's been eleven years since Al-Qaeda's attack on U.S. soil. Since that time there have been three more foiled attempts to down our commercial jets, and two bombs, one successful, that detonated aboard a subway train. Over the last two weeks, the internet has been riddled with excerpts from an unpublished memoir, written by the late Kelli Doyle, former national security advisor under the Bush administration, who was murdered back in December. The excerpts allude to a nuclear detonation on U.S. soil that would lead to an invasion of Iran. My question,

Senator, is whether you give credence to these memoirs, and why you believe you would do a better job than President Prescott in preventing such an attack?"

"Thank you, Katie. First let me say that all of us on Capitol Hill are concerned about the information as well as the associated accusations aimed at the neoconservative movement. It's always been our greatest fear that a dirty bomb or biological weapon could fall into the hands of a terrorist, and any group or individual that would support such a horrendous scenario should be tried and hung for treason. As to the information itself, it's difficult to give credibility to any report whose author is not around to present the evidence. Ms. Doyle was a staunch Neoconservative herself, and this could very well be another fear tactic designed to sway our populace, and we've seen far too much of that since September Eleventh. Do I believe I could do a better job than President Prescott in preventing an attack? Absolutely. The last two republican administrations talked the tough talk but refused to adequately fund security at our ports and borders, Osama bin Laden died and was never captured, and the Persian Gulf remains a boiling pot that has only grown worse since we invaded Iraq. As president, my immediate goal will be to diffuse these tensions; first, by engaging in an exit strategy that will remove U.S. troops from what has essentially become a Sunni–Shi'ite civil war, and second, by moving America's economy off our fossil fuel addiction once and for all. The invasion of Iraq had nothing to do with WMDs or 9/11 and more to do with a neoconservative agenda that seeks to control the Middle East and its supply of oil. By invading Iraq, we only increased the threat posed by Islamic radicals, whereas immediately after 9/11 we could have used our goodwill around the globe to isolate these extremists. We've listened to the last two presidents talk about funding alternative energy during State of the Union speeches, yet nothing is ever funded. Meanwhile, fuel prices continue to skyrocket, and the oil companies continue to reap tens of billions of dollars every week. Well, I have a different agenda, and it's not to engage in endless rhetoric. Together, we will take the necessary steps to once and for all free our nation of our addiction to oil, and that, Katie, will make our country safer."

"President Prescott?"

"Katie, there's a simple reason our country hasn't suffered a major attack since September 11, 2001, and that's because the Bush administration, backed by the support of a republican House and Senate, passed legislation designed to go after the bad guys while keeping our nation safe. President McKuin followed in his footsteps but could not take our security to the next level because the Democrats controlled the House and Senate. Still, one subway attack in eleven years . . . it's hard to debate those kind of results. My opponent and other liberal Democrats like him would argue that wire tapping and identity cards are nothing more than an invasion of privacy, that passage of the Patriot Act was an infringement on our right to live in a free society, and if you believe that, then on November 8 you should cast your vote for the Democrats. Personally, as a law-abiding citizen, I'm comforted knowing my government is doing all it can to prevent another attack, and that the Republicans were in office at the time Al-Qaeda struck. As to these latest rumors, Kelli Doyle served her country honorably, but it's a little too convenient to pin this information on a dead woman, especially right before a presidential election. Personally, I believe the information was released by some 527 group with ties to the liberal wing of the Democratic Party. When I read an e-mail that links a nuclear attack with a group of Patriotic Americans . . . it just sickens me that members of our party and their families have to be exposed to such underhanded politics."

"Senator?"

"When it comes to underhanded politics, Karl Rove wrote the book, and the Republicans published it. As for the Patriot Act, I've yet to see a shred of evidence that indicates those laws prevented an attack or led to the capture of a single terrorist. What the Patriot Act has done is make a mockery of our Constitution. If the American public actually knew what was written into this far-reaching document, there'd be a march on Washington. Simply put, the Patriot Act has legalized Gestapo tactics, allowing the federal government to investigate anyone for any reason, evidence be damned, and if you are investigated, there's even a clause that forbids you to speak about the investigation or face criminal prosecution. The fact of the matter is, the Patriot Act was passed before members of Congress ever had a chance to read it, and it has been used as a tool by the White House to monopolize its powers ever since."

"President Prescott?"

"Again, the senator demonstrates the difference between a liberal view of the world and the actions necessary to protect our democracy from those who would attack us. The simple, frightening situation in the world we live in is that there is a sect of Islamic extremists who are ready and willing to strap bombs onto their bodies in order to kill us, and weaning our economy off oil isn't going to send them packing. I don't like it and you don't like it, but these radicals are out there. We know what they're capable of, we've seen their senseless killing and destruction. Add a rogue power like Iran enriching uranium for nuclear bombs, and you have a recipe for disaster. Remember, we have to rise to the challenge and be perfect every time, they only have to be successful once. The Patriot Act is an essential tool for going after the bad guys, end of story."

"Next question; this one for President Prescott. Mr. President, as mentioned, Senator Mulligan has made it the thrust of his campaign to take our nation off of fossil fuels. How much oil is left in world reserves, and should we be moving to change our nation's energy infrastructure as the senator is suggesting?"

"Katie, before his passing, President McKuin commissioned a new study on world oil reserves. I've seen this classified document, and I can assure you that, based on current world usage, we should have enough oil to last us until 2035 and beyond. Having said that, I believe it's only prudent that we continue to explore all available options to bring alternative energy sources online. I do not, however, share the Chicken Little theory that my opponent has made the thrust of his campaign."

"Senator Mulligan?"

"Well, I have no idea what's in this classified document, nor has anyone in Congress been privy to its contents. Whether we have less than a decade of oil left, as some experts have stated, or two decades isn't the point. Fossil fuels are running out, fossil fuels dictate foreign policy, fossil fuels make us dependent on third-world nations that harbor and finance terrorism, and fossil fuels exacerbate climate change, an extremely dangerous situation that the last two republican administrations went out of their way to refute despite overwhelming evidence to the contrary. Katie, my message to the American people is that this election is about choosing the kind of world and economy we want our children and their children to live in. By investing in clean, renewable energy we can reduce global warming, reduce and eventually eliminate our dependence on hostile regimes, create entirely new industries that will not be outsourced overseas, and eliminate the graft and corruption that the fossil fuel lobby has spawned over the last sixty years. And the only reason, Katie, that the majority of Republicans continue to fight and block these initiatives year after year is that their campaigns are financed by the very corporations that keep us addicted to their product. If a nation like Brazil can switch to ethanol-based E85 fuel and eliminate its dependence on oil, then why can't we? The American people deserve better."

"President Prescott?"

"Changing the infrastructure of a country like Brazil is a whole lot different that changing the largest and most successful economy in the world. We're already running huge deficits, where are we going to get the money?"

"Senator?"

"Besides the terrible loss in lives, we spent a trillion dollars on a war we never should have entered, and the tally for that invasion continues to climb by $80 billion every year. Ever wonder where that money goes? It goes into the pockets of corporations who deal in warfare and industries that want to keep us on the fossil fuel needle. One of my first duties as president will be to pass a law that restricts any business offering its services in a wartime venture from making a profit. Meanwhile, I say let's bring our men and women home and use that $80 billion a year to sow the seeds of a new clean, green economy. The prosperity of the masses should outweigh the greed of the few. Enough is enough."

"Senator Mulligan, you've staked your campaign on tying both your foreign and domestic policy on making radical changes in our country's infrastructure that will wean our nation off of fossil fuels. Specifically, what do you hope to accomplish in your first hundred days in office if elected?"

"Katie, first and foremost, I would put an immediate freeze on CO_2 emissions and a moratorium on new coal-fired plants that don't capture and store CO_2 emissions. Our goal is to reduce atmospheric carbon dioxide by 90 percent within the next three decades. Next, I would eliminate the payroll tax and substitute it for a carbon tax—something Vice President Gore has been pushing for since 2007. The idea here is to create a pollution credit business whereby entrepreneurs would invest in new technologies designed to clean up pollution, turning a nice profit by selling the CO_2 reductions in the open market. I would also demand much higher fuel economy standards for cars, eventually outlawing vehicles that use more than fifty percent gasoline."

"Senator, wouldn't these proposed changes be rather expensive?"

"A trillion dollars, Katie . . . that's what the war in the Middle East has cost us so far. All Americans should ask themselves if they honestly believe we'd have spent that trillion dollars and gone to war if Iraq had no oil. So when you say the programs I've just outlined are expensive . . . we've already payed the price, and that's without even counting the human toll. Once in place, these green programs would more than pay for themselves while greatly reducing carbon dioxide emissions and gradually reversing climate change. But if we wait, if we allow the greedy few to continue to safeguard their own financial interests, disputing the overwhelming evidence that says we must act now, then the costs will be far greater. And that's a cost that none of us can afford to pay."

SMOKEY HILLS, KANSAS
6:49 A.M. MST

SPECIAL AGENT ELLIOTT GREEN FILLS THE Honda Accord's gas tank at the Exxon station, his bloodshot eyes focused on the white van progressing through the drive-thru lane of the McDonald's across the four-lane highway. He contemplates a mad dash for the men's room, but the van is already at the pay window. *Cutting it too close . . .*

He caps the tank, returns the pump, and climbs back in the rental car, turning the radio volume up on the rebroadcast of the presidential debate.

Across the street, the van pulls out of the McDonald's drive-through onto U.S. Highway 83, continuing south—

—the FBI agent's vehicle remaining seven cars behind.

◆ ◆ ◆

Elliott Green has been tailing the van driven by Michael Tursi and Shane Torrence for nearly sixteen hours. After leaving the old garage in Flagstaff, the two suspects had driven east on Route 40 out of Arizona. By the time they entered New Mexico, Green had been on his cell phone with FBI–Phoenix.

Phoenix was not the closest FBI office to Flagstaff, but it was the one Green trusted. Back in July of 2001, two months prior to the 9/11 attacks, Kenneth Williams, a senior special agent from the Phoenix FBI terrorism task force had alerted FBI Headquarters about a radical group of Muslims taking flight lessons in Arizona. Williams's memo to FBI director Robert Mueller specifically mentioned the threat of hijacking aircraft. Williams's urgent request to institute a nationwide survey of aviation schools to discern a pattern was denied. During the subsequent investigation, Director

Mueller would classify the document and refuse to show it to members of the Senate 9/11 panel.

Green gave FBI–Phoenix the location of the boarded-up garage, along with the van's license plate. He also told them about FBI Director Schafer's phone calls to Michael Tursi.

As the van continued north into Colorado, zigzagging across local thoroughfares before reaching Route 70, the Phoenix director had phoned Green to report the garage had exploded and burned to the ground. Because Special Agent Green had been suspended, the Phoenix director was obligated to report the information to his own superiors.

It was late Wednesday afternoon when the white van crossed into Kansas. For a while it seemed they would remain on Interstate 70, until the suspects had exited on Route 83, heading south through Kansas's north-central "badlands."

Elliott is exhausted. He has not slept for more than two hours at a time in weeks, afraid he would lose track of Michael Tursi. He is running on caffeine, adrenaline, and fear . . . fear that a nuclear detonation is imminent, fear that one mistake at this juncture might cost the lives of millions of people.

He has replayed the telephone conversation between Director Schafer and Michael Tursi dozens of times while driving, desperate to break their code.

"The patient's in labor." *The attack is imminent.*

"Where?"

"St. Mary's Hospital."

"So soon?" *The hospital name must determine the date of the attack.*

"Yes or no, is the doctor ready to deliver?" *Professor Bi.*

"He's ready. I hear twins." *Bi has constructed two bombs, ready to be delivered to the target sites.*

Two vans, two bombs. To prevent the second he must stop the first.

◆　◆　◆

The urge to urinate becomes overwhelming. Elliott wiggles his legs back and forth, his bladder feeling ready to explode. He starts to pull over when the van suddenly turns left, heading east on Jayhawk Road.

They have entered a desolate valley known as Smoky Hills. The first area ever chosen by the U.S. Department of the Interior as a national natural landmark, these midwestern flat lands date back more than 100 million years to the Cretaceous Period, when Kansas was covered by treacherous seas populated by fifty-foot plesiosaurs and other prehistoric monsters. Now a fossilized desert, the valley contains towering chalk formations that reach heights of seventy feet, interspersed with incredible buttes and sandstone arches.

Elliott glances at the calendar he purchased three rest stops ago. *The patient is in labor . . . any holidays coming up?* He checks the calendar again.

Halloween . . . could be, wait, Monday is Columbus Day, could it be that soon? What would St. Mary's have to do with Columbus Day? Christopher Columbus . . . 1492 . . . three ships, what the hell were their names? The Nina, the Pinta—

". . . the Santa Maria! St. Mary's hospital! The attack is on Monday!"

He almost veers off the side of the road as the van turns again, this time heading south. Green follows, suddenly finding himself on a deserted stretch of roadway, the van and his rental car the only vehicles around.

Careful Elliott . . . He slows, but there is no where to hide.

Dust clouds roll up ahead as the van pulls off the road onto the shoulder.

Damn . . . did they make you? Too late, just keep going, double-back when you can.

Green shoves his electronic gear and the evidence incriminating Schafer under his seat. He accelerates past the van on his left, staring straight ahead—

—never noticing the gunman poised on one knee on the right side of the road.

A swarm of bullets bursts through the passenger side window, splattering Elliott Green's remains across the dashboard. The rental car veers off the left side of the road, continuing another sixty yards across the flatlands before coming to a halt.

Shane Torrence jogs across the tarmac, joining Michael Tursi. The two SSB officers approach the stalled vehicle, guns in hand.

Tursi opens the driver's side door and nudges the corpse back into its seat. Urine streams from the dead man's crotch.

Torrance stares at Green's bloody face, the dead man's eyes still open in shock. "Aw, hell!"

"What? You know this guy?"

"It's the FBI agent, the one who was staking out Bi."

"Schafer?"

"Who else?"

"Incompetent bastard!" The Turk shoots Green's corpse four more times in the chest, sending Torrence backing away for cover.

"Easy, Turk!" Using the barrel of his gun, Torrence prods and feels along Green's clothing. Locates the cell phone in a pants pocket. Carefully extracts it, wiping the blood off with the loose end of the dead agent's tee-shirt. "We'll check his outgoing calls, see who he's been talking to."

"Yeah, good." Tursi looks around, the flatlands running forever, yielding to an occasional monument of rock. He points southeast. "Send him out there while I change our license plate."

Torrence nods, then searches the ground. He collects several heavy rocks—

—while Tursi returns to the van. From an envelope under his seat he removes a new license plate, this one registered in Ohio. Grabbing a screwdriver from the glove box, he removes the old license plate, swapping it for the Ohio tag—

—as Torrence restarts the FBI Agent's rental car and adjusts the steering wheel, aiming it for the open flat lands. Weighing down the gas pedal with the rocks, he puts the vehicle in gear, sending Elliott Green's remains bounding over a sea of desert for parts unknown.

"Where was the military? General Richard Myers [Acting Chair of the Joint Chiefs of Staff] and Mike Snyder [NORAD spokesperson] both said no military jets were sent up until after the strike on the Pentagon [9:38]. Yet American Airlines Flight 11 had shown two of the standard signs of hijacking at 8:15. This means that procedures that usually result in interception within ten or so minutes had not been carried out in eighty minutes. That enormous delay suggested that a stand-down order, canceling standard procedures, must have been given."

—Professor David Ray Griffin,
The 9/11 Commission's Incredible Tales

"A report by Transportation Department inspector general Kenneth Mead said the manager for the New York air traffic control center asked controllers to record their experiences a few hours after the crashes, believing they would be important for law enforcement. Sometime between December 2001 and February 2002, an unidentified Federal Aviation Administration quality assurance manager crushed the cassette in his hand, cut the tape into small pieces and threw them away in multiple trashcans [sic], the report said. The manager said he destroyed the tape because he felt it violated FAA policy calling for written statements from controllers who have handled a plane in an accident or other serious incident."

—Leslie Miller,
Associated Press writer,
May 6, 2004

CHAPTER 39

RED SEA PALACE HOTEL
JIDDAH, SAUDI ARABIA
OCTOBER 6, 2012
SATURDAY 1:26 AM LOCAL TIME

A STEADY BREEZE BLOWS IN FROM the open balcony doors overlooking the Red Sea. Scott Santa lies spreadeagled across one of the room's two double beds, finishing a joint, his eyes glazing over the live broadcast of the presidential debate. In the second bed are the Asian prostitutes, the two women curled next to one another like spoons. He turns the TV louder as one starts snoring.

A double knock. "Room service."

"About time." He puts the joint out, slips on his boxer shorts, and opens the door—

—the Saudi police bashing their way inside, guns aimed at his face. "Down! On your knees!"

"American! I'm an American! My company works with—"

"Quiet!" One of the police strikes him with a baton across the back of his head.

The two naked women cower as their client is forcibly handcuffed and dragged out of the room.

ABQAIQ OIL REFINERY
SAUDI ARABIA
4:16 AM LOCAL TIME

"TONIGHT WE CHANGE HISTORY! FIRST WE reclaim our nation's stolen resources, then the Arabian nation!"

Four thousand laborers, half of them foreign nationalists, cheer the live Internet feed of Prince Alwaleed bin Talal and their brothers-in-arms—members of the Ashraf movement.

Since 2005, Al-Qaeda and other Islamic extremist groups have launched a dozen unsuccessful attacks on the Abqaiq refinery, the most secure site in all of Saudi Arabia. Tonight's assault was a bloodless coup—the culmination of eight months of selling the revolution to workers who have always despised the House of Saud, combined with three weeks of working without paychecks due to "technical problems" at the National Bank.

Now, hours after the takeover, supporters have been streaming into the compound by the hundreds, many carrying weapons, cheering the arrival of the Saudi army and their military vehicles.

In Saudi Arabia, it is the National Guard, made up of loyal Bedouin, that is entrusted with protecting the Royals and the kingdom's major cities. Far smaller, the Saudi Armed Forces are purposely positioned outside the major centers of government, making it more difficult for the soldiers to overthrow the king.

But keeping these disgruntled soldiers isolated made it easier for Ashraf's leaders to sway them to their side. With the successful takeover at the Abqaiq compound, the military has mobilized, sending dozens of long-dormant Bradley Fighting machines and armored personal carriers through the refinery's open gates—

—while in an administration building, Ramzi Karim meets with his military advisors who are coordinating the revolution.

"The compound is secure," reports General Al-Jaber. "Seven wounded, nothing serious; all were members of the Interior Ministry. The American workers will remain locked down in their dormitories as we agreed. Aramco personnel harboring loyalty toward the Royals have been segregated from the group and placed under guard in the cafeteria."

Ramzi nods. "And the infrastructure?"

"All separation stations and natural gas plants are being rigged with explosives," says Mohammed Zayed, a disgruntled Saudi Aramco official. "Demolition teams are heading out to the pumping stations now."

"Be sure the televison crews film this when they arrive. Tell me about the military bases."

"Eastern Area Command reports Dhahran has been secured."

"Northern Command at Hafr al-Batin as well. Four Saudi pilots were arrested, the other Royals haven't shown up for duty since their bank accounts were purged."

Ramzi smiles. "What about the bases in Tabuk and Khamis Mushayt?"

"Northwestern and Southern Command Centers have been secured. But we knew the bases would not be a problem. How will the clerics respond?"

"They will wait and see."

"We still have the element of surprise," the general reminds him. "Perhaps we should consider making a move on Riyadh. With the king and his ministers in France—"

Ramzi shakes his head. "Move on Riyadh now and we invite the U.S. Armed Forces to enter the arena, and a direct confrontation is the last thing we want. The refinery may be our bartering chip, but this is only one battlefield, and there are things going on in America that must be resolved before we take the next step in the revolution. The last thing we need is to appear like a regime of Islamic extremists. Let the Royals appear desperate. Our first goal must be to win the battle of perception among the western media and the confidence of our own people."

BOCA RATON, FLORIDA
OCTOBER 6, 2012
7:40 AM EST

JENNIFER WIENNER DRIVES SOUTH ALONG SCENIC route A1A, the pristine aqua-blue of the Atlantic Ocean on her left, high-rise condominiums on her right. She is happy about her campaign efforts but far from satisfied.

The latest polls indicate Senator Mulligan has increased his lead over President Prescott by a 52 percent to 44 percent margin. More important, the country clearly favors the immediate withdrawal of American troops from the Middle East as well as moving forward with a green energy plan.

But poll numbers mean nothing when dealing with a win-at-all-cost GOP machine—one she knows is capable of pulling off its own "October surprise" at any time.

◆ ◆ ◆

The original "October surprise" dates back to the 1980 presidential election, when the release of American hostages from Iran would have all but guaranteed a re-election win to democratic incumbent Jimmy Carter, whose administration was preparing to implement a second rescue attempt in the event negotiations broke down.

When the Reagan-Bush campaign heard about the rescue, they launched a major publicity blitz warning the public that President Carter was timing an "October surprise" solely to win the election. Meanwhile, former CIA director George Bush and other members of the Reagan team were secretly meeting with high-level Iranian and Israeli representatives in a hotel in Paris, forging an agreement that promised to award Iran with arms and spare military parts in return for agreeing not to release the American hostages until after the election.

On October 21, Iran publicly broke off negotiations with the Carter administration, dispersing the hostages to several different locations a day later in order to dissuade another rescue. Two days later, a planeload of F-4 aircraft tires arrived in Iran from Israel without the Carter administration's knowledge. Reagan won the election, and the hostages were released on January 21, 1981, only minutes after the republican nominee was sworn in as president.

◆　◆　◆

Turning off A1A at Palmetto Park Road, Jennifer parks in front of a deli. Inside, she orders a breakfast sandwich and a coffee to go, then walks back across A1A to an oceanfront pavilion to enjoy her food.

There are a dozen benches beneath the roofed structure, one occupied by a couple in their seventies, another by a scantily clad female jogger tending to her miniature poodle. Teens mill about by the rail, watching surfers catch the occasional four-foot swell. Down the beach, a yoga class finishes their sunrise meditation.

Claiming an empty bench, she eats her sandwich.

Twenty minutes pass.

"May I?" Without waiting for a reply, Kenneth Keene Jr. parks himself on the end of her bench, removes his bicycling helmet, and retrieves a bottled water and banana from his waist pouch. "Potassium break."

"You're late."

"There's a series of commercials running on Senator Downing at the top of every hour. It's like a friggin' soap opera; I just couldn't miss it. This last one reveals private medical records of his wife's abortion six years ago, only it wasn't his wife, it was an exotic dancer."

"Maybe a man who runs on an anti-gay adoption platform should make sure his own closet is clean, huh?"

"It just amazes me where they come up with this stuff. It's like . . . it's like they could read his mind."

"Anything on our boy?"

"Chatter. Nothing solid. We're shutting down soon, it's getting tight."

She stares at the ocean. "Before you do, I need you to locate someone for me. Name's Armond Proctor, goes by the nickname Dale. Caucasian, late fifties, a former sailor who worked explosives on offshore oil rigs for Dresser Atlas in Louisiana. Went to work for the NSA as a computer systems analyst in '94. Spent five years with the spooks before Diebold hired him. He disappeared during the 2000 election."

"You sure he's still alive?"

She stands, tossing him the uneaten half of the sandwich. "He's alive. I want him found . . . before the election."

WASHINGTON MONUMENT
WASHINGTON, DC
OCTOBER 6, 2012
7:38 AM EST

THE WHITE OBELISK TOWERS JUST OVER 555 feet, its image sparkling in the waters of the reflecting pool, which runs west toward the Lincoln Memorial.

Scott Swan spots Howard Lowe seated on a park bench reading a newspaper. The Homeland Security director never looks up as the defense contractor moves within earshot, pretending to talk on his cell phone.

"I'm listening."

"I have information," Lowe says, "but it will cost you."

"Name your price. Sultan's desperate."

"Not from Sultan. This has to come from you. A deuce."

"Two hundred thousand? You're insane."

Lowe continues reading.

Swan swears at the phone. "Fine. Just tell me what you've got."

"We've tallied almost a trillion dollars in stolen funds. Most of it's dirty money, so the financial institutions are keeping it quiet, at least the ones in the West. In some of these other countries, bankers are turning up in body bags."

"How are the funds being moved?"

"Promis. Someone created a very clever worm. Remember Kelli Doyle?"

"The NSA staffer? I thought she was taken out?"

"She was, but apparently not before she passed Promis off to her husband. Resourceful little prick. We had him twice, then lost him in Canada, and his kids have gone AWOL. Seven weeks ago he turned up in Riyadh, in the National Bank."

"Dammit! Do you have any idea—"

"Yes."

"Can the process be reversed? Can the funds be traced?"

"Not without the worm."

"Where's Doyle's husband now?"

"The Saudis have him. They don't know who he is or what he's done."

"Just tell me where the prick's at."

"Inakesh."

"We have discovered how to hit the Jews where they are most vulnerable. The Jews love life, so that is what we shall take away from them. We are going to win because they love life and we love death."

—SHEIK HASSAN NASRALLAH,
Hezbollah leader
(The European Union has steadfastly refused to place
Hezbollah on its list of terrorist organizations.)

"We have not succeeded making our children love life. We have taught them how to die for Allah, but we haven't taught them how to live for the sake of Allah."

—ABD AL-HAMID AL-ANSARI,
Former Dean of Islamic Law,
Qatar University,
2005

"They are a persistent bunch. They just keep coming at you when they have a good idea."

—STEVEN SIMON,
Former White House National Security official
and author of "The Next Attack,"
Newsweek,
August 21–28, 2006,
on al Qaeda and Islamic jihadists, after their failed attempt
to explode U.S. commercial jets departing from London

CHAPTER 40

The stranger's face is harrowed and thin, the eyes sullen, sunken deep into their sockets. The hair is longer, grayed heavily around the temples. The mustache and beard remain unkempt, dark, with bizarre, silver streaks.

Ace stares at his own reflection in the bathroom mirror and shudders.

The guard hands him the razor and motions with the gun.

Take it easy; at least you survived another Friday. With a trembling hand, Ace shaves.

♦ ♦ ♦

Twenty minutes later, he emerges, freshly showered for the first time in almost two months, his scarred wounds hidden beneath his now neatly ironed suit. Free from shackles, he is led through the courtyard and into a different administration building, one reserved for outside visitors.

Ace catches a heavy whiff of a familiar European aftershave a moment before he enters the small conference room.

A guard stands near the door, looking bored.

The warden watches from behind a two-way mirror.

Kelli Doyle's killer is seated at the far end of the table, smoking a cigarette. The man looks up at Ace and forces a smile. "There he is. Lost a few pounds, huh, champ? Bet you'll be glad to get back to the States."

Ace says nothing, but his eyes burn holes in the assassin's face, the adrenaline coursing through his body, setting every muscle to quiver.

Scott Santa's mouth twitches nervously. "I spoke with the Saudi police. They've graciously accepted your confession. I'm here to get you out. Be smart and in a few hours, we'll have you on a plane heading home to see Leigh and Sammy—"

At the mention of his children's names, Ace is airborne, leaping across the table. He topples Santa backwards in his chair, his hands finding the assassin's throat, his thumbs puncturing flesh as they crush the man's windpipe.

OVAL OFFICE, THE WHITE HOUSE
WASHINGTON, DC
OCTOBER 6, 2012
SATURDAY 9:46 AM EST

HOMELAND SECURITY DIRECTOR HOWARD LOWE ENTERS the Oval Office, President Prescott already meeting with Joseph Kendle. The secretary of defense has laid out the latest satellite reconnaissance photos taken over Saudi Arabia.

Prescott looks up. "You heard?"

"Caught it on CNN. What do these Ashraf rebels want?"

"A Royal-free democracy."

"Crazy bastards."

"Sultan had me on the phone all morning. He's demanding we move in with U.S. troops or he'll cut off the oil—"

"—only Ashraf controls his biggest refinery," finishes the defense secretary. "We move in now, and they blow up the entire infrastructure . . . it would take years to rebuild."

Prescott waves Lowe to come closer and lowers his voice. "We'd be free to deal with the Ashraf if something happened that might implicate the House of Saud. What about . . . you know?"

"Things are progressing, that's as far as I've heard."

The president looks to his secretary of defense. "Joe?"

"Two birds with one stone? Easily sold and done."

"Then my job is to address the media. Brief them on Ashraf. Maybe seed something—"

"No, sir."

"Mr. President, it's Saturday. Go to Camp David, let your new press secretary handle this. You've spoken to Sultan; his national guard has stabilized the situation, we support our allies, blah, blah, blah, but there is no need to involve our military at this juncture."

"Good . . . good, and you're right: I do need the break. Some great games on this weekend. Redskins play the Cowboys."

Lowe nods. "Try to get some rest, sir. It's going to be a busy week."

DUNDALK MARINE TERMINAL
BALTIMORE, MARYLAND
OCTOBER 6, 2012
SATURDAY 11:25 PM EST

THE 2009 CHEVY TRAIL BLAZER ENTERS the security gates, its occupant flashing his identification badge to the guard on duty.

Jamal al-Yussuf follows the access road back toward the river, then parks in the staff lot. He has been working the graveyard shift for the last two months.

Tonight will be his last at the cursed port.

The "delivery" had arrived two hours earlier in a white van parked beneath an overpass under Interstate 95. Jamal had lugged the heavy suitcase and duffle bag to his car, along with the copy of the Koran that his "contact" had left for him.

He selects a parking space close to his destination and removes the duffle bag from the backseat, registering its internal heat as he slings it over his shoulder. He lights a cigarette to calm his nerves, then heads for the open overseas pier.

The bright yellow shipping container had arrived last night. The gantry crane had lifted it from the cargo ship's hold, Jamal directing the operator to leave it in a row and space he knew would have little traffic on tonight's shift.

The steel container is forty feet long, eight feet high and wide, with a maximum cargo capacity of forty-four thousand pounds. It occupies the bottom position beneath a stack of four. The authorities who will eventually track its journey will learn that it had originated in Tehran, loaded aboard an Islamic Republic of Iran cargo ship from the Imam Khomeini Port in the Persian Gulf. It was then relegated to a China-India Service, making stops in Hong Kong and Singapore before reaching its first destination in the Philippines, where its shipping documents had been swapped for forged invoices. From there the container had traveled through the Panama Canal and gradually up the Atlantic coastline of the United States to its final destination in Baltimore.

Jamal verifies no one is around before unlocking and opening the container's door. The inside is filled to capacity, cardboard boxes stacked to the ceiling on one side, long rolls of Persian rugs wrapped in plastic sheeting on the other. He begins removing the lightweight boxes as instructed, working his way to the center—

—where he finds the lead box, bolted to the floor. He unhinges the top and looks inside.

Empty.

Opening the duffel bag, Jamal dumps its contents into the lead box—wires, housings, plastic wrapping, metal brackets—everything covered in telltale radioactive residue.

He shuts the lid and leaves the cardboard boxes as instructed, then hurries to the edge of the pier and tosses the empty duffel bag into the Patapsco River, watching it fill and sink.

An hour later, he is driving north on Route 83 on his way to the Pennsylvania Turnpike.

Venice Beach, California
October 7, 2012
Sunday 11:15 am PST

The Bohemian walkway is lined with tall palm trees, the late morning crowd pausing to enjoy the street performers and gawk at the scantily clad men and women in bathing suits, everyone soaking up the California sunshine.

Omar Kamel Radi holds Susan Campbell's hand as the couple strolls south on Ocean Front Walk. The green-eyed thirty-six-year-old aerobics instructor slips her arm around her steady boyfriend of two months. Registers the contraction as he tenses up.

"Omar, is something wrong? You've been so quiet."

"I received word from back home. Two of my sisters were killed, shot by American soldiers."

"Oh my!" She stops walking. "How could something like this happen? Were they in Cairo?"

"Baghdad." He turns, wiping away tears. "I am not from Egypt, Susan, I am from Iraq. This bothers you?"

"It bothers me that you lied."

"People judge."

"I'm not judging. My cousin, he's over there now, fighting for your people's freedom."

Omar's eyes narrow, growing angry. "Freedom? Do you know what you are saying? Because I don't think you know."

"Maybe we shouldn't talk about this right now."

"No, we will talk now!"

People turn to look. Susan walks away, Omar in pursuit.

"You know nothing about what we want, Susan! We never asked for your help or your freedom; we just wanted security. We just wanted to be able to live our lives in peace."

"Calm down—"

"Maybe it was your cousin who shot my sisters, eh? Maybe he thought they were a threat?"

"Stop. Stop it right now. My cousin would never shoot a helpless civilian. Never."

"How do you know? Your military drops bombs that kill families, is this the freedom you speak of? The Shi'ites take control of our city, they kill civilians, is this the freedom you also enjoy? You know nothing about war. You are an ignorant woman with no hardship who . . . who dances, and drives her car, and surfs. What bloodshed have you experienced in your life to earn your freedom? What would you sacrifice to keep it?"

"I love my country—"

"You love your country? I love my country. What would you do, Susan, if foreign soldiers broke into your home and shot your parents? Would you smile at your liberators as they killed your little sisters? Or your grandfather, helpless in his wheelchair? Would you say 'thank you' when the butchers offered you an apology and $2,500 for each family member killed?"

Her eyes fill with tears. "Omar . . . I'm sorry, I didn't know—"

"No, what you mean is you do not wish to know. As long as it does not affect you, as long as you have gasoline to sit in traffic and cool your apartment, then the price of Iraqi freedom is affordable."

She reaches for him but he backs away. Chokes on his words. "I love you . . . but this cannot be. Too much has happened, too many deaths." He jogs several steps, then turns, anger in his eyes. "Do you want to know what freedom really is, Susan Campbell? Freedom is the power to inflict justice upon your enemies. That is freedom."

He gives her one last look, then takes off running down the beach.

WASHINGTON, DC
OCTOBER 7, 2012
SUNDAY 4:17 PM EST

"And the Cowboys recover the fumble on the Redskins 35 yard line. And that should do it . . . "

The barflies boo, the crowd thinning out to avoid the late afternoon traffic.

Howard Lowe taps Gary Schafer on the shoulder. "Game's over. Let's walk."

♦ ♦ ♦

The two men stroll along the Tidal Basin around the Jefferson Memorial, the walkway lined with hundreds of cherry trees—a gift, dating back to 1912, from the Japanese government.

The head of the FBI massages the tightness along the back of his neck. "When did our friend contact you?"

"Late last night. Gary, you should have told me about Springfield. The colonel's orders were quite clear—"

"Howard, I swear, I thought I had it under control."

"You didn't. Green contacted Phoenix, now they're involved, which means something has to be done, a sacrifice made to protect your office . . . and the rest of us."

"I'm listening."

The director of Homeland Security pauses to pick a bud off a cherry tree. "Gary, do you remember the movie *Sophie's Choice?* Meryl Streep's character survived the holocaust; she was brilliant in the lead."

"Yes. She had to choose, right? Between two of her children."

Lowe nods. "One twin lives, the other dies. Contact our friend with your decision. Then save the child . . . personally."

"I share a deep disgust that those prisoners were treated the way they were treated."

—President George W. Bush,
on torture in Abu Ghraib prison.
(Bush later threatened to veto an amendment to the $450 billion
Military Appropriations Bill because it adhered to the Geneva
Conventions' prohibitions on torture.)

"In a memorandum dated January 19, 2002, Secretary of Defense Donald Rumsfeld ordered the Chairman of the Joint Chiefs of Staff to inform combat commanders that 'al Qaeda and Taliban individuals . . . are not entitled to prisoner of war status for purposes of the Geneva Conventions of 1949.' He ordered that 'commanders should'. . .treat them humanely, and to the extent appropriate and consistent with military necessity, consistent with the Geneva Conventions of 1949. That order thus gives commanders permission to depart, where they deem it appropriate and a military necessity, from the provisions of the Geneva Conventions."

—International Law of War Association

CHAPTER 41

"DO YOU UNDERSTAND WHAT I AM telling you, Ashley? This man is a friend of Al-Saud. It is you who will be tortured to death, not him."

Ace is again in the death chamber. He is naked, his legs and arms strapped to the chair without the seat.

Nahir kneels next to him, pleading with him to confess. Instead he stares straight ahead, focusing not on the woman but General Abdul Aziz, who is busy in his office with the two visiting princes and their entourage of body guards. The Royals are berating the warden, cursing him and demanding answers—

—and Ace can understand every word.

For nine weeks he has played dumb, the former petrol-geologist never letting on that he could speak Arabic. Now, as the Saudi Royals rattle on about stolen billions he hears one word that tells him all is lost, one word spoken from the Royal's mouth—

Promis.

They know. Someone got word to the Saudis, and they know . . .

The muscles in his legs tremble within the leather strappings, each inhaled breath acrid with stress.

"Ashley, I have witnessed what Ali Shams will do. He will begin by tearing off each one of your fingernails, then he will work on your eyes. Tell them what they want to know, and your death will be merciful."

They know what I did. What can I possibly tell them?

"Ashley, you have proven yourself twice, but the game has changed. Please, Ashley!"

They want their money back. They will torture me until they realize the money is gone forever, then they will keep me alive as long as they can—

—unless . . .

"They won't believe me, Nahir."

"Tell me and I will make them believe."

Surround the lie with truth.

"The man I attempted to strangle—Scott Santa—he worked with my wife. Her name was Kelli Doyle. Before she was a national security advisor she worked with the CIA. She was murdered nine months ago. Scott Santa came to me and told me the men who had her killed were Saudi Nationals, members of the Royal Guard. Scott said he knew of a way to hurt those who hurt me, that if I downloaded a special CD program he had designed into a computer terminal at the National Bank in Riyadh, I would have my revenge."

"What was on the CD?"

"I don't know. He refused to say."

"You attacked him. Why?"

"While in prison, I had time to think. I know now that he used me, that it wasn't the Saudis who had Kelli murdered. It was this man . . . this CIA assassin."

"Ashley, you are certain of this?"

He looks into her eyes. "Yes."

She leaves his side, hurrying to the warden's office. She knocks on the open door, then speaks quickly, pointing at Ace.

The men listen intently. The general dials a number on his desk phone.

Minutes later, Scott Santa is led into the chamber, his bruised throat bandaged. "Now what? Prince Turki. Good. Perhaps you could explain to—"

The guards force him to sit before the warden. One man fixes the blood pressure cuff around Santa's arm while the other attaches the remaining monitors of the lie detector machine.

"Prince Turki! Is this how you treat a friend? Prince Turki, *minfadlik!* *Minfadlik!*"

The warden slams his open palm on his desk. *"Ma ismok?"*

"Santa, Scott J. I am a U.S. citizen, subcontracted by the House of Saud to train—"

The warden cuts him off with a string of Arabic.

"His wife?" Santa looks over his shoulder at Ace, his expression falling as he hesitates to answer. "Yes, I knew her."

The guard operating the lie detector nods as Ali Shams walks through the chamber and enters the warden's office, circling the proceedings like a predator in heat.

General Abdul Aziz asks another question.

The Russian-American stares at the rotund Saudi torturer, fear in his eyes as he spots the flathead pair of pliers in the man's left hand. "CD? What CD?"

The guard shakes his head.

Ali Shams smiles.

Ace's eyes widen as the sadist grapples with the Russian's left hand, separating the middle digit from the rest as he positions the tool—

—the flathead wrench biting down . . .

"Aaaah! You bastard, Futrell! You stupid fu—"

More Arabic from the warden.

"No . . . no wait! Okay, yes, I was in the bank that morning, but I had nothing to do with any plot to steal your money! No . . . no! Please—"

Ace turns away as the tortured screams reverberate in his eardrums.

◆ ◆ ◆

In Earth's 4 billion–year history, only one species has evolved that inflicts pain and suffering upon its own kind. Is this evolution? Intelligent design? If we were cast from the dye of our maker, does that make God a tyrant?

For the mother forced to watch her infant perish of starvation, there is no God. For the family wiped out by religious fanatics, nothing can remain holy. For the mother of the soldier who loses his life in a battle unjust, no flag-draped coffin can offer her comfort.

For the many who find themselves facing inhuman abuse, only death is humane.

For Ashley "Ace" Futrell, there is no logic or hope, no more cause for prayer, there is simply the promise of relief that will come after a long, painful death.

As the room reverberates with Scott Santa's screams, Ace's mind races, searching desperately for a distant memory he can hold on to—a life raft in this sea of insanity.

He is in his backyard, as a boy. Tossing a football with his father, Brownie . . .

Older now . . . the strawberry-blonde fifteen-year-old he met at overnight camp—his first kiss . . .

High school . . . his first real football uniform. That first game . . .

The thrill when he threw the winning touchdown pass . . .

The screams grow louder, shaking loose the memories.

School, think about school! High School . . . no, go straight to college, life at Georgia. Making the team as a walk-on . . . playing in that first game . . . the screaming fans . . . the two touchdowns! Meeting Kelli . . . love at first sight. Taking her to Tasty World, five-dollar giant margueritas at the Blind Pig . . . making love in the front seat of my old Chevy Malibu—

Men yelling. Arabic curses stealing his thoughts once more.

Focus on Kelli, you'll see her soon. Maybe we'll be young again? No cancer, no pain . . .

His eyes have been gazing at the aluminum table only inches from his left wrist, seeing nothing, seeing everything. Now, as Scott Santa's howls fill his ears, his vision refocuses on the tray and the sharp steel probes only inches away . . . six-inch skewers designed to inflict pain—

—or liberate one's soul. He stares at the three white scars running lengthwise down his left wrist, three white scars calling to him from the past.

Suicide . . . do it; it's your best option!

With every last ounce of strength, he wrenches and flexes his left forearm within its velcro straps, gaining precious inches of slack . . . retracting and flexing until he can slip his wrist free. The rest of his arm remains taut against the chair, but his fingers reach for the tray, straining to pull it closer, to snag one of those precious probes . . . his second and third fingers pinching one . . . losing it to the tray . . . touching another one . . . easy, Ace—

Got you!

His index finger maneuvers the skewer closer, his middle finger pinching the steel, palming it, pulling it back toward the chair.

Flexing his forearm, he gradually loosens the strap around his elbow, just enough to reach his throat . . . to plunge the instrument deep into his carotid artery.

The Russian screams again.

Do it! Lean forward and jam it home!

"It was a long time ago, Leigh. You don't have to worry . . ."

Ace freezes.

"I'm coming back, Leigh, I promise. Watch out for Sammy, okay?"

Ace breaks down, unable to do it, unable to break his promise to his daughter.

Okay, baby girl, okay . . . maybe there's another way.

The screaming stops.

They're coming for you, hide the skewer!

He stares at the three white scars. Gritting his teeth, he maneuvers the probe within his hand, then forcibly pushes the sharp steel tip so that it penetrates the soft flesh below his wrist, drawing blood as he uses the wrist strap as leverage to slide it deeper just beneath the surface of his skin . . . until the entire six-inch probe is embedded within his arm.

Ace tucks his left wrist back inside the velcro strap and turns his arm palm-down as Scott Santa's bloodied body is carried out of the warden's office.

Now it is his turn.

One more shot, Ace, one more tick of the clock. God's giving you a chance to throw a Hail Mary, to get back in the game—

—all you have to do is survive.

"Tomorrow is zero hour."
"The match is about to begin."

—ARABIC MESSAGES,
intercepted by the NSA on September 10, 2001 and
translated on September 12, 2001

". . . to commit mass murder on an unimaginable scale."

—PAUL STEPHENSON,
London Deputy Commissioner,
on the attempt by Islamic radicals to
blow up commercial jets over the Atlantic.
Newsweek,
August 21–28, 2006

"Then the sixth angel blew his trumpet, and I heard a voice speaking from the four horns of the gold altar that stands in the presence of God. And the voice spoke to the sixth angel who held the trumpet: 'Release the four angels who are bound at the Euphrates River. And the four angels who had been prepared for this hour and day and month and year were turned loose to kill one-third of all the people on earth. . . .' "

—REVELATION 9:13–15

CHAPTER 42

"Aruba, Jamaica . . . ooh I wanna take you to Bermuda, Bahama . . . come on, pretty mama. Key Largo, Montego . . . baby why don't we go and snort some blow . . . way down in Kokomo!"

Michael Tursi laughs at himself, tapping away at the steering wheel to the Beach Boys' tune as he follows the airport signs to the rental car return. He smiles to the Avis attendant, offers his seat on the return bus to an African-American mother and her two young children, and says "good morning" to airport security.

Ninety minutes early for his flight to the Grand Caymans, he purchases a bagel and cream cheese and a *Philadelphia Inquirer,* then sits and enjoys his breakfast at gate E-22.

After a few minutes, Tursi tosses the paper, his mind too cluttered, too excited to read. *Twenty-two million in the bank, and everything moving like clockwork. Just goes to show, if that know-it-all Rummy had listened to me ten years ago, there'd be a McDonald's on every corner in Baghdad by now.*

Like a kid on Christmas morning, he opens his laptop and accesses the Internet, needing to see his bank account one more time.

Types in his password and code.

Looks at the statement—Balance: $0.00

"What the . . ."

He tries it again, slamming his fist on the empty chair next to him when he gets the same results.

Heads turn.

Tursi is frantic as he simultaneously re-boots the laptop and dials the bank's customer service number on his cell phone. He curses at the automated machine, punches in his account number when prompted, then presses zero over and over again, the sweat pouring from his body as a male service rep in India finally comes on the line.

"Good morning. How may I—"

"My account, I need to know the balance right now!"

"I can help you with that, sir. I just need to ask you a few quick security questions—"

He gives him his name, account number, his mother's maiden name . . .

"Thank you, Mr. Tursi, I see you have a zero balance in that account."

"What the hell are you talking about, Gandhi? Look at your records! Doesn't it show recent deposits totaling over $22 million?"

"Yes, sir. And a transfer this morning of $22,347,890, as per your instructions."

"I did not—" He lowers his voice as two police officers approach, "I did not transfer a dime! Not one dime, you stupid, godless—"

The line goes dead.

Tursi curses and dials Gary Schafer's cell phone number. He hears the "line has been disconnected" message and nearly throws up his breakfast.

He hurries to the men's room. Takes the handicapped stall and washes his face, his hands quivering. *Think it through, Turk; think it through. Can't reach the Colonel, and he never would have screwed me . . . never. That leaves Schafer. Incompetent prick. He's covering his own ass, leaving me out to dry.*

The Turk stares at his pale reflection in the mirror. "Game's not over yet, my friend. Not by a long shot."

Michael Tursi exits the bathroom and jogs to the airline counter a floor below to exchange his ticket for a new destination.

CHICAGO, ILLINOIS
12:15 PM CST

"WHAT'D I TELL YOU GUYS, SUE's the tallest T-Rex in the world!"

Mitch Wagner leads Leigh and Sam Futrell into the Chicago Field Museum, leaving his wife, Yvonne, at the ticket counter to take care of business. "Sammy, what do you think? Pretty cool, right?"

"Yeah, if it was twenty years ago, before *Jurassic Park* came out."

"What? You don't want to even look around?"

"We've been here before."

"Twice for me," says Leigh.

Yvonne joins them. "Okay, we ready?"

"Now they don't want to go."

"What are you talking about? I just bought IMAX tickets. *Mission Deep: Mariana Trench*. It's supposed to be great."

"We saw it last year on a school field trip," Sammy says. "I told Uncle Mitch that yesterday."

"Yeah, well us old farts suffer from a disease called CRS . . . Can't Remember Sh—"

"Mitch!" Yvonne pats Sam on the shoulder. "Go with your Uncle Mitch, and return these tickets while your sister and I figure out what we're going to do until the game starts."

Los Angeles, California
1:45 PM PST

SUSAN CAMPBELL ENTERS HER STUDIO APARTMENT, her blood sugar low from having taught four aerobics classes since seven that morning. She grabs a bottle of orange juice from the refrigerator and swigs several gulps, then notices the note taped to the cabinet door.

Susan,

Forgive me, please. I should never have lost my temper with you. I have some important things I need to discuss. If you could meet me this evening in San Diego at the zoo at 5:30 (at the gorilla house) I will explain everything and be most grateful. Pack an over-night bag, I have a special surprise.

I love you,
Omar

South Bend, Indiana
5:37 pm EST

Shane Torrence steadies the steering wheel with one hand and drains the remains of his soda with the other, hoping the caffeine and sugar rush will provide him with a much-needed late afternoon jolt. The Strategic Support Branch officer is tired, having followed Jamal al-Yussuf in his Chevy Trail Blazer over nearly twelve hours and eight hundred miles of driving, the last five on Interstate 80. Traveling west, the turnpike skirts the northern borders of Ohio and Indiana before circling into Chicago . . . another two hours ahead in rush-hour traffic.

Torrence has two cell phones on him, the SADM's detonator numbers programmed into both. He also has the number memorized, just in case.

Passing signs for South Bend, he instinctively rechecks his timeline backwards from zero. *We detonate at 8:11 Central, that's still three and a half hours, plenty of time to catch 65-South out of Gary, even in rush-hour traffic. Unless there's an accident. If there's an accident, I'm screwed. But it'd have to be a really bad one, no movement for hours. What about the wind? If the prevailing winds are blowing south, then I could catch some radiation. Still, I'd be so far out by that time, at least to Indianapolis . . . that should be far enough.*

He accelerates, closing to within six car lengths of Jamal's vehicle.

Stupid bastard, I wonder if he actually still believes it's just a dirty bomb. Leave the car, then take cover and watch the show . . . if only he knew. Explosion should take out Masoud Ali Masoud and the rest of the Bridgeview Muslims . . . a little bonus.

Godless Islamic radicals . . .

Soldier Field
Chicago, Illinois
5:05 pm CST

Doug Dvorak maneuvers his golf cart through the throng of tail-gaters, keeping an eye out for any excessively drunk fans. The Aurora Police Area Commander has been working security at Bears games for the last three years, moonlighting for Homeland Security.

He has never worked a Monday-night game, but he's been told the expected 61,500-capacity crowd will be far rowdier than on Sunday games.

Doug checks his watch: 5:15. *Still three hours to go before kickoff and the place is already a zoo.* Accelerating past the rows of campers, he heads south to check on the Waldron Drive Parking deck, the traffic outside the stadium complex bumper to bumper.

U.S. BANK TOWER
LOS ANGELES, CALIFORNIA
3: 37 PM PST

THE WHITE VAN DRIVEN BY MARCO Fatiga enters the building's underground parking lot. The SSB agent follows the ramp down to the lower level, then backs into an empty space close to the row of trash dumpsters. Shutting off the vehicle, he unlocks the rear doors and walks to a silver Lincoln Town Car parked several rows away. He keys in and slinks low in the driver's seat, keeping vigil on the maintenance elevator.

Traffic getting out of the city's going to be hell, at least an hour. Add another two hours to San Diego . . . could be cutting it close. Where is he?

Another fifteen minutes pass before the elevator doors open and Omar exits, pushing a four-wheeled trash bin. He tosses several trash bags into the dumpster, then guides the cart to the back of the white van. Looks around. Opens the rear doors.

A moment later, the Iraqi drags the heavy SADM out of the vehicle. He wraps it in a triple layer of garbage bags, then places it at the bottom of the cart, covering it with several full trash bags.

Omar wheels the bin to the service elevator and presses the button.

By the time it arrives, the silver Town Car is gone.

SOLDIER FIELD
CHICAGO, ILLINOIS
6:22 PM CST

JAMAL AL-YUSSUF'S PULSE RACES AS HE exits the Dan Ryan Expressway onto Lake Shore Drive. He stares in wonderment at the massive stadium looming up ahead, its bright lights creating an almost halo effect in the darkening heavens.

Tonight I will die shahid. *Tonight I will go to a place in heaven near God's other messengers. And though I will perish, my body will not rot nor cool. Tonight I will be taken to paradise where seventy-two virgins wait to service my every need for all eternity.*

Ignoring the blaring horn of an irate driver, Jamal recites the Koran's Aal-e-Imran sura, verse 169. "Think not of those who are slain in Allah's way as dead. Nay, they live, finding their sustenance in the presence of their Lord."

◆ ◆ ◆

Two cars over, Mitch Wagner lays on the horn again as traffic slows to a crawl.

Yvonne shoots him a look. "What are you doing?"

"What does it look like I'm doing? I'm trying to park the damn car."

"I told you we should have left the restaurant earlier."

"Hey, I didn't even want to go! Plenty of great food in the ball park, I told you that!"

In the backseat, Sammy looks over at his sister, feeling lost.

Leigh squeezes his hand.

U.S. BANK TOWER
LOS ANGELES, CALIFORNIA
4:25 PM PST

THE MAINTENANCE ELEVATOR STOPS ON THE fifty-third floor. Omar pushes the cart out into the lobby, the top twenty floors only accessible from a different set of elevators.

"Hey . . . you!"

Omar turns, confronted by his supervisor, Cleve Wilson. "Where you been? I've been calling you on your walkie-talkie for twenty minutes. Get down to the real estate office on thirty-six; a fire extinguisher went off and made a mess of everything. "

"Yes, sir." He pushes the cart back toward the maintenance elevator.

"Whoa, leave the trash cart here, they need you now!"

Omar nods. "Let me just park it out of the way." Without waiting for a reply, he pushes it down a side corridor toward the restrooms. He keys open a maintenance closet, digs through the bin and hoists the heavy suitcase out, stowing it in the closet.

LOS ANGELES INTERNATIONAL AIRPORT
LOS ANGELES, CALIFORNIA
4:43 PM PST

THE FBI LEAR JET TOUCHES DOWN, brakes, then taxis rapidly to an awaiting SWAT team helicopter. Moments later the door opens and FBI director Gary Lee Schafer bounds down the steps.

Los Angeles FBI director J. C. Rodriguez shakes his supervisor's hand as he leads him toward the chopper. "We've sealed off a two-block area. No one gets in or out. Sir, how certain are you—"

"We've been tracking the suspects for ten months, coordinating their activities with messages intercepted from Tehran. Had to wait until we knew when and where the bombs were coming in. They arrived in a shipping container two days ago, Port of Baltimore. Missed the suspects by twenty minutes."

"Damn."

The two men climb aboard the chopper, slipping headphones on to communicate as the airship lifts off.

"Sir, forgive me, but you're absolutely certain about the detonation time? Because we can force a limited evacuation—"

"It's 6:11 Pacific, 9:11 Eastern, and yeah, we're sure. We intercepted a communication about two hours ago between the two suspects. Besides, you'd need twelve hours minimum to evacuate LA in all this traffic."

"Yes, sir . . . but what about the second bomb?"

SOLDIER FIELD
CHICAGO, ILLINOIS
7:26 PM CST

JAMAL AL-YUSSUF INCHES THE CHEVY SPORTS truck forward, rolling his window down to speak to the traffic cop, "Please, I wish to park in here."

"Deck parking's full; go down to the south lot."

"But I must—"

"South lot, that way! Move it, pal, you're blocking traffic!"

Twenty feet away, Doug Dvorak stares at the driver of the Trail Blazer, his skin tingling with the sudden rush of adrenaline. *It's him . . . the Iraqi kid!*

Doug takes three quick steps closer, the driver pulling back into traffic, continuing south on Lake Shore Drive.

"Hey, you, hold it!" Doug turns to the cop. "Where's he heading?"

"South lot."

Doug sprints back to his security cart, fumbling with his radio. "Central, this is Unit One. Code Red! Suspect is a Middle Eastern male, mid-twenties, driving a black Chevy Trail Blazer. Last seen moving south on Lake Shore Drive, possible destination is the south parking lot. Likelihood of terrorist activity is high. Repeat: high!"

Dvorak accelerates the golf cart south along a pedestrian walkway, his lights flashing, horn blaring.

"Unit One, Unit Seven, I'm moving toward the south entry. Stand by."

"Central, Unit One, contact Chicago PD! Get a bomb squad over to the south lot—"

"One, this is Seven. I'm at the Lake Shore gate. No sign of a Chevy Trail Blazer. He must have bypassed the lot."

"Damn it!"

U.S. BANK TOWER
LOS ANGELES, CALIFORNIA
5:48 PM PST

ALONE IN THE ELEVATOR, OMAR CHECKS his watch, cursing to himself. He is behind schedule, having spent the last hour cleaning up the mess on the thirty-sixth floor.

The elevator stops at the roof. Omar pushes the trash cart across the massive helopad, its perimeter outlined by a large, glass "crown" that sits atop the tower, its lights illuminated at night. He hurries over to a series of satellite dishes anchored along the far side of the roof and drags the heavy suitcase out of the cart—

"Evening."

Michael Tursi steps out from behind a satellite dish, the silencer on his gun pointed at Omar. "You're late."

The gun spits out three flashes of light, punching Omar in the chest.

The stunned Iraqi looks at the spreading crimson stains on his uniform. Then the dead man's legs fold beneath him as he collapses in a heap.

The Turk spits at the corpse. "Can't trust an Arab to do anything right."

SOLDIER FIELD
CHICAGO, ILLINOIS
7:56 PM CST

"ALL UNITS, WE HAVE A CODE Red. We are searching the immediate vicinity for a Middle Easterner, male, mid-twenties, driving a black Chevy Trail Blazer. All police and stadium security personnel are to sweep the street-level parking lots and side streets within a five-block radius of Soldier Field."

Doug Dvorak is in the south lot, a half-mile from the south entrance of the stadium, watching a dozen cops double-time it on foot through rows of cars. *Something's wrong, they would have found him by now. Think! Assuming it is a dirty bomb, he'd want to take out as many people as possible, which means—*

"He must have doubled back closer to the stadium!" Dvorak guns the golf cart, racing north along Museum Campus Drive.

◆ ◆ ◆

The Chevy Trail Blazer is double parked by a fire hydrant next to Soldier Field, the vehicle's grillwork pointed east, facing Mecca.

Jamal al-Yussuf checks his watch: 8:04 p.m. *Seven minutes . . .* He prays aloud.

◆ ◆ ◆

"Those four, right there, kids." Mitch Wagner points to the four empty seats. "Lower bowl, thirty-five yard line. Not bad, huh, Sammy? Bet your old man would have loved these."

"Mitch!"

Sam's eyes tear up.

"Ah, jeez." Wagner squeezes the boy's shoulder. "I didn't mean it like that, kid. I just know you're gonna see your dad again real soon."

◆ ◆ ◆

Ninety-six miles to the south, Shannon Torrence pulls his car off the highway into a rest stop, preparing himself for a history-changing phone call.

◆ ◆ ◆

"Get out of the car! Now!" Doug Dvorak presses the barrel of his revolver against the driver's side window, aiming it at Jamal al-Yussuf's face.

The Iraqi stares at the police commander in disbelief, his mouth twisting into a half-snarl, baring his teeth.

Dvorak shoots out the window, splattering shards of glass across the front seat. In one motion he drags the suspect out of the car and onto the asphalt, handcuffing his wrists behind his back.

"Unit One to Central, I have the suspect. Museum Campus Drive, one hundred yards north of Waldron." Doug scans the front seat, then hoists the suspect onto his feet and shoves him toward the rear of the SUV as a crowd gathers.

"Everyone, stay back!" Doug yanks open the rear hatch. Grabbing the Iraqi by the back of his neck, he slams him face-first against the side of the truck, knocking him woozy, buying himself a moment of freedom to crawl into the back of the vehicle.

Witnesses gasp. Several aim their cell phones to record the abuse.

Doug sees the lead suitcase bomb anchored to the floorboard. He reaches inside and slides the heavy SADM out of the rear gate.

"One to Central, I need that bomb squad here, A-SAP!"

"It's a bomb!" Word spread, the nosey crowd quickly dispersing.

Dvorak leaves the bomb by the tailgate, then jams the barrel of his gun in the Arab's face. "Is it a timer or radio controlled? When's it supposed to go off?!"

Jamal's eyes catch Dvorak's watch.

"You bastard!" Doug knees the suspect in his face, breaking his nose, incapacitating him. He turns his attention to the SADM. Unlatches the casing.

"Heaven help me . . ."

8:09 . . .

The roar of the crowd rises out of the stadium, the Giants kicking off to the hometown Bears.

Doug Dvorak scans the nuclear device. Sees the cell phone—

8:10 . . .

—and instinctively powers it off.

U.S. BANK TOWER
LOS ANGELES, CALIFORNIA
6:09 PM PST

MICHAEL TURSI DRAGS OMAR KAMEL RADI'S lifeless body aside, then opens the SADM and powers the cell phone off. Re-latching it, he drags it back to the trash bin—

—as the thunder of rotors echoes across the rooftop in all directions.

The Turk looks up. The dark silhouettes are coming in fast from the southwest, the setting sun making it hard for him to see. "Move!" He muscles the SADM inside the cart and pushes it as fast as he can across the helopad—

—the SADM's unevenly distributed weight toppling the bin onto its side, spilling trash everywhere.

"Damn it!"

He reaches for the suitcase, but something bites him in the right hamstring. He tries to drag the heavy SADM, but suddenly he's lying on his face, blood pooling beneath him—

—as the SWAT team helicopter lands, blowing garbage-filled trash bags across the roof like plastic tumbleweeds.

Minutes pass. A heavy boot rolls him over. He looks up to see a circle of faces—Gary Lee Schafer and Marco Fatiga among them.

The SWAT team members converse with the SSB agent, but Tursi can only hear the pounding of rotor blades. One by one, they back away to examine the bomb, leaving only Marco Fatiga, who takes a knee by Tursi's face.

The Turk coughs up a mouthful of blood. "Why?"

Marco speaks into the dying man's ear. "Last-minute call. One twin lives, the other dies. Figured I'd play the hero. What the hell are you doing here?"

"Schafer . . . double-cross. Stole our money."

Fatiga's face turns ashen gray.

The SWAT team demolitions expert carefully opens the metal case. "This isn't just a dirty bomb, it's a nuclear device! It's wired to a cell phone, everyone kill your radios, we don't want to set this thing off!"

"Wait! Let me handle it!" Marco Fatiga pushes through the crowd. Then, without looking, he hits the power button on the cell phone . . . turning the cell phone on!

Gary Schafer looks down at Michael Tursi, who is grinning a blood-stained smile—

—the fingers of his right hand searching his pocket . . . hitting the pre-programmed number on his cell phone.

Startled looks as the cell phone on the SADM rings just once—

—stopping time.

"Then the seventh angel blew his trumpet, and there were loud voices shouting in heaven . . . Lightning flashed, thunder crashed and roared; there was a great hailstorm, and the world was shaken by a mighty earthquake."

—REVELATION 11:15, 19

CHAPTER 43

Life. Conceived in an instant, birthed in an instant, and in an instant we die, our lives those precious moments in between.

In the first millionth of a second that is the SADM's conception, a spark from the bomb's ringing cell phone detonates its C-4 plastic explosive, unleashing a speed-of-light chain reaction that blows a small portion of enriched uranium into a larger volume of U-238, birthing 10 trillion calories of energy in an intense, blinding flash of light five thousand times brighter than a Palm Desert noonday sun. Asphalt melts and paint burns off walls, metal buckling until—

—fission's first official breath, an inhaled gasp a millisecond later that captures every molecule of air over a twenty-mile radius. Trees and telephone poles uproot, windows shatter in their frames, as downtown Los Angeles is inhaled into ground-zero's vortex, becoming a purple-gray mushroom cloud whose heart glows bright red as its core superheats into a fireball—a mass of hell so hot that it briefly reaches 200 million degrees Fahrenheit, five times the temperature of the sun's core.

Fission's "afterbirth" is an electromagnetic pulse, the EMP created when the nuclear explosion's gamma radiation strikes air molecules and dislodges "free" electrons, producing strong electric and magnetic fields that damage every electronic system they come in contact with—

—including the commercial passenger jets landing and taking off only miles away at Los Angeles International Airport.

♦ ♦ ♦

"Ladies and gentlemen, this is Captain Primosch speaking from the flight deck. We are beginning our approach into Los Angeles. Clear skies, calm winds, and a temperature of seventy-two degrees. It's been our pleasure having you on board this afternoon. Thank you again for flying US Airways, and we hope to see you again real soon. We should be on the ground shortly."

High school teacher Holly Owen adjusts her seat, stealing a glance at the nervous flier next to her. The Asian man has been sweating profusely since their flight had taken off from Phoenix, but now he looks positively pale.

"Sir, are you alright?"

"Huh?"

"We're almost in LA, just a few more minutes."

Professor Eric Mingjuan Bi looks at the petite woman, fear in his eyes. "I was foolish, I should have flown out of San Francisco, but there was a three-hour layover."

She looks at him, puzzled, then shrugs it off, returning her attention to grading papers.

From his vantage in the cockpit, Ian Primosch and his first officer, Robert Slack, have a clear view of the Pacific coastline. LAX is due east, its runway in sight, the city of Los Angeles nestled farther north below the San Gabriel Mountains.

FLASH!

The explosion of light ignites the sky a brilliant white, instantly blinding both pilots, who clutch their eyes, their damaged retinas completely fried. A second later the 727 is jerked sideways as if caught in hurricane-force winds. Captain Primosch gallantly fights the controls he can no longer see, somehow managing to activate the automatic pilot, never knowing the nuclear blast's electromagnetic pulse has already crippled his aircraft's electronics.

Power shuts down.

For several long seconds the commercial jet glides in a vacuum of silence. A moment later, a chorus of screams fills the cabin as the massive plane falls nose-first from the sky like a wounded, steel bird.

◆ ◆ ◆

Infancy. It began in the second millionth of a second as a thin shell of high-pressure gas formed before exploding into a fireball more than a half mile in diameter. Vaporizing the U.S. Bank Tower down to a thousand-foot crater, the growing monster expands outward at 750 miles-per-hour, a conflagration of wind that combusts every object within a two mile radius—save only the strongest concrete structures—into superheated dust. Farther out, cars are blasted into the air like leaves on a windy day, torched into mini-explosives as the wave of hell ripples outward at the speed of sound, overtaking the USC campus and Koreatown, Dodger Stadium, and Hollywood in temperatures so hot that it burns buried coffins and the remains of their dead.

Pedestrians on the Miracle Mile blinded by the flash scream in agony as their hair bursts into flames and their charred skin peels away from their bones. Farther down Le Brea Avenue, the ancient tar pits combust, belching thick, black smoke that turns day into night. Vehicles backed up on the Interstates are heaved one over the next like flaming dominoes.

Dexter Khan and his wife, Brenda, are sitting in traffic on Santa Monica Freeway when the couple from Trinidad and Tobago are instantly engulfed in fire, their vehicle hurled off the highway along with ten thousand other passengers and five thousand cars—everyone cremated before their vehicles strike the scorched earth.

Seconds pass into minutes as fission enters its childhood, fueled by vast amounts of thermal energy. Entire neighborhoods ignite. Beverly Hills and Watts, UCLA and Cal State, Sherman Oaks and West Hollywood . . . and tens of square miles in between—all engorged infernos. As these enormous volumes of superheated air rise, cool air is drawn in from the Pacific, creating a pumping action that revs up hurricane-force winds, further intensifying the firestorm. Structures collapse, adding more flammable material to the already spreading holocaust that is the Los Angeles nuclear inferno.

Back at LAX, a stunned P. J. Walther looks out from the remains of his control tower 277-feet above a tarmac that is now on fire. Bay windows he had been gazing out only seconds ago have been blasted into shrapnel, everything around him smoldering. The FAA air flight supervisor has lost most of his hearing, yet his ears still reverberate every few seconds as commercial jets that had been lined up on runways and by gates detonate in a cascade of powerful explosions that reverberate the black, smoke-clogged air. Walther's skin feels heavy and hot—his state of shock numbing him to the fact that his flesh has been engulfed in third-degree burns, charred black beyond recognition. His co-workers lie dead and dying on the floor.

He will join them before the day is done.

Miles out, a safe distance from the weakening EMP, the rest of LAX's incoming aircraft have broken from formation, their pilots engaging emergency procedures, climbing their jets to higher altitudes as they race away from the ominous mushroom cloud now rising like a malevolent genie on the eastern horizon.

In Venice Beach, surfers have been blasted backwards off their boards by a superheated matrix of molecules that now include the subatomic remains of hundreds of beach-goers. Surfer Theron Turman is underwater, having been tossed aside by his wave seconds before the blistering wind had struck. He surfaces now to a scene out of a *Terminator* movie, the shoreline littered with charred bodies, the promenade and surrounding infrastructure a blazing inferno, the eastern horizon billowing clouds of black smoke. So hot was the blast wave that great swaths of sand have been transformed into glass.

On Santa Monica Pier, Sharon Harris-Hill had been looking out to sea when the sky had illuminated its lethal white. She had screamed in horror as the big commercial jet had plunged into the Pacific only a half-mile away. Her last thought—that terrorists have used rockets to shoot down planes—

—then the mother of three had turned in horror to see a mushroom cloud rise fifty thousand feet above downtown Los Angeles—a second before a wall of hot gas, propelled by gale force winds, had blasted her sideways into the sea, collapsing the pier beneath her like kindling.

◆ ◆ ◆

Two hours south of Los Angeles, Susan Campbell waits at the San Diego Zoo's gorilla house. She has been looking for Omar for over an hour, and now her initial excitement about the getaway is turning to anger. She tries his cell phone again . . . still no answer—

—unaware that the nuclear storm clouds on the horizon contain the remains of her boyfriend.

◆ ◆ ◆

Moments have passed into minutes, the fission beast now approaching adolescence. Since its creation twelve minutes ago, more than a million people have been incinerated. Now the blast wave has dissipated and more than a million tortured souls lie in agony along death's periphery. Many are blind, all are in agony, their flesh a quilt of festering blisters and bleeding sores. For these victims there will be no relief, everything around them a wasteland of radioactive debris. Help will not arrive, medical personnel hesitant and ill-equipped to enter the radiation zone. Badly burned, their organs laced with radioactive particles, the luckiest of these living dead will drift back and forth in a coma-induced state until death finally relieves them from their sentence.

And now the first hour passes, moving the nuclear genie into adulthood. Frightened southern Californians who had been well beyond the blast wave venture out of their homes to gawk at the atmospheric maelstrom, only to be caught within its purple rain—radioactive particles of pulverized dust and debris that descends from the heavens—a fallout that will burn their skin and scorch their eyes as its toxins are inhaled into their lungs. For these unfortunate souls, death will come within twenty-four to seventy-two hours, for others, cancer will eat them slowly away during their dramatically shortened lives.

Ground zero is ash.

Los Angeles is a dead zone.

The fission monster has struck America, its legacy—a radioactive lifespan that will languish for decades to come.

"The government consists of a gang of men exactly like you and me. They have, taking one with another, no special talent for the business of government; they have only a talent for getting and holding office."

—H. L. MENCKEN

"President Bush, who used specious claims about a nuclear threat to launch his disastrous war in Iraq, agreed to a deal—in blatant violation of international accords and several decades of bipartisan U.S. policy—that would enable India to double or triple its annual production of nuclear weapons."

—BOB HERBERT,
New York Times,
March 11, 2006

"I would characterize current U.S. nuclear weapons policy as immoral, illegal, militarily unnecessary, and dreadfully dangerous."

—ROBERT McNAMARA,
Former Secretary of Defense,
from *Foreign Policy* magazine,
May/June 2005

"No snowflake in an avalanche ever feels responsible."

—UNKNOWN

CHAPTER 44

WEST PALM BEACH, FLORIDA
OCTOBER 8, 2012
9:22 PM EST

JENNIFER WIENNER IS IN HER OFFICE, reviewing a new series of 527 commercials when her assistant, Collin Bradley, barges in, shuts off the DVD, and turns on CNN.

". . . the nuclear device exploded at 6:14 Pacific, just eight minutes ago, wiping out most of downtown Los Angeles."

Jennifer goes numb.

"No word yet from President Prescott, but CNN correspondent Teri Smith is standing by at the White House. Teri, is the president aware of the explosion?"

The red-haired reporter looks as if she's been crying. "Katherine, we've received word that the president has been informed of the attack, that he and his family are being moved to a secure facility, and that he will be addressing the nation as soon as he learns more."

"Any indication whether this was Al-Qaeda?"

"The only thing we're being told is that this was a terrorist strike, most likely involving foreign nationals, and that—"

"Teri, stand by . . . we're getting a report out of Chicago that a second terrorist strike may have just been foiled. Bill West is in Chicago . . . Bill?"

The correspondent is an island of calm amid chaos as tens of thousands of football fans race out of Solder Field. "Katherine, this story is still unfolding, but here's what we know so far: at approximately 5:30 this evening local time, a Homeland Security officer recognized a suspect wanted on questioning by the FBI. The suspect is a Middle Eastern man in his mid-twenties. The officer chased down the man's vehicle, apprehended the suspect, and deactivated some kind of explosive. We are not being told whether the device was a nuclear device, only that it was safely deactivated. As a precaution, the Monday Night Football game between the Bears and the Giants has been postponed, but the crowd began dispersing almost immediately as word of the Los Angeles attack hit the Internet."

"Bill, I want you to stand by, joining us via satellite from his home in San Diego is CNN terrorism analyst Dr. John Rogers. Dr. Rogers, you're two hours south of Los Angeles. Were you able to see the explosion?"

"No, I was inside my office at the time, but a few of my neighbors saw the mushroom cloud. Right now, if you look behind me, the northern horizon is covered in black smoke from fires that are burning out of control. With the prevailing winds moving out of the northeast, we'll be evacuating, heading as far east as possible to escape any nuclear fallout."

"Doctor, we've just learned that Chicago averted what looks like a similar attack. Are our cities under siege?"

"I hadn't heard about Chicago . . . if that's true . . . then yes, it's possible." The analyst suddenly looks pale, unnerved.

"Sir, over the last month the Internet has been rife with blogs and anonymous reports predicting this attack, pointing the blame squarely at the neoconservative movement and its influence in the Middle East."

"Katherine, I think it's a mistake to assign blame before we know the facts. At this juncture our first responsibility is to make sure our cities are secure, that our ports are being checked—"

"With all due respect, shouldn't that have been done back in 2001?"

"Yes, absolutely. Experts have been preaching this for years, but Congress repeatedly failed to address the situation or adequately fund port security, preferring to focus their attention on the war in Iraq. Tonight, it seems, we paid dearly for that shortsightedness."

"Last question, Dr. Rogers, and I know you have to leave . . . any idea how large a nuclear device this was, and how many people may have perished in the blast?"

"Until we can inspect the devastation, there's no telling how large this bomb was, but as a basis of comparison, the device that was dropped on Hiroshima was a fifteen-kiloton bomb, and the one that followed on Nagasaki, twenty-kilotons. Twenty kilotons would be the equivalent of twenty thousand tons of TNT. Compare that to our modern-day hydrogen bombs, which yield 50 million tons of TNT, and you realize the ungodly potential danger of nuclear war. Based on the damage we've seen, I'd put the Los Angeles blast within the Hiroshima range. Keep in mind, those were air blasts, the bombs dropped from a plane. This was clearly a surface blast, the effects and concentration of radiation are totally different. As for the number of dead . . . untold millions."

BLUEMONT, VIRGINIA

THE HELICOPTER TRANSPORT CARRYING PRESIDENT PRESCOTT, the first lady, Homeland Security director Howard Lowe and Joseph Kendle, Prescott's hawkish secretary of defense, soars west over the town of Bluemont and Virginia Route 601. In the distance, landing lights illuminate, guiding the chopper towards the fenced-in compound.

This is Mount Weather, a top-secret military base located forty-six miles outside Washington, DC. Managed by Homeland Security, the eighty-five-acre compound contains a subterranean city equipped with private apartments and dormitories, cafeterias and hospitals, a water purification and sewage treatment plant, a power plant, a mass transit system, a television communication system, and even an underground pond. While no member of Congress has ever publicly claimed knowledge of the facility, many Senior House Representatives are in fact tenured members of this subterranean capital's "government-in-waiting." Nine federal departments have been replicated within the facility, as well as five federal agencies. Secretly appointed Cabinet-level officials serve indefinite terms, without the consent of Congress and far from the public eye, their purpose—to govern the United States in the event of an all-out nuclear assault.

The helicopter touches down. Prescott's party is escorted through a security building, his wife taken on one elevator, the president and his staff in another.

The elevator descends into the bowels of the facility.

Prescott's eyes are rimmed red with emotion. He barely nods to the MPs as he steps off the elevator, allowing Director Lowe to lead him to Mount Weather's equivalent of the West Wing and its Oval Office.

Joseph Kendle closes the door behind them.

The president snaps, "I was told a dirty bomb, not a ten-kiloton nuke!"

"A dirty bomb implicates Al-Qaeda. Remember, our target is Iran."

"We could have connected the dots . . . made the connection."

"After everything Bush and Chaney went through? Sir, a dirty bomb wouldn't have justified our response. There was no other choice."

Prescott paces, shaking his head. "This is bad. They say 2 million people may be dead . . . all of Los Angeles—"

Kendle and Lowe exchange looks. "Sir, let me remind you what we're dealing with. Militant Islamic regimes controlling available oil reserves, supplying terrorists with potentially dozens of suitcase bombs like the one that took out LA. Imagine New York, Chicago, Miami, Philadelphia . . . our major cities—all smoldering like Los Angeles. Our economy would collapse, Americans would be starving in the street . . . it would be anarchy. By being proactive we prevent that disaster from coming to fruition; we change the Middle East once and for all. Today we amputated a foot but saved the patient."

"A foot? I don't think the bereaved would quite appreciate that analogy, do you, Kendle?"

"What the secretary meant, sir, was that tonight America sacrificed a million souls to save 100 million. By beating them to the punch, we took control of the game, now we control the variables . . . we can take them out of the equation. Yes, it was a devastating decision to make, but history will recognize that we had no other course of action."

Prescott nods, tears in his eyes. "We did what was necessary."

"Yes, sir. Under your watch, the nation was saved."

The president looks around the windowless room. "I hate this place. At least let me address the nation from the real Oval Office."

Lowe shakes his head. "We're under attack, we follow protocol. The last thing we need is another *My Pet Goat* incident. The American public needs to see a man in charge of his faculties and his nation. A president who follows proper procedures is a man in charge. They need to see your strength."

"Okay . . . I'm doing better." He looks at Kendle. "Why LA?"

"Honestly . . . we don't know, sir. It was supposed to be Chicago."

"LA is better," Lowe says. "Chicago controls an important sector of the stock market. It's more vital to our economy. With Los Angeles, you lose the movie industry along with a hotbed of liberalism."

"Ugh . . . no more talking like this, I can't hear it. We're all one nation tonight, end of story. And I better not be blindsided by anything else."

Howard Lowe pats him on the shoulder. "Trust me, sir, everything's under control."

SAUDI ARABIA

ON HANDS AND KNEES, ACE CRAWLS across the desert, delirious . . . close to death. The sand burns his swollen feet and chews his fingers raw. He is feverish from the heat, the flesh on his exposed back baking and blistering beneath the merciless sun, his left forearm sizzling in acid.

He finally collapses, then rolls over on his back, the pain unbearable. "Futrell . . ."

No . . . just leave me to die already.

"Futrell!"

◆ ◆ ◆

Ace opens his eyes, back in his cell. His right hand is heavily bandaged, throbbing in pain, the nails of his middle three fingers having being torturously torn off with pliers.

"Futrell? I know you're still alive, I heard you moaning."

The man's voice is coming from behind the concrete wall.

"Go to hell."

"We're in hell." Scott Santa is lying on a mattress in the next cell. Both of his hands are heavily bandaged, the empty socket where his left eye had been now plugged with bloodied gauze. "I didn't murder her, Futrell."

"I was there! I saw you." Ace examines his left forearm. The probe is still there. Gritting his teeth, he gingerly begins pushing it back out through the wound.

"Listen to me . . . she paid me to do it! It was part of her plan . . . a setup . . . to get you to carry the ball over the goal line. Her words."

Ace freezes, his pulse jump-starting. "You're lying . . . she wouldn't do that!"

"She was dying, Futrell. The cancer had spread to her brain, she only had days, maybe a week. She wanted her death to have meaning. She wanted it to motivate you . . . to provoke you into finishing what she had started . . ."

"No!" Ace tears the skewer free from his flesh, then rolls painfully onto his knees, shouting at the wall. "She wouldn't use me like that! I don't believe you!"

Scott Santa closes his remaining eye, feeling dizzy. "Think it through. She knew how to get to them, how to defeat them. She arranged everything. Promis. Ramzi. Her own death. She even pulled strings years ago to move you up the chain of command at PetroConsultants."

"What . . . ?"

"You didn't know this? Ha." Santa breaks into a fit of coughs—

—as Ace slumps down to his knees. He strikes the back of his head against the concrete wall. Recalls how he had "miraculously" landed the promotion at PetroConsultants, how it was Kelli's idea to apply, that he never wanted to travel that much in the first place but she had insisted, the opportunity too good to pass up.

Random thoughts rush through his mind. "Her cousin . . . Jennifer . . . was she involved?"

Santa moans. "Butch and Sundance. They planned everything."

Tears of anger roll down his cheeks.

"Women, huh? Cunning as cats and just as vicious. Got to hand it to them . . . they got you to play along, and you did. Because of you, the House of Saud's collapsing, but in the end, everything will still play into the Neocons' agenda. Iran will be carpet bombed with chemical weapons, wiping out the extremists' hives while leaving the oil, and the Saudi fields will be ours for the taking."

Ace is too weak, too drained emotionally to answer.

"You and me . . . we're worse than dead. They'll keep us alive, torturing us like this for weeks. The fat one . . . he's good at his work. And the girl . . ." Santa's voice trails off.

"What about the girl?!"

The CIA agent mumbles something incomprehensible, then slips back into a pain-induced unconsciousness.

Ace stares at the steel pick for several long moments. Finally he wipes the blood off the instrument, then sets to work on the cell door lock.

"The political mind is the product of men in public life who have been twice spoiled. They have been spoiled with praise and they have been spoiled with abuse. With them, nothing is natural, everything is artificial."

—PRESIDENT CALVIN COOLIDGE

"That question touches upon a highly sensitive and classified area . . . May I most respectfully request that the matter not be touched upon, at this stage. If we wish to get into this, I'm certain arrangements can be made for an Executive session.'"

—SENATOR DANIEL INOUYE,
Iran-Contra Committee chairman,
in response to Texas Congressman Jack Brook's questioning of Oliver North regarding a secret plan developed by the Reagan administration and the National Security Council that would, in the event of an emergency, suspend the American Constitution, establish martial law, and have military commanders running state and local governments.
December 1986

"To those who scare peace-loving people with phantoms of lost liberty, my message is this: your tactics only aid terrorists."

—JOHN ASHCROFT,
U.S. Attorney General

CHAPTER 45

PRESIDENTIAL ADDRESS
OVAL OFFICE, MOUNT WEATHER
OCTOBER 8, 2012
11:17 PM EST

"... AND IF WE'VE LEARNED ONE thing since September 11, 2001, it is that terrorists know how to use America's freedoms as weapons against us. Tonight our enemies targeted the populations of two major cities. Thanks to our intelligence community and the fortifying powers of the Patriot Act, one of these attacks was averted.

"It wasn't nearly enough. We should have done more to prevent this catastrophe. When it comes to fighting our enemies, there can be no mercy. I promise you, we will find out who was behind today's acts of evil and those perpetrators shall be punished. Until then, our priority must be to the security of our nation. As such, I have raised the terror alert to Code Red. Until further notice, all U.S. borders and ports will remain closed, all containers opened and checked. All flights have been grounded. A state of martial law is now in effect, which includes a 10:00 p.m. nationwide curfew. The military will be establishing roadblocks on major U.S. highways, all vehicles subject to search and seizure. Finally, as per Executive Orders 11310 and 11921, I am canceling the scheduled November 8 national elections until an acceptable level of security can be re-established. Senator Mulligan is a decent man and a patriotic American, and I know he will accept and support these measures so that we may move forward, as one nation, in the days and weeks ahead, to ensure the safety and welfare of all Americans. Thank you, and God bless the United States of America."

WEST PALM BEACH, FLORIDA

JENNIFER WIENNER HURLS HER DESK CLOCK at the television, shattering the plasma screen and sending her assistant ducking for cover. "Damn Neocons!"

"Take it easy, boss." Collin Bradley picks particles of glass out of his hair.

"Those bastards manipulated the attack. They set the whole thing up!"

"You got the word out, the media won't let them off the hook."

She turns to him, venom in her eyes. "You don't get it, do you? Those executive orders Prescott just rattled off, they allow him to do anything he wants. The first order requires the Justice Department to enforce any and all powers granted to Homeland Security by the president, the last prevents Congress from reviewing the president's actions for at least six months."

"Okay, so we organize Mulligan and the Dems . . . we march on Washington."

"Those things only work in an open society, Collin, not during martial law and red alerts. You think post 9/11 was bad; that was nothing. This time dissenters won't be booed at their podiums, they'll be arrested and moved to secret detainment camps, beginning with any politician with the balls to stand up to these murderers. By week's end, the White House will present its gift-wrapped package of lies to the American people, and long before those fires in California are ever put out, we'll have chemical-bombed Iran and declared war on a billion Muslims."

She shakes her head in disbelief. "We're witnessing history, Collin, the end of democracy . . . the birth of the United Corporation of America."

FBI–CHICAGO
CHICAGO, ILLINOIS
OCTOBER 9, 2012

THE BULLET-PROOF LIMOUSINE PARTS THE CROWD, its police escort leading the vehicle down a ramp to the underground garage.

FBI director Adrian Neary greets Homeland Security director Howard Lowe with a warm handshake. "Sir, I'm glad you're here. As you can see, word got out that we're housing the suspect and it's all we can do to control the crowd."

"We'll move him to a more secure facility as soon as we can. This is Special Agent Shane Torrence. Agent Torrence is on loan to us from the SSB, he's been tracking the two suspects' whereabouts, coordinating with Director Schafer."

Neary shakes Torrence's hand. "I was real sorry to hear about Gary."

Torrence nods. "Sometimes life comes down to a matter of inches. The last report we had was that LA SWAT had shot the suspect on the roof, that they had taken him down. Gary had coordinated the arrest, he wanted to be there in person."

Lowe squeezes Torrence's arm. "He died a hero. Let's make sure it wasn't in vain."

Neary leads the two men inside. "The arresting officer's waiting upstairs in my office. The suspect's in a holding cell. We can move him to an interrogation room—"

"Not necessary," says Lowe. "Agent Torrence will see the prisoner while I speak with Commander Dvorak."

◆ ◆ ◆

Doug Dvorak is waiting in Director Neary's office, wearing his dress uniform. He has not slept in more than thirty-six hours, and the adrenaline rush of the last twelve has been replaced by waves of fear—what might-have-been—as he stares at the gruesome scenes on TV.

Satellite reconnaissance using thermal sensors cuts through the heavy smoke to reveal ghostly shots of ground zero. A massive crater is visible, its heat signature still radioactive-hot and glowing. Three square miles surrounding the crater have been pulverized to dust, the remains of steel girders and concrete skeletons all that is left standing in this petrified urban forest. Helicopters dropping pond-size caches of water are focusing on the still-sizzling La Brea tar pits while forestry planes drench the periphery thirty miles out, attempting to stop the spread of fires.

Perhaps the most frightening images come from the MASH units that have been set up in gray zones—intermediate areas between the blast site and the surviving population. Medical personnel sealed within self-contained radiation suits are treating thousands of shocked and dying men, women, and children, their numbers so overwhelming that they are being lined up in rows along scorched lawns and fed IV drips of morphine and sodium pentothal—an anaesthetic that is also a radio-protective agent designed to minimize the effects of radiation. When a CNN camera focuses on a burned child, Doug turns off the television, unable to handle anymore.

What kind of world do we live in . . . what kind of animals—

"Commander Dvorak?" Director Neary enters the office with his guest. "This is Howard Lowe, director of Homeland Security."

"A pleasure commander. Please sit." He nods to Neary, who leaves the office. "What you did . . . your country owes you a great debt. We'd like you to join us in Washington where the president will be awarding you the medal of honor."

Doug breaks into tears.

"I know . . . it's hard to think about such things when we're dealing with so much death, but your presence would help us heal."

Doug nods.

"I need to ask you a few important questions . . . about Jamal al-Yussuf."

◆ ◆ ◆

Heavily-armed FBI agents stand guard at a security desk check point. Shane Torrence's weapon is confiscated, his body scanned using a metal detector wand. A closed circuit TV monitor reveals the interior of a holding cell, a man lying face down on a cot.

An FBI agent leads Torrence down a short corridor to the cell door. "The drugs we shot him up with initially made him talkative. Told us about his training in Iran, started to mention something about working with a sleeper cell in Baltimore, then he clammed up. We were ready to administer more drugs when Washington put a stop to everything."

Torrence nods. "We find it more effective to use the same questioners in an interrogation. The suspect actually forms a bond."

"Understood." The FBI agent leaves. Torrence pulls up a chair. "Jamal, rise and shine."

Jamal sits up. He is dressed in an orange prisoner's jumpsuit. No shoes or socks. No belt. The cot is anchored to the floor. The sink lacks a mirror.

"Seventy-two virgins awaited you in paradise, Jamal. You had it all. You were so close to paradise, but you failed."

◆ ◆ ◆

"And you're certain the suspect said nothing?"

Dvorak rubs at his eyes, trying to remember. "My focus was on the bomb. By the time I deactivated it, Chicago PD had arrived. We secured the suspect and sealed off the area, there was no time to question him."

Director Lowe smiles . . . relieved. "You did well. Go home and get some rest, I'll have Director Neary make arrangements to fly you into Washington on a private jet."

◆ ◆ ◆

Jamal moves to the bars, standing only inches away from Torrence. "How can I still die *shahid*? Tell me!"

"You die *shahid* by preventing the Americans from questioning you, from turning your words into lies."

"I want to die. Will you help me?"

Torrence stands, using his body to shield his actions from the closed circuit TV camera. He tears at the lining of his suit, his fingers extracting an empty hypodermic needle. He passes it through the bars. "Wait several hours, then fill the needle with air and shoot it into your vein. Do it several times, then shove the needle deep inside your mattress without the camera seeing you.

"When you open your eyes, you'll be in paradise."

OVAL OFFICE, THE WHITE HOUSE
WASHINGTON, DC

KING SULTAN BIN ABDUL AZIZ AND his son, Prince Bandar, sit uncomfortably on one sofa, facing the president and his new secretary of state, Richard Diefendorf. The former Arizona prosecutor and United Standard Oil executive flashes a false smile at his guests. "Your Highness, what has always separated the Saudi Kingdom from the rest of the Arab nations has been your ability to remain flexible during times of strife. It's been this flexibility that has allowed our two nations to serve each other so well as business partners over the last seventy-plus years—"

Sultan cuts him off with a wave of his hand, directing his comments to Prescott. "The House of Saud has been robbed of nearly a trillion dollars. Rebels control our largest refinery, further paralyzing our economy. Revolution is being whispered on our streets. What kind of business partner allows these things to take place? I am here at your request, Mr. President, but my patience is worn thin. If the United States will not remedy this situation, the Chinese will."

Diefendorf continues. "Your Highness, the United States is not responsible for the illegal transfer of assets that have affected your nation as well as ours. Seven of our top fifteen defense contractors have been victimized, along with a dozen of our largest financial institutions and countless private businesses. Every intelligence agency is working on the problem, as well our banks. What we are proposing will bring financial aid to your country while allowing the Saudi monarchy to remain in power for generations to come, without fear of a hostile Islamic invasion."

"Go on."

"The United States will retaliate for the Columbus Day attack by bombing Iran's military installations, terrorist training camps, and nuclear sites. We will also target and kill the Ashraf rebels currently controlling your refineries. The nature of these strikes will not harm the infrastructure. Saudi Aramco will then take over Iran's oil fields, reselling the oil to the United States at $45 a barrel."

Prince Bandar's eyes widen.

"In exchange for a $100 billion loan, 70 percent of which must be directed to the Saudi economy, the House of Saud will guarantee 80 percent of its current natural gas and oil reserves to the United States. The term of that loan and contract will extend twenty years, with negotiated ceilings placed on pricing."

Diefendorf sits back and waits, the offer on the table.

Sultan shakes his head, his cherub cheeks twitching with emotion. "You steal our money, you steal our oil, and in exchange you offer us a twenty year lease on our kingdom?"

The secretary of state runs a manicured hand over the knot that highlights his cleanly-shaven scalp. "With all due respect, Your Highness, we have not taken your money, we have purchased your oil and made you billionaires, we have sold you advanced weaponry, allowing your royal agents to pocket billions more in illegal commissions. Furthermore, we have stood idly by while your monarchy has suppressed even the most basic of human rights from your population, while your treasury funds radical Islamic groups that attack our people. What we offer you now is not a twenty year lease, but a final solution that will remove Iran from the Middle East equation—the last challenge to your sovereign rule."

Prince Bandar speaks to King Sultan in Arabic. "This is an insult. Let the Chinese court us, the offer will change."

Diefendorf leans forward, his expression all business as he responds in Arabic. "The offer will change, Your Excellency, but not how you think. The moment you meet with the Chinese, our Intelligence Services will release evidence that implicates the House of Saud in supplying the uranium fuel rods used in the bomb that destroyed Los Angeles. We'll recognize Ashraf's leaders as the founders of a new Saudi democracy while you and your family are criminally charged with conspiring in the death of millions."

Diefendorf sits back, enjoying the look of shock on the two Arabs' faces. "Decades more of decadence, or a public execution? Think it over, Your Highness. But the president addresses the world in six hours, and we will have your decision before you leave this room."

INAKESH PRISON

SWEAT POURS FROM ACE'S FACE AS he continues probing the cell door's keyhole with the steel skewer, unsure what he is doing, the deadbolt refusing to budge. After twenty minutes he stops, his right hand throbbing from the effort.

Don't give up . . . if you can't pick the lock then find another way out.

He re-examines the heavy metal door. Focuses on its three hinges.

Maybe . . .

He looks around his cell, searching for something he can use to strike the steel probe like a hammer. But there is nothing, not a rock nor loose chunk of mortar, just the defecation hole and the sink.

He walks to the sink, then unceremoniously jumps in the air and lands on its rim with his buttocks—

—his weight tearing the porcelain bowl nearly free from the wall. Cold water sprays from a lone, iron pipe, all that is keeping the dangling sink from crashing to the floor. Grabbing hold of the pipe with both arms he tugs, then, meeting resistance, he lays down on his back and props his bare feet against the wall for leverage—

—ripping the sink loose.

The basin now rests on his belly, water trickling out the severed pipe. Leaving the sink on the floor, he returns to the door and peers out the barred window.

Looks. Listens. All clear.

He returns to the sink, raises it above his head, and drops it on the cement floor.

The bowl shatters into a dozen pieces.

He selects a baseball-sized chunk with a flat edge, checks the corridor again, then sets to work on the middle hinge, placing the steel pick along the open bottom of the pin, tapping it from below with the chunk of porcelain.

Rusty with age, the hinge refuses to yield, then slowly, gradually, the pin's head separates from the top of the hinge. A dozen more strikes and it pops free!

Ace's heart races with adrenaline as he moves to the lower hinge. He strikes it again and again, the pin rising from the hinge—

"Futrell!"

The Russian-American's voice startles him.

"What are you doing?"

"Carving my initials for posterity, keep your voice down." Ace continues striking the lower pin until it pops free, then sets to work on the remaining upper hinge, all that separates him from escaping his cell.

"Futrell, take me with you!"

Ace ignores him. Taps at the pin, inching the head loose.

"You'll need my help! I can get us to safety."

Ace frees the top pin. The heavy door wobbles, now held within its frame only by the dead bolt. Pressing against the loose side, he pushes the door open—

—catching it before it collapses into the corridor.

Scott Santa watches from the barred window of his own cell door. "Outstanding. Now free me!"

Ace carries the door back into his cell, then checks the corridor again before approaching Santa's cell. "I have no key, and even if I did, why should I help you?"

"You're not free yet. Two have a better chance than one. And I can get us to Ramzi."

Footsteps! Someone descending the stairs at the end of the corridor!

Ace hurries back to his cell. Stands the door within its frame, the fingers of his left hand holding the cut-out window's bars to maintain its balance, his right hand gripping the chunk of porcelain like a weapon as he crouches, ready to spring.

The footsteps grow nearer. The guard pauses at his door. Presses the brass key into the lock—

Now!

Ace pile-drives the door into the guard and clear across the corridor, registering a heavy *thud* with the contact. Flipping the door over, he rears back to pound the Arab with the chunk of porcelain.

"Nahir?" She is dressed in her black burka and matching head scarf, her broken nose gushing blood from the blow.

Ace sits her up. "Nahir, are you alright?"

"You don't have time for this," Santa whispers urgently. "Grab her key, and free me!"

"Shut up."

Nahir's eyes open, the woman still woozy. "Ashley?"

"Nahir, we're getting out of here."

The hazel eyes refocus. "How did you escape?"

"I'll explain later. Where are the guards? Are they posted upstairs?"

Nahir regains her feet, backing slowly away from Ace.

"Futrell, don't trust her! Can't you see she's with them?" Santa's face is pressed to the bars.

Ace stares at Nahir's hazel eyes, suddenly predatory . . . nervous. "Nahir?"

She matches his gaze, then turns and runs.

"Stop her!"

Without thinking, Ace winds up and throws the hunk of porcelain— a fastball that smashes dead-center into the back of Nahir's scarfed head. She goes down as if shot.

"Well done! Now get the key!"

Ace lifts the fallen door. Finds the key and frees Santa. "How did you know?"

"It's an old trick. Using females to gain a prisoner's confidence."

Ace kneels by Nahir. Verifies she's breathing. "She's coming with us."

"You're insane. We'll be lucky just to make it to the courtyard."

"I said she's coming."

"Fine, play your game of Sir Galahad if you wish, but if she comes to, be prepared to silence her or I will."

Lifting the girl over his shoulder, Ace carries her to the end of the corridor. Santa signals for him to wait while he climbs the steps to take a look.

The Russian returns a moment later. "Luck may be on our side. It's dark out, must be late. Only one guard posted at the gate, which has been left open. Another guard is making his rounds. He's two buildings over. That gives us three to five minutes tops. There's several vans parked about fifty paces from this building, but they're out in the open, with no way to reach them other than crossing the courtyard. Any ideas?"

◆ ◆ ◆

Ace stands by the prison block's entrance facing the courtyard. He is dressed in Nahir's burka and black scarf, the woman's loose fitting garment a foot too short and skin tight across his broad shoulders, chest, and arms. He waits until the guard enters the next building over before emerging from the shadows. Hands tucked deep in the burka's pockets, head bowed, he walks toward the van, trying to stoop as he moves, hoping to conceal his bare feet and exposed calf muscles.

He is halfway to the nearest vehicle when a large man in a nightshirt exits from his quarters on the opposite side of the compound.

Ali Shams lights a cigarette.

Ace continues walking, trying to look small, inconspicuous.

The torturer sees him. Calls out in Arabic, "Nahir, come here, I need you to walk on my back!"

Twenty yards . . . Ace pretends he cannot hear the sadist.

"Nahir, you little whore, do not ignore me!" Ali Shams staggers toward the two vans. "Nahir!"

Ace picks up his pace. Reaches the nearest van. Opens the driver's side door—

"You pigeon-brained whore, what are you doing?"

—checks the ignition . . . no keys. Checks the sun visor, the seat, the floor . . . nothing.

"Do you wish to be beaten?" Ali Shams is ten paces from the van's passenger side door when he realizes something is not right. "What is this?"

Ace flips open the ashtray . . . grabs the keys! Climbs in and starts the van.

"Hey . . . hey!"

Shifting into drive, Ace presses his bare foot to the gas pedal, the van's rear tires kicking up dirt as he executes a tight U-turn and races back toward the prison block—

—slowing as Scott Santa jumps out from the shadows, dragging Nahir's semi-naked body with him. The Russian tosses the girl through the open cargo door then leaps inside—

—as Ace accelerates back across the compound, the prison yard suddenly flooded with light.

Ali Shams runs toward the prison entrance, yelling at the guard to close the main gate—

—as the van's headlights switch on, the left beam illuminating the fat Arab's nightshirt as he runs. Ace swerves after him, jamming the pedal to the metal as he bears down on his torturer—

—who turns around just as the van's grill plows into him doing fifty miles an hour, the front bumper rupturing Ali Sham's internal organs and crushing his rib cage before impaling him as a hood ornament—

—freezing the guard at the gate, who has a dead-on shot with his AK-47 assault rifle.

The van veers toward the startled guard, then swerves out the open prison gate, bashing through the perimeter chain-link fencing.

Ali Sham's mouth projects a stream of blood and vomit across the windshield before the corpse slides off the hood, only to be dragged twenty feet more before being released . . . and run over by the van's left front tire.

Ace grapples with the wheel as the vehicle crushes the sadist's skull, popping the front left shock in the process. Steering free of the dead Arab's body, Ace accelerates down an asphalt road to the main highway, heading east.

"A democracy cannot exist as a permanent form of government. It can only exist until the voters discover that they can vote themselves largesse from the public treasury. From that moment on, the majority always votes for the candidates promising the most benefits from the public treasury with the result that a democracy always collapses over loose fiscal policy, always followed by a dictatorship. The average age of the world's greatest civilizations has been 200 years. These nations have progressed through this sequence: "From bondage to spiritual faith; From spiritual faith to great courage; From courage to liberty; From liberty to abundance; From abundance to selfishness; From selfishness to apathy; From apathy to dependence; From dependence back into bondage."

—ALEXANDER FRASER TYTLER,
from *The Decline and Fall of the Athenian Republic*,
published in 1776

"All dreaded it, all sought to avert it . . . and the war came."

—ABRAHAM LINCOLN

CHAPTER 46

"Mr. Speaker, Madam Vice President, members of Congress, my fellow Americans: On September 11, 2001, the enemies of freedom committed an act of evil against our country and everything we stand for. Thus began the War on Terror, a war that has cost us the lives of thousands of American men and women and almost a trillion dollars—a war we cannot afford to lose. And now all of us know why. Four days ago, on a day set aside to honor the courageous explorer who discovered our great nation, our enemy struck again. Four days later, as the world sits in shock, I come to you tonight with answers.

"The two men involved in the Columbus Day atrocity were radical Islamic jihadists who were recruited out of Iraq and trained for their deadly suicide mission by members of Iran's Qod forces. Jamal al-Yussuf arrived in the United States sometime in early February of 2011, and Omar Kamel Radi followed a few months later. The two met up in late September of 2011 in Aurora, Illinois, where they were instructed and financed by Iranian sleeper cells. These well-connected cells enabled Jamal al-Yussuf to obtain a security job at the Port of Baltimore, while Omar Kamel Radi moved to California to work maintenance at the U.S. Bank Tower in Los Angeles—ground zero.

"Let me repeat: the two men involved in the Columbus Day massacre were recruited and trained by Iran's Islamic Revolutionary Guard, known as the Qods Force. Iraqis were specifically chosen over Iranian nationals because they come from a land now liberated from oppression, allowing them to enter the United States without causing suspicion. At the Qod terrorist training camps these men were brainwashed by their Iranian trainers into believing the death of millions of innocent Americans would serve their people. While they trained, the Iranian government that supported their mission commissioned two nuclear devices to be built using enriched uranium-238 taken from spent nuclear fuel rods.

"We have in our possession the unexploded device that was captured in Chicago as well as radioactive debris from the bomb that destroyed Los Angeles. In both cases, the enriched uranium used in these nuclear suitcase bombs matches uranium taken from Iran's nuclear reactor. We now know these suitcase bombs, or SADMs, arrived in the Port of Baltimore on October 5. We have found the container they arrived in and the bomb's radioactive residue. We have traced the overseas shipping container to a port in Iran. There is no doubt who was behind the attacks, any prosecutor who even glances at the evidence would tell you this is an open and shut case. And we have all seen news footage of the Iranian people rejoicing in the streets of Tehran as downtown Los Angeles burned.

"The two Iraqis used in the attacks were pawns of a sinister government plot—a government that remains part of the axis of evil that President Bush described days after the 9/11 attacks. The nation of Iran had targeted America long before the attack of October Eighth, the roots of their hatred dating back to 1979 when Iranian students, serving as proxies for the ayatollah, attacked our embassy and kidnaped sixty-six of our citizens.

"Over the last seven years, Iran's President Mahmoud Ahmadinejad and his radical clerics have openly and blatantly defied the world's will by developing nuclear weapons. Moreover, Iran's leaders have threatened to use them against Israel, America, England, and our allies in the Middle East and in Europe. And now they have struck.

"How do we, a civilized nation, deal with an oppressive regime who employs its most radical element to slaughter the innocent? How do we safeguard our nation and our citizens so this can never happen again?

"First, we must remove the shackles of radical liberalism that places limitations on our own intelligence services. Tonight we are honored to have with us Commander Douglas Dvorak of the Aurora Police Department. Commander Dvorak and the Homeland Security agents operating out of Chicago saved millions of lives when they caught Jamal al-Yussuf only minutes before he could detonate his nuclear device. Commander, we are honored to have you with us."

The cameras turn to an embarrassed Doug Dvorak, who waves from his seat beside the first lady as he receives a sixty-second standing ovation. *Damn politicians . . . using me to sell their brand of snake oil.*

"Because the two bombers were not on our intelligence agency's known terrorist list, they were allowed to live and operate within our borders free of restrictions. Had the counter-terrorist program that once allowed the NSA to monitor suspicious phone calls been in place, we could have stopped the Los Angeles attack. To those Democrats who continue to criticize these necessary intelligence tools I say: What good is freedom if we fear living in our major cities? What good is liberty if our laws fail to restrict our enemies from crossing our borders?

"In order to protect our citizens from ever experiencing another nuclear attack, I am sending Congress a list of mandates that must be incorporated into the Patriot Act—mandates that will close intelligence loopholes in the system and allow Homeland Security to do its job properly. Be wary of those who oppose these measures, for their weakness places your family directly in harm's way.

"To the majority of peace-loving Arabs and Muslims sharing our world, I wish to convey that we respect your faith, that many of our own law-abiding citizens follow the teachings of Islam. But hatred holds no place in Islam anymore than it does in Christianity, Judaism, Buddhism, or any of the other practiced religions. Hatred rarely begins as a boiling pot. It is instead a simmer that heats up when communities fail to stand together against oppression. Radicals have hijacked the teachings of Muhammad. What we ask of moderate Islam today is to condemn the radical elements of your culture that led to the heinous events of October Eighth, to direct your intolerance not to the freedoms that come with an open society but to those who force you to live in fear.

"To all Americans, I ask you to continue to support the victims of this tragedy with your contributions and your prayers. I ask for your patience in dealing with the restrictions that remain in effect. While martial law will eventually come to an end, there will still be delays and inconveniences that will accompany tighter security.

"Our economy was strong before October Eighth, and it will be strong again. To that effect, we are honored to have with us King Sultan bin Abdul Aziz of Saudi Arabia and his son, Prince Bandar. The king has agreed to jump-start the United States' economic recovery by selling America oil at a substantially reduced rate—at least until we can overcome the setbacks of the Columbus Day attack. Thank you, King Sultan, you are a true ally and friend."

The king offers a half wave to the applauding crowd.

"Finally, to the nation that plotted and executed the murder of 2 million of our people, I issue this decree: Citizens of Iran, your self-appointed leaders and mullahs have led you astray, your acquiescence to their iron rule has empowered them to take you down a dark path—a path that will lead to your own destruction. Rise up now against your oppressors, or suffer the consequences of their actions."

The chamber rocks with applause.

"A previously undisclosed meeting last year of President Bush's most senior national security advisors was the higest level discussion about how to rewrite the Cold War rules. . . . Among the subjects of the meeting was whether to issue a warning to all countries around the world that if a nuclear weapon was detonated on American soil and traced back to any nation's stockpiles through nuclear forensics, the U.S. would hold that country 'fully responsible' for the consequences of the explosion."

—DAVID E. SANGER & THOM SHANKER,
New York Times,
May 8, 2007

CHAPTER 47

Majority of Americans Favor Nuclear Strike

Associated Press: October 13, 2012

A recent poll found an overwhelming majority of Americans favor a nuclear strike on Iran in response to the terrorist attack on Los Angeles.

"Iran trained these people, Iran sent the bombs, as far as I'm concerned, Iran deserves to be nuked," said Lynn McDonald, a teacher in Houston, Texas. "I know there are innocent people in Iran . . . families, but you can't just sit idly by and allow your government to support these kind of atrocities."

Iran to Launch Nuclear Missiles If Attacked

New York Times, October 14, 2012

TEHRAN—Following President Prescott's speech on Capitol Hill, Iranian President Mahmoud Ahmadinejad responded by threatening to launch nuclear missiles at Israel and Saudi Arabia if attacked. "The great nation of Islam was not responsible for the devastation in Los Angeles. If the United States thinks they can create new lies to justify another invasion as they did in Iraq, then they are making a grievous error. At the first sign of an attack, we shall launch nuclear-tipped Shahab missiles at the Zionist cities as well as the American Green Zone in Baghdad."

Israel's prime minister responded to the Iranian threat by stating that Israeli Defense Forces were updated two years ago with the Arrow 3 theatre ballistic missile defense system, and that the first Iranian nuclear missile fired, whether successful or not, would lead to a "significant response."

Code-named Homa, or Fence, Arrow 3 is deployed in two batteries, one near Tel Aviv and one to the south of Haifa. The anti-missile missile system has successfully completed sixteen intercept tests. Iranian forces are believed to be in possession of a dozen operational nuclear missiles, with Israel's nuclear arsenal numbering well over two hundred.

AL UDEID AIR BASE,
QATAR
OCTOBER 17, 2012
7:22 PM LOCAL TIME

THE AL-UDEID AIR BASE IN QATAR is the forward headquarters of U.S. Central Command (CENTCOM), the Unified Combatant Command military group responsible for rapid deployment of U.S. forces in the Middle East, East Africa, and Central Asia.

CENTCOM's commander, General Mike Tristano, began his military career in the United States Army's Special Forces. Unlike the president and secretary of state to whom he reports, the battle-tested general feels the invasion plans for Iran are far too ambitious, especially when his combat troops are already so overextended. He knows a nuclear strike option for Iran is on the table, but he has yet to be briefed.

Tristano enters his war room, joining his chief of staff, Major General Ben Serviss, his deputy commander, Vice Admiral Brandon Herbert, who is overseeing naval operations in the Persian Gulf, and Major General Cynthia J. Zizzi, the director of ground operations and the highest ranking female officer in the armed forces.

Detailed maps of the Middle East line the walls of the chamber. Facing the conference table is the room's centerpiece—an eight-foot-high, multi-layered transparent digital display board, offering CENTCOM real-time data of friendly and hostile troop movements, air support status, atmospheric weather conditions, and the location of the super-carrier, *USS Ronald Reagan* and her battle group, now steaming northwest through the Persian Gulf.

The general takes his place at the head of the table. "Do we have an updated target list?"

"Yes, sir." General Zizzi types in a command on her laptop, a revised target list appearing on the computerized map, broken down by category:

Nuclear Facilities:

Bushehr Nuclear Power Plant
Esfahan Uranium Conversion Center
Saghand Uranium Mining Site
Natanz Uranium Enrichment Facility
Arak Heavy Water Plant
Arak Radioisotope Facility
Ardekan Nuclear Fuel Unit
Isfahan Uranium Conversion Facility
Tehran Nuclear Research Center
Tehran Molybdenum, Iodine and Xenon Radioisotope Production
    Facility
Tehran Jabr Ibn Hayan Multipurpose Laboratories
Tehran Kalaye Electric Company
Lashkar Abad Uranium Enrichment Plant
Karaj Radioactive Waste Storage Unit
Anarak Radioactive Waste Storage Unit
Qods Force Garrisons:
Ramadan Garrison—Kermanshah
Nabi-Akram Garrison—Zahedan
Hamza Garrison—Orumieh
Ansar Garrison—Mashad

Saudi Arabia:

Abqaiq refinery*

Shahab Missile Launch Sites:

Targets A–G (Persian Gulf)
Targets H–M (Caspian Sea)

Military Bases:

Mehrabad air base
Parchin
Khorramabad
Pessyan
Borujerd
Zagheh
Malayer
Sahneh
Kangavar

Qods Training Centers:

Imam Ali Training Base (N. Tehran)
Khomeini Training Base (N. Tehran)
Bahonar Base (Chalous highway, Karaj Dam)
Nahavand (Forty-five kilometers from the town of Nahavand, west of Iran)
Beit ol-Moghadas University (Qom City)
Farahzad district (Tehran)
Hezbollah Base (Varamin, southeast of Tehran)
Madani Base in Dezful (southwest Iran)
Bisotoun Base in Kermanshah (western Iran)
Tangeh Kenesht Base in Kermanshah (western Iran)
Ghayour Training Base in Ahwaz (southwest Iran)

General Tristano removes his hat, massaging the tension building along the back of his neck. "I'll be blunt, people, we're still being kept in the dark by the secretary of defense, and it's got me pissing mad. Air strike, nuclear strike . . . no one's saying. But this whole operation reeks of 2003, the White House jumping in with both feet before thinking things through."

"It's no secret Prescott's people have been lobbying for a nuclear strike on Iran for years," says General Serviss. "Kendle spent time in Iraq, he knows full well we don't have the manpower to police another hostile nation."

Vice Admiral Herbert concurs. "Prescott has no intention of occupying Iran. This is death on a massive scale, any way you slice it. Even if we don't go nuclear, bombing a nuclear reactor with conventional weapons is still a dangerous venture. General Zizzi, you spoke with Los Alamos, what did the eggheads have to say?"

"They agreed saturation bombing, or even a lone Tomahawk strike on Iran's nuclear installations could create a Chernobyl-like radioactive cloud. The Indian Ocean is still experiencing monsoon season, even a small storm would draw radioactive fallout southeast over India's coastal cities. Calcutta, Rangoon, Dhaka, Mumbai, Chennai, and Colombo would all be exposed, with the higher humidity leading to even more adverse effects. Obviously things get worse if Prescott orders a tactical nuclear strike on Tehran. Radioactive fallout could effect both Pakistan and India, even moving into China, Russia, and as far east as Japan. Musharraf's government is already in trouble in Pakistan, a nuclear strike would ensure his demise, and his replacement would most likely be an Islamic radical. That would provoke a military response from India. We're also bracing for a major Shia retaliatory attack in Iraq, once the invasion begins."

"General Serviss, how certain is Intel that we've targeted all the Shahab missile sites?"

"At this juncture, confidence is only running at 75 percent. The Shehab III has a maximum range of eight hundred miles. If they manage to launch, their most likely targets are Camp Doha base in Kuwait, Al-Seeb airbase in Oman, any number of targets in Saudi Arabia, and the Israeli cities of Tel Aviv, Eilat, Haifa, Beersheba, and the nuclear complex at Dimona. The Israelis have the ARROW defense system, the other sites remain exposed. Oh . . . and of course, our site here in Qatar."

"What about the Chinese?"

"I think we have to expect some response. Iran is China's second largest source of imported Middle East oil, they also use the Iranian terminal for the export of natural gas from Turkmenistan. A large-scale invasion would likely spell the end of NATO as well."

"Damn politicians. Let 'em all rot in hell." General Tristano checks the local time: 8:12 p.m. "I'm scheduled to speak with Defense Secretary Kendle again at twenty-one hundred hours. We'll reconvene then."

The CENTCOM senior staff exits the chamber.

General Tristano grabs the admiral's arm, wanting him to remain behind. "What have you heard, and don't blow sunshine up my ass, Brandon, we go back too far."

"I spoke with Fisher, the *Ronald Reagan*'s CO. A supply ship made a delivery earlier this morning, Kendle's orders."

"What kind of delivery?"

Persian Gulf
October 17, 2012
10:28 pm Local Time

The United States Aircraft Carrier *Ronald Reagan* (CVN-76) plows through the gulf at a steady fifteen knots. A thousand feet long, displacing ninety-seven thousand tons, the steel fortress towers twenty stories above the waterline, its hulking presence on the Arabian horizon foreshadowing death.

Escorting the carrier are sixteen combat ships, ten support ships, and two *Los Angeles*–class attack subs. Two 567-foot Ticonderoga-class warships flank the boat, each equipped with the Aegis Theater High Altitude Air Defense (THAAD) program, a highly sophisticated battle-management system designed to shield the carrier from attack. The two *Ticonderogas* are also equipped with Tomahawk cruise missiles—long-range projectiles capable of destroying targets up to a thousand miles away.

Captain Scott James Fisher, the carrier's commanding officer, has spent most of the last twenty-four hours in the ship's Combat Information Center (CIC), the carrier's nerve center. Within this dark, heavily air-conditioned chamber, dozens of technicians focus their attention on tactical computer screens, monitoring the carrier battle group's position, the surrounding defense zones . . . and the electromagnetic emissions emanating from hostile forces in the area.

The captain appears a rock on the outside, but his thoughts are back home with his family—his parents and sisters, residents of Ventura, California . . . all missing.

Commander Tony Ordonez, Fisher's executive officer, weaves his way between computer stations, carrying sealed orders. He hands the encoded message to his skipper.

Fisher glances at the note. "Assemble the senior officers."

Ten minutes later, the CO joins his senior staff in a small conference room adjacent to the CIC. The evening's target list has been divided geographically, each area assigned a sortie.

"We're a go. First wave of sorties launch at zero–three hundred hours. Second wave, six hours later. Questions?"

"Second wave payload, skipper . . . is it a nuke?" Commander Ordonez asks the question everyone wants to know.

Fisher hesitates. "Officially, the decision is being held back while the bureaucrats continue haggling at the U.N., but my sources tell me the nuclear option on Tehran is off the table. The repercussions from the radioactive fall-out were just too risky." Fisher looks into the faces of each of his senior officers. "We're going with chemical weapons, VX nerve gas. The rebels who captured the Saudi refinery will get the first taste at oh-three hundred."

The senior officers nod, everyone's adrenaline pumping.

Fisher bows his head. "What happened in Los Angeles, what nearly happened in Chicago . . . it affects all of us. Nobody likes war, gentlemen, but when attacked, when the enemy brings bloodshed to our homeland . . ."

The captain looks at his men, tears mixing with the fire in his eyes, "Tonight, we teach our enemy a lesson—paybacks are a bitch."

ABQAIQ OIL REFINERY
SAUDI ARABIA IRAQ
1:07 AM LOCAL TIME

FOR WEEKS THE SAUDI NATIONAL GUARD has taken up positions out-side the fortified gates of the Abqaiq refinery, squaring off against a well-armed platoon of Ashraf freedom fighters. Not a shot has been fired, the impasse ensured by explosives the rebel's have planted around the refinery's highly-flammable pipelines and storage tanks.

Inside the compound, Bradley Fighting machines and Abrams tanks—stolen from the House of Saud's own military depots—stand guard over the perimeter fence, the administration buildings and dor-mitories. The revolution, which had been gaining momentum, has lost support since the nuclear attack in Los Angeles, an event that has enabled the House of Saud to paint the Asraf rebels as just another violent terrorist organization.

♦ ♦ ♦

A reflexive jerk awakens Ace from a restless sleep. For several long seconds he searches his surroundings until he recognizes the infirmary.

Nine days have passed since Ace, Scott Santa, and the Saudi woman had escaped Inakesh Prison. They had raced east on the highway to Riyadh before pulling off at a petrol station to switch vehicles. Santa had hot-wired a car while Ace restrained Nahir.

By dawn, they had arrived at the outskirts of the oil refinery.

Ramzi's men had interrogated Nahir. Santa was right, she had been lying. Years earlier she had been arrested by Saudi officials for her involvement in a vodka smuggling ring (alcohol is illegal in the kingdom), earning her scars from a public flogging. Her father, General Abdul Aziz—the Inakesh warden—had managed to commute her jail sentence in exchange for her work at the prison. They had made an especially effective team—Ali Shams the sadistic torturer, the beautiful yet compassionate Nahir Abdul Aziz providing a shoulder the prisoner could lean on while confessing his sins. Even the Friday execution had been a ruse, everything designed to win Ace's trust.

She remained in the compound under lock and key.

Day by day, the worst of Ace's physical wounds had begun to heal. He is now able to keep down solid foods, and the intravenous drips have fought off an infection and fever that had developed after three of his fingernails had been torturously extracted.

Adding to his mental burden are the scenes of devastation being broadcast from Los Angeles, along with the sobering realization that his children could have suffered or even perished had not the second bomb been defused in Chicago. Despite his efforts, despite the torture he has had to endure, his wife's worst fears are coming true—America is under siege from within, the Neocons firmly in control, an attack on Iran imminent, the Asfraf rebellion all but over.

He checks the time: 1:22 a.m. Unable to sleep, he laces up the khaki army boots the rebels had given him, slips on the matching jacket, and heads outside.

The moon is full, high over the desert plain, its luminescence casting an eerie light upon the armored vehicles in the compound. It takes him several moments before he realizes something is amiss—

—the Saudi national guard is gone!

◆ ◆ ◆

Ace locates Ramzi Karim in the basement of one of the administration buildings. The Ashraf leader is with his military commanders, discussing the national guard pullout. Scott Santa is there as well, the CIA agent chain smoking and listening in, a makeshift "pirate's patch" now covering his empty left eye socket.

"The Guards' withdraw means the American attack will come tonight," Ramzi restates for Ace's sake. "We need to be prepared."

"They will not bomb the compound," one of the younger rebels responds. "The Americans cannot afford to lose the refinery."

"While they may not use explosives, Khaled, they will strike using chemical or biological agents. Thousands of families—women and children among them—remain in Abqaiq's dormitories. If we stay in the compound they will wipe us out."

"We have a dozen functional biohazard suits," an Army general reminds him. "Give the suits to my squadron, we will maintain a vigil at the gates. The rest of you—lead the exodus into the desert."

Ramzi nods. "Khaled, organize the evacuation, you must leave before dawn. I will remain behind with the general."

"Wait." Ace limps toward the group. "So maybe you'll survive this attack, but it won't change a thing. You're running low on food, and the House of Saud has obviously made a deal with Prescott. How long do you think you can hold out?"

"The longer we hold out, the stronger we become in the eyes of our people. Rebellions only succeed when the will of the populace rises as one. We were close once, the American attack may yet serve to win us more support."

"Martyrs don't lead rebellions, Ramzi. If you want to take back your country, you have to do it now, by exposing Prescott and his machine. We have to connect the dots for the media, link the White House to the attack on Los Angeles. Incriminate Prescott and his warmongers and we give the American public what they need to start their own rebellion."

"Ace, Prescott's lies are far stronger than any evidence we could produce. These people don't play by the same rules, they'll do anything to stay in power."

Anything to stay in power . . .

A seed of thought takes root. Ace closes his eyes, his mind fighting to reel in a distant memory. *Anything to stay in power . . . where had he heard that statement before?*

Jennifer . . . that day in her apartment!

"And if 9/11 was the biggest intelligence screw-up of all time, how come no one ever lost their job? My friend's dead because a lot of people failed to act, and now my wife's dead because of what she knew, and you just got done telling me that the people in power will do anything to stay in power."

"You want to know how the Neocons win, Ace? They begin with the message, a lie they can sell. Message gets candidates elected. Not truth, not policies, not resumes or war medals. Message."

"Ramzi, we don't need evidence, we just need to drive home the right message. Kelli's murder, the money trail, McKuin's death . . . get me in front of the news media, I can sell this!"

"It won't stop the invasion."

"No, but it will force the American media to raise the issue, it will cast doubt on who's really to blame. After 9/11, everyone was afraid to question Bush, and those that did were publicly disgraced, branded traitors. But if we come out in force now, playing up on what we've already disseminated over the internet—"

Ramzi looks at his commanders. "Where are the news crews?"

"Gone. The national guard forced them to leave the area."

"I think I know a way we can bring them back."

"An 'emergency response exercise' is scheduled to take place at 9:00 a.m. the morning of 9/11, involving the simulated crash of a small corporate jet plane into a government building. The exercise is to be conducted by the National Reconnaissance Office (NRO) in Chantilly, Virginia—just four miles from Washington Dulles International Airport, from where Flight 77 took off, and 24 miles from the Pentagon. The NRO draws its personnel from the CIA and the military. The exercise is to involve the jet experiencing mechanical problems then crashing into one of the four towers at the NRO. In order to simulate the damage from the crash, some stairwells and exits are to be closed off, forcing NRO employees to find other ways to evacuate the building. However, according to an agency spokesman, 'as soon as the real world events began, we cancelled the exercise.' After the attacks, most of the agency's 3,000 staff are supposedly sent home."

—ASSOCIATED PRESS,
August 21, 2002

"The world's top ten energy companies are failing to find enough crude to replenish their reserves."

—WOOD MACKENIZIE,
Oil consultant,
from *Times of London*,
January 2004

"Follow the money."

—FBI INFORMANT W. MARK FELT,
a.k.a. "Deep Throat,"
in bringing down the Nixon presidency.

CHAPTER 48

SMOKEY HILLS, KANSAS
6:32 AM MST

THE SHERIFF'S HELICOPTER KICKS UP A twister of limestone dust as it lands near the camper. Deputy Caleb Kennedy-Smith allows the air to settle before exiting the chopper to join the two couples gathered by the base of a limestone rock.

The wrecked Honda Accord's grill is buried deep in the escarpment. The deputy looks inside at Elliott Green's decaying remains. Grimaces. "Alright, who called this in?"

One of the men, a heavyset biker, raises his hand. "Kevin Graham. Me and the wife were out riding when we saw the car. I told her not to touch anything, but she might have left a print or two on the door."

"Okay, Mr. Graham, wait by the camper, I'll take your statement in a minute." The deputy speaks into his radio. "Base, this is 902. I'm out at Smokey Hills, approximately six miles north of Jayhawk Road. We've got a dead body, Caucasian male, mid-forties. Multiple gunshot wounds. Gonna need the FBI in on this one."

ABOARD THE RONALD REAGAN
PERSIAN GULF
1:37 AM LOCAL TIME

CAPTAIN FISHER IS IN THE ARMORY, a high-security chamber located in the bowels of the aircraft carrier. As instructed by the secretary of defense, the CO is personally overseeing a handpicked weapons crew in the fusing and loading of dozens of specially made binary chemical bombs. Once finished, the canisters will be loaded onto the freight lift, designated for the sortie scheduled to bomb the Abqaiq oil refinery and its rebel extremists.

Hundreds more of these weapons of mass destruction line the armory, waiting to be dropped on another target—

—the population of Iran.

A B Q A I Q O I L R E F I N E R Y
1:43 AM LOCAL TIME

THE BLAST SENDS SHOCK WAVES RIPPLING throughout the compound, igniting night into day in a fiery explosion that can be seen and felt for miles. Secondary detonations follow like incinerating dominoes as pockets of liquid natural gas ignite, dispersing fiery mushroom clouds into the heavens.

Six men, all dressed in biological suits, watch the fireworks from one of the compound's golf course fairways. Ramzi removes his hood to speak with Ace, "You can feel the heat even at this distance. Imagine if we detonated the entire refinery."

"This'll do for now. What about that call?"

Ramzi digs through an exterior pocket. Hands him a cell phone. "Remember, the NSA is monitoring everything. You've got about three minutes before they intercept the call."

Ace dials the overseas number.

◆　◆　◆

"Hello?"

"Jen?"

Jennifer Wienner nearly drives off the side of the road. "Ace! Are you all right? Where are you?"

"Saudi Arabia, the Abqaiq Oil Refinery. Jen, listen carefully. Where's the senator?"

"He's in an emergency meeting with members of Congress. They're trying to force Prescott into making concessions."

"Forget concessions, Prescott's going down tonight. What time is it there?"

"Almost nine."

"Contact Mulligan. Have him call a major news conference for ten o'clock. Tell him I'm going live within the hour to present criminal evidence against the Neocons, linking them to the attack on Los Angeles. Then call our boy in Atlantic City . . . hello? Jen? Hello?"

The line goes dead.

ABOARD THE RONALD REAGAN
PERSIAN GULF
2:54 AM LOCAL TIME

HAVING BEEN DEBRIEFED, TEAMS OF PILOTS exit their squadron ready rooms, joining the controlled chaos of the four-and-a-half-acre flight deck. Crews are identified by their colored shirts—green for mechanics, yellow for the catapult crew, red for munitions; hand signals are used to communicate on this, the noisiest, most dangerous piece of real estate in the world.

Lieutenant Rudi Anger climbs inside his F-35C Joint Strike Fighter (JSF), a stealthy $28 million killing machine designed with the latest cutting-edge avionics, propulsion systems, and firepower. The panoramic cockpit is alive with a matrix of liquid crystal monitors, all linked to the lieutenant's helmet-mounted display.

As the pilot moves through his checklist, a munitions crew loads a dozen of the special binary bombs into two parallel bays located in front of the JSF's landing gear. A mechanic signals the pilot to start his jet's engine. The cockpit is closed, the fighter's surface given a final check. Hand signals warn crewmen about the jet's hot exhaust while the flight deck handler signals the "all clear."

Seconds later, the JSF launches vertically into the night. At five hundred feet the afterburners kick in, hurtling the killing machine west toward Saudi Arabia.

ABQAIQ OIL REFINERY
2:57 AM LOCAL TIME

THE CNN CREW IS FIRST TO ARRIVE.

Field reporter Rebecca St. Croix is on her first stint in the Middle East. Her cameraman, Larry Kelly, is doubling as her director, his younger brother, Sean, their soundman. As Larry films the blaze, the gates of the compound open, and they are greeted by Ramzi Karim, still wearing his biological suit.

"My name is Ramzi Karim, I am a former member of the CIA and one of the Ashraf leaders. I have with us an American citizen who has evidence that President Prescott and a neoconservative faction were involved in the plot to blow up Los Angeles and Chicago."

Rebecca's grey-blue eyes widen. "Where is he? Will he allow us to interview him?"

"Yes, but it must be a live interview. Can you arrange this?"

Before she can respond, Larry Kelly is dialing his cell phone.

♦ ♦ ♦

Ace, dressed in his biohazard suit, enters the administration building basement where Nahir Abdul Aziz is being held in a locked meeting room. Keying open the deadbolt, he opens the door.

She is seated in a padded chair, the burka having been replaced with an oil worker's orange jumpsuit. Her long hair is braided, hanging free behind her back. The hazel eyes soften as he enters the room.

"Ashley . . . are you here to kill me?"

"No."

"You understand, there was nothing I could do. Saudi women have no power, marked women like myself are a scourge—"

"I understand."

"Inakesh is a terrible place, I too was its prisoner—"

"I said I understand. Nahir, for whatever reason, you were the one who kept me alive, the one who nursed my wounds. In the middle of the insanity, you were my only beacon of hope. For a while, a part of me actually, well—"

"Love?"

"I don't know . . . maybe."

"It was part of the illusion, Ashley. Trust me, I am not worthy of your love."

"People can change."

"I am not so sure."

"If that's true, then civilization may already be over." He hands her the key. "I came to release you. Ashraf's abandoning the compound, American fighters are on the way. You can follow the others into the desert, then it's up to you."

"And you?"

"I'm staying here. News reporters are on their way. I'm going to try to stop a nuclear holocaust."

"If it's alright, I will stay with you." She squeezes his hand, then looks up as Scott Santa enters the room, wearing his own biohazard suit.

"Conspiring with the enemy?"

"What is it you want?"

"A word. Alone."

Ace nods to Nahir, who leaves.

"Think about what you're about to do, Futrell. Think about the repercussions."

"I have."

"No, I don't think so." Santa circles the conference table, his lone eye irritated and red, twitching nervously. "You're about to announce to the world that the president of the United States willfully allowed millions of Americans to die in order to justify the bombing of Iran."

"The world needs to know the truth."

"The truth? You don't know the truth! Do you even understand what this conflict is about?"

"Oil."

"Oil is nothing but a by-product. This is about two different ideologies, one an open society promoting freedom and commerce, the other a closed society dominated by religious fanatics who kill indiscriminately in order to control their own populace. These people live to die, Futrell. They've been taught to hate since birth—it's all they know. You can't rationalize with terrorists who have been convinced that blowing up innocent people is their ticket to paradise."

Santa pauses. "Listen."

Ace hears a low rumbling sound . . . bombs exploding in the distance.

"It's begun," Santa says. "Tonight we cut off the head of Islamofacism. Make your little speech and you dishonor the deaths of those Americans whose sacrifice will lead to a greater good."

"Not every end justifies the means. What kind of democracy allows its president and advisors absolute power to wipe out entire populations because they alone decided it was the best course of action?"

"This isn't about democracy, it's about war . . . the war on terror."

"Not every Iranian is a terrorist. There are innocent people out there, families who have no interest in your rules of conflict or your idea of democracy, they just want to live out their lives in peace. These are moderates who want to live a civilized life, our actions are what pushes them to accept radical Islam. Winning their hearts is the key to defeating radicals. We should be supporting their efforts, not slaughtering them."

"In war, innocent people sometimes die. What history honors is the cause."

"What cause? Capitalism? Is that your justification for slaughtering millions?"

Santa shakes his head. "You know nothing about the real world. Millions die every year, we just ignore the headlines. They die of war and abuse, they die of starvation and disease. Americans ignore their plight, filing it away as another global cause allocated to celebrities. My family's roots trace back to Russia, to the time of the czar. You have no idea what it means to live under an oppressive regime. I served in the Company, the CIA, for twenty-six years. What you call murder we called liberating societies. And that's what we do tonight. Yes, the cost is high, but if we do nothing, then the cost is a hundred-fold. Think it through! The world is filled with oppressive regimes . . . Islamic radicals who won't hesitate for a moment to wipe out as many westerners as they can. What happens when a nut like Mahmoud Ahmadinejad or his Hezbollah goons actually launch a real WMD, not some ten-kiloton suitcase nuke, but a fifty-megaton warhead. Maybe they'll wipe out Israel, maybe the entire island of Manhattan! What will you say then?"

Ace loosens the upper catches on his Racal suit. "I agree there's a real threat, but we're making it worse. Afghanistan was necessary, by invading Iraq we forced Muslim moderates to choose sides instead of helping us to isolate the extremists. Today's actions will signal the official start of a holy war that will only end with the destruction of civilization. Violence never truly stops violence, only peace can do that."

Santa sneers. "Peace? Peace is an illusion. This is good versus evil, a black-and-white issue, and those of us who see the world for what it is cannot afford to wallow in a liberal's shades of gray."

Ace steals a glance over Santa's shoulder, then stares at the man's cold eye. "Whose idea was it to blow up an American city? Prescott's?"

"Prescott knew something was on the horizon, but presidents are never directly involved, they don't want to know, they just want it done. The men I work with . . . these are men with vision who understand America's role in leading the industrialized world. They recognized long ago that America's military might have weakened, that by shirking our responsibilities we were actually inviting the rise of fundamentalism. Corporations move the world, Futrell, not peace activists. What you label Neocons are the world's movers and shakers, the ones determined to control events before the events control us."

"September Eleventh? Was that such an event?"

"It could have been stopped, but there would have been more attempts. By allowing the hijackings to take place we changed the rules of engagement. If you want to move the flock, invite the wolf. Prescott will use the Columbus Day attack to crush the nuclear threat in Iran. Without state support, fanatical Islam will fall."

"And the House of Saud?"

"When the time is right."

"You left out Venezuela."

The Russian-American's eye widens, then he offers a wry smile. "Like warfare, oil is a catalyst, a means to an end. Chavez's nation will be labeled the linchpin in the war on drugs. He must be controlled."

"You mean like the druglords the CIA control in Afghanistan? See, the problem in your theories is that you always fall short in the execution. You never actually defeat evil; you simply trade one oppressive regime for another, and you never hesitate to make deals with the devil. The heroin's in bloom, profits are up . . . you're doing a heck of a job, Brownie. Freedom's on the march . . . my ass. You hypocrites could give a damn about democracy. The only cause you truly understand is money. Money and power."

Santa reaches inside his jacket, retrieving the 9mm semi-automatic. "Your wife once shared the same ideals as the PNAC, did you know this? It was the cancer that changed her perspective, it made her weak, a bleeding-heart liberal. I took great pleasure in putting her out of her misery."

The agent aims the gun at Ace's head—

—his good eye exploding in a blast of blood and bone fragment as the bullet tears through the back of his skull.

Ace looks up, his limbs quivering. Ramzi is standing outside the meeting room door. Nahir and the CNN film crew are with him, all in bio-hazard suits. "Jeez, Ramzi, think maybe you were cutting it a bit close?"

Ramzi re-holsters his weapon. "His rants made for a better interview."

The CNN cameraman continues to film, his soundman nudging the female reporter, who is still in shock. The woman regains her composure.

"Mr. Futrell, Rebecca St. Croix, CNN. Sir, could you tell us who this man was?"

Ace takes a breath, fighting to collect himself. "His name was Scott Santa. He murdered my wife, Kelli Doyle, a former national security advisor under the Bush and McKuin administrations. The two of them were involved in a neoconservative contingency plan . . . to allow terrorists to use a nuclear device on an American city so that we could disarm Iran. My wife documented everything, we're sending some of the evidence over the internet to the major media outlets. Congress needs to act now to impeach Prescott before he and his lunatics start World War III."

◆ ◆ ◆

The Joint Strike Fighter soars over the desert, racing for the burning infrastructure in the distance. The jet's Lockheed Martin electro-optical targeting system (EOTS) configures its multiple targets, its undercarriage yawning open . . . ejecting its payload.

◆ ◆ ◆

Ace, Nahir, Ramzi, and the CNN crew instinctively look up as bombs explode three hundred feet over the oil refinery . . . bathing the small city in VX nerve gas.

"Officials at NORAD have stated when the hijackings first occurred they initially thought it was part of the Vigilant Guardian drills running that morning. Despite some confusion, once Flight 11 struck the World Trade Center at 8:45 a.m., everyone should have known this was not a test. . . . Scrambling aircraft simply means providing an Air Force escort to survey the situation. This has nothing to do with shooting down an aircraft. Such scrambling procedures had occurred sixty-seven times in the year prior to 9/11. The concept of this simple standard operating procedure failing from 8:28 a.m. when Flight 11 made an unplanned one hundred–degree turn to the south, until 9:38 a.m. when the Pentagon was struck, is inconceivable without a military order. Such an order, or multiple orders causing 'confusion,' may have been scripted into the war game scenarios that morning. We do not know if this is the case, and it seems the 9/11 Commission doesn't want to know.

—MICHAEL KANE,
from *Elephants in the Barracks:
The Complete Failure of the 9/11 Commission*

"House Republican leaders have quietly scaled back their plan to limit the political influence of lobbyists, dropping proposed requirements that lobbyists disclose which lawmakers and aides they have contacted and how they have raised money for politicians."

—*USA TODAY,*
May 2006

Book Excerpt:
To the Brink of Hell: An Apology to the Survivors
by Kelli Doyle,
White House National Security Staff Advisor
(2006-2010)

The Neocons' solution to disarm a nuclear Iran meshed with another global concern appearing quickly on the horizon—the end of oil.

When it comes to the human ecosystem, energy is everything, societies ultimately succeed or fail based upon their ability to process energy. That the planet's population explosion coincided with the industrial revolution is no mere coincidence, the two are intrinsically tied together—a result of the impact of fossil fuels, specifically oil.

A quick but vital lesson: It is oil and its by-products that allow machines to complete tasks formerly performed by human or animal muscle power. A century ago, horses and humans had to live off the crop they farmed, the capacity of land they could work quite limited. It was the advent of gasoline-powered vehicles and their introduction into agriculture that suddenly enabled industry to plow, plant, and harvest massive acres of land quickly and economically, making it possible for 2 percent of our population to feed our entire country . . . allowing civilization to expand.

Without gasoline, goods cannot be transported by truck to central collecting and processing points, or distributed to cities and remote areas. Without oil, we could not populate vast regions of our own country. Imagine living in desert states like Arizona or New Mexico, or the cold northern areas in Minnesota and Wisconsin without energy to cool and heat our homes, feed the populace, or supply goods and other services. Oil makes it all possible.

What most people fail to realize is that it takes energy to get energy, gasoline to drill an oil well, electricity to manufacture a photovoltaic solar panel. Can we replace oil? Nuclear power is expensive and creates dangerous radioactive waste. Wind, while an effective alternative source of electricity in some regions, cannot bring a truck carrying perishables to market. Photovoltaics, long underfunded, remain expensive. Hydrogen is not an energy source, it is an energy storage medium, and the production of hydrogen requires fossil fuels. Natural gas is running out and, again, cannot mobilize an economy.

The harsh reality: When it comes to energy production and profit ratio, nothing competes with the economics of oil—the primary reason America has failed to invest in other alternative energy resources. Combine that fact with the all-powerful fossil fuel industry, which uses its billions in profits to leverage politicians, and you have a steep mountain to climb in order to effect quantum change.

That oil is running out is no great secret, though economists will debate endlessly into the night as to the exact year the last drop will be drained. Controlling that last drop had always been at the crux of the Neocons' "Plan for a New American Republic," but the sudden realization that Iraqi oil reserves (and others) had been greatly exaggerated forced the radical right to readjust its plans and ponder another harsh reality:

How many of us can actually exist on this planet at the same time without fossil fuels?

The law of unchanging energy supply states that a growing economy must eventually consume more energy than it can produce. World oil peaked back in 2003 and consumption is soaring, effectively burning the candle at both ends. The effects are already being felt. More than 3 billion people worldwide are malnourished and living in poverty. Grain production and arable land per capita has been declining steadily since 1984, along with fish production and fertilizers essential for food production. Inversely, water, air, and land pollution has increased, along with global warming. As the U.S. National Academy of Sciences has pointed out, humanity is approaching a crisis point.

For decades Earth's carrying capacity had been artificially increased because of an abundance of oil—oil that supported industrial agriculture and technological advances in key sectors, including transportation networks, medical care, and sanitation. With our primary energy source running out faster than anticipated, our leaders faced a sobering reality—at current reserves, there are simply too many people living on our planet to feed and house everyone.

Here's the basic math: six billion of us exist today, and that number must be reduced by roughly 66 percent over the next two decades or severe famine, induced by the end of oil, will do it for us.

That's 4 billion people who must be strategically eliminated to avoid anarchy.

And so society's gluttons came up with their own contingency plan, one they didn't exactly publish on their web site. Instead of using their influence over the majorities in the House, Senate, Executive and Judiciary Branches to wean America off fossil fuels and invest in safe alternatives and the infrastructure to support them (jeopardizing their voting base), they instead decided to seek out alternative methods to selectively "thin the herd."

The two most effective ways to reduce population centers are pandemic and war. As I type this passage, genetically-manipulated epidemics are being developed in government-controlled labs, along with cures that will be selectively administered by key allies in the pharmaceutical industry. As for those annoying scientists who might potentially "cure" a future pandemic—many of these individuals have already been "eliminated."

After the occupation and resultant struggles in Iraq, and faced with the reality of America's depleted armed forces, a New Republic Doctrine was created. In essence it states, "The most cost-effective way to invade and control a foreign land is to initially employ methods that will radically reduce the populace while preserving the country's infrastructure."

Translation: instead of invading with troops, use tactical chemical weapons to destroy the will of your enemy . . . and its people.

When it comes to systematically murdering hoards of human beings while leaving buildings and oil wells intact, there is nothing quite as lethal or effective as a chemical nerve agent. Nerve agents are toxins designed to disrupt the transmission of cholinesterase, an enzyme nerve cells use to clear themselves of acetylcholine, the chemical that causes muscles and glands to contract. By inhibiting cholinesterase, the muscles of the diaphragm will contract uncontrollably, leading to death by suffocation.

The most lethal family of chemical agents ever created is the V-series—ten times more toxic than sarin gas. VX is the worst of the lot, an odorless, colorless, oily agent that does not wash away easily. Even a small dose of VX on the skin or inhaled will cause severe convulsions, respiratory paralysis, and death within several minutes.

Because VX is so lethal, the Defense Department must deploy it in binary bombs—canisters designed with separate chambers, each holding the two VX chemical precursors. When fired or dropped at elevation, the bomb's acceleration causes the partition within the capsule to break, the VX nerve gas mixed as it races toward its intended victims.

The end of oil.

A nuclear Iran, led by an extremist with an agenda.

The threat of radical Islam, fueled by a hatred of western society.

The Neoconservatives' desire for control.

The variables of destruction are in place, the game of chess coming down to its last fatal moves—

—check-mating the end of our civilization as we know it.

"The president has the power to seize property, organize and control the means of production, seize commodities, assign military forces abroad, call reserve forces amounting to 2.5 million men to duty, institute martial law, seize and control all means of transportation, regulate all private enterprise, restrict travel, and in a plethora of particular ways, control the lives of all Americans. Most of these laws remain a potential source of virtually unlimited power for a president should he choose to activate them. It is possible that some future president could exercise this vast authority in an attempt to place the United States under authoritarian rule. While the danger of a dictatorship arising through legal means may seem remote to us today, recent history records Hitler seizing control through the use of the emergency powers provisions contained in the laws of the Weimar Republic."

—Senators Frank Church (D-ID) and
Charles McMathias (R-MD),
September 30, 1973

"Vice President Dick Cheney vigorously defended a secret program that examines banking records of Americans and others in a vast international database, harshly criticizing the news media for disclosing an operation he called legal and 'absolutely essential' to fighting terrorism."

—New York Times,
June 24, 2006

CHAPTER 49

Senator Mulligan stands before the podium, fists balled in anger, as the CNN live feed featuring Ace Futrell and Scott Santa is abruptly cut off . . . seconds before Ace was interviewed!

The democratic candidate turns to address the hastily gathered group of reporters. "Prescott knew, he allowed the attack on Los Angeles to happen! Tonight, I call on all members of Congress to join me in an emergency midnight session on Capitol Hill to investigate charges that members of this administration were directly involved in the Columbus Day attack. Tonight I call on the Senate to take back control of our nation from an administration hell-bent on abusing its power!"

Al Udeid Air Base,
Qatar
3:51 am Local Time

CENTCOM's commander, General Mike Tristano, listens to Vice Admiral Brandon Herbert as he barks orders over the video speaker phone at Captain James Fisher aboard the aircraft carrier *Ronald Reagan.*

"Exactly how many of these binary bombs did the secretary of defense order the supply ship to bring onboard, Captain?"

Fisher's complexion seems to pale over the monitor. "Sir, just over three hundred."

General Tristano swears under his breath. "Captain, under my direct order, no more VX bombs are to be loaded aboard any aircraft, is that understood?"

"Sir, Defense Secretary Kendle has already issued orders to the contrary."

"Captain, the secretary of defense is under suspicion of treason," the Admiral shoots back. "If the secretary of defense contacts you, you will refer him to me, is that clear?"

"Yes, sir."

"Major General Zizzi, what's the status of the Phase I targets?"

"Nuclear targets have been destroyed, Iranian Air Force has been immobilized. Fourteen sorties now on approach to terrorist training camps."

"Captain Fisher, you will complete Phase I of the mission, then await orders from CENTCOM."

"Yes, sir."

WEST PALM BEACH, FLORIDA
11:35 PM EST

JENNIFER WIENNER IS WATCHING CNN ON her cell phone when her assistant calls out from his office, "Jen, turn on CBS, they're breaking another story!"

She changes the channel to a live scene at FBI Headquarters in Chicago, where Director Adrian Neary is being grilled by the press.

". . . the suspect, Jamal al-Yussuf, was found dead about two hours ago. Preliminary autopsy reports indicate it was a heart attack."

"Sir, the suspect was only in his late twenties. How is it possible—"

"As I said earlier, we are investigating all possibilities, including foul play."

"Did anyone visit the suspect prior to his death?"

Neary contemplates his answer carefully. "I'm sorry, I can't comment at this time."

"You just did!" Jennifer hugs her assistant as he enters the room. "It's happening, Collin! It's all coming down like a house of cards!"

Collin Bradley's expression gives her pause as he hands her the phone.

CAPITOL HILL,
WASHINGTON, DC
12:12 AM EST

THE POLICE PRESENCE IS ENORMOUS, OFFICERS and Homeland Security arresting any dissenter so much as wearing an anti-war T-shirt. The media is kept at bay, no cameras allowed within a quarter mile of the Capitol Building.

Inside, a deeply shaken Senator Joseph Mulligan looks out upon an empty chamber as an aide hurriedly approaches. "Seventeen Democrats, three Republicans—that's all that showed. Homeland Security arrested every one of them, sir."

The doors burst open, three armed Homeland Security agents making their way toward them from down the center aisle.

"This is a sad day," Senator Mulligan says. "A sad day for democracy."

"Senator Mulligan, we are placing you under arrest, the charges—treason. Under the statutes of the Patriot Act, you are not entitled to counsel. You will be detained until further notice."

AL UDEID AIR BASE,
QATAR
4:22 AM LOCAL TIME

THE MPs ENTER EN FORCE, THEIR guns drawn.

General Mike Tristano looks up from his desk, his blood pressure boiling. "What's going on here? Holster those weapons!"

"I'm sorry, sir. You're under arrest."

"Arrest! Under who's orders?"

"The president of the United States."

ABQAIQ OIL REFINERY
6:47 AM LOCAL TIME

FIRST LIGHT UNVEILS A LANDSCAPE OF death—thousands of bodies, the dying gasping final breaths their lungs cannot breath, the poisoned nerves of the deceased still twitching.

Cloaked within their protective garments, the CNN crew moves carefully amid the fallen as they film the heart-wrenching carnage: locals . . .

fathers and sons, mothers clutching infants . . . part of an exodus that began a blink in time too late.

Ace hyperventilates behind the plastic hood of his biohazard suit as he staggers through the refinery, his insides emotionally ravaged, his anger raging at the senselessness of an act that he was utterly powerless to prevent. Nahir is by his side, wearing Scott Santa's biohazard suit.

Ramzi Karim stumbles from one body to the next, sweeping suffocating children up in his arms, carrying them inside a building, the act of desperation far too late against the man-made toxin.

More news crews arrive on the scene, all wearing protective biohazard suits. Within hours their shocking images will appear on news networks across the globe.

OVAL OFFICE, THE WHITE HOUSE
WASHINGTON, DC

PRESIDENT PRESCOTT SITS BEHIND HIS DESK, wringing his hands as he watches the cable news broadcast of Abqaiq. "How bad is this?"

"Bad." Howard Lowe mutes the television's sound.

"We're in damage control," replies Jim Miller, Prescott's new press secretary. "We spin this back to LA, link Ashraf to Iran. Tell the American public these rebels were trained at Qods."

Prescott raises his eyebrows. "That would work, right?"

Defense Secretary Kendle enters. "CENTCOM's back under control. I was forced to arrest General Tristano."

Miller is livid. "You can't just do that without clearing it with the president! This entire process has got to slow down. There's only so much you can sell the public at one sitting, even if we are at red alert."

"Tristano was insubordinate, he cancelled Phase II."

"What's Phase II?"

"Our response to Los Angeles," Lowe replies. "Destruction of key Iranian population centers."

"Destruction how?"

"VX nerve gas."

Jim Miller winces, the former Olympic baseball player suddenly wondering why he accepted the press secretary job in the first place. "Mr. President, with Mulligan's arrest, with these images of dead children coming out of Abqaiq, I strongly advise you to put this attack on the back burner."

"Out of the question." Defense Secretary Kendle stares down the press secretary, a man half his age. "I have sixteen warships in the Persian Gulf—"

"Which succeeded in destroying Iran's military bases and nuclear installations. Threat over, mission accomplished. Stop the war now and we win in the arena of global politics. Slaughter tens of millions of Iranian civilians and we declare open war on a billion Muslims."

"Enough!" Kendle spats. "You're the press secretary, you're not here to dictate policy. People a lot more experienced than you have devoted the better part of their careers working on a game plan—"

"To do what? Invade Iran by neutralizing its populace? It's all over the internet, kill the radicals and take the oil, brilliant plan. Well, it didn't work in 2003, and it—"

"Quiet!" The Homeland Security director points to the television, turning up the sound.

It's a CNN report, broadcast live out of Phoenix.

FBI Regional director Marc McDuff is speaking at the podium. ". . . coordinating the investigation with agents in Kansas, we were able to identify the body of FBI Agent Elliott Green. Agent Green had been involved in an ongoing investigating of a nuclear physicist, Professor Eric Mingjuan Bi. After searching the vehicle, FBI agents recovered recorded telephone conversations made by Agent Green of FBI director Gary Lee Schafer and a yet-to-be-identified terror suspect. It should be noted that the director was in fact on the scene in Los Angeles just prior to the detonation of the nuclear weapon on October 8, and was killed in the attack."

Ellis Prescott stares at the television, his heart palpitating, his skin bathed in a cold sweat, the blood vessels in his left arm constricting.

"Mr. President? Sir, are you okay?"

A crushing weight impales Prescott to his chair—an elephant squatting on his chest. "He's having a heart attack! Get a doctor up here!"

ONE WEEK
LATER

"It would be a terrible disservice to those Muslims who are liberal, who are Democrats, who are modern, who want to live a civilized life . . . to throw them in with the barbarians, because they are on the right side, and more than that, they have a great deal to offer in the war against militant Islam."

—DANIEL PIPES,
Middle East Forum Director

CHAPTER 50

DOVER AIR FORCE BASE
DOVER, DELAWARE
OCTOBER 24, 2012
9:38 AM EST

THE MONSTROUS 247-FOOT GALAXY C-5 TRANSPORT circles Dover Air Force Base on its final approach before landing. Ace Futrell is seated in the upper deck, along with sixty-two wounded soldiers and a cargo lined with the flag-draped coffins of the dead.

The last seven days have been a whirlwind of intelligence briefings and backroom deals, the U.S. military action in the Persian Gulf called off after succeeding in destroying Iran's nuclear facilities, along with its military bases and suspected Qod training centers. After around-the-clock negotiations, the UN Security Council announced a cease-fire, with Iran's mullahs agreeing to clamp down on all radical Islamic sects, and cut off all military and financial aid to insurgents in Iraq. Iran and Syria also agreed to cease all military aid to Hezbollah and other terrorist organizations, with the United Nations "vowing" to keep the offending nations to strict timetables.

At least that was the "official" story.

In the wake of the Abqaiq massacre, the Ashraf movement had spread, leading to waves of demonstrations in Jiddah and the eastern provinces. The Royals continue their hold on power . . . but only for the moment.

Back at home, all "political detainees" have been released, the nation's red alert status reduced to orange. The president of the United States remains in serious but stable condition after surviving a heart attack, but Ace knows from his own debriefing that he has secretly agreed to step down, in exchange for the "burial" of critical evidence implicating members of his administration.

As for Ace, he has made his own deal with the powers-that-be, agreeing to quash Kelli's memoir in exchange for his life back. Should an "untimely death, disappearance, or act of God" claim his life or that of a family member, then Ace's "merry men" will release the information via the internet.

And so he finds himself returning to the States, his mind still in a state of shock over what has transpired. He cannot conceive of the devastation in Los Angeles. He grapples with his wife's involvement in the plot, at times he despises her, at times he wonders if her efforts may have changed the world. Physically, mentally, and spiritually burned out, he no longer cares about oil or politics, the chaos going on in the world, or the wreckage of his life. He no longer wonders why he was spared from the torture chamber at Inakesh, or why he is still alive. When he looks in the mirror, he is bewildered by the person staring back at him.

Nahir is a fading memory. Freed from her existence at Inakesh Prison, she had decided to relocate to India where her mother's family resides. Ace had let her go, deciding it was best to close that chapter of his life.

◆ ◆ ◆

The military transport taxis across the runway, coming to a halt at one of the open hangars. Ace gazes out the window at the crowd—families and loved ones of America's wounded and dead.

He has journeyed through hell, but for so many, the journey continues.

He thinks about his children, wondering how he can get in touch with them after such a long absence. Will they recognize him? Will they forgive him?

The black government-issue limousine rolls to a stop beyond the crowd. Ace sees David Schall exit the vehicle, the CIA director walking toward the C-5 transport, accompanied by two heavily armed MPs.

So that's the way it's going to be . . .

Nine months ago Ace had stepped off a plane in New York, a man in full, anxious to see his wife, blissfully unaware of the storm gathering on his horizon. Now the storm has struck and passed, leaving everything that was his life in shambles.

How do I pick up the pieces?

Stepping out of the plane into the sunshine, he looks out at the crowd, at the widow who awaits her husband's remains, at the children who will go on without their father, at the father who has lost a son. At the combat veteran who has sacrificed a limb . . .

He pinches away tears, feeling ashamed.

David Schall greets him as he steps off the ramp. "Walk with me."

"Do I have a choice?"

David Schall sees the glazed over stare. He dismisses the MPs, then leads Ace back across the tarmac to the awaiting government vehicle. "Some of the things that happened between us . . . I had to keep up appearances. You understand it was nothing personal. As for what happened in Saudi Arabia, I had nothing to do with that. I just wanted you to know."

Ace says nothing.

"Your wife and I were friends. You were away on business when Kelli found out how badly the cancer had spread. She decided to keep it from you. Probably never told you I came to see her the day she received her death sentence. I remember the vacant look in her eyes, it was the same look you have now."

He pauses, grabbing Ace's arm. "A man is not finished when he's defeated, he's finished when he quits. You know who said that? Nixon. Right after the Watergate scandal."

"You brought me here for a history lesson?"

"I'm here to get you to understand. Kelli's last eighteen months . . . she knew she had lost the battle but she never gave up. She kept fighting, she made every day count."

Ace's eyes narrow. "You were in on it, weren't you? Her plan?"

"Who do you think gave her access to Promis?"

Ace continues walking, his blood pressure ticking higher.

Schall follows him out the gate. "I gave her what she needed . . . a cause. A second wind. This country's a mess, Ace, but at least we see the problems for what they are, and that's a step forward . . . at least it's a start. What the two of you accomplished . . . it was a good thing."

"A good thing?" Ace turns on him, pushing him back on his heels. "Tell the hundreds of thousands of cancer victims who will suffer until the day they die that this was a good thing. Tell it to the victims' loved ones, see if they buy it, because I sure don't. "

"No argument, but it could have been worse. The situation had to be defused."

"You know what the problem with you and Kelli and Prescott, and the rest of your ilk is? No matter how bad things get, no matter how many times you screw up, you assholes always think you're right. Well guess what? There wouldn't be any Islamic extremists if we weren't addicted to oil, there wouldn't be an Al-Qaeda if we hadn't funded an Afghanistan resistance against the Soviets, Saddam would have never been a threat if we hadn't armed him, or Iran, or the other puppet regimes the CIA set up so our administrations could pull their strings. We're the United States, Schall, we're supposed to be the good guys! What if our leaders had insisted on human rights and accountability in places like Saudi Arabia in exchange for their oil? Better yet, what if Congress and the White House actually got together and decided to force our nation off fossil fuels once and for all . . . to hell with big oil, to hell with the auto industry, let's reinvent the wheel and do it right. Imagine what a different world we'd be living in today. I guarantee you, Los Angeles would be a lot greener."

Ace bypasses the limousine, heading for the airport exit.

"Dad!"

He stops and turns, his heart leaping in his throat as Sam bursts out of the back door of the limousine and race into his arms. Tears of joy flow from Ace's eyes as he hugs his son, the vacuum in his soul suddenly overflowing with emotion.

Leigh approaches, unsure.

Sam wraps his arms around Ace's neck in a bear-hug. "Dad, we saw you on the news, Dad . . . you were on the news!"

His daughter stares at him, still feeling betrayed. "Dad? What did they do to you? Look at you, you're a train wreck."

"Felt like I was in one. Guys, I am so sorry for leaving you, and I promise I will never leave you again. Ever. Do you forgive me?"

Sammy nods.

Leigh's face breaks into sobs as she hugs him.

"It's okay, sweetheart. Daddy's home again—

—I'm home."

"Then I saw a new heaven and a new earth for the old heaven and earth had disappeared."

—Revelation 21:1

"The thing the sixties did was to show us the possibilities and the responsibility that we all had. It wasn't the answer. It just gave us a glimpse of the possibility."

—John Lennon

EPILOGUE

THE MOVING TRUCK IS PACKED TO its roof, the movers wedging in the last of their belongings. Leigh and Sam are out front saying good-bye to their friends. Their grandparents are inside, speaking with the real estate agent.

Jennifer parks in the cul-de-sac. She tosses a scarf around her neck before heading up to the house. "Hey, kids. Where's your dad?"

"Where else?" Leigh says, "saying his good-byes."

♦ ♦ ♦

A harsh March wind whips spray across the Atlantic, churning the surf into endless foam-crested waves. Ace adjusts his collar, staring at the ocean . . . ready to move on.

He and his family had spent most of November in Washington, DC, Ace testifying in Senate hearings on the Columbus Day attack. As predicted, the heavy-handed public investigation had implicated Iran and the House of Saud in the destruction of Los Angeles . . . preventing anarchy in the United States and hostilities throughout the Arab world.

Seven members of the Strategic Support Branch were eventually indicted for "failing to protect the citizens of the United States." Homeland Security director Howard S. Lowe and secretary of defense Joseph Kendle stepped down for "family reasons." Details of how the two suitcase bombs actually arrived in the States were never publicly disclosed, nor was the recruitment process of Jamal al-Yussuf and Omar Kamel Radi.

The democratic minority leaders agreed to these secret arrangements to "preserve the state of the union" in exchange for sweeping changes in the election process. Campaign contributions were banned, all monies would now be drawn from a pool of federal funds that would be divided equally among the parties and their candidates based on predetermined amounts assigned to the particular office they were campaigning for. No other monies were permitted, 527s outlawed . . . along with all lobbyists. A wartime bill was enacted, preventing private companies from reaping profits. More changes were on the horizon, pending the upcoming presidential election.

In late December, following an "anonymous tip," a man named Armond "Dale" Proctor was arrested in the Cayman Islands by CIA agents. Proctor would later turn state's evidence against two manufacturers of voting machines that had been rigged to alter the count in key counties in Florida, Ohio, and Pennsylvania. Proctor's testimony would lead to another new election rule mandating all touch-screen voting machines be equipped with paper ballot receipts.

On February 22—George Washington's birthday—Senator Joseph B. Mulligan was elected forty-sixth president of the United States. His first act was to pass a farm and energy bill designed to systematically replace gasoline with E85 ethanol by the end of 2013. His second act was to begin withdrawing troops from the Middle East. A United Nations peace-keeping force took over U.S. military bases in Saudi Arabia—preparing for the former kingdom's first open democratic elections. The interim government—headed by Ramzi Karim—was supported by $600 billion in missing funds that had been sequestered into private bank accounts all over the world.

Having accepted a small "settlement," the Royal Family abandoned their palaces and relocated to Europe.

With the more radical mullahs forced to give up power, Iranian students once more began organizing peaceful demonstrations against the ruling parties. A short time later, the president of Iran died of what was reported to be a massive stroke.

◆ ◆ ◆

"Ace!"

Jennifer joins him, her earlobes bright red from the cold. "It's freezing out here. Keep me warm." She hooks her arm between his and tucks her hand back into her jacket pocket, using his body to block the wind. "Have you heard the latest? They decided to turn downtown Los Angeles into a Redwood park. They say it should significantly reduce radiation levels."

Ace says nothing, his eyes transfixed on the horizon.

"So, South Florida, huh? I guess we'll be close. What made you—"

"Southeast Wind and Power, they offered me a job. I figured we could all use a change in scenery."

"What about me? Am I part of that change?"

Ace swallows the lump building in his throat.

"Ace . . . that night on the beach, I meant what I said . . . about having feelings for you. Do you suppose when you're in Florida—"

"You'll always be part of our family, Jen."

"But nothing more?"

"What do you think?" He turns to face her. "You and Kelli . . . the two of you set me up."

"It was your wife's idea, not mine."

"But you went along with it. You lied to me."

"Yes. Yes, you're right, and I'm sorry. I'm sorry for all you went through. Believe me, if we had known—"

"Stop."

They continue to stare at the ocean in silence. A slice of sun shines its way through a gray cloud, casting its beam upon the water.

"Ace . . . I truly am sorry."

He swallows hard. "Back in college, the first time I saw Kelli, the first time I met her, it was love at first sight. I guess first loves are special that way. When we met again years later . . . maybe I was looking for something I had lost, maybe we both were." He brushes a strand of dark hair from Jennifer's eyes. "I'm not looking for that anymore, Jen, that person's long gone. You know what I'm saying?"

She nods, tears in her eyes. "Have a safe trip." Adjusting her scarf, she heads back down the beach.

Ace watches her go, then returns his gaze back to the sea.

Their new home is located on the same ocean, fifteen hundred miles to the south. The water is different, the Atlantic an azure-blue. Yes, as his father-in-law has repeatedly warned, there will be the occasional hurricane threat to contend with, but no sea stays calm forever, no paradise remains unblemished. He will miss Montauk, and the house that he and his wife made into a home.

Change is hard.

The company he will be working for is one of the businesses Kenneth Keene had secretly funded with the House of Saud's money. Ace is a partner in the firm, the managing director.

From oil to wind . . . sometimes change is good.

The green movement is well underway in America, spurred on, no doubt, by the nuclear devastation in Los Angeles. By late 2014, it is predicted E85 ethanol will officially replace gasoline at the American pump. A year later, new high-tech wind mills are expected to sprout up along the Atlantic, Gulf, and Pacific coastlines. By 2017 these high-tech machines should provide clean, affordable electricity to nearly 50 percent of American homes in the continental United States. Scientists expect carbon dioxide levels to drop significantly, reducing the effects of global warming while improving the quality of air that has been causing severe asthma problems among children living in areas located near coal-powered plants.

Some scientists actually predict fossil fuels could be phased out globally by 2033.

Ace recalls his last moments with his wife at the John Lennon memorial.

Imagine . . .

Wiping a tear, he takes one final look to the east, then walks back to the house, anxious to begin his life anew.

"We're not going to plunge into an irresponsible action just because a fanatical fringe in this country puts so-called national pride above national reason. Do you think I'm going to carry on my conscience the responsibility for the wanton maiming and killing of children we saw (playing) here this evening? Do you think I'm going to cause a nuclear exchange—for what? Because I was forced into doing something that I didn't think was proper and right? Well, if you or anybody else thinks I am, he's crazy."

—PRESIDENT JOHN F. KENNEDY

"I'm trying to say to you—be part of the change! No one else is going to do it. The politicians are paralyzed. Our democracy hasn't been working very well . . . that's my opinion. We've made a bunch of serious policy mistakes. But it's way too simple and too partisan to blame the Bush-Cheney administration. We've got checks and balances, an independent judiciary, a free press, a Congress . . . have they all failed us? *Have we failed ourselves?*"

—FORMER VICE PRESIDENT AL GORE,
2007

"Be the change that you want to see in the world."

—MAHATMA GANDHI

Final Excerpt:
To the Brink of Hell: An Apology to the Survivors
by Kelli Doyle,
White House National Security Staff Advisor
(2006-2010)

Where will you be when the world changes? When the gas lines are miles long and the grocery store shelves run bare. How will you cope? Do you have the land to farm your own crop? The means to protect it?

How will you react when suitcase nukes replace commercial jets as the new terror threat, and the first mushroom cloud rolls toward the heavens. Will you be caught in the maelstrom? Traveling on business? At home with your loved ones? Enjoying the night out? If you reside in a major city, will you stay at home or flee? Stuff your belongings in the car and race to the interstate, only to find it clogged in bumper-to-bumper traffic . . .

Will you ever trust your elected leaders again?

Will you ever feel safe?

What will you do when civilization and sanity goes up in radioactive smoke, when anyone resembling a brown-skinned Muslim is dragged into the street and beaten to death. When nine o'clock curfews and Big Brother's eyes become the rules of the day, and our borders remain permanently closed to all but the elite.

How will you feel when the retaliation begins? When 70 million Iranians pay the ultimate price for being born under an oppressive regime . . . for the lies they were spoon fed since birth, for the hatred it festered under the guise of religion.

Will the purple rain wash away the threat? Will the world just call it a day?

Will we ever learn?

—Kelli Doyle-Futrell
December 9, 2011

This novel is dedicated in memory to my father-in-law

James Franklin Roof
(July 11, 1933–June 19, 1996)

Served proudly in Korea 1950–1954
Recipient of two Purple Hearts

and

to my friend and technical editor

Charles "Chuck" Eugene Jones
(May 28, 1962–December 29, 2006)

Served proudly as a ballistic missile technician and police officer.

FACT OR FICTION

WHILE *The Shell Game* REMAINS FICTION, some of the more disturbing passages and threads of information incorporated into the storyline are indeed real. While I cannot begin to cite every reference used for every detail woven into the manuscript (the studies and published articles alone number well over six hundred) I have included (below) comments on some of the more controversial references appearing in the novel. As an author, I reserve the freedom to select those references (and slants) that allow me to move the story forward, however, unlike the cherry-picking of information conducted by the Bush White House, the references cited service the truth, and not a hidden agenda.

"Numerous Sources" means the references are far too numerous to list and that the subject matter can be easily found through an Internet search. "Bibliography" refers to the list of key books that follow. "Classified" is a confidential source who has requested not to be identified. For those subjects or threads I have not covered, I suggest an Internet search.

For those of you who seek more detailed answers regarding the end of oil and the involvement of key officials in the September Eleventh attacks, I highly recommend *Crossing the Rubicon,* by Michael C. Ruppert. It is a disturbing, extremely well-documented accounting that makes transparent what those involved do not wish the public to see. For those of you who still have comments or questions, my personal e-mail link is available at www.SteveAlten.com

PROLOGUE

"I reported that Bin Laden had escaped to the Hadhramaut of Yemen, that he was being protected by Sayyid tribesmen." Reference: classified. (Note: While it is impossible at this time (June 2007) to know if this is really true, I have absolutely no doubt that the Middle Eastern Muslim confidant who told me this tidbit was telling me what he believed was true.)

"And the Reserves and National Guardsmen? Nice surprise, not telling them deployment doesn't officially begin until their boots hit sand, meaning the six months their unit spent at the MOB stations didn't count." Reference: U.S. soldiers.

Author's Note: Just as disturbing as reports of depression and suicide is the fact that soldiers returning from Iraq and Afghanistan are not being given proper time to "detox" before being assimilated back into society. Nor is the needed psychiatric assistance being made available. This is a dangerous reality that is impacting our veterans and their families and we owe them far better than to sweep this under the rug.

"Roosevelt knew the Japanese were readying an attack on Pearl Harbor, and guess what—he allowed it to happen!" Reference: numerous historical articles.

CHAPTER 1

"I'm not sure we're any different, after all, how many tens of billions of dollars worth of aid to New Orleans was secretly diverted to rebuild oil rigs damaged by Hurricane Katrina?" Reference: classified.

Stats and references about oil usage can be found in numerous resources and bibliography.

CHAPTER 3

Alternative energy sources and oil info can be found in numerous resources and bibliography.

"Syn-fuel is nothing more than a giant tax dodge created by a handful of greedy companies who found a way to take advantage of a tax incentive enacted by Congress back in the 1980s." Reference: see references in the text.

CHAPTER 4

"It was a neoconservative initiative, pushed by Dick Cheney, who believed Iran-Contra failed only because the CIA and Pentagon were involved and secrecy couldn't be maintained." Reference: Op-Ed (March 31, 2007) written by Jim Mullins, Senior fellow at the Center for International Policy in Washington, DC, backed by numerous cross-references.

CHAPTER 5

"The opening scene, taken by a hand-held camera, is of a classroom of Arab grade schoolers, ages five to seven . . . singing a song. Neary listens carefully. Translates: "Arabs are beloved and Jews are dogs." Reference: *Obsession: Radical Islam's War Against the West.*

CHAPTER 7

Carlyle Group information: *House of Bush, House of Saud,* by Craig Unger, along with numerous sources.

CHAPTER 8

"Homeland Security is no longer required to have a search warrant when dealing with acts intended to intimidate or coerce a civilian population." See Patriot Act.

KELLI DOYLE EXCERPT

"On the day of the attacks, the joint chiefs, under Vice President Cheney's personal direction, scheduled and conducted five separate war game drills that purposely pulled interceptor jets away from the northeastern airspace corridor while deliberately inserting false blips on air traffic screens to simulate, of all things, hijacked airliners. Military jets that routinely intercept aircraft within minutes were delayed an unfathomable eighty minutes, most never even entered the fray. . . ." Reference: numerous sources and *Crossing the Rubicon: The Decline of the American Empire at the End of the Age of Oil*, by Michael C. Ruppert.

"A day before the attacks domestic and foreign investors placed an unprecedented number of 'put calls' (a leveraged bet a stock will drop) on the airlines and companies that would suffer devastating losses, in some cases over ninety times higher than normal trading. These financial transactions netted upwards of $15 billion in insider trading that was half-heartedly investigated before they too were dismissed by investigators and the media, the later manipulated by the Bush administration who were dictating which stories to run and which to kill. Meanwhile, key members of Congress who opposed the administration's plans received packages of anthrax in the mail, the lethal spores later determined to have originated not overseas, but from labs used by the CIA." Reference: numerous sources and *Crossing the Rubicon: The Decline of the American Empire at the End of the Age of Oil*, by Michael C. Ruppert.

"In an effort to stymie the Shi'ites in both Iraq and Lebanon, the Bush administration covertly began channeling billions of 'rebuilding' dollars into Sunni resistence groups—otherwise known as Al-Qaeda." Article in March 5, 2007 *New Yorker* by Seymour Hersh.

CHAPTER 9

"Enlisted men not cutting it can be sent home, every so often a few opt to kill themselves rather than be shamed into quitting. During Tursi's eight weeks his squadron experienced one attempted suicide and one that succeeded when a recruit took a nose-dive out a third story window during morning formation." Reference: confidential (AF recruit).

CHAPTER 10

"Patriot Act, section 213: Any Federal law enforcement agency can enter your home or business, whether you are there or not or whether they tell you about it or not, then use any confiscated evidence to convict you of a crime. Section 202 states the Feds can read your e-mail, section 216 allows them to intercept your cell phone calls." Reference: Patriot Act.

CHAPTER 11

All information cited about the assassination of Meir Kahane, the Muslim terrorist cell that planned the murder, and the eventual targeting of the (first) World Trade Center attack that should have been prevented is factual, backed by numerous sources.

CHAPTER 13

The incident described at Little Rock Air Force Base that nearly wiped out a significant portion of central Arkansas is factual. Reference: confidential (the source was one of the BMATs who witnessed the event).

KELLI DOYLE EXCERPT

Historical information presented on Ibn Saud and the history of the House of Saud, along with their purchasing of U.S. and other weapon systems is factual, backed by numerous sources, including *The House of Saud,* by Said K. Aburish.

CHAPTER 14

"Rove's primary mantra, besides WMDs, was that Iraqi oil would pay for the entire cost of the war. Andrew Natsios, the Administrator of the U.S. Agency for International Development, actually appeared on Nightline quoting a maximum cost of invading Iraq to the American taxpayer of $1.7 billion. That same message and dollar amount was

repeated, over and over until even Congress believed it. Here we are, ten years later, and we just passed a trillion dollars in spending!" Reference: numerous sources.

Author's Note: Current war spending to date totals over $200 billion. Federal money spent on Hurricane Katrina victims: $6.9 billion (presently $2 billion shortage). Money requested in 2005 to raise levees and prevent the devastation: ($11 million, plus an additional $22.5 million to complete the job.) Money received in 2005: $5.5 million. Projected cost to fix levees post-Katrina: $9.5 billion. Money allocated by GOP Congress: $2 billion. Additional monies requested by Bush administration: $2 billion. Reference: Environmental News Service: March 31, 2006.

CHAPTER 16

"Part of a highly classified stealth satellite program known collectively as the Future Imagery Architecture (FIA), ONYX was severely criticized by members of the Senate Select Committee on Intelligence for its extraordinary price tag ($40 billion) and its inability to penetrate underground bunkers where Iran and North Korea house their nuclear facilities. Despite these objections, the program was funded by the GOP-controlled House and Senate appropriations committees." Reference: numerous sources and *Space Review*.

CHAPTER 17

Haditha massacre: *TIME* magazine and numerous other sources.

KELLI DOYLE EXCERPT

Historical information on Iran-Contra, Iran-Iraq War, Kuwait, etc. Reference: numerous sources.

"When (April Glaspie, U.S. Ambassador to Iraq) asked the dictator what else he wanted, Saddam replied that his country's aim was to reclaim the Shatt al-Arab, a region of Iraq that was now part of Kuwait. Glaspie's response was

that 'the Kuwait issue is not associated with America.' In essence, the United States had just given Saddam a green light to invade Kuwait." Reference: numerous sources.

CHAPTER 21

Historical information on Promis is factual. Numerous sources and *Crossing the Rubicon: The Decline of the American Empire at the End of the Age of Oil*, by Michael C. Ruppert.

CHAPTER 22

"More vocal and proactive than their moderate contemporaries, the Brotherhood (Bridgeview, Chicago Moslem community) began a fundraising campaign several years ago, asking Arab governments to help them 'prevent the undoing of Islamic society at the hands of the west.' More than a million dollars poured in from Kuwait, the Saudi government, and the religious ministry of the United Arab Emirates. In addition, Jordan's religious affairs ministry sent over Masoud Ali Masoud, a 57-year-old Palestinian, to work to at the Bridgeview mosque as an assistant prayer leader. Soon, a strict interpretation of Islam infiltrated the mosque, women ordered to cover their hair, segregated from their men during social events." Reference: based on numerous sources and *Obsession: Radical Islam's War Against the West.*

"When I was in Tehran I heard rumors that many of the Magnificent Nineteen were still alive. Mohamed Atta and Salem al-Hazni . . . that these men were never even onboard the planes. They had been traveling on false passports, instructed the night before the attacks to get publicly intoxicated and to scream insults at the infidels so as to attract attention to themselves. We were told these men were no one's fools, that they had purposely allowed their driver's licenses to be photocopied, that they even used public library computers to send e-mail using unencrypted messages, all to leave false trails to the FBI."

Author's license: Not based on any fact. Similar reports have surfaced on numerous websites and blogs, including www.WhatReallyHappened.com and www.MadCowMorningNews.com

"See, even with oil, the planet only has a feeding and energy capacity for about 2 billion people. We manage now because 4 billion of our fellow human beings are slowly starving to death in Africa and Asia. That leaves about a billion or so of us lucky ones who get to lead the charmed life, only the rules change when the pumps run dry. Divide 6 billion into what little food and fuel resources are left after the Big Rollover and you come up with approximately 500 million people, give or take a few hundred thousand." Reference: "Confronting The 21st Century's Hidden Crisis: Reducing Human Numbers by 80 Percent," by J. Kenneth Smail, professor of anthropology, and "Food, Energy and Society." by David and Marcia Pimental, professors of ecology and agricultural science, 2000.

CHAPTER 28

"Enter the Mu chip, a tiny invader the size of a grain of sand. Mu allows the government to scan you, track you, and determine what hazardous materials you've come in contact with. The next generation Mu will enable Washington to eavesdrop on our very thought process." Reference: numerous sources.

"Nineteen dead scientists in four months—all experts in the field of viruses. No arrests, everything kept out of the news and conveniently swept under the carpet." All true. Reference: numerous sources, including *Crossing the Rubicon: The Decline of the American Empire at the End of the Age of Oil,* by Michael C. Ruppert.

"There were two influential Democrats poised to thwart the Patriot Act—Tom Daschle and Patrick Leahy—and they were the only ones on Capitol Hill to receive packages of anthrax. The anthrax used in those packages was traced back to the Ames strain taken from Fort Detrick, yet John Ashcroft refused to follow up on that little piece of evidence."

All of the anthrax packages came from within the United States with origins that trace back to CIA-run covert research programs. Reference: numerous sources, including *Crossing the Rubicon: The Decline of the American Empire at the End of the Age of Oil,* by Michael C. Ruppert.

KELLI DOYLE EXCERPT

"A hardline group of Neoconservatives, headed by Dick Cheney, Paul Wolfowitz, Richard Pearle, Jeb Bush, and Donald Rumsfeld, all members of an organization calling itself the Project for a New American Century (PNAC). Using the Defense Planning Guidance as its blueprint for America's future, the group created their own strategic military document, entitled Rebuilding America's Defenses. *Admonishing the Clinton administration for its adherence to the 1972 ABM Treaty and for cutting military spending, the plan outlined a grand strategy that sought to exploit America's newfound position as the world's lone superpower."* Reference: numerous sources, including the two cited documents.

"Within months Vice President Dick Cheney was organizing secret energy task force meetings involving some of the biggest players (and donors) in the fossil fuel and nuclear industry. My role in these meetings was to supply maps of Iraqi oil and natural gas fields, as well as the locations of pipelines, refineries, and terminals . . ." Author's License (but I'll tell if Dick Cheney will tell!)

"Afghanistan is the world's largest producer of the opium poppy, used to make heroin. It is estimated $500 billion flows from poppy fields annually, the drugs ending up on the streets of the United States and other western nations, the profits washed through banking systems across the globe. Plain and simple: Drugs finance crooked banking ledgers and the world's debt." Reference: numerous sources, including *Crossing the Rubicon: The Decline of the American Empire at the End of the Age of Oil,* by Michael C. Ruppert.

Author's Note: According to a 1996 IMF report, money laundered from drugs and other criminal activities accounts for 2 to 5 percent of the world's GDP (about $800 billion to $2 trillion).

CHAPTER 32

"And yet the Saudi slave trade remains common knowledge around Washington power circles, a tolerated "look the other way" crime that has been going on since King Fahd and his sons first ran child sex rings from their private

mansions in Beverly Hills." Reference: numerous references, denied by the State Department.

CHAPTER 33

Inakesh Prison, Saudi Arabia. Reference: *The Defilers: Sowing the Seeds of Terrorism,* by El Sirgany.

CHAPTER 34

"At least half the monies taken originated from commissions skimmed by the House of Saud on arms contracts. Patriot Missiles, F-15s, AWACS, Canadian Halifax frigates, French Helec torpedo boats, the British Yamama sale . . . as well as off-the-book deals that can be traced as far back as the Reagan years." Reference: *The House of Saud,* by Said K. Aburish. Also backed by multiple cross-references.

CHAPTER 39

"The original 'October surprise' dates back to the 1980 presidential election when the release of American hostages from Iran would have all but guaranteed a re-election win to democratic incumbent Jimmy Carter, whose administration was preparing to implement a second rescue attempt in the event negotiations broke down. When the Reagan-Bush campaign heard about the rescue, they launched a major publicity blitz warning the public that President Carter was timing an 'October surprise' solely to win the election. Meanwhile, former CIA director George Bush and other members of the Reagan team were secretly meeting with high-level Iranian and Israeli representatives in a hotel in Paris, forging an agreement that promised to award Iran with arms and spare military parts in return for agreeing not to release the American hostages until after the election." Reference: multiple articles and published books.

Author's Note: This one admittedly divides along party lines and is very controversial, having been the subject of several investigations, the results of which are split. If you're a Dem you probably agree it happened, if you're a Republican you'll call it a "conspiracy." My opinion: both sides were certainly attempting to "spin" the Iranian hostage situation in an attempt to win the election. Reagan won. You decide.

CHAPTER 45

"Those Executive Orders Prescott just rattled off, they allow him to do anything he wants. The first order requires the Justice Department to enforce any and all powers granted to Homeland Security by the president, the last prevents Congress from reviewing the president's actions for at least six months."
Reference: Presidential Executive Orders 11310 and 11921.

SUGGESTED READING

Aburish, Said K. *The House of Saud*. New York: St. Martins Press, 1994.

Brock, David. *The Republican Noise Machine: Right-Wing Media and How it Corrupts Democracy*. New York: Crown Publishers, 2004.

Campbell, C. J. *The Coming Oil Crisis*. Essex, UK: Multi-Science Publishing Company & PetroConsultants SA, 1988.

Diamond, Jared. *Collapse: How Societies Choose to Fail or Succeed*. New York: Penguin, 2005.

El Sirgany, Emad. *The Defilers: Sowing the Seeds of Terrorism*. Summer Publishing House, 2004.

Hall-Jamieson, Kathleen. *Deception, Distraction, and Democracy*. New York: Oxford University Press, 1992.

Heinberg, Richard. *The Party's Over: Oil, War and the Fate of Industrial Societies*. Gabriola Island, BC: New Society Publishers, 2003.

Heinberg, Richard. *Powerdown: Options and Actions For a Post-Carbon World*. Gabriola Island, BC: New Society Publishers, 2004.

Johnson, Chalmers. *The Sorrows of Empire: Militarism, Secrecy, and the End of the Republic*. New York: Metropolitan Books, 2004.

Kane, Michael. "Elephants in the Barracks : The Complete Failure of the 9-11 Commission." Centre for Research on Globalisation, March 27, 2004. http://globalresearch.ca/articles/KAN403A.html.

Klare, Michael T. *Resources Wars: The New Landscape of Global Conflict.* New York: Henry Holt, 2001.

Kunstler, James Howard. *The Long Emergency: Surviving the Converging Catastrophes of the Twenty-first Century.* Boston: Atlantic Monthly Press, 2005.

Mooney, Chris. *The Republican War on Science.* Jackson, TN: Perseus Book Group, Basic Books, 2005.

Packer, George. *The Assassins' Gate: America in Iraq.* New York: Farrar, Straus & Giroux, 2005.

Pimental, David and Marcia. "Food, Energy & Society," *Bioscience.* May 2000.

Ruppert, Michael C. *Crossing the Rubicon: The Decline of the American Empire at the End of the Age of Oil.* Gabriola Island, BC: New Society Publishers, 2004.

Smail, Kenneth J. "Confronting the Twenty-first Century's Hidden Crisis: Reducing Human Numbers by 80 Percent." *NPG Forum Series.* Kenyon College, May 1995.

Unger, Craig. *House of Bush, House of Saud: The Secret Relationship between the World's Two Most Powerful Dynasties.* New York: Scribner, 2004.

Webb, Gary. *Dark Alliance.* New York: Seven Stories Press, 1998.

Yergin, Daniel. *The Prize: The Epic Quest for Oil, Money & Power.* New York: Free Press, 1991.

Suggested Websites and Multimedia

http://www.aspo-usa.com

http://www.TheOilDrum.com

Obsession: Radical Islam's War Against the West (www.
    ObsessionTheMovie.com).

0 26575 70947 6

DEC   2008